UNDER THE COVER OF DARKNESS

K.D. RICHARDS

DANGER ON THE RIVER

TARA TAYLOR QUINN

MILLS & BOON

First Published in Great Britain 2023
by Mills & Boon, an imprint of HarperCollins*Publishers* Ltd
1 London Bridge Street, London, SE1 9GF

www.harpercollins.co.uk

HarperCollins*Publishers*
Macken House, 39/40 Mayor Street Upper,
Dublin 1, D01 C9W8, Ireland

Under the Cover of Darkness © 2023 Kia Dennis
Danger on the River © 2023 TTQ Books LLC

ISBN: 978-0-263-30754-2

1223

UNDER THE COVER OF DARKNESS

K.D. RICHARDS

Chapter One

Detective Yara Thomas hadn't had time to grab a cup of coffee or boot up her computer before her lieutenant bellowed for her from his office.

So it was going to be that kind of day.

She stood in front of his desk as Lieutenant Ted Wilson gave her a brief rundown of the new case he was assigning to her. His exact words were, "Dead body in a car on old Route 30. Go."

She went.

Forty minutes later, she slowed around a curve and parked her standard-issue unmarked police sedan at an angle next to a police cruiser with its red and blue lights still flashing. Together her car and the cruiser created a barrier completely blocking the southbound lane of the road. A tow truck from one of the area towing companies that the department contracted had blocked the northbound lane. Not that anyone was traveling this stretch of the highway at night. The faster, better-paved and more centrally located interstate had long since enticed most of the traffic that might have made the trek down this dark, forlorn road.

A frigid wind blew as Yara stepped from the unmarked police sedan. She wore what she thought of as her work uniform—black slacks, a button-down shirt, blue with thin white stripes today, but the color and pattern varied from day to day, and black low-heeled boots. As usual her long, dark brown hair was pulled back in a tight, tidy bun. As a concession to the early November weather, she'd added a black pea coat to her usual ensemble along with a black knit cap, which she pulled down over the tops of her ears as she strode toward her sometimes partner, Martin Rachlin, who stood talking to a uniformed officer and another man. As she did, she made note of the scene.

A second uniformed officer stood guard next to a red Mercedes sitting on the side of the road, the driver's side door open. The plate read "Flyin'" and Yara couldn't help but wonder how many times the driver had been pulled over for speeding.

No flares around the car. The hood was closed. None of the three tires she could see were flat. No indication that the driver had stopped because the car had become disabled in some way.

If the car didn't break down, why had the driver chosen to pull over on this desolate road?

"What do we have?" she asked, stopping next to Martin.

Martin was a couple of inches shorter than her five-ten and outwardly self-conscious about his stature. He compensated for it by donning a tough-guy attitude that often grated on her nerves, although she did her best to be a team player and not show it.

Martin gestured toward the older man, who looked more than a little shell-shocked. Yara put him in his early sixties. Medium height, thinning brown hair, bushy eyebrows. "This is Nelson Freeman. He stopped when he saw the car to see if the driver needed help."

"I saw the blood and I freaked out. I called 911," Mr. Freeman said.

She gave the man what she hoped was a calming smile. "That's exactly the right thing."

He wrung his hands. "Maybe I should have tried CPR. Maybe she could have been saved if I'd tried."

She put a hand on the man's shoulder. "You did exactly the right thing. Sir, do you live around here?"

He nodded. "Yes, ah, my wife and I. I was on my way home from work this morning when I saw the car. I work security at an office building on the Upper West Side. The night shift. I prefer taking this side road because it's quiet. Only a few cars ever use it."

She glanced at Martin. "Do we have Mr. Freeman's statement and contact information?"

Martin nodded.

She motioned for the uniform standing near the Mercedes. She read his nameplate when he joined the group. Kilingham. "Officer Kilingham, can you make sure Mr. Freeman gets back to his car? Sir, you can go home now. If we need anything more from you, we'll be in contact."

The officer led Mr. Freeman away.

She turned back to Martin and the uniform he'd been talking to when she walked up.

Martin was older than her by two years but she'd joined the force right out of college and doggedly worked her way up to detective in only five years. Two years better than the average, but still a year longer than it had taken her older brother, Henry, who was now a sergeant with the San Francisco Police Department and, according to her other brother, Eddie, soon to be a lieutenant. Always the little sister chasing her smarter, braver, stronger big brother and not quite catching up.

Personal problems were for another day, so she forced her focus back to the present.

"Officer Connell." Martin jerked his head at the officer. "First on scene."

Connell had the buzz cut that so many of the young uniforms seemed to favor. As was her habit, she noted his stats—average height, dark hair and eyes, stocky, but not fat. May have been a wrestler in school. "Ma'am, my partner and I were first on scene. We arrived at 21:12 hours." Connell threw his shoulders back and met Yara's gaze directly.

She appreciated the show of respect. Too many of the guys on the force still held misogynistic views about female superiors even in the twenty-first century. It looked like Connell wasn't one of them.

"The car looked to be disabled," Connell continued.

"Was the driver's side door open like it is now? Yara looked up from the notepad she'd taken from her pocket when Connell had begun talking.

He shook his head. "No, ma'am. I opened the door to ascertain the possibility of giving first aid. It was too late."

She made a note. "Okay, go on. The car appeared to be disabled when you got here…"

"Yes. I called in the tags and they were clear. I couldn't see it when I first pulled up, but as I approached the vehicle on the driver's side with my flashlight out, blood was visible on the window. I called for the driver and anyone inside the car to show their hands. When there was no movement from inside, I approached." He paused, swallowing hard.

Yara surmised it was his first time seeing a dead body. He looked young, but then all the uniforms were looking younger and younger these days. "It's okay, Officer Connell. Take your time."

Connell swallowed again before continuing. "I could see there was only one person in the car and that…she was covered in blood. It didn't look like she was breathing. I tried the door and it opened. She was slumped over the steering wheel. I could tell she was gone but I felt for a pulse. When I didn't find one, I called for EMTs and major crimes."

Yara nodded. "Good work." She jerked her chin in the direction of the tow truck. "Could you let the driver know we will be here a while yet."

Connell marched off to take care of the task.

Yara turned to Martin. "Have you taken a look yet?"

"Just a quick one. CSI has gotten all the photos and the medical examiner's people are ready to move the body so we should be good to do a more thorough look-through. I figured you'd want to haul the whole car back to forensics and have them do their thing there."

"Sounds good."

She stuffed her notebook back into her coat pocket and followed Martin to the luxury sports car.

An air freshener shaped like a tree hung from the rearview mirror. It must have been pretty new because the smell of pine hung heavy in the interior of the car even with the open door.

A white woman, mid to late twenties, with blond hair now matted with crimson blood rested against the steering wheel. One arm hung on either side of her body, pink manicured nails sparkling. She wore a long, gray bubble coat and pink strappy heels. Her long pale legs were bare, but the hem of a pink skirt peeked through the opening where the two sides of her coat gaped open at her knees. Her head was turned toward the driver's side window, which made it easy to see the bullet wound in her right temple.

Yara's eyes traveled over the interior of the car. A gun lay on the console between the two seats next to the gearshift.

Suicide?

Possible. She didn't see a note but that wasn't unusual at all. Despite what people were used to seeing on television, most people who committed suicide did not leave a note explaining why they'd decided to take such an extreme, and final, step.

A purse lay on the floor on the passenger footwell. Yara stepped around to that side of the car and opened the door with a gloved hand. "Her purse is still here so that reduces the chances this is a robbery gone bad."

A look of confusion traveled across Martin's face. "Robbery? I'm surprised you're even considering it. This looks like a clear-cut case of suicide to me. Dark road. Gun in the car."

Yara grabbed the purse from the car and glanced at Martin over the roof of the car. Yes, she'd worked her tail off to make detective in record time, but one of the reasons that Martin had struggled with the same task, only earning his shield a little more than a year ago, was that he had developed the habit of jumping to conclusions.

"I'm considering everything until the evidence tells us otherwise."

Martin frowned but didn't say anything more. He was one of the men in the department who couldn't quite hide their displeasure with working with a more senior woman. Too bad. If she had her way, she'd always work alone, but the powers that be had determined that pairing detectives up was a good idea, at least in certain cases. Assigning two detectives to every case just wasn't feasible. She could only hope that Martin would catch his own case and leave her to work this one, whether it turned out to be a suicide or something more insidious, alone.

She pawed through the medium-sized Louis Vuitton bag that ran in the thousands of dollars. The car, the purse. Whoever this woman was, she had money.

Yara found the woman's wallet, also a Louis Vuitton and also costing a good chunk of change, and pulled out the driver's license.

"Name on the driver's license is Tanya Rutger." She bent down, looking across the vehicle's interior to compare the face in the driver's license photo with the one she saw on the other side of the car. "Looks like her."

She handed the license off to Martin and stepped back so he could do his own comparison. "She's twenty-nine. Lives in Manhattan." As she spoke, she went through the other items in the purse. "Has got lots of credit cards. Let's see. I've got an employee identification for the Stryder Medical Clinic. Same name as the license. Says she's a nurse there."

Martin straightened and handed Tanya's driver's license back to her. "My mother was a nurse. They must be making a lot more money than they made back in the day if Tanya can afford this car and a place in Manhattan."

"Don't forget the purse." Yara held it out in front of her. "It retails for a couple grand and the wallet is another grand."

Martin cocked an eyebrow.

"According to *People* magazine. I myself am a lowly public servant who can only dream of such luxuries. Hence the *People* magazine subscription and no Louis Vuitton."

Martin chuckled.

Yara frowned. "What do you think about Nelson Freeman? Is he involved in this?"

The man had seemed like a Good Samaritan just trying to do the neighborly thing and help a stranded motorist, but it wouldn't be the first time a killer had hung around the crime scene. For some it was part of the thrill.

Martin shook his head. "No. He seems credible. He was definitely shaken. Didn't detect any alcohol on his breath and he didn't have a record when I ran him. I think it happened just like he said it did."

She agreed with Martin's assessment. She'd take a look at Nelson Freeman but she didn't expect him to be anything more than a guy who was in the wrong place at the wrong time.

She crouched down, giving the interior of the car another once-over. The forensic guys would have a look for fingerprints on the gun and gunpowder residue on Tanya's hands but the blood-spatter patterns were consistent with someone sitting in the driver's seat and shooting themselves in the right temple. As best she could tell, there was no blood on the outside of the car, which would be consistent with a suicide.

What was so bad that you thought this was the best choice, Tanya?

That was the question. Assuming this was, as it looked, a suicide.

Something tickled at the back of Yara's mind. She opened the purse again. Wallet. Keys, probably for her apartment and maybe work. Lipstick. Half a dozen receipts. Earbuds. And a business card for Brandon West, Attorney at Law.

Her breath hitched. Why did her victim have Brandon's business card? He was one of the best attorneys in town, which meant he was likely one of the most expensive. He also did mostly corporate work. So what would the victim, a nurse, need with a corporate lawyer?

Then again, the connection didn't have to be professional. It could be personal. Maybe Tanya and Brandon were seeing each other.

The thought wrapped around her chest and squeezed the air from her lungs.

She sucked in a deep breath and pushed thoughts of Brandon away.

"It's what I didn't find. What twenty-nine-year-old doesn't have a phone?"

Martin looked at her like she'd just sprouted a second

head. "Every twenty-nine-year-old in the galaxy has a phone. I know some six-year-olds with a phone."

"Right. So where is Tanya's?"

"It's not in her purse?" Martin shined his flashlight in the back seat of the car.

"Not in her purse and not anywhere in the car that I can see," Yara said, following the trajectory of Martin's flashlight over the empty backseat area. Neither of them attempted to open the back doors. Searching for the phone wasn't worth potentially destroying evidence.

"Huh, well, maybe it slid under one of the seats. The forensics guys will find it if it's in there."

"I've got a faster idea." She dialed a number in her phone.

Detective Paris Vaughn answered with a, "Yo."

"Yo, yourself. Can you look up a cell phone number for me right quick?"

"Got a name?"

"Tanya Rutger." She gave Paris the home address, too, just in case there was more than one Tanya Rutger in New York City. It took a couple of minutes but Paris came back with a phone number.

"Paris found a cell phone number?" Martin said when she'd hung up.

"Yep, now let's hope it works." She dialed the number and put the phone on speaker so Martin could hear it ringing. She let it ring until the voice mail picked up. The recording didn't give a last name but they were told they'd reached Tanya, for whatever that was worth, which wasn't much at all.

"That doesn't mean the phone isn't in the car. It could have died or been damaged when she shot herself," Martin said. "Or if she may have just not wanted to take the chance of a friend or family member calling her and talking her out of what she planned to do."

Yara frowned. Not because he was wrong but because he continued to assume that Tanya Rutger had committed suicide. Working the case alone was looking better and better.

"Let's get a couple more uniforms out here to scour the area. Look for the phone and anything else that might be of value."

"Yes, sir." She knew the *sir* was not a sign of respect but she let it go. Martin's expression telegraphed his thoughts. This was a waste of his time. Tanya Rutger had driven to a remote area and shot herself in the head. End of story.

Too bad for him she was the senior detective.

Yara headed back to her car.

"Where are you going, Thomas?" Martin called out.

Butterflies fluttered in her stomach. A missing cell phone wasn't the only loose end in this case. "To speak to a lawyer."

BRANDON WEST STOOD in a corner just outside the courtroom he'd just recently left with his client, Lakeisha Curtis. He hadn't been sure Lakeisha would show for the 9:00 a.m. hearing. This wasn't the first time she'd asked him to file a restraining order against her abusive husband. Each time she'd changed her mind before the hearing. But she'd not only shown up, she'd exhibited a resolve in the courtroom that morning that had renewed his hope that she was finally ready to leave her spouse.

He huddled with Lakeisha and her mother, making sure they were clear about the terms of the order and what they should do if her husband violated those terms.

Glancing up, he spotted a woman standing at the other end of the hall and his pulse raced.

Detective Yara Thomas of the Silver Hill, New York, Police Department. Her eyes were trained on him.

He took stock of the woman he hadn't seen in months

but couldn't seem to stop thinking about. Tall with a heart-shaped face, dark hair pulled back in a sleek ponytail, dark eyes that looked serious but not unkind and plump lipstick-red lips that appeared thoroughly kissable. Hot in a "could kick your butt" sort of way.

Maybe it was the gun.

The badge hooked on the opposite side of her belt said she was on duty. Probably visiting the courthouse on some official police business. His heart sank to his stomach at the realization that she was almost certainly not there to see him.

"Thank you so much, Mr. West," Lakeisha said, pulling his attention away from Yara. "The kids and I have moved in with my mother so you can reach me there if you need to. I haven't gotten a new cell phone yet. I'm changing my number so David can't keep calling me at all times of the day or night."

"That's a good idea. Be careful, though. I'm sure he knows you're at your mother's."

Lakeisha nodded and smiled. "Oh, he knows. But he won't come near there. He also knows my two brothers live with Momma and they'd just as soon shoot him as talk to him."

"Well, I hope it doesn't come to that. I've got to run, but you give me a call if you need me."

He turned and headed for the elevator without sparing Yara a glance and was surprised when she caught up with him as the door slid open.

"Mr. West, can I speak to you for a moment?"

So they were going formal. Well, he couldn't say she hadn't been clear about not wanting a personal relationship with him, so formal it was. Even if his heart was thudding in his chest like a snare drum.

It was early but the courthouse was buzzing with activity already. People streamed off the elevator.

He took a step back out of the way but kept his focus on the detective. "Detective, how can I help you?" He held the door and let Detective Thomas step onto the elevator before he did. Three other people were in the car going down with them.

"I was hoping to speak to you about a case I'm working on."

He searched his memory for a case of his that she could be working on. With the exception of the work he did with the women's shelter, most of his caseload was corporate work. Mergers. Buyouts. Loan facilities. While he was well aware that many corporate types were as criminally minded as any common gangbanger on the street, he did his best to weed them out during the extensive conflicts and background checks he did on each client before agreeing to representation. And since he had one of the country's premier investigative firms at his service, he hadn't had any trouble with the clients he chose to represent.

So what did the lovely Detective Thomas want with him?

"Well, I'm happy to help if I can." He emphasized the last word. If this was about one of his clients, he'd be bound by attorney-client privilege as to what he could tell the detective. "I only have a few minutes before I have to meet a client. How about I buy you a cup of coffee? There's a place on the corner that's good."

She bit her bottom lip, thinking.

Her hesitation irritated him further. "Or we can talk right here in the busy courthouse hallway."

"No, coffee sounds good."

The walk was short. The coffee shop was technically in the same building as the courthouse but had to be entered from the outside. He let Detective Thomas claim them a table, which wasn't hard to do. It wasn't quite 10:00 a.m.

and most people hadn't yet felt the need for a coffee break or early lunch.

He ordered two regular coffees and two Danishes. He'd overslept that morning and hadn't had time to grab anything to eat before heading to the hearing. If the detective didn't want hers, he'd gladly take it.

Coffees carefully balanced on the plates next to Danishes, he made his way to the table. Yara was scrolling on her phone but when she saw him heading for her she dropped it on the table and rose to take one of the plates from him.

"Thanks. I wasn't sure I was going to make it."

One of Thomas's perfectly shaped eyebrows arched. "You could have asked for help."

"That would have been one way to go." He smiled. Asking for help wasn't exactly his thing. He was getting better at it, though. Or at least he thought he was.

Now settled across from the detective, he reiterated the question he'd asked her standing at the courthouse elevators. "So, Detective, how can I help you?"

"Do you know Tanya Rutger?"

His gut clenched. She worked major crimes and if she was asking about his client, it wouldn't be for anything good. "Yes. She's a client."

"And why did she need your services?"

That was the million-dollar question. He wasn't quite sure himself.

He'd met Tanya Rutger a week earlier. She'd been jumpy, obviously scared of something or someone. At first he'd thought she'd come to him on referral from the women's shelter. Most of the time the shelter's director, Joy Wynn, would call and make the appointment for the women at the shelter who wanted to file a restraining order against their abuser or, occasionally, initiate divorce proceedings. But not always. Many women stayed at the shelter for a very short period, sometimes as little as a night. Those women often came immediately after an assault, desperate to escape the violence. But a night in an unfamiliar bed surrounded by battered women—women they didn't see themselves in despite the similar bruises—left them feeling even more afraid. This was a life they didn't know. A future that was unsure. Most returned to their abusers figuring he'd have calmed down during the night. He was sorry. It had been her fault for being too loud, coming home late, talking back. And the cycle would continue.

Although she'd admitted to getting his name from a former client whom he'd helped escape an abusive relationship, Tanya hadn't been looking to file a restraining order, she'd made that much clear. What she did want to hire a lawyer for remained a little murky. She'd seen something that worried her, he'd gotten that much out of her. Something she was sure was illegal, but she hadn't known what to do about it. She wanted to make sure she was protected but she also needed time to think.

He hadn't been comfortable committing to represent her with such scant information but he'd allowed her to fill out the form he had all potential clients complete so he could make sure there were no conflicts of interest between a potential client and his current ones. And she'd insisted on leaving him a retainer with a promise to call him the following week and fill him in on the details of the case.

"Mr. West? Tanya Rutger? Why did she hire you?"

Under the circumstances, he felt it was best to keep his cards close to his chest. He leaned back in his chair. "You understand that attorney-client privilege keeps me from disclosing what my client and I spoke about."

She frowned. "I understand privilege."

"Then you know why I can't answer your question. Why are you asking me about Ms. Rutger?"

The look on her face answered his question.

"Tanya Rutger was found dead earlier this morning."

His heart sank. Though he hadn't really known Tanya, she'd seemed like an intelligent young woman who'd found herself in a tough spot. And now her young life was over almost before she'd really gotten a chance to begin it.

"I'm sure this has come as a shock, but it's important we get as much information as we can," Yara said. "I was under the impression you practiced corporate law. Has that changed since we last met?"

He smiled tightly.

"A lot of things have changed since we last met, Detective. But no, I still mostly practice corporate law. Occasionally, I take on cases outside of that area, though."

"When was the last time you spoke to or saw Tanya Rutger?"

The dismissal of his previous quest still rankled. For a moment, he thought about throwing out the privilege claim again but he suspected she knew the law, at least in this respect, wasn't on his side. When he spoke to his client wasn't a confidential communication. "About a week ago."

"In your office?"

His lips quirked up. "Yes, that is where I typically meet clients. West & Williams LLP does have two offices and typically clients find it easier to meet in the Lower Manhattan headquarters, but Tanya and I met in the Silver Hill office."

"Did she say why she wanted to meet with you there instead of in Manhattan?"

He shook his head. "She didn't. And I didn't ask."

Her frown deepened. "And you haven't spoken to her or seen her since?"

"No." Something was up and it involved Tanya Rutger. He wouldn't find out talking to Yara. Fortunately, he was related to a few people who could probably help him find out what was going on.

He dusted invisible crumbs from his hands. "I'm sorry, Detective. It seems we've reached the limit of what I can tell you about my client and, unless you're willing to share why you're interested in her, I have to be going now."

He stood and she followed suit.

"Thank you for the coffee and Danish," she said. "I'll be in touch."

Something to look forward to under any other circumstances but now, not so much.

She turned and marched from the coffee shop as if she had been the one to end their conversation.

Yara Thomas was a woman who liked to be in charge. Maybe it was time she learned to share the reins.

Chapter Two

Breathing seemed to come easier once she walked away from Brandon. She had managed to stay out of his orbit for the past several months but she hadn't anticipated how awkward it would be when she inevitably saw him again.

They'd met in this very courthouse after she'd spent a grueling day on the stand in a drug trafficking case. He wasn't one of the attorneys involved in the case, but he had caught some of her testimony and had complimented her after court adjourned for the day on having kept her cool under the defense attorney's barrage of questions.

Whether it had been fatigue or his chocolate brown eyes, she'd consented to letting him buy her a cup of coffee. And when he'd called the next day and asked to take her out to lunch, she'd agreed. A couple of more coffee dates and one very romantic dinner and she'd felt herself falling under the thrall of the handsome, successful attorney.

So she'd cut him off. Stopped taking his calls, returning his messages and texts. Cold turkey. Usually, if she got past a second date with a guy, she'd take him for a roll or two in the hay. A woman had needs, after all.

But even though there had been loads of sexual tension, like bucketloads, big hulking Mack truckloads of sexual tension, between her and Brandon, they'd never taken that

step. And she had kind of liked it. Getting to know him on
a deeper level and letting him know her a little more than
she usually did with men as well. It had happened almost
without her realizing it, but when she did, she put a stop to
it right away.

She had a rule. No relationships.

They were simply too hard when one person was a cop.
And it wasn't fair. Not when she could be hurt or worse.

It was better to keep things casual. And when you
couldn't, to end them as quickly and cleanly as possible.

She called Martin on her way to the Stryder Medical
Clinic and updated him on her brief and unfruitful conversation with Brandon. Twenty minutes later, Martin met her
in the clinic's parking lot and they spent the next few hours
questioning the two doctors who ran the practice and several of Tanya's coworkers. Word had already reached the
practice about Tanya's death.

They spoke to the clinic's co-directors, Dr. Steven Manning and Dr. Anand Gristedes, as well as several other employees. Everyone said Tanya was a great employee and a
good coworker, and though several people mentioned she
had seemed somewhat preoccupied in the last couple of
weeks, no one suspected depression or that she was suicidal. They all suggested they speak with Bailey Dunlap, a
fellow nurse and Tanya's close friend. Unfortunately, Bailey had gone home, wracked with grief after finding out
about Tanya.

She and Martin returned and they spent the rest of the
morning finding out as much as they could about their victim.

Tanya Rutger rented a one-bedroom luxury apartment in
Lower Manhattan, in a neighborhood where rents started at
more than three thousand dollars and went up from there.
When she and Martin arrived at the apartment around

midafternoon, the building was quiet. Most of the residents were probably still at work slaving away to make their rent. She'd called ahead to inform the building manager of Tanya's death and the need to search her apartment.

A fortysomething woman in a conservative dark green suit and kitten heels waited next to the doorman's desk when she and Martin pushed through the revolving door into the lobby. The woman held a black-leather-covered folio and stood so straight Yara suspected the woman had spent time in the military.

"Detective Thomas?"

Yara extended a hand. "Yes. And this is Detective Rachlin."

"I'm Una Snowden, the building manager. We spoke on the phone earlier today." Ms. Snowden quickly shook each of their hands.

"Thank you for your cooperation," Yara said. She'd requested a search warrant for the apartment and faxed it to the building manager as a means of expediting entry into Tanya's apartment. She'd dealt with enough apartment managers to know that the real estate company would want the formal search warrant in order to cover themselves for letting the cops into a resident's home. Even a dead resident. Getting the warrant had taken longer than she'd have liked. There wasn't much urgency to an investigation when the victim appeared to have committed suicide, but the warrant had finally come through.

"Of course. Let me show you to the apartment." She led them to the elevators, which carried them to the sixth floor.

Tanya's unit was about midway down the long corridor of apartments.

Una unlocked the door and stepped aside.

Martin strode into the unit ahead of Yara, who hung back to question the apartment manager.

"When was the last time you saw Ms. Rutger?" Yara asked.

The other woman's forehead furrowed. "I don't have much contact with the residents unless they have a problem. Ms. Rutger was relatively new to our building. The last time I remember speaking to her was just after she moved in and I ran into her in the lobby. I asked her if she was settling in and she said she was. I don't think I've spoken to her since then."

"The warrant included the rental paperwork on the unit."

"Yes, I have that." Mrs. Snowden flipped her leather folio open and handed over a sheath of papers.

Yara flipped through them. The rental application was in Tanya's name and detailed a monthly rent of $4,300 a month. There was no way Tanya could afford that on her salary as a nurse, not even one working for a successful private practice.

"How did Ms. Rutger afford this place?"

"She was a nurse," Una said timidly.

Yara pinned the manager with a narrow-eyed gaze.

"There was a man with her. He didn't want to be formally listed on the application, but he said he would be paying the rent."

She studied the other woman. "And you allowed that?"

The woman shrugged, but her cheeks were beet red. "He paid the year up front. In cash. There was no risk on our end so I didn't see the harm."

A year up-front? She did the math in her head. That was almost $52,000. In cash. Not including any fees the building assessed. If this mystery man was throwing that much money around, he had probably thrown a little at Una Snowden to sweeten the deal.

"Did you get the name of this man?"

She shook her head. "No. He did not want his name connected to the apartment in any way."

Which almost certainly meant he was married and Tanya was his sidepiece. Since the apartment was in the financial district that could mean that he worked down here somewhere. At one of the many investment banks maybe? Of course, he could have chosen to set his mistress up as far away from his wife and everyday life as possible, which could mean he worked anywhere other than the financial district. The proverbial needle in a haystack.

"Do you think you could describe the man?"

The lines etched on Una's forehead deepened. "It's been months. I can't really recall. Average height and build. He had brown hair or dark blond, I think."

Her tone carried too much uncertainty for the description to be relied upon.

"Okay, Ms. Snowden. We'll let you know if we need you for anything further."

The manager let out a sigh of relief. Turning on her heels, she marched back toward the elevators.

Yara entered the apartment. She pulled a pair of gloves from her pocket and put them on. She could request a tech out to the apartment to lift fingerprints but she wasn't sure Lieutenant Wilson would approve it if the medical examiner came back with a conclusion of suicide. It might be the only way they'd find out who Tanya's mystery man was so she was determined to make the case for it. Right now he was one of the many loose ends she wanted to tie up.

The kitchen was small but functional. There was a dirty bowl and a glass in the sink as if Tanya intended to take care of cleaning up when she returned from work, but she'd never had the chance.

She opened the fridge. Veggies, milk, fruit, yogurt, eggs. It looked like Tanya had recently made a trip to the grocery store. Would a woman contemplating suicide bother stocking her fridge? She didn't think so.

She stepped into the bathroom, which like the rest of the apartment was pretty upscale. It had a prefab tub but tiles lined the walls around it and the vanity countertop was granite. A purple razor and a jumble of bottles—soap, perfumes, deodorant, nail polish, a cup holding a pink toothbrush and toothpaste—cluttered the vanity top. In the cabinet above the sink, she found hundreds of dollars of makeup and grooming utensils. A bottle of aspirin and over-the-counter allergy medicine were the only drugs in the medicine cabinet. Under the sink she found mouthwash, body wash, lotion, feminine products, a hair dryer, flat iron and several curling irons. Nothing she wouldn't have expected to find in a twenty-nine-year-old woman's bathroom. Right outside the bathroom was a linen closet that held nothing but towels, sheets and other linens.

Martin stepped out of the bedroom a few feet down the hall. "Did you get anything from the building manager?"

She filled him in on the cost of the apartment and the mystery man who'd paid for a year up-front.

"And I'm guessing you want to find this guy even though this is looking more and more like a suicide."

She frowned. "We don't know what this looks like. That's why we are investigating, so yes, I'd like to talk to the man who paid for Tanya to live here."

He shook his head, the expression on his face saying he thought she was wasting her time. "Maybe he broke up with her. Maybe he was throwing her out of the apartment and she became despondent over losing her lover and her home. It happens."

"Tanya only moved in three months ago. The apartment was paid through for a year and in her name only. I doubt she could have been thrown out even if her guy had wanted to do so."

Martin crossed his arms over his chest. "So maybe the

breakup was enough to drive her over the edge. We've both got a dozen more cases on our desk. Let's not turn this into more than it is."

She felt her frown deepen. His penchant for cutting corners was one of the reasons she hated it when Lieutenant Wilson assigned her and Martin to work together. "I'm not turning this into anything. I want to find the truth."

Martin rolled his eyes. "Well, I didn't find anything helpful in the apartment."

There was no way she was going to rely on Martin's search so she slid past him and into Tanya's bedroom.

The room was bright with light coming in through the open curtains. The room smelled faintly of strawberry and she recalled noting that the body wash, shampoo and conditioner Tanya used were strawberry scented. She scanned the space, taking in the neatly made bed and the shoes lined up on a rack next to what she presumed was the closet. The nightstand was bare of clutter holding only a single paperback, a romance. She opened the drawer in the nightstand. A power cord for a phone was coiled inside.

Tanya did have a phone. So where was it?

She stepped over to the dresser and opened the top drawer. Neatly stacked long-sleeved T-shirts and scrub tops were inside. Each of the remaining drawers was equally as organized and held nothing of evidentiary interest. She turned to the closet. Tanya sorted her clothes by type—shirts, dresses, skirts—hung side by side in a tidy row. The shelf above held sweaters and an assortment of jeans. Tucked below the hangers was a single silver roll-on suitcase with three more expensive handbags tucked away inside.

Out of everything she hadn't found in the apartment, the most conspicuous was the absence of a cell phone, computer or any other device. No way a twenty-nine-year-old woman didn't have at least a phone and a computer.

She returned to the living area and found Martin scrolling on his phone.

"There's not a single indication in this apartment that Tanya was distraught enough to want to end her own life," she said.

"Sometimes people don't show how disturbed they are to the outside world," Martin replied without looking up from his phone.

Maybe, but she didn't think that was the case here. No, the more she learned about Tanya Rutger, the less she thought the woman had committed suicide.

What then?

An accident seemed unlikely. So that just left...murder.

She had nothing more than a hunch, but it felt right.

Someone had killed Tanya Rutger and done their best to make it appear that she'd taken her own life.

The question was who would have wanted the twenty-nine-year-old nurse dead.

She couldn't help but think the answer lay with Tanya's mystery man.

Voices in the hall pulled her attention from her thoughts. She crossed the apartment and pulled open the door.

A woman was opening the door to the apartment directly across the hall with one hand and holding a cell phone to her ear with the other.

"Excuse me. I'm Detective Yara Thomas with the Silver Hill Police Department. Do you mind if I ask you a few questions about your neighbor Tanya Rutger?"

The woman's face morphed into an expression of concern. "I'll call you back," she said to the person on the other end of the line before dropping the phone in her open purse. "Is Tanya okay?"

This was one part of the job that she hated. "I'm sorry

to have to inform you but Ms. Rutger was found deceased earlier this morning."

"Oh, my God." The woman slapped a hand over her mouth.

Yara gave the woman a moment to compose herself and pulled her notebook from her pocket before asking, "Could I get your name?"

"Ah, Sharon. Sharon Taylor."

"Ms. Taylor, did you know Tanya well?"

"Well, no. Just to say hello and make small talk if we were in the elevator together, you know? She was a pretty private person."

"When was the last time you saw her?"

"Last night, actually. She was on her way out when I was on my way in."

"And what time was that?"

The woman cast her eyes up to the ceiling. "Oh, about eleven thirty. I had a date. It went well," Sharon said absently.

"And did you talk to Tanya?"

"No." Sharon shook her head. "She seemed like she was upset and was in a rush. And she was on the phone."

So Tanya did have her phone with her last night.

She was already going to request Tanya's phone records but Sharon's details would help if she faced pushback from the lieutenant.

"Did Tanya have a lot of guests?"

Sharon shrugged. "Can't say I notice who comes and goes from my neighbors' places. We all pretty much keep to ourselves."

It was the blessing and the curse of living in the city. You could live side by side with someone for years and never really know anything about them.

"Thanks. If you recall anything that might help, please give me a call." Yara handed over a business card.

"Detective? You never said how Tanya died."

Yara looked into Sharon's anxious eyes. "I'm working on that."

Chapter Three

Detective Paris Vaughn had her long legs propped up on the seat of Yara's black desk chair. Seven months pregnant, she was on desk duty shuffling paperwork, running background checks and finding phone numbers for detectives in the field. And hating every minute of it.

"I don't think that's how ergonomic chairs work, Vaughn," Yara said, dropping her coat on the rack next to the door to the large room that housed four of the six detectives on the Silver Hill major case squad. The other two detectives shared a slightly larger office, two doors down on the same floor.

"It's working for me. At least for the moment. I've tried to tell this kid I'm doing him a favor, you know, letting him use my body to be birthed and all. The least he can do is go easy on me, but noooooo."

Yara smiled across the desk at her friend. The fiery redhead was doing possibly the biggest favor one woman could do for another. After years of trying, Paris's older sister had been told that the chances of her ever getting pregnant and carrying a child to term were vanishingly small. Paris had volunteered to be her sister and brother-in-law's surrogate.

"You'll forget all these aches and pains the moment you

hold your nephew in your arms." Yara rolled Martin's chair from his desk to hers and sat down.

"Don't you know it." Paris grinned. "I can't wait to meet the little guy. Did you find the lawyer?"

Paris had tracked down Brandon West for her at the courthouse.

Yara frowned. "Yeah, I found him."

Paris laughed. "Went well, then."

It was frustrating to say but Brandon had been the best part of the day even with his insistence on being unhelpful. The medical examiner refused to fast-track Tanya's autopsy. The cell phone company was taking its time pulling her phone records. And she had made no headway on finding Tanya's phone or the name of her mystery man.

"He wouldn't tell me anything else except that Tanya was his client."

"Well, I looked at her record when you were away. A single pop for disorderly conduct when she was nineteen. She hasn't had so much as a ticket since, so nothing there will tell us why she hired a lawyer."

"I'll find out one way or another." She smoothed a flyaway hair that had come free from the bun at the nape of her neck.

Paris's gaze was piercing. "Oh, ho ho. It looks like the lawyer got under your skin. I know I wouldn't mind getting under his—"

"Paris!"

"Sorry, sorry." She threw one hand in the air as the other rubbed her belly. "This pregnancy has got my hormones surging all over the place. That said, I have seen Brandon West. He was the defense attorney on a civil case that had a tangential connection to one of mine. He's smok'n hot."

Yara kept her eyes trained on the file in front of her. "I hadn't noticed."

Paris snorted. "Yeah, right."

Of course she'd noticed, but she had been very careful to keep her relationship—no, not relationship, the few dates they'd gone on—under wraps. Both because he was an attorney and because she'd only ever expected it to be a casual fling at best. That it hadn't even made it that far, well, she was glad she'd never mentioned the coffee dates to Paris or anyone else.

She glanced over the top of the file folder and caught Paris's amused expression.

"What?" she grumbled.

"Nothing. I just thought you should know that there was an incident report filed under Tanya's name. She reported a break-in at her apartment a few weeks back. The perps made a mess, but Tanya reported nothing of value was taken. NYPD responded. Tanya couldn't tell them who might be after her. The building only has security cameras in the lobby and however the perp got in it wasn't that way. There was nothing to go on."

Definitely not a B&E. There were much easier targets than a sixth-floor apartment, and in light of Tanya's death, she had to consider whether there was something to it. Maybe Martin wasn't wrong about Tanya having broken up with the boyfriend. And if he'd prepaid for a year's rent, maybe he felt justified in getting some of that money "back" by destroying Tanya's things. All great questions to ask the mystery boyfriend when she found him.

Martin entered the bullpen.

"Just got back from the lab. Only fingerprints found on the car and on the gun were Tanya's, the uniforms that were first on the scene and Nelson Freeman's."

Yara's ears perked up. "Freeman's? Did he mention touching the car in his statement?"

"No—" Martin shook his head "—and his prints were

found on the outside of the trunk. I still don't see him being involved. You saw how shaken he was, Yar. He probably touched the car and didn't even realize he'd done it."

She frowned. More assumptions. "We need to follow up with him anyway. I pulled his record. It's clean. Let's go deeper. Talk to his neighbors. Friends. See if there's any connection at all between him and Tanya. Maybe they were having an affair."

Martin's eyebrows shot up. "A woman who looks like her doesn't date a sixty-something-year-old man. Hey, where's my chair?" His eyes skirted over Paris and narrowed.

"Just grab Jimmy's." Yara made no attempt to hide the irritation in her voice. "We both wondered how Tanya could afford an apartment in Manhattan, an expensive sports car and thousands of dollars in handbags. Maybe Freeman is her sugar daddy."

"Sugar daddy?" Martin plopped down in his purloined chair. "Did you read the background on Freeman? He's been married for thirty-nine years. Has two daughters and a grandson. Worked at the same place for forty-two years before retiring two years ago."

Yara sighed. "I'm not accusing the man of anything but we need to look into it. Forensics get anything else from the car?"

"No hair or fibers," Martin grumbled. "Still working on the blood spatter but so far it's all the same type so it's looking like it is all going to be Tanya's."

"Did they find a phone?"

Martin gave a thumbs-down.

No phone. That was the thing that bothered her the most. Everyone had a phone. Tanya had a charger for an iPhone in her night table, and her neighbor had seen her leave the apartment talking on her phone. So where was it?

Most people had their entire lives on the devices.

What was on Tanya's phone that someone didn't want them to see? And did that same someone kill her and make it look like a suicide?

There was no sign of anyone else in the car. That might be possible if the perp wore gloves and a hat. But how had he or she gotten away from the scene? The area wasn't exactly walking distance to anything.

There was also the question of how the killer had lured Tanya to the dark, desolate road so late at night. She was a female city dweller. It was unlikely she was naive enough to take a drive down a dark road alone for no reason.

But if Tanya and Freeman were in some kind of relationship that could explain it. He admitted he frequented that road. Maybe it was their regular meeting place. Things got out of hand. Freeman ends up killing his mistress and then freaks out. Calls the cops.

Possible, but it was nearly impossible for Freeman to have killed Tanya in the heat of the moment and leave no forensic evidence at all.

She'd look into Freeman but she had to agree with Martin, he didn't fit.

"Thomas. Rachlin." Lieutenant Wilson strode into the bullpen. "Tanya Rutger's mother is here. I put her in the large conference room."

Martin groaned. "Sometimes I hate this job."

That was another thing she agreed with him on.

Chapter Four

West Investigations was housed in a three-story building on the Upper West Side of Manhattan. The interior was decorated in rich tones of deep beige and burgundy. Leather sofas and armchairs and tasteful abstract art decorated the waiting area.

James West Sr. had started West Investigations more than thirty years ago with work focused primarily on providing alarms and security systems for commercial buildings. Brandon's younger brothers, Ryan and Shawn, had expanded the business when they took over the day-to-day operations into a full-service security management firm that handled residential, commercial and personal security needs, as well as investigations of all types, for some of the world's most prominent businesses and individuals. While his older brother, James Jr., took on select investigative projects, Brandon had opted to keep his role with the family business firmly rooted in his expertise—legal work. He handled all the company's contractual business and served as their primary legal counsel, but left the security and investigative work to his brothers.

At least most of the time. A dead client seemed like a good reason to make an exception.

West's newest receptionist, Emily Kwan, greeted him with a wide smile as he strode toward the receptionist's desk.

"Mr. West, how nice to see you. Are your brothers expecting you?"

He smiled at the recent college graduate. "Emily, now, I've told you to call me Brandon. And no, my brothers aren't expecting me, but I'm hoping one or both have a moment."

"Let me just check." She reached for the phone, but before she raised the receiver, his youngest brother, Shawn, appeared from around the faux wall separating the reception area from the rear of the office where business got done.

For as long as he could remember, he and his brothers had been told how much they resembled each other and their father. The older they got, the more Brandon had to agree. Looking at Shawn now was like looking at himself five years ago. They had similar, medium brown coloring and dark brown hair and eyes, but his youngest brother was broader in the shoulders and sported a more muscled physique. His style was more casual and laid-back. Today, he wore dark jeans and a ribbed shirt under a dark sports coat.

Shawn's eyes landed on him and a boyish smile spread across his face. "Brandon. To what do we owe this surprise?" They shared a quick one-handed hug with a backslap. Shawn stepped back, his eyes roaming over the bespoke suit and black leather briefcase in Brandon's hand. "You're looking mighty serious. Are you here on business?"

"Actually, I am."

"Are we getting sued?"

Brandon quirked an eyebrow. "Not that I know of. Have you done something to get sued for?"

"If you don't know, I'm not telling." Shawn laughed. "Come on back."

He followed his brother back through the corridor, calling out greetings to the staff members who were in the first-come, first-served cubicles as he went. Private investigation and security work didn't lend itself to a typical office environment. Employees at West came and went as they saw fit, but the freedom to do their work without the boss unnecessarily hanging over their shoulders had created fierce loyalty in West employees. Most of the people who worked for West had done so for years, some having been with the firm since their father ran things. James Sr. had managed the company as if his employees were part of his extended family and Shawn and Ryan had continued the tradition when they'd taken over.

They finally reached Shawn's corner office, the walk having taken twice as long as it should have. Brandon wasn't surprised to find Ryan waiting in Shawn's office when they arrived.

"Took you long enough," Ryan said, looking up from his phone. He sat in one of the visitor's chairs with his feet up on one corner of Shawn's desk.

"What can I say? Everyone wants to say hello to their favorite West brother," Brandon quipped.

He unbuttoned his suit jacket and sat on the black leather couch that formed part of the cozy sitting area in Shawn's office.

"In your dreams." Shawn knocked Ryan's feet from his desk and sat in his red-and-black high-backed leather executive chair behind his chrome-and-glass desk. "So what's the business that has you interrupting our very busy day here at West Investigations?"

"I need you to look into someone for me. A client of sorts."

"A client of sorts?" Ryan frowned.

"It's a long story. A woman came to see me. She was

scared of something or someone but wouldn't give me details. She left a retainer so that's good enough for me to call her a client."

"Okay, so why do you need us to find her? Don't you have her contact information?"

"Unfortunately, she's dead. I got a visit from a major crimes detective earlier today."

He caught the look on Ryan's face. Months earlier, he'd told Ryan about Yara and that he thought he could develop real feelings for her. He was willing to admit he'd moped a little when she'd stopped taking his calls and he knew Ryan had noticed. There wasn't much Ryan didn't notice. But he hoped his brother would refrain from asking which major crimes detective had come to see him.

Thankfully, Shawn spoke first. "This is official, right?" He turned to face the computer monitor at the desk and began tapping on his keyboard, opening an official file, no doubt.

"All official. I'm hiring West as a consultant. As far as I'm concerned, Miss Rutger is a client until I'm informed otherwise by a representative of her estate." Bringing West on officially as consultants on Tanya's case meant that attorney-client privilege would also protect West's communications taken on his behalf.

"Tanya Rutger," Shawn said typing. "Address, phone number, social security number and whatever else you have. You know the drill."

He did, which was why he'd brought along a copy of the file he'd opened on Tanya Rutger. He took it from his briefcase and stood to hand it to Shawn.

"I'll scan all this info into the system later but for now…" Shawn typed furiously, no doubt pulling up all the information he could find on Tanya Rutger. It was why he'd come to his brothers. He did background checks on all his clients, before taking them on, but he didn't have access to the kinds of databases that West subscribed to.

"Could she have been involved with a violent partner?" Ryan asked.

"Tanya wasn't clear about exactly what her concerns were, but she wasn't looking to file a restraining order and I didn't get the sense that she was being abused. She dodged a lot of my questions at our initial meeting. I just know that she'd seen something that troubled her and she felt she might need a lawyer."

Ryan shot him a pointed look. "Whatever it was, it must have been big. You think she was involved in something shady or dangerous? Maybe she's on the run?"

"Maybe." But he didn't think that was it, either. That wasn't the vibe he'd gotten off her. What he'd gotten was abject fear. "I want to know what was going on. She was supposed to get in touch with me later this week, but she was killed before that happened. Why was she killed? What *had* she gotten herself into?"

Shawn looked over the top of his computer screen. "I can't tell you what Tanya Rutger is into but I can tell you about the new case the major crimes division caught yesterday. A body was found in a car on the side of a remote road earlier this morning." He turned the monitor so Brandon and Ryan could see it.

An article from a local news blog filled the screen. Under the headline "Dead Body Found" was a photograph of a red car being lifted onto the back of a tow truck.

He recognized the profile of the woman in the corner of the shot so he wasn't surprised by the probing look Ryan shot at him or Shawn's next words.

"Detective Yara Thomas is primary on the case. Was she the detective you spoke with?"

ENGROSSED IN WHATEVER he was reading on his phone, Brandon West didn't immediately look up when she entered the conference room, giving Yara a few precious moments to study the man. He wore the same suit he'd been wearing when she had met him at the courthouse that morning, but now he looked slightly ruffled. But ruffled worked on him. Hell, everything worked on him. It was the lean, wide-shouldered frame and expressive brown eyes that made her heart stutter when he turned them on her. The man was the definition of fine.

A faint warning bell went off in her head. She shouldn't be thinking of Brandon as an attractive man. Or thinking about him at all.

He sat in the chair with his shoulders hunched forward and frown lines creasing the skin at the edges of his mouth. She was good at reading other people's faces and body language. It was part of what made her so good at her job. And she knew Brandon West was worried.

After a moment, he looked up, finally seeming to realize he wasn't in the conference room alone anymore.

"Detective, I'm sorry. I didn't realize you had arrived."

She placed her notepad on the table and slid into a seat on the opposite side of the table from him. "It's not a problem. Can I get you anything? Water?"

He flashed a quick small smile. "That would be great, thanks."

She stepped out of the room and grabbed two bottled waters from the small kitchenette area at the end hall. She slid one across the table to Brandon and set the other one next to her notepad.

He twisted the top off the bottle and took a long sip, his Adam's apple bobbing.

"I must say I was surprised when the front desk clerk called to say I had a visitor," she said. "After our conversation this morning I didn't think you'd be cooperating with me."

He frowned. "I never said I wouldn't cooperate."

She shot a pointed look across the table. "Yet, you didn't cooperate when I asked for information."

"I have a duty to keep my client's confidence. I told you what I could given the circumstances then."

That sounded just like something a lawyer would say. Which was why they weren't her favorite people. Even the incredibly handsome, smolderingly sexy ones.

She mentally slapped herself and refocused. "And have the circumstances changed?"

"I think they might have. Tell me, is the body you found on the road this morning that of my client, Tanya Rutger?"

He set his phone on the table and turned it so she could see the article he had pulled up.

She swore under her breath. She'd thought the remote location would have bought them more time outside of the press's intrusive glare, but she should have known better.

She scanned the article. It didn't appear the vultures had Tanya's name, at least not yet. They would soon, Yara had no doubt. Thankfully, they'd been able to confirm Tanya's identity through her fingerprints and they'd already notified Tanya's mother of her daughter's death. The department media office was working on a press release as they spoke that was scheduled to go out later that afternoon but at this point there didn't seem to be much reason to keep Brandon West in the dark.

"I'm sorry to have to inform you, but the body we found this morning has been positively identified as Tanya Rutger," she said, falling back on her standard line for delivering news no one ever wanted to get.

Brandon let out a breath so deep it shook his broad shoulders. The sadness she saw in his eyes ran deep. He'd cared for Tanya Rutger.

An emotion flared in her chest but she'd have sooner taken a bullet than to call it out as jealousy.

"Were you and Ms. Rutger close?" She worked to keep her expression neutral, but flinched at how brittle the words came out.

If Brandon noticed, he didn't show it.

It would have been unethical for an attorney to get involved with his client but if he'd taken her on as a client because they had a personal relationship, that would explain how a nurse could afford his services. She'd done an internet search on Brandon West before their first coffee date months earlier so she'd known he had offices in Manhattan and Silver Hill before this case landed on her desk.

"Close as in personally? Not at all." He shook his head for emphasis. "I only met her once. A week ago, as I mentioned to you earlier, in my office."

The tension in her chest dissipated. She took a deep breath and got her thoughts back on track, on the case. "And you wouldn't tell me why she'd hired you."

"Couldn't and wouldn't aren't the same things. I'm not sure it would have helped you anyway."

Annoyance knotted her stomach. That wasn't up to him to decide. "Why don't you tell me and let me decide that for myself."

He gave a slight smile, revealing dimples in his cheeks that made her knees go weak. Good thing she was sitting.

"I'm not here to aggravate you, Yara. Once I realized that Tanya might be the poor woman you found this morning, I decided it was in her best interests if I provided you with whatever help I could."

Yara clicked her pen to ready mode. "I'm glad you made that determination. So, why did Ms. Rutger hire you?"

"I'm not sure exactly."

She knew what she'd been expecting him to say but it wasn't that. How could he not know what he'd been hired to do? Her face must have said what she was thinking because he held up a hand as if warding off her question before she could ask it.

"I know it sounds a little weird. Let me start from the beginning. Ms. Rutger came to my office in Silver Hill a week ago yesterday. She was visibly anxious about something and, though she didn't actually say this, I suspected she was more than a little bit afraid, which would have explained why she wanted to meet in Silver Hill rather than at the Manhattan office where I normally meet clients."

"Afraid? Afraid of what?"

He shook his head. "I don't know. She was very evasive in her answers to my questions. All she'd tell me is that she'd seen something illegal and that she thought she might need an attorney, but she wouldn't go into specifics."

"And you took her case without knowing what it was she wanted you to do for her?"

Most of the lawyers she came into contact with were either criminal defense lawyers or prosecutors but Brandon did not practice criminal law as one of his areas of specialty.

"My firm does a little of everything. Including my partner and I, there are ten lawyers at the firm and a dozen paralegals and support staff. We're a small firm with varied practice. It's how we survive the industry's ups and downs. I do mostly corporate work—mergers, acquisitions, loans, securities. But I also do a lot of pro bono work with women who are victims of domestic abuse. I thought maybe whatever she'd seen had something to do with that. While I don't normally take on clients without knowing the specifics of their representation, this was an unusual case."

She was surprised. Not many attorneys of his stature

would do pro bono work on behalf of abused women. It made her like Brandon West more, and that was dangerous, because she already liked him a lot. Too much.

"Okay, so you thought Tanya might be a victim of domestic violence?" She jotted the letters *DV* on her notepad.

"I didn't say that. It's just that she gave off the same vibe as the women I represent. The same waves of fear and desperation. It's why I took her on without knowing exactly what she wanted from me. She was so upset about something, I couldn't just turn her way. She signed the retainer agreement and was supposed to contact me this week to discuss details. If her issue wasn't something that fell into one of my specialties, I would have made sure to connect her with an attorney in my firm that did specialize in her issue. Or, if need be, connect her with a firm that would take her on."

"Do you have any idea who referred her to you?"

He shook his head. "There's a spot for that on the intake form, but she left it blank. She did mention that she got my name from a friend who used my services in a domestic violence case, but I don't know which client. I don't usually push if a prospective client doesn't want to answer that question. They have their reasons."

Brandon might not have been sure about the domestic violence theory, but it was a possibility she'd have to explore. Especially given what she knew about Tanya's mystery man. Although public perception of domestic violence usually centered on lower-income and marginalized women as the primary targets of abuse, she knew that far more middle-class and upper-income women were victims than anyone wanted to admit. Tanya's expensive car and apartment might be explained by a boyfriend, maybe one who was abusing her? But Tanya's mother hadn't given them a lot to work with. She hadn't thought Tanya was seeing anyone and she hadn't been to Tanya's new apartment. To be honest it didn't seem like mother and daughter were particularly close, although the woman had been devastated to learn of her daughter's death. It wasn't unheard of for an abused woman to hide the abusive relationship from their family and close friends.

"Okay," she said, going back through the notes of the conversation she'd had with him earlier in the day. "And you said you hadn't spoken to her since that day in your office. Was that the truth?"

She looked up to find his face stormy.

"Detective Thomas, the rules of my profession may not allow me to tell you everything I know, but I do not lie."

She saw that he was genuinely angered by her implication that he'd lied to her. "I'm sorry. Let's go back a step. The last time you spoke to Miss Rutger was a week ago, correct?"

"Yes," he bit out. "Last Tuesday to be precise. The day she came to my office and I began the paperwork to formally begin our professional relationship. I did leave a message for her a couple of days after that, last Friday, asking her to call and set up another appointment so I could get more information on what she wanted me to do for her, but she never returned my call. After speaking with you this morning, I tried calling her again but, of course, there was no answer."

"You tried calling her on her cell phone?"

"Yes. It's the only number she gave me. Why do you ask?"

"We didn't find Ms. Rutger's cell phone with her belongings."

His eyes narrowed. "She definitely had a cell phone. She had it in her hand the entire time she was in my office. When she filled out the intake form, she used it to pull up information."

"What do you ask on your intake form that she needed to look up on her phone?"

"Just information on next of kin and close relatives. I have to make sure that the interests of any new clients don't conflict with the interests of any of my current clients."

Yara nodded her understanding. "Can you give me the number you called and any other contact information you have for Ms. Rutger? I want to make sure it's the same as what we have for her." She turned to a clean sheet of paper and slid her notepad across the table to him. "I also wouldn't mind having that client intake form and your notes from the meeting with Ms. Rutger."

He glanced up from writing with a wry smile. "Nice try, Detective."

She felt herself smile back. "It was worth a shot."

He copied Tanya's information. When he was finished, he slid the notebook back to her. "Can I ask you something?"

It was unlikely she'd answer, but she was curious about what he wanted to know. She gave him a little nod. "Go ahead."

"The article said you'd found Tanya's body in her car on the side of the road. It didn't look like there was any damage to the car, at least not from the photo in the article. You're a major-case detective. Can I take it that Tanya didn't die of natural causes while driving?"

She instinctively rebelled against telling him anything about an open case, but the press release would be out any minute stating that Tanya Rutger had been shot.

"Tanya didn't die as a result of a car accident. She was shot."

His eyes widened and he jerked away from the table a little, as if trying to put more distance between himself and the information she'd imparted. "Shot? As in murdered?"

She shook her head. She didn't need him getting ahead

of her investigation. "We don't know that. Not yet. We are investigating the case as a suspicious death at the moment." Another piece of information that would be shared with the public in the press statement being released.

"What is the other option?" His brow furrowed in thought. "Suicide? You think she could have shot herself?" He shook his head. "I don't think so. I know I only met her in person once, but Tanya Rutger didn't strike me as suicidal."

"You said she was very worried about something."

"Yes, she was. And scared if I read her right. But if she was planning to commit suicide, why hire me?"

"I don't know. Maybe she didn't start contemplating suicide until after she left your office."

"You think it's possible she went from scared but hiring a lawyer to suicidal in a week's time?" He shook his head, disbelief written over his face.

She agreed it wasn't likely, but as he'd said, he only met her once and only briefly then. He couldn't possibly say for sure Tanya wasn't suicidal when she'd walked into his office.

"I assure you, I will be investigating all possibilities, Mr. West."

He sighed. "Yara, given the situation, I think we can put aside the awkwardness from our brief prior association. Just call me Brandon."

Prior association. Something about categorizing whatever they'd started months earlier so coldly stung. But if he could move on, so could she.

"Sure, Brandon." She gave a tight smile. "Let me walk you out."

Chapter Five

"Police found the body of a woman parked in her car off of Interstate 95 yesterday morning. Details remain scant, but authorities say that Tanya Rutger was found having suffered at least one gunshot wound. The case is being investigated as a possible homicide. It's time for us to take a short break, but when we return Dan Coates will be here with your five-day forecast."

Brandon used the remote to turn off the television, then powered down the stationary bike he'd been cycling on in his home gym.

Ryan and Shawn lived in New York City, but he'd bought a townhome in the tony suburb of Silver Hill, New York, less than an hour from Midtown Manhattan. It was ironic. Both Ryan and Shawn were married. Ryan had a young daughter and Brandon was sure that Shawn and his wife, Addy, would be adding to the West clan any day now. But both of them had elected to live in the city while he, the single, childless brother, had purchased a two-thousand-square-foot townhome in the suburbs. His brothers loved to tease that he was the most married unmarried man they'd ever met.

He didn't mind the teasing. He'd known from the first moment he'd stepped into the house that he had to have it. The first floor boasted an open-floor-plan kitchen that flowed into the dining room, which in turn flowed into the living area that looked out onto a backyard where he'd lovingly planted roses, hydrangeas, lilies and any other flower that caught his fancy. As a boy growing up in a three-bedroom apartment in Harlem in a concrete city, he'd dreamed of one day having a home that he could spread out in, with each room having one primary purpose, and a backyard where he could run around with a dog. The hours he worked kept him from having the dog, but he'd made sure his home fulfilled every other requirement. The large master suite was his sanctuary, the place where he relaxed and let all the stress of his job go. There were two additional guest rooms and a small room he'd turned into his home office. On the lower level of the three-level home, he'd set up his man cave and used the last bedroom as his home gym. It was perfect.

He moved now from the gym to his office, stopping in the gourmet kitchen to refill his water bottle with filtered water. He slid behind his desk and opened an email from his investment adviser. He'd done dual graduate degrees at Columbia, earning his law degree and his MBA at the same time. It had seemed prudent given his intention of going into corporate law, and in the years since he'd graduated and started practicing, it had paid off several times over. Understanding the world of finance had made him a wealthy man, independent of the money he made practicing law, and it meant he didn't have to think twice about working with the domestic violence shelter and taking on clients who couldn't pay his usual hourly fee.

A quick scan of the email from his adviser told him that he was in no danger of falling into destitution anytime soon. He clicked out of the email and into the secure system the firm used. West & Williams LLP had two offices, one in Lower Manhattan and a second in Silver Hill. Last year, he'd taken on his sister-in-law, Addy Williams-West, as a partner and she ran the office in Manhattan like a well-oiled machine. He had an office in the Manhattan space, which he visited when he needed to, but he spent most of his time in the Silver Hill office staffed by one associate and paralegal. It was a setup that worked for him.

An email waited from Shawn. Brandon had called Ryan and Shawn after his talk with Detective Thomas and confirmed what they'd already suspected. The body found earlier that day was his client's. Ryan hadn't seen a purpose in continuing to dig into Tanya's past, but Brandon had insisted and Shawn had agreed to take on the project himself. He'd attached everything he'd been able to pull up on Tanya as of five that afternoon and promised to keep digging.

Shawn had only been on the case less than a day, but the report he'd sent was characteristically thorough. Tanya Rutger had been born and raised in Hackensack, New Jersey. After graduating from high school, she'd earned her nursing degree and certifications. She'd worked in a number of places before landing a job with Stryder Medical Clinic, a private medical practice on the Upper East Side. The report listed her address and phone number as the same ones she'd given on the intake form. Shawn had also noted that Tanya didn't appear to have a roommate and that the typical one-bedroom apartment in the luxury building she lived in started at three thousand dollars. Very pricey for a nurse. There was a Mercedes sports car registered in her name. Another pricey item, not just because of the cost of the car, but add in the cost of renting or buying a parking space in Manhattan, gas and insurance and it was clear, without even knowing how much she made, that Tanya was living well above the means of a nurse.

What were you into, Tanya?

He skimmed past the photos of the various social media posts that Shawn had included. He'd read them before the night was over. Social media was always a gold mine, but if there was anything in particular that stood out above the rest, Shawn would have called his attention to it. Instead he moved to the section of the report titled Criminal Record, Reports and Proceedings.

Tanya's criminal record was clean; he knew that from the background report he'd had done on her. What the standard report hadn't turned up, and why he'd gone to his brothers, was an incident report filed on Tanya's behalf. Three weeks before her death, someone attempted to break into her apartment.

Irritation churned in his chest. Detective Thomas had undoubtedly known about this incident and hadn't told him of it. Of course she hadn't. They weren't a team.

Emotion swirled inside him at that thought. Something primal. Yara's repeated failure to respond to any of his messages or texts after their third date was a clear "uninterested" signal. He was not the type of man who pursued a woman who didn't want to be pursued. But he couldn't deny she'd gotten under his skin in those three dates.

He wasn't even sure how she'd done it. She was prickly and short-tempered. She took herself far too seriously and she was a cop for goodness' sake. He should be glad she'd blown him off. But he wasn't. He'd tried dating other women to get over whatever she'd done to him but it hadn't worked. He still thought about her months after their brief relationship had ended.

He didn't need this right now. He needed to focus.

Her job was to find Tanya's killer. And his job was to…?

He wasn't sure anymore. He had no idea what Tanya had wanted him to do for her and it didn't matter now anyway. Why was he spending precious billable hours on a case that had no living client?

Because Tanya Rutger hadn't deserved to die the way she had. Alone. On a dark road. Shot.

He didn't believe for one second that she'd committed suicide. The young woman who'd hired him had been upset, yes, but suicidal? Not a chance.

Whatever situation Tanya had found herself in, it most likely had led to her death. She'd come to him for help and that's what he was going to provide.

He turned back to the incident report. The apartment had been broken into, but according to Tanya, nothing was stolen. The place had been destroyed, however. The sofa cushions had been slashed as had the clothes from Tanya's closet. Food had been thrown on the kitchen floor and walls. The mirror in the bathroom shattered. These weren't actions of a typical burglar who was most concerned with getting in, grabbing a few valuables and getting out before anyone was the wiser. The cop had noted as much, stating in the report that the incident appeared personal, but that Tanya had sworn that she had no angry ex-boyfriends or other enemies who would destroy her home.

But someone had done just that. And three weeks later she'd come to him, terrified.

It had to be related.

The question was, how?

It was a question he was determined to answer.

He grabbed his phone and hit the speed dial for his brother. Shawn picked up after two rings.

"I got the report you sent. Thanks for getting on this so fast."

"No problem. It seemed like a priority for you."

"It was. Is. Listen, could you look into the break-in at Tanya's apartment some more? Since nothing was taken, I know it wasn't a priority for the cops."

"It's likely to get another look now, though."

"I know, I know, but Detective Thomas is not going to tell me anything so I need to do this myself."

There was a long silence on the other end of the phone.

"Do you think you might be getting too involved with this case? I get that she was your client, but this really is a police investigation now. Getting involved, for you and for West Investigations, could have consequences."

"I don't want you to do anything that would jeopardize the firm in any way. It's just that Tanya came to me. She was worried and scared and I agreed to help her."

"And you would have if she hadn't been killed. You have nothing to feel guilty about."

"It's not guilt exactly. I don't know what it is. I can't stop thinking that if I'd pushed her a bit harder on why she wanted to hire a lawyer, maybe I could have done something. Maybe she wouldn't have been killed."

"My sources are saying it's looking like a suicide, Brandon."

"It wasn't." He heard the forcefulness in his tone and tempered it. "It wasn't. I talked to Tanya a week before her death. She was not suicidal."

Shawn sighed. "Okay. I'll see what I can find out and get back to you."

He hung up the phone, still thinking about Shawn's words. What was driving him to look into Tanya's death? Obligation? A savior complex? If that was it, he was too late.

He wasn't sure what it was, but he knew he wouldn't stop. Not until he knew why the scared young woman who'd come into his office a week ago was lying on a slab in the morgue now.

And who had put her there.

THE SILVER HILL Police Department's forensics division occupied a two-story warehouse about a twenty-minute drive from the main police headquarters. The lower-level garage served as a workspace for evidence that was too large to process in the lab. Tanya's red Mercedes was parked at the rear of the large space.

Becca Chandler worked at a desk next to the door. "Detective, welcome to my humble abode."

"You don't live here."

"Well, it sure feels like I do sometimes."

"I get that. I got your message. I hope you've found something in the car that I can use because right now I've got a whole lot of nothing."

Becca grinned. "I've got something." She tapped an empty plastic bag on her desk. "Bad news first. I found this caught in the locking mechanism on the back right side of the door."

Yara stepped closer to the desk and peered at the bag more closely. That's when she noticed it wasn't empty. A small scrap of black material just a little wider than a piece of thread.

"Since this is the bad news, I'm going to guess you didn't find blood or DNA on it."

"That would be a good guess. It's clean."

Yara thought back on the scene. "A pink skirt, white blouse and gray coat. That's what Tanya was wearing when we found her. Nothing black."

"Well, I can't even tell you how long the material had been there, but given its size and its precarious placement, I'd say not too long."

"Okay, but a scrap of material is not going to be much help unless we can tie it to someone."

"That's why I called it the bad news, although *bad* is not exactly right." Becca crooked her index finger. "Follow me."

Yara followed her to the car. All four doors were wide open. It had been too dark when they found Tanya and the car to get a good look at the interior. Under the harsh bright lights of the warehouse, the crimson was a shock against the expensive beige leather of the seats.

"As you can see—" Becca pointed to the front passenger area "—most of the spatter was concentrated in the front right side of the car. That's consistent with your victim sitting in the driver's seat and being shot in the right temple."

Yara felt her stomach drop. "So you're saying it was suicide."

Becca wagged a finger. "Not so fast." She moved from the front of the car to the rear seat. "See here and here." She pointed to a spot of blood on the back right door and another on the midsection of the back seat.

"Yeah, more blood, but wouldn't you expect some to get in the back of the car?"

"I would. But what I wouldn't expect is for there to be a big break in where it landed."

"A break?"

"There's blood on this side window and on the leather seat here but nothing in this area between."

"No blood at all?"

Becca shook her head slowly. "Not a drop."

Yara tingled with anticipation.

"Taken with the material I found on the door…" Becca paused.

Yara finished the thought. "Someone was in the car with Tanya Rutger when she was shot."

Chapter Six

Florence Rutger still resided in the Hackensack home where she'd raised her two daughters alone after her husband walked out on her twenty-three years earlier. Shawn hadn't done a deep dive into Tanya's mother's life, but his report had revealed that Florence Rutger was a retired school bus driver, avid Powerball player and devoted churchgoer.

Brandon parked in front of the one-story home, walked up the concrete walkway and rang the doorbell. The buzz of the television ceased abruptly, replaced by the sound of heavy footsteps heading for the door. The white lace curtain covering the window in the door was pulled back by a round-faced man in his mid-twenties.

The man peered out at him with suspicion. "Yes? Can I help you?"

"My name is Brandon West. I'm an attorney who was hired by Tanya Rutger. I was hoping to talk to Mrs. Rutger about her daughter."

The man let the lace curtain fall back into place. For several long moments nothing happened. Brandon could see him on the other side of the door and hear murmuring voices inside but he'd angled away from him, talking to someone he couldn't see in the house. He was beginning to think he wasn't going to be let in when the locks tumbled and the door opened.

The man wore a forest green sweat suit and running shoes. "Now is not a good time for Ma to have visitors. There's been a death in the family, and…"

A female voice came from farther inside the house. "Nick, I said to let the man in."

Nick's face pinched and he gave Brandon a dark look before holding the door open just wide enough to let him slide through. As he did, the man whispered, "You best not upset her. She's been through an awful thing these last twenty-four hours."

Brandon looked into the man's eyes. "I know and I'm sorry. I have no intention of upsetting her. I want to help."

His statement did nothing to remove the suspicion from the man's expression.

Brandon walked through the narrow foyer and into a living room. The floral scent in the small space was nearly overwhelming. Flowers covered every surface in the room. A tiny woman sat on a large floral-patterned sofa. Or maybe she just seemed tiny. Grief circled her like a vulture. Her eyes were bloodshot and she clutched a tissue in her hand.

"Mrs. Rutger, my name is Brandon West. I'm an attorney. Tanya hired me before she died."

"Please have a seat," the woman said in a low voice. She waved him toward the armchair across from the sofa. "And please forgive my son. He's protective of me."

Nick, still giving Brandon a wary eye, sat on the couch next to his mother, wrapping an arm around her shoulders.

Florence Rutger wore a colorful blue-and-white caftan and matching head wrap. The resemblance between her and Tanya was striking. Tanya had been the spitting image of her mother, only thirty or so years younger.

"Thank you for seeing me at a time that I know must be

extremely difficult for you. And let me just say how truly sorry I am for your loss."

Nick huffed. "If you know how difficult it is, why did you come?"

"It's all right, Nick." Florence patted her son's hand absently. "You said my Tanya hired you, Mr. West?"

"Please, call me Brandon. Yes, about a week ago Tanya retained me to represent her."

Surprise flashed across Florence's face. "Represent her with what?"

Brandon scooted forward in the uncomfortable armchair. "To be honest with you, Mrs. Rutger, I don't exactly know. I was hoping you could help me with that. We only met once and Tanya said she'd seen something illegal and she thought she might need a lawyer. She seemed afraid and said she needed a little more time before she could tell me more but that she wanted to make sure she didn't get into any trouble. Do you have any idea what she could have been talking about?"

Florence shook her head. "No. None at all." Then her eyes turned sad. "Tanya and I hadn't been getting along well in the last few months."

"If you don't mind my asking, why was that?"

"And if she does mind," Nick snapped, "why are you so interested anyway? You cops spoke to my mother yesterday and asked a bunch of questions. I know you think Tanya committed suicide, but there's no way."

Brandon wished he could talk to Florence alone, but since that didn't seem to be on the menu, he opted for placating her son. "I'm sure the police are doing everything they can to get the answers you deserve. That's all I want as well. Tanya came to me for help and even though she's no longer here, I want to help her."

"Nick, would you be a dear and make a pot of coffee,

please. Oh, and Darlene bought that apple pie. Would you heat up a few slices, please?"

Nick shot a look at his mother that made it clear he knew that she was trying to get rid of him. But he rose, doing a sideways shuffle between the couch and the coffee table, and headed for the kitchen.

"I'm sorry," Florence said, keeping her voice low. "Nick is very protective of me at the moment. He won't leave my side, even though there's nothing I want more right now than for everyone to just leave me alone with my grief."

Brandon couldn't help feeling like a heel. The woman had just lost her daughter. He should have waited at least another day or two before barging in and asking questions. "Maybe I should go. I don't want to add to your grief."

He started to rise, but she waved him back down into his seat. "No. No. Tanya came to you. She trusted you and you want to help. Nick is right about one thing. The police seem to think Tanya killed herself. I know she and I were going through a rough time of late, but I know my baby. She would have never killed herself. Never. And the way…" She pressed the tissue to her eyes and guilt kicked him in the gut again.

"Mrs. Rutger, do you remember the names of the officers who questioned you yesterday?"

The sound of a cabinet slamming came from the kitchen followed by the tap coming on.

Florence dabbed at each eye one last time before lowering the tissue. "Ah, there was a male and a female. Thomas and Martin something. I remember the man's first name was Martin because he said it, like, with a French accent. Mar-teen, not Mar-ten. He was also the one who seemed intent on saying Tanya committed suicide even when I told him that there was no way."

Knowing that Detectives Thomas and Rachlin were

headed toward writing Tanya off as a suicide assuaged some of the guilt he felt for ambushing Florence. If the cops weren't going to do their jobs and investigate thoroughly, he would.

Time to get this interview back on track. "Why weren't you and Tanya getting along?"

Florence sighed. "Tanya has been going through something lately. She wouldn't tell me what. I get it. She is...was twenty-nine. A grown woman, but I'm still her mother and I could see something was eating at her. She and Jasper had broken up some months ago so I thought that might be it, but when I asked her about it, she told me that she'd broken up with Jasper and that it was amicable."

He pulled his phone from his pocket to take notes. He could hear the coffee maker bubbling in the kitchen. They didn't have a lot of time before Nick returned. "What's Jasper's last name?"

"Reinholt. Jasper Reinholt. He's an assistant professor in the anthropology department at NYU."

"When did they break up?"

Her eyes tracked to the ceiling as if she was thinking. "About six, maybe seven months ago."

"Did Tanya ever have any problems with him? Did he ever hurt her?"

"You mean, like, did he hit her? No, never. Jasper wasn't that type of guy. He loved Tanya. I'd hoped they might marry and give me some grandbabies one day, but then Tanya just announced they'd broken up. Said he wasn't the one for her."

"Tanya was a nurse. I know that they aren't always paid well. Did she ever have money problems?" Based on Shawn's report, Tanya was living well above her means so it wasn't so much as she didn't have money, but that she seemed to have money that couldn't be accounted for. He was working his way up to the questions that might have Florence kicking him out of her house, but he had to have answers.

She hesitated a beat too long for him to accept her subsequent answer as truthful. "No. No money problems."

"Mrs. Rutger, I only want to help Tanya. I know she was driving an expensive car and living in a luxury apartment downtown. That seems well out of reach of a nurse's salary."

Florence glanced over her shoulder into the kitchen. From where Brandon was seated, he couldn't see Nick, but the racket that had been coming from that direction had died down considerably. She turned back to face him.

He could sense her holding back and decided to press a little harder. "Mrs. Rutger, the police look like they plan to close Tanya's case as a suicide if they can. I met Tanya. I don't believe she committed suicide. The more information I have, the more likely it will be that I can convince the cops to keep investigating her case."

Florence's gaze dropped to the tissue in her hand. "I didn't tell the police about this when they came. I thought maybe if they saw what a good person Tanya was, they'd rethink their silly theory about suicide."

"I understand." It wasn't uncommon for people to paint loved ones in a favorable light after they'd lost them. Even loved ones they hadn't been all that fond of while they'd been living.

"Tanya and I argued over the car and the apartment," Florence said. "I don't know exactly how she paid for it, but I suspected it was a man."

"A man? Jasper?"

Florence's laugh was without mirth. "Definitely not Jasper. Like I said, he's an assistant professor. He had Tanya and I over to his place in the Bronx for dinner once and, well, I ate to be polite, but his place should have been condemned as unfit for habitation by man and beast."

"Okay, not Jasper, then. Is there anyone else you can think of who could have been paying for her new lifestyle?"

Florence shook her head, wringing the damp tissue in her hands until it tore into two pieces. "I don't know. I really don't, but she moved after she started her new job."

He recalled the employment section of Shawn's report. "With the Stryder Medical Clinic, right?"

"Yes, she was so excited." A smile bloomed on her face, then fell just as quickly. "She moved into that new apartment and bought that fancy car. I worried that she was overextending herself. I knew the new job paid more than her old one, but she was spending so much so fast."

"Did you ask her about it?"

Florence nodded. "She got mad at me. Told me she was grown and knew how to manage her money. And she did. Tanya was always very good with money, but still. I'm not so old that I don't realize how much things cost."

"What did you suspect?" He had his own suspicions so he wasn't surprised by her answer.

"I thought she was dating a rich, married guy. Lord knows there are plenty of them in New York City. I asked her point-blank whether she was letting some man pay her way. Told her I hadn't raised her like that. That's when she stopped speaking to me." Florence tore the tissue into smaller and smaller pieces that landed on her lap.

"And you have no idea who this man could be?"

Florence pinned her gaze on him. "I have no idea if this man exists, Mr. West. Tanya didn't take my calls for a month after our argument. When she started speaking to me again, I didn't want to drive her away so I let it go. I figured if… when the relationship with the man went south, she could always come back home and live with me if it came to that."

She looked at him with eyes filled with tears. "I should have kept asking questions. I should have made her tell me. Now she's gone and I may never have answers."

Chapter Seven

The office was empty when Yara got back from the forensics lab. She tossed her suit jacket over the back of her chair and woke her computer, still thinking about the implications of Becca's findings. The medical examiner had emailed his preliminary report while she'd been driving back to the station and she was eager to see if his findings added anything to the evidence they'd collected so far.

The phone on her desk rang.

"Thomas. My office. Now." It looked like the ME's report would have to wait. She shrugged into her suit jacket as she made the short walk from her shared office to his corner one.

His door was open. She knocked on the door frame before striding in.

"Have a seat." Lieutenant Wilson pointed to the pair of visitor's chairs opposite his desk without looking up from the paperwork on his desk. Wilson was a former college football player, many years removed from his playing career, but he'd done well keeping in shape. Large in stature and personality, he was affectionately called a curmudgeon by some in the department while others held far lower opinions of the man.

Yara fell into the latter camp. Wilson worried too much

about the bureaucracy and the politics that came with the job and not enough about the job itself, as far as she was concerned. He had his eye on moving up the ranks and he wasn't about to let little things like fairness or justice get in his way.

Half a minute passed before he took his reading glasses from his face and sat them primly on top of the report he'd been reading. "I saw the medical examiner's preliminary report on the dead woman you caught yesterday. Looks like a suicide just like Rachlin said."

She sucked in a harsh breath. Martin shouldn't have been saying anything to the lieutenant about a case she was the primary detective on. Especially, when he knew she disagreed with his rush to judgment.

"Sir, I'm not convinced this is a case of suicide. I just got back from forensics and there's some evidence that might suggest someone was in the car with Tanya Rutger when she was shot."

One of Wilson's eyebrows arched. "What evidence?"

"A small piece of material was found on the right rear passenger door and gaps in the blood-spatter pattern suggest the possibility that someone was in the back seat."

"That's hardly conclusive." He slid his glasses back onto his face and looked at the computer screen on his desk. "The ME says the head wound is consistent with the victim shooting herself. I understand the only prints on the gun found in the car were the victim's, correct?"

"Yes, sir, but there are other circumstances that also make me think that there is more to this case."

Wilson pinned her with a look. "Such as?"

"I haven't been able to find the victim's phone. It seems peculiar to me that a twenty-nine-year-old wouldn't have her phone on her. Nor was I able to find it at her apartment."

"She could have lost it. It certainly has no bearing on

the medical examiner's finding that the wound is consistent with suicide."

Irritation bubbled in her chest. She wished she'd had time to read the medical examiner's report before Wilson called her into his office. She would have been better prepared.

Lieutenant Ted Wilson had risen up the ranks quickly due more to his political savvy than any outstanding achievement in police work. What he understood better than most was that perception was the key to reality. A high case-close rate for the major case division fed into the police commissioner's tough-on-crime persona and boosted the lieutenant's political aspirations. And that in turn boosted Wilson's professional cache. Wilson wasn't shy about telegraphing his desire to one day sit in the commissioner's seat. Having the current commissioner and the mayor indebted to him would help get him there.

"That's one explanation. It's also possible someone was in the car with Tanya and they took it."

"You don't even know there was anyone in the car. A scrap of material and the absence of blood are not enough to make a case."

Her jaw tensed. "I'm aware of that, Lieutenant. The victim also appears to have been living outside of her means. Fancy car. Expensive apartment. I'd like to find out who exactly was paying for her lifestyle. That might help give a fuller picture of who Tanya Rutger was and whether she was actually suicidal."

Wilson pulled his glasses off again and threw them on the desk in front of him. It was his signature move, a show of irritation. "Detective Thomas, you have nearly a dozen open cases on your desk at the moment, am I correct?"

He knew he was correct. No doubt he'd checked the system to see just how many other cases she had before he'd called her into his office.

"Yes, sir."

"So digging around in, what for all accounts, looks like a straightforward case of suicide, would not seem like the best use of your time."

"With all due respect, I wouldn't call it digging around. I'm pursuing all possible leads so that we can assure the Rutger family that no stone was left unturned."

"You spoke to the family?" At her nod, he continued. "Did they give you any indication that the woman was afraid of anyone? In some kind of trouble that might have led to her death?"

Frustration churned in her stomach. "No."

"What about friends? Neighbors?"

"No. She had hired a lawyer, though. He said she seemed worried about something. That she'd seen something illegal and thought she might need an attorney."

"Well, if she was mixed up in something illegal, that could be her reason for committing suicide. It wouldn't be the first time a criminal took the easy way out."

"Yes, but the lawyer said she'd seen something illegal, not that she was involved in it."

He shot her an incredulous look. "If she was close enough to illegal activity to see it, she was most likely involved in it. Maybe she lost her nerve."

She had to fight the urge to reach across the desk and smack him. That was the kind of attitude among some law enforcement that got innocent people railroaded into jail. You were there so you must have been involved in the crime somehow. Funny how that same logic never seemed to apply to the bankers, corporate CEOs and politicians who were perpetually unaware of what was going on right under their noses.

Wilson leaned forward and tapped a finger on the papers covering his desk. "Detective Thomas, unless the medical examiner or forensics people come back to you with some new evidence that conclusively puts someone in the car with your victim, this is a suicide. I don't have enough time or resources to let my detectives run around turning over rocks in the faint hope of finding a crime."

"Sir—"

"Thomas, this case is not a priority. I've already released the woman's apartment to the management company so they can notify the mother she can clear out the place. I've assigned Rachlin to another case. It's time for you to move on." He snatched his glasses from the desk, his focus now back on the papers in front of him. It was clear she'd been dismissed and she didn't like it one bit.

Her blood boiled. "Sir, with all due respect, releasing the apartment was my call to make as the primary on the case."

Wilson peered at her over the top of his rimless lenses. "Everything that goes on in this station is my call to make, Thomas. And I made it. The owner of the building called this morning complaining that the seal was unnerving to the other residents and causing unnecessary stress to people in their own homes. You already said you didn't find anything of evidentiary value there."

There was something else going on here. Seven years as a detective had honed her instincts enough that she knew when something was off. She'd look into it when she got back to her desk, but she wouldn't be surprised to find out that the owner of the building was well connected. Whoever it was would have to be to make it in New York City real estate.

She'd worked under Wilson for the last four years. She knew when his mind was made up. He'd decided Tanya Rutger was a case of suicide and wasn't worth his detectives' time and she wasn't going to change that opinion today.

But maybe she could at least get him to allow her to track down the phone.

"What about the phone? It's a big loose end. Can I at least request the call and GPS records from the phone company? If you're right and she just lost the phone along her daily route to work, I could find it and wrap up the loose end."

Wilson glared but she could tell he was considering it. After a moment he said, "Fine, but your workday needs to be focused on closing the string of robbery cases you have on your desk. That's your priority until it's closed."

She had four cases of break-ins at homes in an upscale part of Silver Hill and the local media had started to take notice.

"Yes, sir," she answered through gritted teeth.

She rose and headed for the door. Before she got it open, Wilson spoke again.

"And Thomas? The mayor has taken an interest in these robbery cases. Citizens having their homes invaded is not good in an election year. It's in your professional best interests to get your priorities straight and focus on what matters."

FLORENCE RUTGER HAD only hesitated a moment when Brandon asked if she minded if he took a look at Tanya's apartment. She gave him the spare key that Tanya had given her and promised to call the doorman to let him know that she was sending someone over to collect some of Tanya's belongings. He didn't know if the detectives had sealed off Tanya's apartment and he wasn't willing to go as far as breaking a police seal in his quest for answers. He'd never liked driving in the city so he headed home and called the car service the firm kept an account with. He checked in at the office while he waited for the car, and a half hour later he was on the way to Lower Manhattan.

Florence was good to her word. The doorman let him up to Tanya's sixth-floor apartment without delay. There was no notice warning that the apartment had been sealed by police order, so he slid the key into the lock and let himself inside. Tanya's one-bedroom wasn't spacious and its only view was of the neighboring apartment building, but the kitchen appliances were brand-new, the fixtures were high-end and the floors were marble tile. Apartments might have started in the thousands of dollars a month, but whoever was paying for this place was shelling out quite a bit more than that.

"What did you get yourself into, Tanya?" he whispered.

The police report on the break-in had stated that the place had been torn apart, but in the three weeks since the incident, Tanya had made great strides with the decor. A dark brown suede sofa anchored the living room and a round glass-top table took up most of the small eating area. The walls, free of decor, and the faint smell of paint lingering in the air were the only signs that there had been anything amiss in the apartment recently.

He made his way to the bedroom. A queen-size sleigh bed was flanked by nightstands on either side. Tucked into the corner by the en suite bathroom was a five-drawer dresser.

He'd always been careful to keep his work separate from his personal life. And this, well, it was definitely not separate. It felt intrusive being in a client's bedroom even with Florence's permission to look through Tanya's things. But it seemed inconceivable that Tanya could have been seeing a married man, one willing to pay for an apartment like this, and there be no hint of who he was in her apartment.

He opened the drawer in the bedside table and looked through the items inside. A notebook with a few vague comments about dreams. Pens, a box of checks and a few other things that held no interest to him. There were a few business cards scattered in the drawer, as if they'd been thrown inside without much thought. He laid them on the bed and took a photograph just in case. He doubted she'd have kept her lover's business card. Why would she? But stranger things had happened.

He made a mental note to stop by the management office and see if he could find out who was on the lease. No doubt that a man who went as far as setting a woman up in a fancy apartment knew better than to put his own name on the lease and the management company probably wouldn't tell him anyway, but there was no harm in asking.

He bet Detective Thomas already knew the answer. Had it made her more or less sure Tanya had killed herself?

The other nightstand was empty.

He closed the drawer and headed for the closet, wondering if a place like this did a full walk-in or one of those deals where, yes, technically you could walk in if there were no clothes hanging inside and you were no bigger than the average twelve-year-old.

He was reaching for the knob when the door flew open, banging into his head and sending him reeling backward.

Before he could catch his breath or get his footing, a fist slammed into the side of his face that the door had missed.

Stars swam behind his eyes, but he managed to stay on his feet. His vision blurred but he was still able to see the malice in the brown eyes that stared out at him from behind the black ski mask.

He shifted his weight, avoiding another roundhouse punch, and charged his attacker, grabbing the man around the waist and driving into the wall next to the bed.

The man let out an *ooof*, then another when Brandon's fist connected with his jaw.

It wasn't his best showing. His head rang from the two blows.

The masked man feinted left, avoiding the next punch, then launched his own, catching him in the stomach.

Brandon doubled over, all the air having left his body with the gut punch. The intruder pushed him aside and ran for the front door to the apartment.

Footsteps pounded. The creak of the door opening and slamming shut. Then nothing. The apartment was utterly quiet.

It took a few more minutes before his lungs were working properly again. He didn't bother chasing after his assailant. Whoever had been in the apartment was long gone.

Instead, he pulled his phone from his pocket, glad he'd never erased Yara's phone number.

Chapter Eight

Yara strode into the apartment, her expression a mixture of irritation, exhaustion and concern. Brandon sat on the sofa, an ice pack on the bump on the side of his head where the closet door hit him courtesy of the EMTs who'd come and gone after he'd refused transport to the hospital. He watched as her gaze swept over every inch of the space before landing on him.

His heart raced and his body heated.

Now he listened as the detective got an update on the situation from the officers. The assault hadn't merited dispatching a New York City detective to the scene, but she had immediately taken charge, ordering the officers to gather the security tapes from the building management. The officers scurried to do as instructed and Yara turned her attention to him, her fashionable but functional black boots clicking against the tile floors.

"Brandon." She looked him over, her expression one of distinct displeasure.

"Yara." He lowered the ice pack and pressed his fingers to the bump, measuring its width. It didn't seem to be too large, thankfully.

"You want to tell me what happened here?"

He sighed. He knew when he called her and told her what had happened, she wouldn't be happy with him.

He gave her the quick summary of how he'd come to the apartment to see if he could find anything that might point him in the direction of who might have wanted to hurt Tanya and how a man in a mask had jumped out of the closet.

Yara took notes as he spoke. "Did you see any identifying features?"

"Not much. He was a couple inches shorter than me, maybe five-eleven, six feet. I could see enough of his skin around his eyes to tell that he was white. He was wearing gloves. And he had brown eyes."

"Clothing?" she asked, still writing.

"Black pants. Black shirt. Black mask."

"Shoes?" she said, looking up from her notebook finally.

He closed his eyes and tried to bring the memory of the man into focus. He hadn't really been concentrating on anything other than not getting hit in the face again, but when he'd been hunched over after taking the punch to his gut his gaze had been trained downward.

"White sneakers. Can't tell you a brand, sorry."

"No, that's good. Now tell me, how did you get into the apartment?"

"Tanya's mother gave me permission and a key." He pulled it from his pocket. "I didn't break in. And come to think of it, I don't think the intruder did, either. I mean, the door was locked when I arrived. I used the key, and it didn't seem like the lock had been tampered with, although I guess you guys can check on that."

Yara's expression darkened. "Whoa, wait a minute. You went to see Tanya Rutger's mother?"

He didn't care for the feeling of her hovering over him like a displeased parent, so he stood. The upward motion sent a stab of pain ricocheting through his already throbbing head. He winced.

"Sit down," she snapped, placing a hand on his arm. Despite the bite to her words, her grip was gentle as it guided him back onto the couch. Once he was back down, she sat next to him.

One of the uniformed officers returned, interrupting them.

"Detective Thomas, the management is pulling the video for you. They'll email it to you."

"Great. Thank you, Officer." The man retreated into the hallway.

"Now, you were explaining why I shouldn't arrest you for interfering in my case."

He smiled despite himself. He always had liked strong women and everything he'd seen of Yara Thomas said she didn't suffer fools easily. "I went to see my client's mother. To express my condolences and to see if I could make any sense of why Tanya hired me in the first place."

"And did you?"

"Yes and maybe. Tanya's mother told me that she believed Tanya had begun dating a man who she suspected was married and paying for Tanya's new lifestyle."

Yara's back stiffened. "Her mother didn't mention anything about a boyfriend when my partner and I questioned her."

"She admitted she hadn't told you. She said she felt like you and your partner had already made up your minds that Tanya had committed suicide. She was afraid if she said anything it might make it seem more likely that her daughter took her own life."

Yara swore and stood. She paced to the bar separating the kitchen from the living area and turned around. "To be clear, I do not believe Tanya committed suicide. I can't say the same for my partner or my lieutenant, but I have not written this case off as suicide."

Maybe Yara could be an ally after all. "I'm glad to hear you say that."

She held up her hand. "Unfortunately, my lieutenant does not share my belief. He thinks this is a clear-cut case of suicide and he wants me to focus my attention on my other cases. He's already released the apartment, which is the only reason you haven't been arrested for breaking and entering."

He pushed to his feet now, the pain of doing so dimming in the face of his outrage. "How can he do that? I mean, Tanya had someone break into her apartment only three weeks ago. That alone should raise suspicions that there's something other than a suicide here. And now this guy attacks me in the same apartment."

Yara's eyes narrowed. "How do you know about the break-in?"

There was no reason to hedge. "I got my brothers to do a bit of research for me. There's no one better at finding out things people would rather keep under wraps."

She shook her head, curiosity and disbelief at war in her expression. "Why get so involved in this case? I get that Tanya was your client, but you'd met her once and didn't even know what she wanted from you. Is it guilt? Obligation? A hero complex? What? Why not just let it go?"

"I don't know, and trust me, I have asked myself the same questions." He rubbed his throbbing temples. "Maybe it's a little of everything. Maybe it's just that no one was there for Tanya when she needed it most and it cost her everything. I can't save her life, but I can save her reputation. I can make sure that if she was killed, her killer doesn't get away with it."

Yara cocked her head to the side, studying him.

He didn't know her well enough to read her expression,

but he suddenly wished he did. Seeing her again despite everything reminded him of how much he'd liked spending time with her. She was the only woman he'd dated since his divorce he could say that about. But now wasn't the time to explore those thoughts.

"I don't think I'm the only one who can't let this case go," he said. "Your lieutenant ordered you off the case, so why did you come when I called?"

She frowned. "I wish I knew. Maybe I'm a glutton for punishment."

"I'll tell you what I think. I think you're not the kind of detective, the kind of woman, who would let an injustice go unsolved if she can help it."

She studied him intently for a moment. "The New York City cops were happy to let me step in here because you weren't seriously hurt and there's a connection to my case, but my boss was clear. If I push this, I'm putting my career on the line."

He threw up his hands. "Even now? It's obvious that guy was here looking for something. Something that might point to why Tanya was killed."

Yara shook her head. "If my lieutenant can close this as a suicide, he will. It's quick and it doesn't impact his crime stats. Plus—" she hesitated for a moment "—there's the medical examiner's report. He found Tanya's wound was consistent with a self-inflicted gunshot to the head."

A lead balloon landed in his stomach. "I don't buy that."

"Whether you buy it or not, my lieutenant does and he's in charge ultimately."

Brandon shook his head. "Not of me, he isn't. Whoever broke in here was looking for something. What? And why? It seems to me Tanya had something that someone wanted enough to kill her for, but for some reason they still haven't found whatever it is so they came back to search for it here."

Yara threw her hands in the air. "Look, there's nothing I can do."

He closed some of the distance between them and stared into her eyes. "That's not true. Your lieutenant can officially order you to focus on other cases, but he can't tell you how to spend your free time. Help me. Help me find out the truth about what happened. Suicide. Murder. Whatever."

She shook her head slowly, but he could see the wheels turning in her head, the interest behind her eyes. "Do you know how hard I've worked for my career? I don't want to stall out at a detective's rank."

"You share whatever you feel comfortable sharing. The truth is, I'm going to investigate anyway, and between me and my brothers, I can probably find out anything you don't give me. It would just take me longer, which would give Tanya's killer more time to cover up and get away," he pressed.

Yara's frown deepened into a scowl, but her eyes were thoughtful.

"This is going to happen one way or the other. But this way we can build a rock-solid case that you can take to your lieutenant and that he can't ignore. Maybe that will help when—if—there's blowback from you having pursued the case in spite of his order."

"You don't know Lieutenant Ted Wilson at all." Yara laughed without mirth.

But he could see it in her eyes before she said the words. She was in.

"This has to stay quiet. You and your brothers know about my involvement and no one else."

"Absolutely, partner." He stuck out his hand.

Yara hesitated for a millisecond before taking his hand in hers. He saw the electric shock that ripped through him at her touch reflected in her eyes.

She dropped his hand and took a step back.

"I didn't find anything before the attack, but I'd only just gotten started. I want to take a more thorough look around."

"I don't know what you think you're going to find. I searched this place after we found Tanya's body. There was nothing here that led me to a boyfriend or anyone else of particular interest, for that matter." She followed him into the bedroom.

"You never know. With more information, maybe things will look different now. Something might stand out."

But after twenty minutes, it was clear there was nothing in the apartment that pointed to Tanya's secret boyfriend. Which was in and of itself a clue.

"You know, if Tanya was rendezvousing with a secret boyfriend here, she went to great pains to erase any sign of him," Brandon said.

Their search had moved from the bedroom to the living spaces. Yara closed a kitchen drawer she'd been searching, and turned to face him in the living room, where he'd methodically removed the couch cushions and searched every inch of the sofa.

"I was thinking that maybe they'd broken up. That maybe the boyfriend was the person who broke in three weeks ago and trashed the place," she said.

"Out of anger or revenge." He turned the idea over in his head.

"Or both."

"Maybe. I'm sure you asked the management for the names on the lease."

"Just hers. And the rent was paid each month by an automated payment from an account in Tanya's name only."

"So if someone else is paying for the apartment, they are making sure to cover their tracks," he said, putting the couch back together having found nothing.

"I have to get back to my neck of the woods before my

lieutenant starts asking questions. Maybe we can meet up later to exchange information?"

He liked the idea of seeing her later more than he wanted to admit to himself. He was going to have to keep reminding himself that they were only working together. But maybe… "Absolutely. Why don't you give me a call when you get off your shift."

"Okay. How about you? You need a ride?"

"I can find my way home."

She looked at him as if he'd just bumped his head, which, technically, he had. "You have a huge bump on one side of your face and a shiner on the other. If you get behind the wheel, I will have the city cops pull you over and take you in for reckless driving."

"Don't worry, Yara. I don't think I could drive even if I wanted to, not with the hammering going on in my head. I took a car here and I'll get one back to Silver Hill."

And he wanted to stop by West Investigations' offices and update Shawn on the situation anyway.

Yara gave him a small smile. "Okay, well, until tonight, then."

The words sent a flutter through his stomach. "Until tonight."

Chapter Nine

Yara spent the rest of the day working the robbery cases and debating whether she was putting herself on the path to career ruin by helping Brandon West. She almost certainly was. Lieutenant Wilson wasn't the type of man who admitted to ever being wrong. Bringing him conclusive evidence, if she found any, would more likely be seen by him as a direct challenge to his authority rather than as an industrious detective going the extra mile. And yet she knew she couldn't let this case be closed as a suicide. Not with all the loose ends she saw just hanging out there.

It had been a very long time since she'd left work on time, but when the clock struck 6:00 p.m., she logged off her computer and grabbed her coat. Martin was out in the field and Paris had left early for a doctor's appointment. The other detective who shared the office was engrossed in a phone call and didn't look up as she strode from the room.

In her car, she started the engine before pulling up the contact in her cell phone for Brandon West.

She tapped her foot while she waited for him to pick up. She was inexplicably nervous, as if she was fifteen calling a boy she had a crush on. Not that she had the courage to call a boy at fifteen, especially one who was as cute as she guessed Brandon West would have been.

Adolescence had been a decidedly painful time for her, most notably because her mother passed away during that period of her life. Her grief-stricken father and two older brothers hadn't had the first notion about how to shepherd a young girl through the thorny patches to womanhood. She'd done the best she could, mostly relying on the wisdom of her teenage girlfriends. And she'd turned out all right. At least she thought so.

"Hello." The low tone of the male voice coming from the other end of the phone line pulled her from her thoughts.

"Hi. Ah, it's Yara. I was just calling to see if we are still going to meet up this evening."

"Of course. Would you like to come to my place?" he asked.

To his house? She'd avoided that step during their brief dalliance and she wasn't sure that was a good idea now. "Oh. That's nice, but…"

He interrupted. "I'm trying to take it easy after my harrowing experience. And it affords us privacy."

Privacy was important. She thought about how Martin had spoken to Wilson about his suicide conclusion behind her back. She couldn't afford to have him or another one of her coworkers catch her out with Brandon West and report back to the lieutenant. It would bring an onslaught of questions she wasn't ready to answer.

"What's your address?" she asked.

He rattled it off. "I'll order Chinese. Anything in particular you prefer?"

"I'll eat anything."

"I shall get a variety, then. See you soon."

His voice slid over her skin like velvet and she shivered before hanging up and backed out of the parking space. The address he'd given her wasn't far from the station, about a fifteen-minute drive, but she got caught in a bad patch of after-work traffic that drew the trip out to nearly half an hour. Her luck changed, however, when she turned onto his street. A car was pulling out of the space in front of the address he'd given her. She parked and followed the red-brick-paved walkway to the arched front door of the town house.

She pressed the doorbell and heard it ring inside the house. Moments later the door opened and Brandon West stood before her. He was dressed casually in jeans, a gray sweater and a well-loved pair of loafers without socks. The bump on his head seemed to have gone down a bit, but his black eye had moved from its early greenish hew to a dark purplish-black color. He was still breathtakingly handsome. So much so that she couldn't stop the tiny gasp that escaped her mouth.

The sexy smile that slid across his face sent her pulse racing.

"Perfect timing." He stood back and held the door open so she could enter. "The food got here thirty seconds before you did."

"How are you feeling?"

"Not too bad. Better than I look, at least."

He looked pretty good to her but she refrained from making that comment aloud. "Did you ice your eye?"

"I did. Don't worry."

She followed him past a floating staircase and into an open-floor-plan kitchen, dining and living space that looked as if it should be in a magazine.

"Wow. This is incredible."

"Thank you. I fell in love with this place the moment I saw it."

She could see why. The kitchen was well apportioned with eggshell-white cabinets and granite countertops. Very modern but he'd toned down some of the modernity by adding a dark brown farmhouse table big enough for ten in the dining space and a deep, incredibly comfortable-looking sectional in the living room off the kitchen. But for Yara, the *pièce de résistance* was the wall of windows looking out onto the back patio and yard.

"I don't think I'd ever leave if I lived here," she said.

"I have to go to work to afford it, but it is nice to come home to each day."

She left him pulling white boxes out of the large brown bag and floated over to the six-foot colorful abstract painting on the dining room wall. It had caught her eye the moment she'd walked into the space, as it was supposed to, but she was still stunned to see the signature in the bottom right corner. "This is a Gerhard Richter."

Brandon turned to her with two plates in his hands and a look of surprise on his face. "You know your art. It is. I bought it some years ago before the rest of the world realized what a genius he is."

"I met him once. A long time ago." She couldn't take her eyes off the piece. "I minored in art history in college and he came to campus to speak. I'd seen some of his work in one of the SoHo galleries. I can't even remember which one now, but you're right, he's always had something, an eye for color and form that is so unique."

Brandon carried the plates to the table. "It seems we have at least one thing in common, then. We both love art."

"I don't know how we missed that before."

"Well, you stopped answering my calls before I could offer to make you dinner." He said the words lightheartedly, but they still sent heat crawling up her neck. He'd planned to make her dinner. Would they have ended the night with dessert in bed?

She'd have probably gone for it. Heck, she was thinking about it now.

"Yara, would you like red or white with dinner? Or both?

You are off duty, correct?" he asked, pulling her thoughts away from the bedroom.

A laugh bubbled in her throat. "I am, but I'm not a big drinker. Let's start with white and see where the night takes us."

She hadn't meant for it to sound as flirty as it had. She knew he'd caught the innuendo by the rise of his brow, but thankfully he only grinned before making his way to the fridge.

She fanned at the heat rising in her cheeks while his back was turned. She'd better be careful or this partnership might turn romantic, and she couldn't let that happen.

She cleared her throat and sat at the table. "So the management company at Tanya's apartment sent me the security recording. A guy matching your description came up through the stairwell in the parking garage to the apartment. Since the garage also allows public parking, we can't limit our pool of suspects to those who had access to the garage." She piled moo shoo pork onto her plate. "He also anticipated the cameras. Had the ski mask on before he entered the garage. The cameras caught him leaving, but it was the same deal. His face was always covered."

"Damn." He set a glass of white wine next to her plate and took the seat next to her, the spicy smell of his cologne tickling her nose and stirring a feeling in her nether region.

Platonic. Professional. She repeated the words several times in her head before speaking again.

"I think it might be worthwhile if you take a look at the recording anyway. Maybe it'll jog something in your memory that could help."

"Not a problem. I made a copy of the file my brother put together for you," he said around a bite of food.

She took a sip of wine before speaking. "You know, your family has quite the reputation. West Investigations is one of the best firms for private security and high-end investigations. I was able to dig up a partial client list and to say it was impressive is an understatement. Basically, who's who of America's wealthiest people."

"Well, I am proud of the company my father and brothers have built. I'm not involved in the security and investigations portion, though I do manage their legal portfolio."

"Your reputation is nothing to look down on, either. Howard undergrad then Columbia Law. Three years in the prosecutor's office then seven years at Farrington & Barr, one of the country's biggest law firms, I might add. But then you chucked it right before you would have been made a partner at the firm and hung out your own shingle. Why?"

"I wanted something of my own. I'd worked so hard to make partner and the closer I got to it the less I wanted it. At least not on the terms that I would have had to accept if I'd stayed at Farrington."

"I have to say I don't know if I could have walked away after putting in all that time and effort."

"It didn't feel like walking away, though. It felt like starting anew." He grinned. "Does that sound corny?"

"A little, but I think I know what you mean." She laughed.

"I'm sure you do. It's why you're here. Why you're pursuing Tanya's case despite the possibility of harm to your career from doing so."

She looked at him, confused. "It is?"

"Certainly. You're not the kind of cop who only cares about pushing the papers and closing the cases. You care about finding the truth. About getting justice for victims, or at least as much justice as the system will allow. You wouldn't have made it as far as you have if you didn't."

"You got all of that in forty-eight hours and a couple of coffee dates?"

He leaned toward her. "I got all of that the moment I met you six months ago."

He held her gaze, the tension simmering between them. His plump lips glistened, probably from the wine, but it was the straw that broke the camel's back, so to speak.

Impulsively, she leaned forward, pressing her lips to his. *Finally.*

The thought flitted through her brain as if some part of her had been waiting for this moment, this kiss, since they'd met. Maybe some part of her had been. After all, her rule against serious relationships had never kept her from enjoying the company of a man. But she'd run from Brandon after only a few dates. She'd known he was trouble and boy did it look like she was right. This one kiss alone had her feeling warm all over, and she was all too aware that there was a bedroom—given the size of this house, likely more than one—only a few steps away.

With a jerk, she broke off the kiss.

She grabbed her wine and finished off the glass in one gulp.

"Would you care for more wine?" Brandon asked, a knowing smile on his face.

"No. I'm fine, thanks." She pushed her plate away and forced herself to focus on the reason she was there. Tanya. "So listen, I'm sorry about kissing you."

He frowned. "I'm not."

"It's important we keep things professional between us, especially since this is not a department-sanctioned investigation. I don't want to muddy the waters any more than they already are."

Brandon's frown deepened. "If that's what you want." He poured more wine in his own glass and took a long swallow.

"It is. And it goes without saying that everything I'm about to share with you has to be kept confidential. If we develop evidence sufficient to show that Tanya didn't commit suicide, I'll have to decide on the best way to tell my lieutenant about your involvement in this case." Or whether to do so at all, but that was a problem for another day. "Until then, no one can know we are working together."

"Okay, I can live with those terms, but I have to be able to use my brothers." He held up a hand when she started to protest. "They don't have to be read in on the specifics of our alliance, but they have access to resources that neither you nor I do. It would be foolish not to use them. And as I've hired them as consultants on Tanya's case, they are bound by attorney-client privilege in addition to their usual promises of confidentiality. West Investigations is used to dealing with delicate situations. I have every confidence in them."

She didn't like it, but she didn't have much leverage. She wouldn't be able to tap into all the usual police sources since Wilson had ordered her to treat the case as a likely suicide, not if she wanted to keep her ongoing investigation from him. "Okay."

"Now." He smiled but it seemed more than a little forced. "I'm ready to hear all your secrets, Yara Thomas."

Chapter Ten

Yara pulled up the security video from Tanya's apartment on her phone, but the camera only caught a grainy shot of a man fitting the assailant's description entering and exiting the building through the garage. He'd kept his back to the camera as if he'd known they were there. The likelihood that his assailant had been Tanya's mystery man went up.

Yara caught him up on what she'd discovered about Tanya's case so far—the apartment paid for by a mystery man, the blood and fingerprints in the car and her lieutenant's determination that this was a suicide.

Brandon suggested they take advantage of the nice evening and continue their conversation on his patio. He grabbed what remained of the bottle of wine and their glasses and led Yara outside.

"Your garden is lovely," she said, settling into one of the four lounge chairs.

"Thank you. I find that gardening is a great stress reliever."

Her face registered surprise. "You did all this?" She'd declined a second glass of wine earlier, but now she held out her glass for him to fill.

He filled her glass, then his own. "All by myself. It took

a while. I made more than a few missteps, but I'm finally getting it to where I want it to be." He sipped.

"It's very relaxing." She let out a sigh.

"That's what I was going for."

"I shouldn't get too comfortable or you won't be able to get me out of here."

The last thing he wanted to do was get her out of his home. More like get her into the bedroom and out of her clothes. But he pushed that thought away.

"So, the case." She set her wineglass on the pavers next to the lounge chair and scooted to a semi-upright position. "You already know we found Tanya's body in her car on the stretch of Route 30. There's nothing around for more than a mile in either direction. Most of the traffic along that stretch sticks to the interstate."

"Which suggests Tanya was out there for a reason."

"Nothing was wrong with her car. We found the weapon that was used in the car on the console between the two front seats where it conceivably could have fallen if she'd shot herself."

"Yet, you didn't believe this was a suicide from the beginning."

She frowned. "I had my doubts. Mostly instinct if I'm honest. If Tanya wanted to kill herself, why drive out to some desolate road? If there's some significance to that spot, I don't see it. But what really gave me pause was her phone."

"Her phone?"

"Yes, so far we haven't found it or her computer."

A light bulb went off in his head. "Ah, that's why you asked me about her phone and phone number when we spoke earlier."

"Exactly. I don't know anyone without a phone nowadays and certainly not a twenty-nine-year-old. My partner suggested she might have left it back in her apartment so that no one could call her and talk her into changing her mind."

"But it wasn't there."

She shook her head. It was a warm night but there was a slight breeze blowing that had wrenched a tendril of hair from the knot at the base of her neck and now blew it across her face.

He scooted forward and tucked it behind her ear. He traced his thumb over her cheek, setting off a ripple of butterflies in his stomach. He was close enough to feel her body heat, smell the soft lilac scent of her perfume. His gaze dropped to her mouth and a buzz started low in his body. He leaned forward, but just before their lips would have met, she jerked back. The air between them chilled noticeably.

"Sorry," he said.

"No, it's fine." But he could tell it hadn't been. She seemed to be feeling the same attraction to him that he felt for her, but she was fighting it. Which made sense. She was a cop and he was an attorney. The flashing red light could not have been brighter. And yet he fought the urge to pick her up and carry her to his room. The impulse was almost overpowering. But she was giving off back-up vibes right and left, so he did.

"What were we talking about?" she asked.

"Tanya's missing phone."

"Right." She leaned back against her seat, putting more distance between them. "No phone and no computer."

"That is suspicious."

"Exactly. And the forensic tech found a small piece of cloth stuck to the back rear passenger side door, which admittedly is not much. But she also noted a gap in the blood spatter that made it into the back seat of the car."

"A gap?"

"Yes, as if something, or someone, had been sitting on the edge of the back seat leaning forward between the seats."

His heartbeat spiked. "Someone sitting like they might if they had a gun to the driver's head."

"Exactly. The only problem is the medical examiner says the angle of the shot is consistent with a self-inflicted wound and Tanya's are the only fingerprints we found on the gun."

"The killer could have worn gloves and wrapped her hand around the gun after he'd killed her. And couldn't someone get the same angle from the rear of the car if they were leaning forward?"

Yara stroked her chin with her hand. "I don't know. I'd have to ask."

"Okay, so that's something we need to nail down. West Investigations has all kinds of experts on staff. I'll see if anyone there can answer the question generally. It won't hurt to have a second opinion. Anything else you think I should know?"

She shrugged. "That's all we've got. It's thin, but when you add it with the break-ins at Tanya's place, my instincts are telling me there's something there."

"I agree. We need to track down Tanya's boyfriend and the source of her unaccounted for income."

"I talked to one of Tanya's neighbors. But you know how it is in the city. Millions of strangers on your doorstep. She didn't remember ever seeing a man coming or going from Tanya's apartment. The doorman confirmed that she rarely had visitors, but we already know they could have come up through the garage without being seen."

"Why would a building where the residents pay out of the nose for the sense of security have such a glaring hole in security?"

"Because those same residents covet the privacy that glaring hole affords them so that they can do their dirty deeds without shame."

He exhaled heavily. "People don't make any sense."

"You are preaching to the choir." She swung her legs over the side of her chair and stood. "I should head home."

He pushed to his feet, too. "We didn't decide on our next steps."

"My next step is to head back to the Stryder Medical Clinic and hopefully catch Tanya's close friend and co-worker. She hasn't returned my calls."

He walked with her to the door. "Were you thinking of dropping in on the coworker before or after work?"

Yara slid him a sidelong glance. "Why do you ask?"

They stopped at the door, but he didn't move to open it. "It would save time if I sat in on the interview with you. And if I just happen to be there at the same time, your boss couldn't fault you for that."

She fought back a smile. "Morning. I'm hoping to catch her before work."

He reached for the door, leaning in close. The air between them was charged. With his lips a breath away from her ear, he responded, "I'll bring the coffee."

Chapter Eleven

Brandon had just finished his morning workout in his basement gym when the doorbell rang. And rang again. And again. He didn't need to look out of the side window to know who he'd find standing on his front porch.

"Why are you ringing my bell like that?" He directed the question to Shawn, who still had his finger poised over the button. "And why are you letting him?" he asked. Ryan leaned against the railing.

"Because it annoys you," Shawn answered with a grin.

"And I let him because you didn't see fit to call and let anybody know you were attacked yesterday. By the way, James wants you to call him ASAP." Ryan shot a second devious grin his way.

Fantastic. All his brothers were going to gang up on him for failing to inform them he'd been jumped in a dead woman's apartment. Sometimes he longed to be an only child. "A call I look forward to." He stood back so his brothers didn't bowl over him as they stomped their way into his home.

He shut and locked the front door, then made his way to the kitchen. "Coffee?"

It was just shy of seven thirty and he'd planned to get an early start at the office before meeting Yara at the Snyder Medical Clinic, but he could tell his brothers had worked themselves into a lather. Hopefully, he could quickly assure them that he was fine and get his day back on track.

"So were you ever planning to tell us you got beat up?" Shawn grabbed the cup of instant coffee Brandon slid across the island countertop and sat on a stool.

"No. That piece of information didn't make it onto my to-do list, funny enough."

"You okay?" Ryan waved off the mug Brandon tried to hand to him.

"I'm fine." He looked from one brother to the next, letting them see that he wasn't trying to play a tough guy. The two ibuprofen he'd swallowed that morning had taken care of what remained of his headache. His cheek was still tender from the blow he took to the face, but the swelling was minimal.

Ryan scrutinized his face. His second-youngest brother was by far the most serious and focused of the four West brothers. It was why there hadn't been any argument when he assumed the helm of the family's security and investigations firm from their father when he retired. They'd all known Ryan was perfect to captain the family business. Shawn was the second-in-command, although technically he co-owned the firm with Ryan.

For his part, Brandon had never wanted to be a part of the family business beyond handling their legal affairs. He'd known early on that the law was his calling. A penchant for seeking justice and righting wrongs seemed to have been ingrained in him for as long as he could remember. He guessed it was ingrained in his brothers as well. James, the oldest West brother, had, until recently, made his career in the military, serving his country and protecting the freedom and rights of his fellow citizens. And both Shawn and Ryan had met the loves of their lives trying to save his now sisters-in-law from imminent danger.

"Okay, then why didn't you call and tell us what happened?" Shawn said, setting his coffee aside. He might have been the most laid-back brother, but when it came to family, he was as fiercely protective as any of the other Wests. "I had to hear about my own brother from a police contact."

"I'm sorry, but I knew if I told you two I'd never hear the end of getting my butt kicked."

"True." Shawn grinned.

Even Ryan let his lips turn up into a small smile. "Heard you called a detective on the Silver Hill force. Yara Thomas."

Shawn's brow formed a V and his forehead furrowed. "Thomas. I don't recall a Thomas on the detective squad."

"Pretty walnut eyes. Perpetual scowl. Severe bun," Ryan said.

"Oh, bunhead." Shawn snapped his finger. "Yeah, she's no fun at all."

"Don't call her that," he growled.

Brandon clutched the coffee mug in his hand.

Shawn's eyes widened and his grin grew twice as big. "You like her. No wonder you called her instead of one of us."

Brandon caught Ryan studying him out of the side of his eye. "She's the one you had a thing with last year, right?"

"It wasn't a thing."

"It was a thing. There were late-night calls. At least one date, if I remember correctly. You liked her. That's a thing."

Shawn pushed to his feet. "Hang on a minute." Indignation dripped from his voice. "You had a thing with bunhead and no one told me!"

Brandon stepped around the counter into his brother's personal space. "Don't. Call her. Bunhead."

Shawn put his hands up in surrender pose. "Okay, okay, sorry. You had a thing with Detective Thomas and Ryan knew and neither of you told me? Why?"

Brandon and Ryan answered at the same time.

"Because I can keep a secret."

"Because he can keep a secret."

"That's just messed up." Shawn sat back down on the stool.

"So?" Ryan said.

"So what?" Brandon grabbed the mug Ryan had waved away and took it to the sink, turning his back on his brothers.

There were only three years between him and Ryan and they were most alike of the four brothers. That engendered a natural camaraderie. It also meant they were able to read each other fairly well. He always knew when Ryan was holding back and Ryan had the same sixth sense when it came to him.

"She was the first woman you showed any serious interest in since your divorce and she stomped on your heart. So why'd you call her instead of one of us when you got your butt kicked?"

"She didn't stomp on my heart." Brandon turned to face his brothers, both of whom were looking at him with rapt attention. "And I called her because we're working on the case together."

"The one you had us looking into for you?" Ryan said.

"Yes."

"It's unusual for the cops to work with an attorney. Especially one who knows the victim and does mostly corporate work."

"I do pro bono work for a women's shelter, representing victims of domestic violence. That's actually what I initially thought Tanya Rutger had come to see me about, but now I'm not so sure."

"How does Detective Thomas figure into this?" Ryan pressed.

"She's the lead on Tanya's case."

Shawn hissed.

"Listen, I know," he said, coming back to stand at the island across from his brother. "But the medical examiner has issued a preliminary finding of suicide and I know Tanya wasn't suicidal."

"I take it the lovely detective feels similarly," Shawn responded.

"She has questions. But her lieutenant wants her to drop it so we've decided to work together off the books."

"Sounds like a plan that has disaster written all over it," Shawn quipped.

Ryan's brows arched. "For more than one reason."

"Look, whatever Yara and I had or might have had in the past, that is not what this is about."

"Dude, you were all in on her," Ryan countered.

Brandon threw up his hands. "We went out on two dates and exchanged exactly twelve phone calls. I wouldn't say that's all in."

"How many text messages?" Shawn deadpanned.

Ryan's laugh reverberated around the room.

Okay, so maybe he'd been enamored with Yara back then, but she'd made it clear she didn't want to see him romantically. Very clear. Like she'd gone radio silent. Stopped answering his calls, responding to his texts or returning his voice mails. He might have liked her but he could take a hint. She wasn't interested.

"You both need to go. I have to get ready for work."

He shoved his brothers toward the front door.

"Okay, we're going. No need to paw at me. This is an Armani suit," Shawn said, dancing out of reach.

"Out. Now."

Shawn hopped off the porch and headed for the sleek black BMW Brandon knew was part of the West fleet.

Ryan stopped in the doorway. "I just want you to be careful. With the case and with the detective. You can say what you want, but you've been hurt enough. That woman hurt you once. I don't want to see it happen again."

He knew Ryan's concern wasn't just about Yara. His divorce had been amicable as divorces go, but he hadn't wanted it. He believed in commitment and he'd wanted to try to fix his marriage. But Camille, his ex, had wanted out, so he'd let her go.

He laid a hand on Ryan's shoulder. Ryan was a man of few words, but he always made the ones he said count.

"I promise I'll be careful with the case and my heart."

He watched his brothers drive away and wondered if he'd be able to keep that promise.

Chapter Twelve

Yara parked in the lot designated for the Stryder Medical Clinic at exactly eight thirty the next morning. As was becoming a habit, her pulse quickened when she caught sight of Brandon getting out of his car with a to-go cup in each hand as she approached. Heavy clouds hung overhead, threatening rain, but Brandon wore only a navy sports coat over a white button-down and black slacks. He still looked like a million bucks.

"Good morning. I brought you a little something." He handed her one of the cups. "This coffee shop near my place makes the best cinnamon chai latte you will ever have. I guarantee it."

She took the cup but eyed it with suspicion. "I'm more of a regular coffee, cream and sugar kind of girl."

"No, no, no. Trust me on this." He held his own cup under his nose and inhaled deeply.

She had to admit, it smelled terrific. She took a sip. It tasted like heaven in a cup. "Not bad."

"See. I wouldn't lead you astray."

The look he gave her said just the opposite. That he'd love to lead her toward a host of decadently delightful acts. And she didn't need a mirror to glean that her expression said she was increasingly open to following him down that path.

Try as she had to keep things strictly professional between them, more and more of her day was being consumed with thoughts of kissing him. Not to mention her nights, when her thoughts went far beyond kissing.

A car door slamming had her shifting her gaze over Brandon's shoulder. "This looks like Bailey Dunlap." She set her cup on the hood of Brandon's car and headed toward the woman from the driver's license photo she'd pulled. "Bailey?"

The woman eyed her warily. "Yes?"

Yara flipped the cover on her badge open. "I'm Detective Thomas. I've been trying to reach you, Miss Dunlap. I have a few questions for you."

"Is this about Tanya?"

Bailey's gaze shifted from Yara to Brandon and back, questions in her eyes.

Brandon flashed a broad smile and Bailey visibly relaxed. "Brandon West." He extended a hand to Bailey and her body language shifted again from simply relaxed to receptive.

It appeared Brandon wasn't a bad guy to have around during female interviews.

That didn't stop the pang of jealousy that zipped through her.

"I understand you and Tanya were close," Yara said, pulling Bailey's attention from Brandon.

"We had become good friends in the months since she started working at Stryder Medical. I can't believe she's gone." Tears formed in the corners of Bailey's eyes.

Brandon pulled a white handkerchief from his inside blazer pocket. "I'm sorry for your loss."

Bailey took the handkerchief and dabbed at her eyes.

"I want to make sure the circumstances surrounding Tanya's death are thoroughly investigated," Yara said. "If you have a moment, I just have a few questions."

Bailey's face scrounged. "Circumstances? No one has told us much about how Tanya died."

"That's what we're working to find out. Do you know if Tanya had any problems with anyone recently?"

Bailey dabbed her eyes again, obscuring her face, but she shook her head. "She didn't mention anything."

"Any unhappy patients or a patient who showed too much interest in her?"

"No, nothing like that."

Bailey's gaze flicked back over to Brandon. He sent her another dazzling smile.

"I understand she recently broke up with her longtime boyfriend, Jasper Reinholt."

"I wouldn't say recently," Bailey said, shooting a glance at a passing car. "Tanya and Jasper broke up right after she started working for Stryder. I met him a couple of times and I don't think Jasper has a mean bone in his body. He certainly wouldn't hurt Tanya. He worshiped the ground she walked on."

"So the breakup wasn't his idea," Brandon said.

"Definitely not. Bailey initiated it. I know Jasper tried to talk her out of it."

"Was Jasper upset about the breakup?"

Bailey's expression clouded. "I don't want to get him in trouble. He's a good guy."

"Nobody is in trouble," Brandon slipped in smoothly. "We just need all the information we can get to put the pieces of Tanya's last days together. To get an accurate picture of what really happened to her."

Bailey hesitated for a moment longer. "Tanya said he tried to win her back. I think they went out to dinner once or twice after she'd called things off, but she wasn't really into it. She said the relationship had run its course."

"Do you know if they were in touch with each other recently?" Brandon asked.

Bailey hitched her purse higher on her shoulder and glanced at her watch. "I don't know. She didn't really talk about him much anymore."

The slight inflection on the word *him* made Yara wonder if there was someone else Tanya was talking to her friends about recently.

"Was there someone else in her life?"

Bailey glanced at the doors to the clinic and bit her bottom lip.

Brandon placed a hand on Bailey's shoulder. "Bailey, any information you give Detective Thomas will help her find out what happened to your friend."

"Okay, yeah. I want to help, but it's just, I'm not sure. Tanya was seeing someone, but she was really secretive about it. She said it was new, but I don't know. In the last couple weeks, though, she'd stopped mentioning her mystery man. That's what she called him, her mystery man."

That was little help. *Mystery man* wasn't a name she could run through the system. "She didn't tell you anything else that might help us identify him?"

Bailey shrugged. "I know he bought her a lot of presents. She was always coming to work with a new bag or new clothes when we'd go out."

"What about her apartment?"

Bailey frowned. "What about it?"

"Have you been?"

Bailey shifted from foot to foot. "A few times."

"Then you must have noticed it's very nice. Well beyond what a nurse would normally be able to afford. Not to mention the Mercedes."

"I did ask her about it, but she said she had some family

money. I mean, we were friends, but she didn't show me her bank account."

"You said Tanya had stopped mentioning her mystery man in the last few weeks. Do you have any idea why?"

Bailey shrugged again. "No idea. She was all excited about this guy for months and then all of a sudden she wouldn't talk about him. I mean, it was pretty obvious what was going on. The guy must have been married. That never works out, you know." Something about the statement made Yara think Bailey was speaking from experience. "I figured the guy had moved on to the next woman or Tanya had gotten tired of being the sidepiece. I stopped asking when it was clear she didn't want to talk about it." She glanced toward the building again. "Look, I have to get to work."

Yara handed her a business card. "If there's anything else you remember, please give me a call."

Bailey gave her a tight smile but turned a brighter one on Brandon before walking away.

"Tanya lied about having family money," Yara said as she and Brandon headed back toward his car. "Her mother was a retired bus driver."

"Yeah, Mrs. Rutger didn't mention anything about family money to me when we spoke," he seconded. "But Bailey did confirm our mystery man theory."

Yara grabbed her now-cold latte from the top of Brandon's car and chucked it into the nearby garbage bin. "And it seems like the mystery man was on his way out. I wonder if that was his decision or Tanya's."

Brandon threw his coffee cup into the trash behind hers. "Well, we know that the breakup with Jasper Reinholt was her decision and that he wasn't happy about it."

She shot him a knowing look. "You think Jasper knows who the mystery man is?"

"If he suspected there was someone else, well, it would only be human nature to be curious."

She studied him out of the side of her eye. Had he wondered whether there was someone else when she'd cut off contact? Of course, there hadn't been. In fact, she hadn't been on a date since him. The feelings that had begun to build for him had scared her enough that she hadn't attempted dating again. But now, with Brandon back in her orbit and those feelings swelling again, a growing part of her was starting to regret giving in to her fear all those months ago.

Later. Right now they needed to speak to Jasper Reinholt.

"Okay, we don't know who Tanya's mystery man is, but we do know the ex-boyfriend's name and where he works. I say we speak to him next."

"Sounds like a smart plan. Not that I'd have expected any less from you."

She used her phone to google Jasper Reinholt. "It looks like Jasper's morning class lets out at noon. Want to meet me at Blair Hall on the Silver Hill Community College campus at eleven fifty?"

"I'll be there."

"Detectives."

They both turned to find a tall blond man in a black rain slicker and carrying a beat-up leather bag hurrying toward them.

Dr. Anand Gristedes. Yara and Martin had spoken to Tanya's bosses and the heads of the Stryder Medical Clinic, Dr. Gristedes and his partner, Dr. Steven Manning, after finding Tanya's body.

Dr. Gristedes swept an assessing gaze over Brandon before dismissing him.

Out of the corner of his eye, Yara saw Brandon's expression darken.

"Detective, has there been any progress? Do you know what happened to Tanya?"

"We're still investigating," Yara answered.

"Oh." Gristedes's face fell. "When I saw you talking to Bailey I thought there might be some news."

"Brandon West. Dr. Anand Gristedes. He's one of the partners in the Stryder Medical Clinic."

Yara made the introduction.

The two men shared a perfunctory handshake.

Male egos. Yara mentally shook her head. "Have you thought of anything else that might help us with the case?"

"No, I'm sorry. I told you everything I knew when you came to tell us about Tanya. I didn't really know her well. She'd been working with us for less than a year. It's just so unbelievable."

"If you do think of anything, don't hesitate to give me a call." She was anxious to get to the station. If she wanted this investigation to fly under Lieutenant Wilson's radar, getting to work late wasn't the way to do it.

Gristedes nodded and walked away.

"Doctors and their egos." Brandon huffed.

Yara walked backward toward her car. "You know, some would say the same about lawyers. I'm just saying." She laughed at his grumbling as she walked away.

BRANDON PARKED IN his designated space on the parking lot adjacent to his Silver Hill law offices and got out of the car still thinking about the interview with Bailey. The nurse had given them a place to start digging with Jasper Reinholt, but there was something about Dr. Anand Gristedes that he didn't like. Something that didn't involve his male ego, despite what Yara thought.

He headed for the entrance to the building.

"Hey! Ah... Mr. West."

Brandon turned to find Tanya's brother emerge from a black pickup truck and jog toward him.

"Mr. Rutger." Brandon held out his hand and Nick only hesitated slightly before he took it and shook. "What can I do for you?"

"Were you serious about looking into my sister's death?"

"I was. I am."

"Okay, then I want to help."

"Let's take this into my office."

Brandon led the younger man inside the building and into his office, asking his secretary to hold his calls.

Nick declined coffee and water and sat across from his desk. "The cops aren't going to investigate my sister's death. They've already decided she committed suicide."

Not all the cops, Brandon thought, settling into his own desk chair, but he didn't correct Nick. Yara was taking a chance continuing to look into Tanya's death and he wouldn't risk her career, not even to allay a grieving brother's concerns. Anyway, he was right about the department's overall take on Tanya's case.

"Well, I don't think she did and I'm going to do everything in my power to find out what really happened. You can help me by telling me everything you can about your sister. Anything could be of help."

Nick let out a heavy breath. "She'd pulled away from the family recently. Ever since she broke up with Jasper. At first, I just figured she needed time to cope with the breakup, you know. But I know my mother told you about the argument she and Tanya had. Not speaking to Ma like that, it just wasn't Tanya. I knew something else was up, but she wouldn't tell me what it was."

"What about her apartment? How did you think she was paying for it and the car?"

Nick scowled. "I didn't know about that. You have to understand, I'm seven years older than my sister. We weren't ever close. I loved her. I watched out for her, but we were always at different stages. I knew she'd moved downtown but mostly we exchanged texts checking in on each other and saw each other at Ma's house for holidays. I'd never been to her new place."

"But you knew Tanya was upset about something?"

"Yeah, just the way she lashed out at my mother. Ma only told me that they'd argued over Tanya's new boyfriend. When I reached out to Tanya, she went on about Ma nosing around in her personal life and how she was a grown woman and could date anyone she wanted. Our mother doesn't always respect boundaries so I kind of understood where Tanya was coming from and I just wanted to keep the peace between them. Ma didn't tell me she suspected Tanya was fooling around with a married man until after…" His voice broke.

Brandon gave him a moment to compose himself. "Do you have any idea who the man might be?"

"I really wish I did. If I knew, I'd confront the cheat myself," Nick growled. "You asked my mother about Tanya's cell phone and computer. Why?"

He had to tread carefully here. He only knew about the missing electronics because of his side investigation with Yara. "They seem to have gone missing."

"Missing? That's…weird. Tanya was attached to that phone. She always had it with her. And I know she had a laptop. A good one. I helped her pick it out. I work in IT."

Brandon pushed a legal pad and a pen across his desk. "Can you write down the type of computer and anything else about it that might make it identifiable as Tanya's? Same with the phone if you know what type she had."

Nick scribbled on the pad before handing it back over.

"You think there might be something on them that could lead us to whoever killed her?"

"I don't know, but I don't like that they haven't been found."

"Wait, Tanya told me she'd started keeping a video diary. I thought it was kind of kooky. There might be something in it that would lead you to her new boyfriend." Nick stood. "I have to get to work, but I know what cloud service Tanya used. I can try to figure out her password and log in. Maybe she saved the diary there. It can't hurt to look, at least."

Brandon hesitated. "It might be best to let the police handle that. If you tell me the cloud storage provider, I'll pass it on to the detective on the case."

Nick shook his head. "No way. They had their chance. And this is something I can do for my sister."

He could tell he wouldn't be able to convince the man. Nick probably had the best chance of breaking into Tanya's cloud storage, certainly a better chance than he or Yara did, but he didn't want the man to do anything that might make him a target of whoever had killed Tanya.

"I think that would be okay, but you need to let me know right away if you are able to gain access."

"Agreed." Nick shook his hand and left.

Yara was not going to like having Nick dabble in the case, but it was something for Nick to do, something to help him through the grief.

And if they were lucky, he might even find evidence that pointed them to Tanya's mystery man.

Chapter Thirteen

The police station was abuzz with morning activity when Yara arrived at nine fifteen. It was unusual for her to get in later than the other detectives with whom she shared an office, but they were all at their desks when she slid into her chair. She knew that forensics had sent her a message about some prints they'd pulled from the last home robbery and she wanted to have a handle on the new developments in the case before Lieutenant Wilson inevitably asked her about it. She turned on her computer and waited impatiently for the screen to illuminate.

"So you finally made it in," Martin said and smiled.

She speared him a look over the top of her computer monitor. "I overslept." The login square popped up on screen and she quickly typed in her information.

Paris slid her chair over to Yara's desk. "You look pretty bright-eyed and bushy-tailed for a woman who overslept. Might there be a handsome reason for your sudden exhaustion?"

"My alarm didn't go off. I must have forgotten to set it. That's the reason," she said, giving Paris a light push back toward her own desk.

Paris's face fell. "Oh, well, that's sad for you." She rubbed her rounded stomach and scooted back behind her desk.

Yara navigated to her emails and opened the one from the fingerprint lab. They'd found a match for one of the prints they'd pulled from the most recent house that had been burglarized. Zachary Brooks.

She pulled Brooks's record. A couple of pops for possession that were several years old and several arrests for assault, one of which got him an eighteen-month stint in jail. And a more serious charge for attempted murder that was subsequently dropped after the victim refused to testify and left the state. His prints on the dresser in Tanya's master bedroom suggested he might have graduated from assault to burglary. Brooks's record didn't list an employer but there was a note in the file that mentioned he sometimes did off-the-book work at a friend's landscaping company, Marymount Garden and Landscaping. It's the kind of work that would give a would-be burglar access to homes, but it wouldn't explain finding his fingerprints inside the house. Zachary Brooks was definitely looking like someone she needed to talk to.

"Thomas!"

She jumped at the sound of Wilson's voice. Turning in her chair, she found the lieutenant standing just inside the door to the bullpen. "Where have you been? I've been looking for you to get an update on those robbery cases."

She stood. "Sorry, sir. I got in a little later than usual today, but I was just about to come see you. We got a hit on a set of prints from the last burglary." She pointed to her screen and Wilson moved closer to get a look. "Zachary Brooks. He's got a record for assault. Got off on an attempted murder charge. He works under the table for a landscaper, so he might have had a reason to be at the subject house."

Wilson's eyes traced over the screen.

"I'm going to contact the homeowners. See if they use

this landscaping company for their yard work and then have a chat with Zachary Brooks."

"Pick Brooks up. Do the interview here. You might rattle a confession out of him." His eyes found Martin. "Rachlin, you go with Thomas to arrest this guy. There are eyes on us. I don't want him slipping through our fingers."

She pressed her lips together tightly, smarting at the implication that she would let a potential arrestee get by her. It had never happened. It would never happen.

Wilson turned back to Yara. "Let me know when he's in the box." He strode away without another word.

She reclaimed her seat and reached for the phone.

A half hour later, Yara had confirmed with the homeowners and Marymount Garden and Landscaping that Zachary Brooks had done work at several of the residences that had been robbed, but that there was no reason his fingerprints should have been inside any of the homes.

The bright side was that maybe if she got the robberies tied up in a nice little bow for the lieutenant, he'd back off her some, giving her a little more wiggle room to investigate Tanya's case without feeling like she was under a microscope. The bad news was that she wouldn't be able to meet Brandon at Silver Hill Community College and speak with Jasper today.

She pulled her phone from her pocket and typed out a quick message.

SORRY. WORK STUFF. CAN'T MEET TODAY. WILL CALL LATER.

Twenty minutes later, Martin pulled the black Crown Victoria to a stop across the street from a run-down clapboard house where Zachary Brooks lived with his mother, Maxine. Gray and dingy, the remnants of snowfall from the prior week still edged the home's small yard. The rain that had been threatening while she and Brandon talked to Bailey came down as a light drizzle now, but the dark gray of the overhead clouds threatened showers on the horizon.

"What do we know about the mother?" Martin asked as they exited the car.

Yara pulled the hood of her jacket up, covering her head although she knew the moisture would find a way to twist her sleek ponytail into a mass of curls no matter what she did. "She's forty-two. An office administrator for a local trucking company for the past seventeen years and has no criminal record," Yara recited from the information she'd read in Zachary's criminal file. A file she'd sent to Martin while she finalized the warrant, but one he obviously hadn't read.

Frigid air stung Yara's cheeks as she stepped from the car.

Martin joined her on the sidewalk in front of the house.

Yara led the way up the cracked and crumbling walkway to the front door. She climbed the two steps of the small stoop and stood to the side of the door. Martin remained at the bottom of the stoop, flanking the other side of the door, the end of his coat hiked up so that he could reach his weapon.

Yara knocked on the door.

Seconds turned into a full minute and when no one responded, she knocked again.

The door finally swung open. She recognized Zachary's mother, Maxine, from her driver's license photo. Her face was a study in angles-jutted cheekbones and a sharp pointed nose. She wore her dark brown hair in an elaborate braided style. Her black skirt and stocking feet signified her recent arrival home from work.

Yara unclipped the badge she wore on her hip and held

it out toward the woman. "I'm Detective Thomas and this is Detective Rachlin." She gestured behind her to Martin.

Maxine's dark eyes narrowed and her mouth puckered before she schooled her face into a bland expression.

Yara's shoulders tensed. The rain began to beat down harder.

"We'd like to talk to your son, Zachary. Is he here?"

"No." Maxine blinked twice. She was lying.

Yara glanced over the woman's shoulder into the house but saw only an empty living room. "Can we come inside and look around?"

Maxine pulled the door closer to her body, cutting off even more of her view of the inside of the house. Her mouth puckered again. "Do you have a warrant?"

Yara sighed internally, but kept her tone professional. "We do not."

"Then you can't come in." Something, fear, maybe, flashed in Maxine's eyes. She flicked a quick glance to her right.

Years of reading witnesses' body language told her Zachary was inside, probably listening. Yara wouldn't have put it past Zachary to have threatened his own mother to keep her from speaking with the cops.

But if Maxine wouldn't consent to let them enter the house, they couldn't go in.

Yara persisted. "When was the last time Zachary was in your home, ma'am?"

"I don't have to answer your questions." The woman took a step backward, preparing to close the door.

Yara wedged her foot between the door and its frame. "No, you don't. But it may be better for your son if you do. We're just looking to ask Zachary some questions about an incident that took place in Green Village."

She didn't want to give away too much concerning the

nature of the questions so Zachary wouldn't have time to think about how he might answer them.

Maxine's gaze flicked to the side once more and frowned. She wasn't going to talk.

Yara fished a business card out of her pocket. "If you see or hear from Zachary, please have him call me."

Maxine took the card and shut the door.

Yara stepped off the stoop and walked next to Martin back to the sedan, the crumbling walkway crunching under their boots.

"You do have a way with people," Martin said, his smile sardonic. They slid back into the car, Yara on the passenger's side, Martin behind the wheel.

Maxine peeked out from behind the living room curtain.

Frustration tightened in her chest. "Zachary's in there."

"Yep. And there's nothing we can do about it," Martin said, starting the car and cranking the dial for the heat.

A blast of cold air hit her in the face.

She hadn't been sure about Zachary's involvement in the robberies when she and Martin had pulled up to the house, but his reaction had boosted him to the top of the list of suspects. She didn't like being put off. And if she was wrong and he wasn't involved, she needed to know that and move on with the investigation. Chasing him down only to find out that he had a rock-solid alibi was a waste of time and resources that they didn't have.

Martin put the car in gear and pulled away from the curb.

Yara spotted the movement out of the corner of her eye. "Hang on. Look there." She pointed to a shadow along the side of the house.

Someone crept toward the front corner of the house. The outdoor light mounted to the neighbor's eave cut through the grayness of the day enough that she recognized the figure as Zachary.

Zachary surveyed the street, his eyes landing on Yara's through the windshield. He pivoted on his heels and ran into the shadows between the two houses.

Martin hit the sirens. "He should have at least waited until we drove away."

Yara grabbed the large Maglite from the glove compartment and reached for the door handle. "I'll follow on foot."

Martin would call for backup and circle the block in the car. Wilson's comments about eyes being on the department concerning these robberies rang in Yara's head. If Zachary got away, he could go to ground and it might be weeks before they located him again.

A narrow alley ran between the backyards of the houses fronting parallel streets. Unfortunately, many of the yards had fences and gave Zachary several places to lay in ambush. The robberies hadn't involved any violence to date, but that didn't mean Zachary didn't have a weapon.

Yara put her back against the nearest fence and drew her weapon. Taking a deep breath, she rounded the fence gun first. Her heart hammered so loud she was sure it would give away her location. She could feel sweat seeping through her undershirt.

She huffed breaths as she scanned the surrounding yards for her suspect.

Why did people leave so much stuff out in their yards? Doghouses. Sheds. A big decorative rock. What was the point?

Martin had killed the siren, but Yara saw the blue and red strobe lights at the end of the alley just before the hood of the Crown Vic became visible. Martin swept the tactical light mounted on the side of the car over the alley, illuminating the space.

Something moved at the opposite end of the alley. Zachary had made it farther down the alley than she'd expected.

But the light must have scared him. He darted from behind a toolshed, through a yard, and ran hard toward the street adjacent to his mother's house.

"Police. Stop," she yelled, knowing it would do no good. She pounded behind Zachary.

The alleyway was really nothing more than a cut-through, too narrow for the Crown Vic to fit, but Yara heard the peel of tires as Martin raced along the side street.

The foot chase had attracted the attention of several neighbors. Outdoor lights flashed on, helpfully illuminating Zachary in the now nearly torrential rain, sprinting some thirty yards ahead of her. Unfortunately, some of the neighbors had decided to get themselves a front-row seat to the action. Doors were opening, curious faces peeking out.

"Go back inside and lock your doors now!" Yara yelled. If Zachary got tired of running and he did have a gun, he could very well decide that his best way out of the situation was to open fire.

She dug deep and forced her legs to move faster. She heard the Crown Vic's engine roaring down the street behind her and caught the swirl of the car's lights as Martin sped past her. Yara anticipated Martin's goal—cutting Zachary off at the end of the block.

Unfortunately, so had Zachary. He cut across the street, so close to the Crown Vic's bumper that she flinched in anticipation of Zachary's body hitting the hood of the car.

Somehow Zachary made it to the other side of the street without getting struck and darted behind yet another house.

What was he doing robbing houses? The guy could have been a track star.

She cut across the yards, slowing now that she didn't have the neighbors' front porch lights to help her make out shapes through the rain. She fanned the Maglite back and forth. She could hear more sirens in the distance. Backup was on the way.

A dog barked to her right and a chain-link fence rattled.

She swung the flashlight in that direction and caught sight of Zachary going over a fence two yards away.

"Police. Get on the ground now."

Just as before, he kept moving.

She ran for the fence Zachary had just gone over, holstering her gun to jump the fence and pulling it out again almost the moment her feet hit the ground. That Zachary hadn't tried to ambush her was a good sign that he didn't have a weapon, but she wasn't taking any chances. She ran through two more yards and over a gravel-strewn driveway, the rocks pummeling her shins as she ran.

The sirens were louder now but Yara didn't see any black-and-whites. She chased Zachary into another narrow alleyway, spying him twenty feet ahead. Maybe Zachary would have been a better sprinter than a long-distance runner. He'd noticeably slowed. Lucky for her, she had run cross-country in both high school and college and had kept up with the sport for exercise.

Yara pumped her legs, opening up her stride and closing the distance between them. She lunged, propelling herself onto Zachary's back and taking them both to the ground. Her left knee slammed into a brick paver, sending pain shooting up and down her leg, but she didn't loosen her grip on Zachary.

Zachary lay beneath her, stunned and out of breath.

She recovered first. She dragged one of Zachary's arms behind his back, snapping a cuff on it as heavy footsteps raced around the corner of the house. Flashlights lit up the patio.

"I got him," Yara said, snapping the cuffs on Zachary's other hand.

The two uniformed officers took over as she pushed to her feet, still breathing hard, as Martin rounded the corner. "You okay?"

They watched the officers pick Zachary off the ground and read him his rights. He shot a look over his shoulder as they led him away that was pure menace.

Yara rubbed her knee. "I'm good. If you'd ever join me on my morning run you could have been right there beside me for all the action."

Martin slid his glasses from his face and gave each lens a swipe. "Naw. I'm too old for all that nonsense." He slipped his glasses back on his face. His eyes narrowed on the hand she was using to massage her knee. "I thought you said you were fine. You need to have that leg looked at."

Yara shook her head, limping toward the front of the house. "It's fine. Just bumped it against the ground. We need to get back to the station and question Zachary."

"I guess he definitely knows something about the robberies," Martin said.

Patrol cars littered what she suspected was usually a quiet street. The red and blue strobe lights had attracted a crowd despite her order to the neighbors to remain inside. Half a dozen people stood on their front stoops or in the front yards of their homes enjoying the show.

"Looks that way." Yara watched the patrol car with Zachary in the back seat maneuver around the Crown Vic, which Martin had left parked catty-corner to the sidewalk. "Lieutenant Wilson will be happy."

Chapter Fourteen

Brandon was disappointed to get Yara's text canceling their noon rendezvous with Professor Jasper Reinholt. After a brief period of consideration, he decided to speak to Jasper on his own. The attack on him at Tanya's apartment had made the situation more than just a quest to do right by his client. It had made the situation personal.

So Brandon was waiting in the corridor of Blair Hall at noon when students began streaming out of the classroom where Jasper had just finished teaching Anthropology 201: Ecological and Evolutionary Anthropology. He waited for the students to clear the door, then went inside.

Jasper Reinholt stood at the lectern at the front of the class stuffing papers into a backpack. He was about five foot six, thin with dark, almost black, hair and square rimless glasses. He wore dark brown corduroy pants and a brown-and-white-checked shirt with his sleeves rolled up to his elbows. There were no scratch marks or bruises on his hands or the parts of his arms that were visible, and Jasper was at least forty pounds and three inches too small to be the man who had attacked him at Tanya's place.

That didn't mean he wasn't her killer, though.

"Professor Reinholt?"

Jasper looked up from collecting his things. "Yes?"

"My name is Brandon West." He plucked a business card from the gold-plated holder in the breast pocket of his blazer and handed it over. "I was retained by Tanya Rutger prior to her death."

Jasper's eyes widened. "Retained for what?"

"I can't get into that, I'm sorry." Literally couldn't get into it, but Jasper didn't need to know that. "I'm hoping you can answer a few questions and help me sort a few things out. I understand you and Tanya dated for a period. I'm sorry for your loss."

"Thank you, that's kind of you to say. But Tanya and I have been broken up for some time now."

"I did hear that you'd broken up. When was the last time you saw Ms. Rutger?"

Jasper played with the business card in his hand. The man was nervous. But that wasn't altogether unusual. Having an attorney show up at your workplace and start asking questions about your dead ex-girlfriend had the tendency to make some people nervous.

"We broke up six months ago."

Brandon noted that Jasper hadn't answered the question, but he was willing to give the man a little bit of rope. "So you hadn't seen or spoken to Tanya in six months?"

Jasper glanced around the empty classroom nervously.

He already knew the answer to the question based on what Bailey had told him and Yara earlier that morning, but he could see Jasper trying to work out whether to tell the truth or to lie.

"I saw her a few times after the breakup. Why are you asking me all these questions?"

He injected warmth into his smile, knowing it would have the effect of calming the jittery man. "As I said, Tanya hired me, and although she is unfortunately no longer here, I want to complete the job I was hired to do." Not an untrue statement even if he didn't know what the job he was hired to do was. "The few times you saw Tanya after your breakup, when was that?"

"I don't know for sure. We broke things off in early March and I think it was a few weeks after that, so late March, early April."

"And what did you do?"

Jasper's expression relayed confusion. "What do you mean?"

"When you met. Did you go out to dinner? Catch a movie? Hit a bar?"

"Oh, ah, well one time we did go out to dinner and a movie. Another time I think we just stayed in and watched something on the television."

"So the breakup was amicable? You remained friends?"

"Yeah, I mean, I guess."

Brandon pressed. "You guess?"

Jasper let out a heavy sigh. "Look, I mean it was amicable as far as breakups go. I didn't want the relationship to end. Tanya did. I thought maybe if I paid her more attention, you know, she'd come back to me, so I convinced her to let me take her to a nice dinner and let me come over to watch a movie. But like, her mind was made up. Said we could stay friends. Well, I don't drop two hundred dollars on dinner for my friends so eventually I just let her go."

"When you two met up at her place to watch a movie, was that her place in Lower Manhattan?"

"No. She was still living in the apartment in Queens when we were together."

Brandon studied the man with a practiced eye. "But you knew about the new apartment in Lower Manhattan?"

Jasper nodded. "Yeah, I knew."

"Did you wonder where she got the money for a place like that?"

"Of course I did. The money for rent and the money for the car."

"And did you do some amateur investigating and find out?"

Jasper smirked. "Okay, I tried. You would have, too. We'd been dating for nearly two years. I was thinking about asking Tanya to be my wife. Then out of the blue she dumped me and is living large in a fancy apartment. Driving a luxury car. So I was curious, but I never found out how she was paying for it. Or who was paying for it for her."

"But you think someone was paying for her new lifestyle for her."

"Well, I mean, yeah. I know how much she made and it wasn't enough to cover that apartment and car. Her mother's pension barely covers her expenses and her brother can't keep a job, so it's pretty clear where the money is coming from."

"And where do you think that was?"

"A new man. Tanya always had big dreams. She loved helping people, don't get me wrong, but she also wanted nice things. Like, really nice things that she could never have afforded on a nurse's salary. She must have found some guy who was willing to foot her bills and she traded up. I thought maybe..."

"You thought maybe what?"

"We were just fine before she got that job with those two doctors. I had a feeling the new guy might work there or at the hospital that the clinic is affiliated with."

Jasper looked away but Brandon didn't miss the hurt on the man's face. He felt bad for him. It appeared that Jasper really had cared for Tanya. Which didn't mean he was innocent. The majority of people murdered die at the hands of someone who professed to love them.

"Did you ever confirm that feeling?"

Jasper sighed again. "Look, I admit I poked around on Tanya's social media pages, asked a few mutual friends if they'd heard about a new guy, but I turned up nothing, and at the end of the day I'm not the kind of guy who doesn't take no for an answer. I moved on."

Brandon believed him. Nothing in Jasper's tone or body language indicated he was being deceptive. And his reaction to being unceremoniously dumped then seeing his ex's lifestyle dramatically change wasn't unreasonable.

"Have you ever driven on Route 30 north?"

Jasper started at the sudden change in topic, but recovered quickly. "Ah, yeah. A bunch of times. I've taken that road to avoid traffic on the interstate. Why?"

"Just curious."

Jasper swallowed hard, making his Adam's apple bob. "I heard Tanya was found in her car on a road somewhere. Is that where…?"

"Yes, along Route 30. Do you have any idea why she would have been out there?"

Jasper shook his head, sending a dark curl falling into his face. He pushed it back into place absently. "No. I mean, Tanya did go with me to have Thanksgiving dinner at my aunt and uncle's place last year, but I can't imagine her going to visit them on her own. Why would she?"

That did seem to be a long shot, but maybe she'd met her new boyfriend while she and Jasper were at Thanksgiving dinner. "Was there anyone at that Thanksgiving other than you, Tanya and your aunt and uncle?"

Jasper shook his head. "Just the four of us."

That didn't mean Tanya hadn't met her mystery man at that time, although it made it less likely. But it meant she knew about the lightly traveled road. Maybe she'd planned to meet someone out there and something had gone wrong. It was a link between Tanya and the place her body had been found, however tenuous. Maybe if he and Yara pulled at the threads a little more they'd find something.

Jasper hooked his backpack over his shoulder. "Is there anything else? It's my lunchtime and I have another class in an hour."

"No. Thank you for speaking to me."

Jasper took several steps toward the door, then turned back. "Tanya and I might not have been together anymore, but I still cared about her. She didn't deserve that. I hope whatever it is you're doing for her, it helps find her killer."

He hoped so, too.

Chapter Fifteen

Zachary's cold eyes locked on Yara as she entered the interrogation room. He sneered but remained silent.

Yara settled into the chair across the table from him.

"How are you doing, Zach?" She tossed a legal pad and opened the file she'd carried into the room. Zachary's rap sheet. He'd had his first encounter with the law at the ripe old age of eleven, picked up for selling weed. His initial contacts with the system had all been with the juvenile courts. But as he'd gotten older, his criminal offenses had become increasingly more serious.

Zachary had completed three years of a seven-year sentence for the grand larceny for stealing several automobiles as part of a car theft ring. He'd been released on parole last September and, from the looks of things, had taken up right where he'd left off. The detectives in the gang unit suspected he was involved in the robberies of several drug dealers since he'd been released from prison. Unfortunately, his stint in prison seemed to have made Zachary a better criminal than when he'd gone in and they hadn't been able to develop enough evidence for an arrest.

"So, Zach," she said. "Why'd you run from me?"

"I ain't got nothing to say to you." He leaned back in the chair in a position that was designed to convey nonchalance.

Zachary was a dangerous criminal, but his round face and sun-kissed blond hair gave him an air of undeserved innocence. In a Ralph Lauren T-shirt, designer jeans and three-hundred-dollar sneakers, he could have passed for a rich college student home for a visit.

Yara nodded. "True. You don't have to talk to me, but I bet if we looked really hard, we could find something for your PO to violate you on. You know these parole officers. Sticklers for the rules. How many years do you have left on your sentence?"

He glared.

"Four years," she answered her own question. "Four years all because you went all Usain Bolt on me."

He shifted in his seat, stretching his legs out in front of him, one of which was chained to a metal hook in the floor. He crossed his legs at the ankle and his arms across his chest.

She mimicked the pose, sending a saccharine smile across the table as he did. "Maybe you wanted to go back so you could spend more time with Aiden."

Zach drew his body ramrod straight. "You keep my brother's name out of your mouth."

It looked like the sibling connection was the right button to push. Aiden Brooks had taken after his brother and was currently serving a seven-year sentence for assault.

"Two peas in a pod. Or two criminals in the clink, as the case may be," she said as if he hadn't spoken.

His eyes flashed something cold and threatening.

She straightened but kept his smile fixed on his face.

Someone knocked on the door and a split second later Lieutenant Wilson stuck his head inside the room. "Detective, can I speak to you for a moment?"

Annoyance tripped in Yara's stomach. She was just getting started with her interrogation, setting the rhythm, getting Zachary wound up. Stepping out of the room now meant he'd have time to recalibrate and she'd have to start all over again, but she really didn't have a choice.

She stepped from the interview room, surprised to find Lieutenant Wilson and Morgan Corbett, assistant district attorney, and another man. "What's going on?"

"Detective Thomas, you know ADA Corbett and this is Jung Hsiung, an investigator with the ADA's office."

She nodded an acknowledgment at each of the men. "Okay. Why are they here?"

"We're taking custody of Zachary Brooks," Morgan said, the slight upward quirk of his mouth letting her know he was enjoying stealing her suspect out from under her.

Two years ago, she'd reluctantly agreed to go out with Morgan on what had turned out to be the date that would not end. He'd taken her to one of the many chic New York restaurants where diners paid a fortune for a meal that wouldn't fill up a hummingbird. Morgan had spent the entire meal talking about himself—his Ivy League undergraduate and law degree, being one of the youngest attorneys in his division, his goals of one day assuming a judgeship. By the time the check had come, she was more than ready to head home. As was Morgan, only the home he'd wanted to head to was hers and he seemed to think she should feel honored that he wanted to spend the night. She'd made it clear in no uncertain terms that he was not invited up, which had not gone over well. Their professional relationship had been frosty ever since and she'd done her best to keep her distance.

She fisted her hands on her hips. "He's being charged with multiple counts of burglary. You can't just come in here and take custody."

"Our case trumps a few home invasions," Morgan said. "You can have him back when we're done with him."

"What's your case?" Yara spat.

Morgan shook his head. "Sorry. Can't tell you that. It's a need-to-know and you don't need to know right now."

"You're taking my suspect, but you can't tell me why?"

"Exactly. All you need to know is that Zachary Brooks is a material witness in a very important and sensitive case."

"A material witness in what case?"

She glanced at Lieutenant Wilson, but for all his bluster about the mayor's interest in the case, he was conspicuously quiet now. "And when will that be?" she asked.

Morgan shrugged. "Don't know. Depends on how much he can tell us and how long the case takes to prosecute."

He gestured toward the interview room and his investigator stepped forward and opened the door.

She and Lieutenant Wilson watched from the hall as Morgan and the investigator explained to Zachary why they were there and that he was now in their custody.

Zachary didn't look surprised by Morgan's sudden appearance, which only stoked the ire Yara felt. It appeared that everyone but her knew what was going on. And she didn't like being on the outside one bit.

BRANDON OPENED THE door as Yara started up the walkway. The zing of excitement he'd felt upon seeing her car pull to a stop in front of his townhome was quickly replaced by throbbing anger. She limped to the door and up close now, he could see that her bottom lip was split.

"Are you okay? What happened?" He reached a hand out to help her into the house. Her hair fell in tousled waves and made him think about all the ways he'd love to tousle it even more.

But she was in no state for those kinds of thoughts, so he forced himself to ignore the tightening in his groin. Closing the door with his foot, he then wrapped an arm around her waist, prepared to lift her in his arms and carry her to the living room sofa.

She stopped him with a glare. "Don't you dare. I'm not an invalid. I can walk."

He bit his tongue and kept his arm firmly around her waist as she hobbled to his sofa. "What happened?" he asked again, moving to the kitchen to grab a bag of frozen peas from the freezer.

"Foot chase. I banged my knee up a bit. Split my lip when I tackled the guy. I'm fine. I've taken harder hits from my brothers growing up."

"Someone needs to talk to your brothers about how to treat a lady, then," he muttered. "Here, lie back and put your leg up on the couch." He moved a couple of pillows so that she could prop herself up on the arm of the sofa and extend her leg, then laid the bag of peas over her knee.

She probably should have gone straight home to rest, but it secretly thrilled him that she'd chosen to come to him. He liked taking care of her, which would have probably been as much a surprise to her as it was to him if he told her, which he was absolutely not planning to do.

"I doubt my brothers thought of me as a lady, at least not when we were young. I'm fine. Physically at least."

He eyed her. "What does that mean?"

"I'm not hurt, not really, but I am angry. I get banged up chasing down the bad guy and Morgan Corbett swoops in and takes custody of him. And he won't even tell us why."

"Morgan Corbett, the assistant district attorney?"

"Yeah, you know him?"

"We went to law school together."

"Well, your old law school chum is a real piece of work. He said my suspect was a material witness in one of his cases but he wouldn't give any more details. So weeks of work and a bruised knee and I have nothing to show for it."

He moved back to the kitchen and grabbed two beers from the fridge, twisting the top off both bottles before returning to the living room. He sat on the coffee table across from her and handed her one of the bottles.

He tapped his bottle to hers.

They both took long sips.

"You know, Morgan and I keep in touch. I could give him a call. See if he'll share more details on his case with an old law school friend than with the cops."

Her hand stopped as she was lifting her beer to take another sip. "You would do that for me?"

He gazed at her. "That's the least of what I would do for you."

A blush bloomed on her cheeks. "Thank you. And sorry I had to cancel on you earlier."

He enjoyed the renewed sexual awareness between them but he sensed that she wasn't as comfortable with it, so he let her keep the conversation on steadier ground. "Not a problem." He knocked back another gulp of beer. "I actually decided to go see Jasper by myself."

"What? I thought we agreed you'd keep me in the loop."

"We did. Which is why I'm telling you now that I went to see Tanya's ex."

She pushed herself up straighter on the sofa. He could tell the movement had hurt even though she did her best not to show it. "That's not what I meant by keep me in the loop. I meant let me know what you are planning to do before you do it."

Rage at the man who'd hurt her threatened to rear up but he tamped it down.

"I didn't agree to that." He raised a hand before she could start in on him again. "Would you like to know what the professor said or would you rather keep yelling at me?"

She shot him a look that should have made him run for

the hills, but somehow he found it endearing. God, she was even more gorgeous angry.

"What did he say?" she bit out.

He relayed the high points of his conversation with Jasper. She took everything in, only stopping him twice to ask clarifying points.

"So Jasper suspected Tanya's new man might be one of the doctors she'd come in contact with at the job. It's not a bad theory given all the money she seemed to have come into after starting that job."

"It's possible, but doctors don't necessarily have the disposable income that people think. Much like lawyers, the cost of the credential eats into your salary significantly and for a number of years."

"Okay, okay. I'm not going to be an elitist on doctors, but it's a theory that is worth looking into."

"I agree. I've started researching the practice, but there are seven doctors who work in the clinic and it is affiliated with a nearby private hospital so it's possible Tanya could have met someone through the clinic who works at the hospital."

Yara sighed. "Our suspect list is going in the wrong direction. Growing instead of shrinking."

"I know. That's why I've asked my brother to help by checking backgrounds. I figured it made the most sense to start with the clinic doctors and work our way outward."

"Agreed."

"I'm also not sure if there's any significance to be placed on the fact that Jasper and Tanya traveled along the road where Tanya's body was found."

Lines formed on Yara's forehead. "I don't know, either." She shifted on the sofa, then winced.

"Here, let me..." He grabbed the pillow from the other end of the sofa and moved to put it under the injured knee.

"No, it's okay. I should be going." She swung her leg over the side of the sofa and to the floor slowly.

He tossed the pillow aside and sat next to her. "You could stay. I have a guest room. Two, actually. You can have your pick."

Or she could stay in his bedroom. In his bed. In his arms. But something told him saying those thoughts out loud would send her running as fast as her bum knee would allow.

The corner of her mouth curved in a hint of a smile. "Thanks, but I can make it home."

He hooked his arm around hers and helped her to her feet.

Her knee threatened to buckle and he steadied her, pulling her in close. Closer than he had to, admittedly.

She looked up into his eyes, her dark brown ones softening, and filling his chest with a need he'd never felt before.

She surprised him by sliding her arms around his neck, going up on her toes and kissing him. Softly at first, but when he slid his arms around her waist, she deepened the kiss. He wanted to take it easy since she'd been hurt, but when he tried to back away, she held him firmly in place.

Her mouth was intoxicating. She nibbled at his bottom lip, an action that was so erotic his knees threatened to give way.

Finally, she pulled her mouth away from his, but remained in the circle of his arms. "Sorry, I don't know what came over me."

"You wound me. I'm not sorry at all. I think we've been building toward this from the first moment we met in the courthouse."

"Maybe." Her eyes swept over his mouth and he pulled her in closer.

"Why did you drop out of my life all those months ago? What did I do wrong?"

She swept a hand over his shoulder. "You didn't do anything wrong."

"Then why'd you walk away from me?"

"My job is dangerous. Every day I leave for work not knowing if I'll make it back home."

Brandon pushed a lock of hair behind her ear. "I've got news for you, Yara. No one knows if they'll make it until the end of the day."

Her eyes locked on his face. "You know what I mean. I never want to put you or anyone through the agony of having to pick up the pieces and go on if something happens to me on the job."

He held her tighter. "What about the agony of never knowing what we could have been because we never tried?"

The internal struggle between her fears and the possibility he'd put before her played out in the expression on her face.

He dropped a light kiss on her lips. "Just…think about what I said, okay?"

She pushed away, taking several steps backward this time.

"Okay," she said again. "But I really should go now."

He set aside his pent-up need. All things in good time.

He helped her to the door, holding it open for her. "You sure you can make it home on your own?"

"I'm sure. Good night, Brandon."

"Sweet dreams, Yara."

Chapter Sixteen

Brandon wasn't surprised that Morgan kept him waiting for nearly twenty minutes. He was surprised that his friend had agreed to see him on such short notice.

He sat on the comfortable leather sofa and went through his ever-growing email messages on his phone. At last a willowy young woman in a black skirt suit strode through the doors separating the offices from the reception area and asked him to follow her.

They walked down a brightly lit corridor lined with offices with glass front walls, her heels clicking on the tile floors. Brandon stayed close behind. It was clear from the day he'd started at the district attorney's office that Morgan was destined to be a rock star and it seemed that he was well on his way. His wasn't quite a corner office but it was definitely corner adjacent. The walls were lined with dark paneled bookshelves and leather-bound books Brandon would have bet good money Morgan had never cracked open. Through the office's glass wall, Brandon could see the man sat at an antique desk he'd had to have brought in himself—no way the government footed the bill for its cost—but Brandon couldn't deny the setup was impressive.

His escort knocked on the door.

Morgan raised his head and waved at them to enter. He

stood as Brandon crossed the expansive office to shake his hand. "Brandon West, what a surprise. How long has it been?"

"It's been a while. Thank you for seeing me on short notice."

"Would you like something to drink? Water? Coffee?"

"Nothing, thanks."

"That will be all, Coleen." Morgan nodded at the woman who'd escorted Brandon to the office.

They both sat, Morgan in the leather executive chair behind his desk and Brandon in the silk upholstered chair in front of the desk.

It had been more than ten years since Brandon left the prosecutor's office, but Morgan looked as if he aged ten years in that time. Litigation work could do that to a person. Morgan had never been good-looking—his face was flat, and his eyes just a little bit too widely set. Now he looked frail, white dress shirt loose around the neck despite being buttoned up to the last button.

"I must admit, I'm curious as to why you reached out."

"It's about one of your cases. One that appears to have a connection to a client I represent."

"Oh?" Morgan leaned forward and placed his elbows on the desk, steepling his hands.

"You took a man into custody yesterday. Zachary Brooks. Yet, no one seems to know why."

Morgan's face darkened. "How do you know that?"

Brandon smiled. "We all have our sources and connections."

"That's confidential information."

"I heard he was a material witness in one of your investigations." He was taking a chance revealing this information, but a small one he figured. Morgan might suspect Yara had told him and that he was here on her behalf, but there wasn't much he could do about it beyond complain to her lieutenant. Yara was a big girl. She could handle a dressing-down if it came to that. She might not even mind if he got useful information here.

"I can't talk about my case."

"Not even to a former colleague?"

"*Former* being the operative word in that sentence."

"Come on, Morgan. Help me out here. You know I'm not going to share what you tell me with anyone."

"Why are you asking?"

He'd anticipated this question. He couldn't come out and tell Morgan that he was doing it for Yara, so he'd come up with another plausible excuse. "It may or may not have some bearing on a client of mine."

Morgan's right eyebrow rose. "One of the domestic violence cases you work on?"

Brandon let the silence do the work for him.

Morgan sighed. "This doesn't leave this room, got it?"

"Got it."

"Zachary Brooks is a material witness in a Medicare fraud and illegal sale of prescriptions case I'm working on."

Brandon wasn't sure what he was expecting, but it wasn't that. "How in the world did someone like Zachary get mixed up in Medicare and prescription fraud?"

Morgan chuckled mirthlessly. "These guys are like the Warren Buffett of crime. They're diversified to mitigate risks. Zachary's brother is serving seven years for an assault. Zachary came to us with information on the fraud in an effort to shave time off his brother's sentence."

"How did Brooks even know about the fraud?"

"His ex-girlfriend works at the practice that's the subject of our investigation. He overheard her talking about the fraud and got the bright idea to capitalize on it."

Brandon's senses tingled. "What's the girlfriend's name?"

"Bailey Dunlap."

PARIS DROPPED A file folder on Yara's desk the next morning as she waddled past.

"What is this?" Yara asked.

"Tanya Rutger's phone records."

Finally. Hopefully, there was something in them that would give her a name for Tanya's mystery man and explain why she'd been out on Route 30 the night she was killed.

The request for Tanya's phone records covered the thirty days prior to her death and included phone calls and texts. The text messages alone spanned nearly thirty pages. Yara flipped to the list of phone calls, relieved to find that it was a much more manageable ten pages.

She scrolled to the end of the phone list, working backward from the last call made. In addition to the number of the incoming or outgoing call, the records listed the date and time of each call, the city the call originated from and the duration of the call. Unfortunately, it didn't tell her the name of the listed owner of the other phone. She'd have to run each of the numbers through the reverse phone directory database and see if they got a hit, and that would take time.

Most of the calls were incoming. She was able to quickly identify and eliminate calls from Tanya's mother and brother. What really interested her were the nearly three dozen calls from a number that came up as the main line for the Stryder Clinic. There were any number of reasons that an employee might receive or make a phone call to their employer, but these calls mostly seemed to come at the end of the workday or well after the clinic would have been closed for the day. And there were far more calls from the clinic number to Tanya's phone than there were calls from Tanya to the clinic. In fact, when she broke the calls out into those that were sent and those that were received, she could see a definite pattern. All the calls that Tanya had made to the clinic occurred during normal work hours. With the exception of two, all the calls that came from the clinic had come after the clinic should have been closed. There might have been nothing to it—maybe someone at the clinic had been calling to follow up on a patient or ask Tanya to come in for extra shifts, a lot of extra shifts—but Yara's instincts told her otherwise.

Unfortunately, there was no way to tell from the phone records alone exactly who'd been calling Tanya. Which meant another trip to the clinic was in order.

The only other number that had called Tanya's phone with any regularity was unlisted to Yara. But the name that popped up when she ran it through the reverse directory was not.

Jasper Reinholt.

Hadn't he told Brandon that he hadn't spoken to Tanya since giving up on winning her back? Yet there were four calls ranging from approximately five minutes to nearly forty minutes listed on Tanya's phone records well after their breakup. One of which had occurred the day before Tanya's body was found.

She flipped to the pages showing the text messages Tanya sent or received over the last month. There were nearly a dozen text messages from Reinholt's number as well. Many of them were mildly to openly flirtatious. None were threatening, but it wouldn't have been the first time someone went from love to hate faster than a speeding bullet. Maybe Tanya had tried to get rid of Jasper once and for all on one of the calls and he hadn't taken it so well. She'd had Reinholt far down on her list of people of interest given the consensus that his relationship with Tanya had ended several months earlier, but now he was someone she wanted to speak to sooner rather than later.

She reached for her cell phone and dialed another number that was becoming more and more familiar to her.

Brandon picked up after the first ring. "Detective, I was just about to call you."

She ignored the flip-flop in her stomach at the sound of his voice. "Didn't Jasper Reinholt tell you that he hadn't spoken to or seen Tanya in a few months?"

"Ah, well, then, right to business are we? Yes, that's what he told me. Six months, to be exact."

She lowered her voice to little more than a whisper. "I got Tanya's phone records and there are a number of calls from Reinholt as well as dozens from the Stryder Clinic."

There was no one in the office at the moment except Paris and she was focused on typing up a report and hadn't so much as looked her way after dropping Tanya's phone records on her desk. Lieutenant Wilson had given her permission to get Tanya's phone records, but she still didn't want him to know that she was working with Brandon to prove Tanya had been murdered and find out who killed her.

"The calls from Reinholt might be something, but it's not unusual for one's employer to call them occasionally."

"How about three dozen times in the last month? And mostly after hours?"

"Okay, that qualifies as unusual. What do you want to do?"

"I need to go speak to Reinholt and then make a stop at the clinic. See if I can't figure out who was making the calls to Tanya and why. Thought you might want to come along."

"I don't have any work that can't wait until later and I can fill you in on my meeting with Morgan Corbett on the way. I'm in."

She smiled into the phone. "Pick you up in ten minutes."

Brandon was waiting when she pulled up in front of his office in a charcoal suit that he looked as if he'd been born to wear.

"How many of those suits do you have?" Yara asked, smoothly pulling the police sedan back onto the street.

Brandon's mouth quirked up into a smile devilish enough to stop traffic. "You're welcome to take a peek in my closet any time."

Heat crawled up her neck. "Just tell me what happened when you talked to Corbett."

He chuckled but began describing his earlier conversation with the assistant district attorney.

"So Zachary Brooks is connected to Tanya. What are the odds?" Yara tapped the brakes, slowing as a teenage male darted across the street against the light.

"Clearly pretty good. Brooks was dating Bailey Dunlap. Morgan said Zach overheard Tanya and Bailey discussing possible Medicare and prescription fraud. He took the information to the district attorney's office, looking for a deal to get time shaved off his brother's prison sentence."

They stopped at a red light and Yara tapped the steering wheel, thinking. "Brooks is a career criminal. It figures he would have worked out a way to use information like that falling into his lap."

"I suggest we speak to the good doctors," Brandon said.

"Exactly what I was thinking. Right after we talk to Professor Jasper Reinholt."

The parking lot on campus was the size of a soccer field and was nearly full when they parked. The sun was high, but there was still a snap to the air that made it feel colder than the thermometer's report.

"Jasper doesn't have a class listed at this time so we'll have to track him down. His office is in Whitmer Hall to the east of the parking lot."

They set out and found Whitmer Hall easily enough. The building looked like every college brochure, soaring columns and lots of aged stone surrounded by a large, green-grassed quad. Yara knew the campus was not old enough for the building to have actually been built during the century when such architecture would have actually been in vogue. But college students, and more importantly their parents who paid the bills, envisioned a certain university experience and Silver Hill Community College was keen on giving it to them.

They climbed a series of stone stairs and entered the building. There was no directory, but the office doors did have names on them. None of the names on the first several doors were Jasper Reinholt and with four floors in the building, walking the halls to find Reinholt could take some time.

Yara was grateful when the end of the hallway opened up into a small alcove where two women sat behind desks. She supposed they were the professors' assistants and, most likely, the keepers of the most important knowledge on campus.

Neither woman acknowledged their approach.

"Excuse me, could you tell me where I could find Professor Jasper Reinholt's office?" Yara asked.

"Never heard of him," the woman sitting at the desk closest to them said without looking away from her computer. The nameplate on her desk read Rena Smith.

"He's with the anthropology department. This is the sociology floor," the other woman said around the pencil in her mouth. Yara couldn't see if there was a nameplate on her desk.

Yara felt her irritation rising. "Okay, well, what floor are the anthropology professors' offices on?"

Rena sighed, looking away from what she was working on, then gave a little gasp when her eyes fell on Brandon.

Her reaction was enough to cause her coworker to stop typing and pay attention as well.

Brandon aimed a dimpled smile at the women. "Ladies, I know how awfully busy you must be taking care of all these insufferable academics. But if you could help my colleague and me out here for just a moment. We're looking for Jasper Reinholt's office. You're correct, he is an anthropology professor."

The woman behind Rena took the pencil out of her mouth as her gaze drank in Brandon. "He'd be on the third floor, then. I'm not sure of his office number," she said with a dazzling smile.

"I can look it up. I've got my building directory right here." Rena reached across her desk, knocking a stack of papers to the floor. She grabbed several sheets of stapled papers that had been stick-pinned to the corkboard on the wall next to her desk. "306B," she said in a tone more appropriate for announcing an Oscar winner than an office number.

"But he's not there." The other woman rose and came to stand next to her colleague's desk, and extended a hand to Brandon, completely ignoring Yara's presence. "I'm Lara."

Brandon took her hand. "It's a pleasure to meet you, Lara."

"Do you know when Professor Reinholt will be back?" Yara asked, fighting to keep the irritation out of her voice.

"No, I mean he's not coming back. Not for a while, at least. The reason I know he's in the anthropology department is that I'm friends with his assistant and she was down here yesterday complaining that Professor Reinholt called the dean yesterday and said he'd be taking a few weeks off for a family emergency effective immediately. As you can imagine, it shook the place up given that the semester had already started and Reinholt gave, like, no notice at all."

"Did he say what the family emergency was?"

"No, at least if he did, he didn't tell Pam. That's his assistant's name. I guess when you have the kind of money he does to fall back on, you don't worry about burning bridges or ticking off your boss."

Yara's ears perked up. "I wasn't aware that Professor Reinholt had any money to speak of."

The two women shot glances at each other.

"Ladies, this is a police investigation. If you know something, now's the time to say it."

The women gave each other another a knowing look and then Lara spoke. "Professor Reinholt doesn't make a big thing about it, but it's not like it is a secret, either. His stepfather is Chauncy St. James, you know, the billionaire tech entrepreneur. He married Professor Reinholt's mother when the professor was a toddler or something so he's basically the man's father. Professor Reinholt makes a big show of living off his salary, driving that hatchback and living in a little house in Kingsborough, but, I mean, it's easy to live like a poor assistant professor when you know you don't really have to."

They thanked the women for their help and then headed to Reinholt's office. As expected, he wasn't in. His assistant was far less forthcoming with information, only sharing that she had no idea when the professor would be back in the office and offering to pass on the message that the police had stopped by to speak with him.

Yara waited until they were back in the car before asking the question that had been on her mind since speaking to the two chatty assistants.

She turned to Brandon without starting the car. "What are the chances that Reinholt just happened to have a family emergency after you asked him questions about his relationship with Tanya?"

"I've never been good at math, but I'd venture to say the odds are low."

She started the car's engine. "Me, too. You have time for a drive by Reinholt's place?"

Brandon graced her with one of his dazzling, dimpled smiles and she felt herself cutting Rena and Lara some slack. It was an ultra sexy smile.

"For you, I have all the time in the world."

Chapter Seventeen

Yara turned on Reinholt's street and searched for his address. The neighborhood seemed familiar and, after a moment, she remembered why. She'd made her first arrest as a cop two streets over years ago. She and her partner had been called to a domestic disturbance where they'd found a man trying to break down the locked bedroom door and get to his wife and child. He'd been hopped up on methamphetamines and it had taken her, her partner and another cop to subdue him. A few weeks after the incident, she'd gotten notice from the district attorney that the charges against the husband were being dropped because his wife was refusing to testify against him.

Despite her initial introduction to it, the neighborhood was a generally safe, run-of-the-mill middle-class enclave. The homes looked well-kept for the most part and there were a fair number of them with signs that young families lived inside, bicycles lying haphazardly on front lawns, swings hanging from the large mature trees in various yards and a virtual bonanza of neutral-colored minivans as far as the eye could see.

She stopped the car in front of a modest Cape Cod with chipping paint and a cracked concrete walkway. "This is Reinholt's place."

"Doesn't look like anyone is home." Brandon peered out of the passenger window. "No car in the driveway."

No car in the driveway and the blinds were pulled on all the windows facing the front of the house.

"Let's go take a closer look." She shut off the engine and met Brandon on the sidewalk.

Brandon glanced up and down the block. "Kind of sad-looking compared to the other houses on the street."

Unlike most of the other homes that virtually burst with signs of the lives being lived inside them, Reinholt's was sterile and bland. Black front door that matched the black shutters and went along with the chipped white siding. Anybody could have lived here. Or nobody, which was what it looked like at the moment.

But she'd been on the job long enough to know that looks could be deceiving and that complacency could get you killed in her line of work. The husband she'd arrested blocks away all those years ago was a mild-mannered accountant when he wasn't hopped up on meth, five foot five and 140 pounds soaking wet, but it had still taken three people to get cuffs on him.

She unsnapped the strap on her holster and shifted her badge so it could be seen clearly as they approached Reinholt's front door. The sound of drums came from the home to the left while a light from a television screen flashed in the window in the one to the right. Reinholt's place was completely quiet. No sound at all from inside. No interior lights visible through the slats on the blinds.

Yara knocked. "Mr. Reinholt? It's Detective Thomas with the Silver Hill Police Department. Open up, please."

Nothing. She knocked again and peeked through a gap in the blinds on the window closest to the door. Nothing inside the house so much as stirred.

"I don't think he's home," Brandon said, peering through the window on the other side of the door.

"I think you're right. And I get the feeling he hasn't been here for a while."

"He informed the dean about a family emergency yesterday so maybe he's staying with relatives."

"Maybe, if he actually did have a family emergency, and I'm not ready to buy that story."

She rapped on the door again, but without any expectation that the outcome would be any different from the previous two times.

"What now?" Brandon asked.

That was an excellent question.

She turned and looked out over the neighboring houses, thinking. There was something going on with Jasper Reinholt. His lies about the calls and texts to Tanya, holding himself out as an average working Joe when he was really the stepson to one of the richest men in Silver Hill, and now mysteriously disappearing when she wanted to talk to him. He knew more than he was saying. Possibly a lot more. She didn't have nearly enough to officially consider him a suspect in Tanya's death, but she was definitely getting closer to making that leap. And, knowing he was part of one of the most powerful families in town, getting him to talk would likely be all difficult.

She checked her watch, annoyed that Reinholt, at least for now, was a dead end. Lieutenant Wilson wasn't riding her as hard since she'd arrested Brooks for the home invasion robberies, which didn't mean her extended absences would go unnoticed. But she wanted to follow up on the calls that had come from the Stryder Medical Clinic to Tanya after hours enough to risk Lieutenant Wilson's wrath. "Looks like no luck with Reinholt for now."

Brandon strolled beside her. "I can do some digging

when I get back to my office. Maybe have Shawn do some as well."

"Your brothers do have a knack for finding out things people want to keep hidden."

Brandon shot her a boyish grin. "It's a living. How about I dig into Reinholt's background, find out everything I can about his family connections and money, and you see if you can't track him down."

"Sounds good." She smiled across the top of the car, reaching for the door handle. "Still have time to take a drive to the clinic and ask the good doctors a few questions?"

Brandon beamed back at her. "I go where you go, Detective."

"Excuse me!"

Brandon turned and Yara shifted to the side so she could see past him to the woman jogging from the house to the right of Reinholt's place.

She was a tall, lanky white woman in black leggings, an oversize sweatshirt and running shoes. Her hair was up in a sweaty knot at the top of her head.

"I don't mean to pry, but I saw you coming from Jasper's house and, well, I watch enough *Law & Order* to recognize an unmarked police sedan when I see one." The woman chuckled. "I'm Marion Knight, Jasper's neighbor. I just wanted to make sure everything is okay." Her brow creased with worry. "I saw Jasper take off out of here yesterday like a bat out of you know where. He didn't even stop when I called out to him."

Yara circled the car and came to stand in front of the woman on the sidewalk in front of her house. "You saw Jasper leave his house last night? Around what time?"

"Oh, seven, maybe a little after. *Wheel of Fortune* had just come on so it couldn't have been too much later than that."

Yara's eyes flicked to the woman's house, where the television could still be seen through the window. She didn't know one game show from the other, but it appeared that a contestant was spinning a large stand-up wheel on whichever one was on at the moment.

"Did Jasper have anything with him when he left?"

"Anything? Oh, like a suitcase. I think so. He threw something across the car into the passenger seat after he opened the door, like he had a duffel bag or something. He was moving pretty quickly so I didn't get a good look."

"Does he often take off like that, unexpectedly?" Brandon asked.

Marion shook her head. "I can't say that he does. At least not that I've ever noticed before."

And since Yara got the sense that Marion noticed just about everything that happened on the block, it was safe to say that Reinholt didn't take off often.

Which meant nothing. He could have still gotten a call about a family emergency. In fact, everything Marion was telling them was consistent with that.

"Have you noticed Mr. Reinholt acting differently lately? Has he been angry or upset?"

Marion looked taken aback by the question. She actually physically took a step away from them. "No, I mean, not that I've noticed. Jasper is a good neighbor, but we aren't close. We speak, just to say 'hello,' you know, if we both happen to be outside at the same time."

Yara pulled her phone out of her pocket and flipped until she found a photograph of Tanya. "Have you seen this woman at Mr. Reinholt's home in the last month?"

Marion studied the phone screen for several seconds before shaking her head. "I can't say that I have. Sorry. What is all this about? Is Jasper in some trouble?"

Yara smiled tightly. "Thank you, Ms. Knight. You've been very helpful."

Marion frowned, likely not missing the fact that Yara hadn't answered her question. "If you really want to find Jasper, you should try his job. He is dedicated to educating the next generation."

"Thanks, we'll do that." Yara pulled a business card from her pocket. "If you do see Mr. Reinholt, could you let him know Detective Thomas is looking for him? And if you remember anything else that you think could be helpful, please give me a call."

Marion took the card, then turned and went back inside her house.

Yara turned to Brandon. "What do you think? Is Reinholt our guy?"

Brandon's shoulders went up, then back down. "He's certainly acting suspicious, but it could be just what it looks like. A family emergency called him away."

Yara started around the car again. "Yeah, or he could be a murderer on the run."

YARA HAD TO circle the clinic's parking lot twice before she spotted a car backing out of a space. They parked in it, then climbed from the car and headed for the clinic.

"Dr. Manning is not going to be happy to see us," Brandon said.

"Good. I'm not happy to be here. I'm sick of people lying and keeping things from me. I'm trying to find a killer and all anyone is concerned with is keeping their silly secrets."

She pulled open the door to the clinic and a blast of warm air hit them as they approached the reception area. A young man wearing a headset complete with microphone sat behind the desk.

"I'm Detective Thomas. I'm here to see Dr. Manning."

"Do you have an appointment?"

Yara's smile was almost feral. "No, but we would appreciate the doctor making the time."

The receptionist gave them a pitying look. "I'm sure you understand Dr. Manning is very busy. Maybe you'd like to make an appointment."

"If I make an appointment it will be with a judge. For a warrant to turn this place inside out."

The receptionist's eyes widened with fear. "One moment, please." He tapped four numbers on the phone's keyboard and swiveled his chair away from them. The space was small so they could hear his conversation. Dr. Manning wasn't happy, but the receptionist's repetition of Yara's threat to get a warrant seemed to do the trick.

The receptionist swung back to them with a faux smile on his face. "The doctor will see you now. Down the hall and to the left."

The door to Dr. Manning's office was cracked open. Brandon knocked, then pushed the door open wider. He was on the phone, his already gloomy expression darkening when Yara and Brandon entered.

"I've got to call you back," Manning said to the person on the other end of the line.

He put the phone down and straightened in his high-backed chair. "Detective Thomas." He nodded at Yara. "And I don't believe we've met as yet," he said, his gaze raking over Brandon.

"This is my associate, Brandon West. Thank you for seeing us without an appointment."

"I didn't see that I had much choice. Not with the threats you were making."

"Not threats, Doctor. Just making it clear what steps I'd be forced to take if you weren't able to speak with me."

"Call it what you want, but I don't appreciate you barging in here like this. I'm only indulging you because I want, as much as anyone, to know the truth about what happened to poor Tanya. Her family deserves that."

"I'm glad you feel that way, Doctor. Then you won't have any problem explaining why you didn't tell me and Detective Rachlin about the federal government's ongoing investigation into the clinic."

Dr. Manning darted a nervous look around the office. "That's not relevant to what happened to Tanya."

"And how do you know that?" Yara pressed.

"Because the whole investigation is nonsense," Manning said with false bluster.

"The feds got a tip that doctors working at this clinic have been selling prescription drugs to patients and nonpatients. That doesn't sound like nonsense to me."

"Well, it is. None of the doctors I work with would ever violate their oaths like that. It's outrageous that anyone would take the word of an anonymous tipster over the words of two well-respected doctors in the community."

"It's funny that you mention an anonymous tip. I didn't think much information about the investigation had been released. How did you know the investigation was opened based on an anonymous tip?"

"Well, I…" The doctor shifted in his chair uncomfortably. "As I said, the whole investigation is nonsense, and I have many friends who understand that and don't want to see this clinic or my reputation tarnished."

"So you have someone feeding you information on the investigation?"

Manning huffed out a breath. "Is this really what you came here to talk to me about?"

"Did you suspect Tanya of being the anonymous source?"

Manning clenched his teeth, his gaze skittering away. "No."

"Very convincing," Brandon deadpanned. "So did you

ask Tanya if she'd contacted the authorities, Tanya's bosses or the medical board?"

"I told you—"

"You lied," Yara interrupted. "And I'm getting pretty sick of being lied to. Maybe it makes more sense to get that warrant. Search this place for the answers I'm looking for myself." She stood and Brandon followed suit.

It actually wasn't easy to get a warrant to search a doctor's office and Yara doubted she had enough to get a judge to grant one, but the threat seemed to have the desired effect on Manning.

Manning popped up out of his chair. "Wait. Wait."

"Doctor, I'm at the end of my patience. Cooperation or a search warrant. What is it going to be?"

Manning looked beaten. "Okay, look, I suspected Tanya was the person who went to the authorities. She came to me with concerns about Dr. Gristedes. She thought he was prescribing medication to patients who didn't really need it and miscoding some procedures."

"And what did you do about her assertion?" Brandon asked.

"I told her that the doctors prescribed medication, not the nurses. I have the utmost confidence in Dr. Gristedes's diagnostic skills. I don't think it is appropriate for the support staff to second-guess a doctor."

"So your theory is that Tanya contacted the authorities after you blew off her suspicions?" Yara pushed back.

"Who else could it have been? This clinic has been serving the community for nearly twenty years and suddenly, after Tanya Rutger begins working here, these scurrilous charges are hurled at us. I'd actually hoped that after Tanya's death this baseless investigation might be dropped."

Yara's lips curled with disgust at the man in front of her. "Is there anything else you haven't told us?"

Manning glared. "I've told you everything I know."

She and Brandon headed for Gristedes's office, but it was dark and empty.

Yara tried the doctor's cell but got no answer.

They had better luck when it came to finding Bailey. She was in the staff lounge having a cup of coffee with another nurse. At the sight of Yara's badge, the second nurse excused herself, shooting an ominous look over her shoulder at Bailey before she left the room.

Yara settled in the chair Bailey's coworker had just vacated while Brandon took the other empty chair at the table. Bailey chewed her bottom lip, her gaze trained on the mug between her hands.

"Bailey, you lied to me."

Bailey lifted her head. "No, I didn't lie."

"You didn't tell me that Tanya thought your bosses were engaged in fraud and illegal prescription sales."

Bailey's face reddened. "I... I didn't think it had anything to do with Tanya's suicide."

"You also didn't tell me you were dating Zachary Brooks."

Her face scrunched in confusion. "Zach? I'm not dating him."

"But you were. And while you were dating him, Tanya told you about the doctors at the Stryder Medical Clinic engaging in Medicare fraud and selling illegal prescriptions."

Bailey's eyes darted to the door, fear swimming in them. She leaned forward and dropped her voice to a whisper. "Do we have to discuss this here? Now?"

"Yes." But in deference to the sensitive situation that Bailey was in and in the hope of getting her to talk, Yara dropped her voice to a whisper as well. "This is a murder investigation. The murder of your friend."

"Murder?" Bailey pressed her hand against her chest. "I thought Tanya killed herself."

"We no longer think that's the case." At least she no longer thought it. And when Lieutenant Wilson found out she was pursuing the case as a homicide, there would be hell to pay, which was why she needed to have a suspect by the time he realized what she'd been doing. "That's why it's even more important now that you tell me the whole truth."

Bailey swallowed hard. "I... I can't believe this."

"Were you and Zachary Brooks dating?" Yara pressed.

Bailey hesitated for a moment before nodding. "*Dating* is probably too strong a word for it. We hooked up for a few weeks before I realized what a loser he was."

At least she'd realized it, Yara thought. "During the period you were hooking up, did Tanya come to you with her suspicion that your employer was committing Medicare fraud and the illegal prescriptions?"

Bailey shrugged and looked down at the table again. "Yeah, but I thought she was way off base and I told her so. I mean, maybe the doctors prescribed medications to some patients who didn't really need it, but all doctors do it, right? It's like the dirty little secret of the profession and it doesn't really hurt anyone. The patients are asking for the medication."

"You have an obligation to report them to the bosses and board," Brandon said, disdain lacing his words.

Yara shot him a sharp look. She didn't want Bailey to stop talking to them.

Bailey glared. "I also have an obligation to pay the rent every month. I need my job. Best-case scenario, the medical board pulls the doctor's license, the practice shuts down and no other practice will hire the nurse who ratted on her prior employers. Worst-case scenario, no one believes me, I get fired and no other practice will hire the nurse who ratted on her prior employers. Either way, I get screwed."

She wasn't off base. That was pretty close to what had

happened when Tanya took her suspicions to Dr. Manning. She'd been slapped down without so much as a cursory investigation into her suspicions.

"Anyway, we thought Tanya had let it go," Bailey said.

"We?" Yara pressed.

"Zach and I."

"So Zach knew about Tanya's suspicions?" Brandon questioned.

"Yeah, he overheard us arguing about what she should do and wanted to know what we were talking about."

Yara had her notebook out and was taking notes. "Think back. When was this?"

Bailey cocked her head, her expression thoughtful. "I don't know exactly. We weren't together long, but we were pretty hot and heavy while we were together. He was around all the time for about a month. Maybe a little more."

"Okay," Yara said, frustrated. "Did Zach seem overly interested in Tanya's accusations?"

"I think he might have asked her some questions, like she was really worked up about it. She wanted to go to the medical board."

"And what did Zach think about that?"

"He was on the same page with me. The world doesn't treat men like Doc Manning and Doc Gristedes like it does the rest of us. We told Tanya she should just mind her own business. She never brought it up again so I thought she decided we were right."

But Tanya hadn't let it go. She knew what the doctors were doing was wrong and exploitative, and she wanted to put a stop to it. And it looked like it might have cost her life.

"You know, one thing was weird, now that I think about it," Bailey said suddenly.

"What?" Yara asked. "One time when Zach came to pick

me up from work, I did see him talking to Dr. Gristedes in the parking lot when I came out."

Yara shared a glance with Brandon. "Was this after Zach knew about Tanya's accusations?"

Bailey's nose crinkled in thought. "I think so. Yeah, it was. I remember. I got worried and I asked what they'd been talking about and Zach said he'd just asked if the guy had a cigarette and that Dr. Gristedes had given him a whole speech about how bad smoking was for his health."

"So it's possible Zach didn't know he was talking to your boss?"

Bailey shrugged again. "It's possible. The doctors didn't usually wear their lab coats out of the office."

"But you don't believe that?" Brandon pressed her.

"All I know is that Zach turned out to be not at all the nice guy he seemed to be at first. I wouldn't put anything past him."

Zachary Brooks was definitely not a nice guy. And Yara was willing to bet that his chat with Dr. Gristedes was about more than the perils of smoking.

Zach had traded the information he'd learned about the doctor's possible crimes to the district attorney. Who's to say he hadn't also tried playing both sides against each other. Maybe earn a few bucks from the doctor in exchange for warning him about Tanya's suspicions. Maybe he'd even offered to take care of the doctor's problem for him. He'd already gotten away with attempted murder. Maybe he figured he could beat the rap again. The problem was she didn't have anything that directly implicated Zach or Dr. Manning and Dr. Gristedes in Tanya's murder.

She and Brandon headed back to the parking lot.

Brandon stopped in front of the car. "You look frustrated."

"I am. I know in my gut that Tanya didn't kill herself, but

this case is nothing but a web of lies and razor-thin connections leading to nowhere."

He put a hand on each of her shoulders and turned her to face him. "Then we'll just have to cut through that web and build out those connections. I trust your gut, Yara. I trust you."

Desire crackled between them.

She stepped back before she did something truly foolish like kiss Brandon West in a public parking lot for the world to see.

Brandon frowned, but turned and walked around the car to the passenger side and got in. "May I suggest we stop by the West Investigations offices and update my brothers on what we've discovered today?"

"I don't like the idea of reading your brothers in on this."

"They are a resource, Yara. One we need. This off-the-books investigation has gotten more complicated, as you noted, web of lies and all," he reminded her pointedly. "We need all the help we can get."

He wasn't wrong. She could feel time running out. Eventually, Lieutenant Wilson would figure out what she'd been up to. She had to have something by then or her career would go up in flames.

"Okay. Maybe West Investigations will have better luck tracking down Jasper Reinholt." She put the car in gear and pulled out of the parking spot.

Brandon removed his phone from his suit jacket pocket. "I'll call and let them know we're on our way. And I'm sure they have their own contacts in the attorney general's office. Maybe they'll be able to get us more details about the investigation into the doctors at Stryder Medical and Zach's role as a material witness."

She hoped so because right now they needed to catch a break.

Chapter Eighteen

The headquarters for West Security and Investigations was located in Harlem, not far from where Brandon and his brothers had grown up. Yara parked in the garage two blocks from the offices where West rented several parking spaces and had a validated parking arrangement for its VIP clients. As they walked to the building, Brandon couldn't help but reflect on how familiar the neighborhood was and how many memories just the short walk between the garage and West's offices brought back. As much as he loved his town house in the suburbs, there would always be a part of him that called Harlem home.

His call had paved the way and the receptionist wasted no time upon their arrival leading them to a conference room where Ryan and Shawn waited. He made the introductions, then pulled out a chair for Yara at the conference table, waiting until she'd settled before he took the seat next to her.

Ryan and Shawn West sat on the other side of the long glass-top conference room table. Brandon looked across the table at his brothers, the family resemblance among the three of them stark in such close quarters.

He shot a look at Yara out of the corner of his eye, wondering whether she'd vote him the handsomest West brother out of the three she'd met, or had one of his younger brothers captured that honor?

He pushed the prick of jealousy away. Now wasn't the time.

"Brandon's told us a little about the investigation you two are working on but it seems like you've run into some trouble," Ryan said.

Yara shot him a look that seemed to say this was his show, so he took the lead. "We've learned a lot of new information in the last twenty-four hours but we've also hit a bit of a dead end."

Shawn leaned forward. "Tell us about it."

He caught his brothers up on Zachary Brooks's arrest and the subsequent discovery of his role in the investigation into Medicare fraud and illegal prescription sales by the doctors at the Stryder Medical Clinic and Tanya's ex, Jasper Reinholt, and his sudden disappearance.

"Looks like you two have covered a lot of ground," Ryan said, looking impressed. "How can we help?"

"The medical examiner came back with a preliminary finding of suicide, so my boss has written this case off," Yara answered.

Shawn cocked his head. "Clearly you don't agree with your boss."

"I do not, but I do want to keep my job."

"We need you to look into Jasper Reinholt. Find out where he's gone," Brandon said.

Ryan wrote the name on the legal pad on the table in front of him. "That shouldn't be too hard. What do you know about him?"

Yara laid out everything they had on Jasper—his address, employer and everything they knew about his relationship with Tanya.

"It would also be great if you could take a deeper dive

into the Stryder Medical Clinic and the lives of Dr. Manning and Dr. Gristedes. Tanya thought Gristedes was involved in the fraud and illegal prescriptions and I definitely don't trust Dr. Manning. And see if there's any connection between the doctors that run the clinic, Manning and Gristedes, and the career criminal, Zachary Brooks."

Ryan's right hand moved quickly over the paper, jotting notes.

Yara's cell phone rang. She pulled it from her purse and frowned. "Excuse me. I need to take this."

She stepped into the hallway before connecting the call. Through the glass wall, he could see that the frown remained on her face.

"Anything else we can do for you?" Shawn said drolly, pulling Brandon's attention back to his brothers.

"Actually, there is. Someone, a man, prepaid a year of Tanya's rent on a one-bedroom luxury apartment in the Financial District."

Brandon gave Shawn the description of the man who had been with Tanya when she rented the apartment.

Ryan looked up from his notes, frowning. "That is not a lot to go on."

"I know, but it's all we have," Brandon said.

"We'll do what we can, but no promises."

"That's all I can ask." He left his brothers still sitting at the table.

Yara punched off her call as he exited the conference room. "Everything is okay."

"Yeah, just my brother's babysitter had a family emergency. My brother is a single dad and is an independent electrician and he's about an hour away on a house call. I need to head over to his house to watch my niece, Sasha, until he gets home."

"Okay, well, I'm sure someone here can give me a ride back to my office."

"Or you can come with me."

He was equal parts surprised and ecstatic at the offer.

"Unless you have to get back to work, which I totally understand," Yara added quickly.

There was no way he was letting her back out of the offer now. He grinned. "I'd love to."

YARA SPENT THE short drive to her brother's Cape Cod home in the neighborhood where they'd grown up waffling over whether bringing Brandon with her was a good idea. On the one hand, he'd seemed more than willing to jump into babysitting duty with her, which was endearing. She wasn't sure she'd ever have children. She didn't think it was fair when she had such a dangerous job. But she loved Sasha as if she were her own. On the other hand, she was giving him a glimpse into her life that she'd never given any other man. She'd never even brought a boyfriend home. Not that she'd kept any around long enough to make it a holiday.

Yet, she'd invited Brandon to meet Sasha and it felt… right.

She couldn't deny it any longer. Not to herself at least. She was falling for Brandon West.

Her six-year-old niece, Sasha, was waiting for her on the porch with Mrs. Hannigan, Eddie's regular after-school babysitter. Sasha stood next to the older woman in sparkly tennis shoes, jean skirt, blue tights, a pink shirt and her hair in a poof-ponytail at the top of her head.

Sasha jumped off the porch and raced toward Yara as she rounded the front of the car. "Hey, kid. How's it going?" She scooped her niece into her arms and planted a kiss on her chubby cheek.

Sasha placed a sticky hand on either side of her face and

smacked an equally sticky kiss on Yara's lips. "It's going good, Auntie Yara. Miss Hanny is making cookies with me."

"I'm so sorry." Jessica Hannigan met them beside the car. "My mother's taken a fall. Her neighbor found her in the kitchen and called an ambulance. She's on her way to the hospital now. I wouldn't abandon Sasha for anything, but…"

Yara reached out and squeezed the woman's shoulder. "Jess, don't worry about Sasha. I've got her. You just go be with your mother."

Jessica swiped a tear from her face. "Thank you." She hurried toward the red van parked in the driveway.

"Let us know if we can do anything. Eddie and I are here for you," Yara called out to the woman's retreating back.

"Auntie Yara?"

"Yes, sweetie?"

"Who is he?" Sasha pointed at Brandon.

"My name is Brandon." He extended a hand to her niece. "What's your name?"

Never a shy child, Sasha grabbed Brandon's hand and shook it up and down like a noodle. "Sasha. What are you doing with my aunt Yara?"

Brandon shot her a glee-filled look.

"Brandon is a friend. Let's get back inside." She lowered Sasha to the ground.

"We have more cookies to bake." Sasha ran for the house.

"Do you know how to bake cookies?" Brandon asked as they followed Sasha.

"How hard can it be?"

Yara's brother, Eddie, had purchased the three-bedroom bungalow, a fixer-upper, four years ago after his wife decided she wasn't cut out to be a full-time mother and wife. An electrician who often worked unpredictable hours, Eddie became a single father overnight. Yara did as much as she could to help her brother and be a strong female figure in her niece's life. And, although their parents had passed away years ago, they were lucky enough to live in a community that was eager to step up and help. Case in point: Jessica Hannigan had been Yara and Eddie's babysitter while they were growing up. Now she did the daily pickup for Sasha and pinch-hit on nights when Eddie got emergency late-night callouts.

The kitchen looked like a tornado had blown through. Sugar, eggs, vanilla, butter, salt, baking soda, brown sugar, flour and chocolate chips were strewn across the small island countertop.

Sasha pulled on her hand. "Auntie Yara, I need four dozen for the bake fair tomorrow."

Yara scanned the mess for a recipe. "Sasha, where's the recipe?"

Sasha's narrow shoulders went up, then down. "I dunno. Miss Hanny just told me what to do, but I can't use the mixer by myself."

Panic fluttered in her stomach. Point her in the direction of a fleeing suspect and she'd run him to ground, but baking? The kitchen really was not her domain. She looked at Brandon.

He was holding back a laugh. "Don't worry. I got this." He clapped his hands together and went down on his haunches so he'd be eye to eye with Sasha. "Chocolate chip cookies are my favorite."

"No eating!" Sasha admonished.

"Not even a tiny, tiny little cookie?" Brandon held his index finger and thumb a half an inch apart.

"No."

"What if we make extra and eat those?"

Sash cocked her head to the side in thought. "I guess that would be okay."

"Let's get to it, then." Brandon extended his hand. Sasha

took it and he helped her onto the step stool already placed in front of the island.

"What did Jess plan for dinner?" Given her brother's schedule and the early dinner time of a six-year-old, Jess usually made sure Sasha ate.

"Spaghetti." Sasha pointed to the box of angel-hair pasta and jar of tomato sauce next to the sink.

"Okay, I'll get that started while you two make the cookies."

Brandon and Sasha got to work, her niece enthusiastically walking Brandon through a minute-by-minute replay of a day in the life of a kindergartner. To his credit, Brandon patiently directed Sasha in combining and mixing the cookie ingredients and listened with rapt attention as she talked.

She wasn't a woman who pined for children. She loved being an auntie to Sasha and if she never had children of her own that would be enough. But watching Brandon interact with her niece, how good he was with her, Yara couldn't help but wonder what he'd be like with his own kids. Kids who were his…and hers.

Annnnnd she was letting her imagination run wild. She blamed it on the scene of perfect domesticity that she appeared to be caught up in at the moment. In reality, she was a cop. And cops and marriage and families did not mix well.

She prepared the spaghetti, one of the few meals she actually knew how to make. By the time Eddie walked through the front door a little more than an hour after she and Brandon arrived, dinner was ready and the last batch of cookies was in the oven.

Yara introduced the two men, ignoring the smug grin that spread across her brother's face as she did. She was in for some teasing from her little brother.

"Thanks for taking care of the cookies. I totally forgot," Eddie said, gently loosening Sasha's grip on his neck. Sasha had jumped on her daddy the moment he'd walked through the door, wrapping herself around him.

"Brandon helped me because Auntie Yara didn't know how."

"Way to support the sisterhood, kid." Yara tweaked her niece's thigh. "Okay, you guys' dinner is ready for you on the stove. Brandon and I are going to head out."

"Why don't you stay for dinner." Eddie looked from her to Brandon and back. If she didn't know better, she'd think it was nothing more than a polite offer, but she knew her brother. She could see the curiosity burning behind his eyes.

"I don't think—"

"We'd love to," Brandon interrupted. He gave her a shrug. "I didn't have lunch and we're here."

Her stomach rumbled loudly at that moment, reminding her that Brandon wasn't the only one who hadn't found time to eat lunch that day.

Eddie lifted the top on the pot with the pasta. "Yeah, sis, stay. You made far too much pasta for two people anyway. Sasha and I will need help eating all this."

"Please, Auntie Yara?" Sasha whined.

Yara knew when she was beat. "Okay. Spaghetti for four coming up."

Brandon and Sasha took the last batch of cookies from the oven while she and Eddie grabbed plates and silverware.

"New boyfriend? Is it serious?" her brother whispered as he helped her set the table.

"Shh." She glanced through the opening separating the kitchen from the small formal dining area. "He's not a boyfriend. We're barely friends."

Eddie smiled teasingly. "You two looked very domestic when I walked in. Are you sure you don't want to give up chasing the bad guys, settle down and pop out a few ornery mini-Yaras?"

Sasha skipped into the room.

"Can we not discuss this right now?" Yara hissed.

Sasha tipped her head, eyeing them solemnly. "It's not nice to whisper when other people are in the room."

"You are quite right, Sasha. So what are you two talking about?" Brandon said entering the dining room with the bowl of angel-hair pasta in one hand and the tomato sauce in the other.

Yara pulled out the nearest chair and sat. "I was just saying how famished I am. Let's eat."

Brandon fit right in with her family, keeping up the dinner conversation with both Eddie and Sasha. She hadn't expected the tornado of feelings that hit her as she'd watched Brandon and Sasha baking cookies.

Because she'd determined it would be selfish to bring another person into her life when her job meant she might not come home one day, much less bring children into such a situation, she'd never given much thought to what having a family of her own would actually look like. But when she was bustling around Eddie's kitchen fixing dinner, listening to the banter between Brandon and Sasha, she'd let herself envision, for the briefest of moments, what it might feel like if Brandon was her husband and the child he was baking with was theirs. And it felt…right.

A mixture of fear and exhilaration churned in her stomach. She glanced across the table, her gaze meeting Brandon's, which was already fixed on her. A buzz of sexual awareness sparked through her.

You okay? he mouthed silently.

She realized she'd been holding her fork inches from her mouth for who knows how long.

Okay was relative. At the moment, her head was filled with visions of babies with the same piercing brown eyes

that stared at her from across the table. And, more specifically, the process of making those babies.

But she just nodded and focused on her spaghetti.

Over the course of working with Brandon, something
had changed. Somehow, while she wasn't paying attention,
he'd burrowed his way into her life and now she was having a hard time imagining a future without him in it. And
she was pretty sure she didn't want to.

The revelation rocked her to her core.

Brandon was unlike any man she'd ever known. A lawyer, yes. She still didn't love the profession, but he cared
about justice and doing what was right. He was a man who
cared about other people—his family, his community, her.

And as hard as she'd tried not to, she cared about him.
Deeply.

Enough to consider bending her rules about getting into
a serious relationship. Heck, whom was she kidding? She
was thinking about throwing that rule into the dumpster
and setting it aflame.

As if he knew what she was thinking, Brandon's lips
turned up into a sexy grin that set *her* aflame.

She avoided making eye contact with him for the rest of
dinner and the twin smirks on her brother's and Brandon's
faces let her know that it hadn't gone unnoticed.

Eddie refused to let her and Brandon help with the
cleanup when they were finished, shooing them out of the
house.

They walked side by side down the driveway to her car,
the tension between them somehow growing thicker in the
night air than it was inside the house. A half-moon shone
in the sky and crickets chirped a discordant tune.

She moved to walk around the front of the car to the
driver's side.

Brandon's hand shot out, stopping her, drawing her close.

The hand around her wrist moved to her waist while he cupped her cheek with his other hand. He lowered his mouth to hers and she stepped in closer, immediately deepening the kiss.

She wanted him with every cell in her body. Tasting him, feeling the pressure of his body against hers, it awakened a need she'd been denying for too long. A need that only Brandon could fulfill. And if the hunger she felt in his kisses was any indication, he was feeling the same as she was. He was driving her wild and they were only kissing. She might not make it to morning if she listened to her body and spent the night with him.

But what a way to go.

Brandon broke off the kiss. "We might want to take this somewhere more private before one of your brother's neighbors calls your coworkers on us."

"Your place?"

His lips turned up into a wolfish grin and desire flashed in his eyes. "You drive."

Chapter Nineteen

She didn't let herself think about anything other than the pleasure she was in for on the short drive to Brandon's house. From the tightness of his pants, he was thinking about the same thing. Good. She wasn't going to overthink or analyze this. They wanted each other and, for tonight at least, that was enough.

Five more minutes and then they'd be at his place. She pressed down on the accelerator, thinking that was five minutes too long.

She parked the car behind his BMW in his short driveway three and a half minutes later and shut off the engine. Hand in hand, they walked to the door and he let her enter first.

She entered without hesitation and when he shut the door, flicking the lock while backing her against the door, she didn't resist. She smiled.

His kiss was firm. His spicy male scent caused desire to flare within her. She parted her lips and he deepened the kiss, exploring her mouth. He pulled her closer and she slid her arms around his neck. She wanted him. Right here and now. She glided her hands over the front of his shirt and around his shoulders, loving the feel of his hard muscles.

He pulled his mouth from hers and she felt the absence so acutely she moaned.

The desire she felt was reflected in his eyes. "Are you sure?"

She didn't hesitate. "Yes. Absolutely. I want you."

This time the sound came from deep in his chest. He took her mouth again and she sank into him.

His hands moved down her sides and he gripped her hips, molding their bodies together.

Every cell in her body shivered with anticipation. Their kisses alternated between soft and searching and deep and needy. And she couldn't get enough.

"Hold on." His arms tightened again and he lifted her off her feet and turned toward the stairs. She wrapped her legs around his waist, grinding her pelvis against his.

He groaned. "We're not going to make it to the bedroom if you keep doing that."

She laughed and did it again. "It's a risk I'm willing to take."

Brandon slapped her gently on the bottom and kept moving. They kissed their way up the staircase and made it into his bedroom.

He set her feet on the floor and snaked his hand up under her shirt while leaving a trail of hot kisses along her neck. She gave a low hum in response.

He explored every inch of her, his hands roaming over her breasts, her hips, down the side of her thigh and then up again toward her core. He pushed her bra to the side and brought his lips back to her body.

"I've wanted to do this since the moment I saw you."

"It took me a little longer to get here, to be honest with you," she said breathlessly.

"Oh, it did, did it? I think I'll have to make you pay for that little jab." She pulled her shirt over her head and unfastened her bra, tossing both onto a chair in the corner of the room.

His mouth went right to her breast, sending shivers rippling through her body.

"I think I'm going to like my punishment," she said, nearly breathless.

"I think you will, too." He walked her backward until the back of her legs hit the bed. "Lie back."

She followed his instructions.

He pulled his own shirt over his head, then slid his hands over her waistband and undid the button, slowly easing down the zipper while he watched her with a look so intent it made her body flush.

Her heart thundered with anticipation. She raised her hips and he slid the pants free of her legs.

He eased down onto the bed next to her, kissing her deeply. She ran her hands over his chest and pulled him close.

He traced a finger from her breast to her navel and lower, making her insides tighten. He eased her panties from her hips and then chucked the rest of his clothes while she watched.

Gently, he eased on top of her, settling between her thighs.

He kissed her again deeply, pressing her into the bed. Her body throbbed with want.

His body felt like heaven on top of hers. He kissed down her neck to her shoulders before lavishing attention on each of her breasts in turn. He lingered there until she was in danger of losing her mind.

She arched against him. "Brandon, please. I need you."

Then he moved lower, driving her over the edge.

He leaned across her and opened a drawer in the nightstand while she came down. He sheathed himself, then pushed into her.

She moaned with the pleasure of it. Feeling him sit himself deep inside her, she wrapped her legs around him and pulled him deeper.

They found a rhythm quickly, the tension building inside her for a second time. "Brandon. Brandon, you feel so good."

"So do you, baby. I don't know how much longer I can hang on."

But it didn't matter because a moment later she crested again and he followed right behind her.

He rolled onto his back and pulled her in close to his side.

She turned onto her side, fighting to catch her breath. She ran her hand lightly over his chest, kissed his shoulder.

"That was spectacular," he said.

"Amazing."

He dropped a kiss on her head, then pushed up from the bed and went into the adjoining bathroom. He was back moments later, drawing her back into his arms.

"Stay the night. Don't think. Just say yes."

She laughed, relaxed to the point of giddy from what he'd just done to her body. "Is this how you sweet-talk all your conquests?"

He shifted, looking into her eyes. "You aren't a conquest. I want to wake up with you in my arms. Say yes."

Her chest tightened with an emotion she couldn't name. She wasn't sure she wanted to try to name it at the moment. She just wanted to enjoy the feeling of being in his arms.

"Yes." She closed her eyes and tucked her head against his chest.

They fell asleep in each other's arms.

BRANDON AWOKE TO Yara's arm draped over his torso, her warm body pressed into his side. Her head rested against his shoulder and her chest rose and fell rhythmically. This was the most relaxed he'd seen her since, well, a few hours earlier when she'd been coming down from their second, or maybe their third, round of lovemaking.

Love.

Damn. He'd be the first to admit he'd wanted to take her to bed since she strode into the courthouse and demanded he tell her everything he knew about Tanya Rutger. Hell, he'd wanted her in his bed since last year. But he'd had every intention of keeping emotions out of the equation. And at that he'd failed miserably because he could no longer deny it, not to himself anyway.

He was in love with Yara Thomas.

The thought made his heart thump uncontrollably in his chest.

Yara opened her eyes and a slow, sensual smile spread across her luscious mouth. "Hi."

"Good morning." He pressed a kiss to her lips but she drew back quickly.

"Uh, I haven't brushed."

"I don't care," he said, going for another kiss.

After a long moment, Yara broke away again. She ran a finger along his stubbled jaw, sending electric currents to his groin. This woman was going to kill him, but what a way to go.

He shifted, pressing her back to the mattress with every intention of going for round four.

Yara wiggled away with a giggle, a sound he never would have expected to hear from her before last night. Now it was a sound he was determined to draw from her as often as possible.

"I have to go home and get ready for work." She pressed a hand to his chest to stop him from pressing his body to hers in the way that every cell of his being cried out for.

"What I have in mind is a lot more fun than work." He

rained kisses down her neck while his hand traveled low, grazing along her hip.

His touch elicited a moan from her that set his libido aflame.

A crash and the sound of glass shattering had them both stilling for a split second before Brandon jumped from the bed. He had an advantage over Yara, having pulled on a pair of pajama bottoms prior to their falling into a satiated slumber hours earlier.

It only took a second to grab the gun he kept for protection from the safe hidden away in the nightstand next to his bed, then he bounded down the stairs.

Glass littered the rug in the rarely used formal living room at the front of the house. A red brick lay next to a cylindrical tube in the middle of the shattered glass. It looked like someone had thrown a brick through the window, then followed it up with a smoke bomb. The vapor was filling the small room quickly and would move to the rest of the house if he didn't do something.

He waded forward, grabbed the tube and tossed it through the broken window out onto the porch. Not ideal, but a smoke bomb was more nuisance than harmful.

He could hear Yara's footsteps beating the stair treads. "Be careful. There's glass everywhere."

She joined him in the living room. She'd pulled on the clothes she'd worn to his house, her yellow dress shirt buttoned haphazardly and untucked. Her service weapon was in her hand. "I can see that and it looks like you cut yourself." She pointed to his foot.

Drops of blood joined the glass on the light-colored rug, likely ruining it. He hadn't felt the tiny sliver that protruded from the side of his foot until she'd pointed it out, but now the sting radiated through his foot.

He swore and hobbled to the kitchen. He set his gun on

the counter, then fell onto one of the bar stools and pressed a napkin against the gash. "It's not bad. Nothing some antiseptic and a bandage won't take care of."

"Whoever did this will need more than a bandage when I get through with them."

"One of the Stryder doctors?" he asked.

"Or Reinholt. I have no doubt this has everything to do with the investigation into Tanya's murder."

"I'd say so. I've lived here for nearly two years and I haven't had any trouble until now. Someone is scared," he said.

"Or desperate. Either way, this is a major escalation. They've attacked your home. It could be dangerous for you."

He shot her a pointed look. "This might not have been about me, or at least not all about me. Your car is in the driveway. Whoever did this could have known that you were here. They may have followed us."

Yara shook her head. "From my brother's house? Doubtful."

But he could see the fear in her eyes. He took great pains to keep his home address under wraps. Technically, the town house was owned by an LLC. It wasn't impossible to discover he was the sole member of that LLC, but it was far more likely that whoever was behind this had followed him or Yara at some point and found out where he lived.

"You're probably right," he said, more in hopes of dimming the fear he saw in her eyes than because he actually believed what he was saying.

"This was a bad idea. Letting you get involved in this. I don't know what I was thinking." She paced in front of him.

He stood and took her by the shoulders. "You didn't let me get involved. I would have gotten involved with or without you." He crouched a bit so he could look directly into her eyes. "Don't bail on me now. We're getting close to answers. I know it."

"You could have been hurt." Emotion swam in her eyes.

For a moment, he dared to dream it might be... No, he knew how he felt about Yara, but he wouldn't rush her. He'd give her however much time she needed to realize they were meant to be together. Just as long as they could be in each other's lives while she figured it out.

"You could have been hurt, too, but neither of us were. Let's just be thankful for that."

"I'm not going to let you get hurt," she replied, pulling him closer and resting her head against his chest.

The sound of sirens cut through the night.

Yara disappeared into the living room and returned seconds later. "Looks like one of your neighbors called 911."

Brandon swept his eyes over her. "Since your colleagues appear to be on their way, you might want to make yourself look a little less comfortable."

Yara swore but headed upstairs.

He placed his gun in the kitchen drawer closest to him and closed it firmly. He was fully permitted to carry, but the last thing he needed was a hot headed cop freaking out at the sight of it.

He was already well into his explanation of what happened by the time Yara came back downstairs. The eyes of the older of the two patrolmen who'd been taking his statement grew comically big when Yara joined them.

In her usual blunt manner, she explained that they'd been in bed when they'd heard the sound of glass breaking and come down to find the shattered window and smoke-filled room.

To their credit, the officers had remained professional as she'd recited the facts, but Brandon didn't miss the looks they shot at each other. Although Yara hadn't been specific about what they'd been doing when the brick had come through the window, it was barely six in the morning and it was clear they'd been sharing a bed.

"I hope this doesn't cause you too much embarrassment," Brandon said after the patrolmen left with assurances that they'd be writing up a formal report that he could request for his insurance company after seventy-two hours.

Yara surprised him by taking three big steps forward and wrapping her arms around his waist. "I'm not embarrassed by my feelings for you."

He felt a goofy grin slide across his face despite the circumstances. "Do you have feelings for me?"

She rolled her eyes playfully. "As much as I have tried not to, I do have feelings for you."

He leaned forward, but she backed away.

"No. I still have to go to work, and it's even more important that I get cleaned up and present a professional facade."

His heart dropped. "You may not be embarrassed by your feelings, but the cops seeing you here with me is going to cause you problems, isn't it?"

She moved in close again, pressing her palm against his heart. "Don't worry, counselor. I can handle it. And more importantly, I think you're worth it."

Chapter Twenty

She wasn't delusional enough to believe that Lieutenant Wilson wouldn't have heard about patrol responding to the incident at Brandon's town house in the early morning hours and finding her there, having obviously spent the night in his bed. She had hoped that he'd at least show a modicum of discretion and keep whatever dressing-down he was primed to give to the four walls of his office. Apparently, that was too much to hope for.

She'd barely stepped into the bullpen when Lieutenant Wilson bellowed her name from his office. He stood in the door frame and made a show of slamming the door the moment she stepped through.

"I told you to close the Rutger case as a suicide," he yelled loud enough that there was no doubt the detectives on the other side of the door heard. He didn't bother to round the desk and sit. Better to stand, lording over her. Much more intimidating, or at least he probably thought so.

She'd dealt with enough cops and criminals who thought they could intimidate her that it would take a lot more than crowding her personal space.

She adopted a parade-rest stance. "You said the home invasions took precedence. With our suspect in custody, I had the time to look more deeply into the Rutger case and

I found a connection between Zachary Brooks and a friend of Tanya's." She quickly filled him in on what Bailey had told her and Brandon and Zachary Brooks's role as an informant and possible participant in the sale of illegal pills at the Stryder Medical Clinic.

"Just so I have this straight, you went behind my back to continue an investigation I ordered you to steer clear of?"

Of course that was all that the lieutenant would take from what she'd told him.

"With all due respect, sir, you did not order me to close the case. As such I treated it as I would any other suspicious death and investigated it until I was satisfied that it was a suicide, which for the record, I never believed."

Wilson scowled. "And your conclusion that this case is a homicide wouldn't have anything to do with the fact that you're sleeping with the victim's attorney?"

She couldn't help it, she flinched. Her fellow detectives had heard that. What were they thinking?

"Brandon West is neither a suspect nor a witness in this matter or any other case on my desk," she bit out. "As such, what we do on my personal time is of no concern—"

"I decide what is of concern in my unit, Detective. And it concerns me that I gave an order and you not only disregarded it, you conducted a rogue investigation with a civilian. Do you have anything to say for yourself?"

With ten years under her belt as a female law enforcement officer, she'd become an expert at forcing her anger into a tiny little box and locking it away. But this time it wouldn't be tangled. "You know what, I do have something to say. You're a crap lieutenant." She kept her voice low so her co-workers wouldn't hear, her only concession to the fact she was currently telling off her boss and likely diminishing her career prospects.

The lieutenant took a step back, shock written across his face.

"The evidence in this case screamed that this was no suicide right from the beginning, but you only care about clearing cases so that you look good to the higher-ups. So that nothing gets in the way of you climbing the bureaucratic ladder. Well, that's not why I became a cop. That's not why the detectives sitting out there bust their humps every day. Tanya Rutger deserves justice. Her family deserves to know why she died and who is responsible. And the community we serve deserves to know that we did everything we could to get a killer off the streets. So I did what I had to do. If there are consequences to be paid, so be it."

Her words, quiet though they were, had sucked all the oxygen out of the room. They stood, silently assessing one another.

After a long moment, Wilson's eyes narrowed and his face twisted into an expression of fury. "Oh, there will be consequences. I'm writing you up and suggesting a lengthy suspension without pay. I wish I could do more but as of right now consider yourself on desk duty, indefinitely. You don't leave your desk for any reason without notifying me first. Do you understand?"

"Yes, sir," she said between gritted teeth.

"Now, get out of my office."

She opened the door, letting it bang against the sidewall. There was no use in trying to keep a low profile. Every eye in the bullpen was on her as she stalked across the floor to her desk and fell into her chair.

The low hum of voices picked up again as she logged on to her computer, careful to keep her gaze from landing on any of her coworkers. She didn't want to see the pity, or glee, in their eyes. She could already guess which of the other detectives were reveling in her downfall and those who felt sorry for her having demolished her career.

She'd done what she had to do to get justice, and despite everything, she knew she'd do it again. And she didn't think that made her a bad cop.

"Hey."

She looked up to see Martin leaning across his desk toward her.

"I wouldn't worry about the lieutenant too much. He's angry now but when this all washes out, he'll probably settle on a verbal reprimand and a note in your file."

Martin was probably right. Taking this any further would mean acknowledging to the brass that one of his detectives ran an investigation under his nose without his knowledge, and he was not going to spotlight his failure to supervise his squad like that. Too bad for her that didn't feel like much right now.

BRANDON'S PHONE BUZZED. He didn't recognize the number. "Hello."

"I finally got in."

He looked at the screen again but the number still wasn't registering. "Who is this?"

"Nick, Tanya's brother. I figured out Tanya's password for her cloud storage. I'm in and I listened to her video diary. I know who killed her." Nick's voice was a mixture of excitement and rage.

"Whoa, whoa, slow down and start from the beginning."

"I told you I was trying to figure out Tanya's cloud password since the police couldn't find her phone or tablet. I did. It was a combination of the address where we were living when she was born and our mom's current address. Anyway, I'm in and I started listening to her diary recordings.

She was dating a doctor she worked with. He was the one paying for her apartment and Mercedes."

Brandon had a feeling he knew which doctor Tanya had been involved with, but he asked the question anyway. "Which doctor?"

"She called him Anand. That's the young one, right?"

"Yeah," Brandon answered, distractedly. The young married one.

"A few weeks ago she walked in on him selling pills to a patient. She confronted him about it and he threatened to cut off the money. She was going to go to the cops. That's why he killed her."

"Did she say that in the diary? That she was going to the cops and Anand threatened to kill her if she did?"

"She said she was going to the cops. She said he'd been good to her, paying for the apartment and car, so she wanted to give him a chance to tell his wife and get his affairs in order. She didn't…" Nick's words caught on a sob. "She didn't want to hurt him. That bastard. I'm going to kill him."

"Nick, you have got to calm down. Don't let your emotions lead you to do something you'll regret. You need to take Tanya's diary to the police. I'll go with you."

"The cops don't care," he screamed. "They think Tanya killed herself. I told them she would never, but they wouldn't listen."

"Nick, listen to me. Detective Thomas doesn't think Tanya committed suicide. She and I have been working together to prove it. If you take the diary to her, that will be enough to force her superiors to let her formally investigate Tanya's death as a murder."

"No. No, the cops had their chance." His voice was shrill. "I'm going to do what needs to be done now. That doctor's address is in Tanya's contacts. I've got my father's old gun.

I'm going to go to his house and kill him and no one is going to stop me."

"Nick!"

The only answer was dead air. Nick had hung up on him.

Brandon pulled up the file Shawn had sent to him on Anand Gristedes and jotted down his address. He turned to the wall behind his desk and pressed a finger to the top left corner of the third panel of wainscoting lining the bottom. The panel popped free, revealing the safe behind it. He pressed his palm to the faceplate and seconds later the safe unlocked.

His Ruger lay in the safe already loaded. He might not have an official role in West Security and Investigations, but he was still a West. James West Sr. had made sure all his sons knew how to defend themselves. He was more than proficient with a gun.

He stuck the weapon in his waistband, then darted from his office. His paralegal was on the phone but he glanced up as he raced from the office.

He started his car and pulled into traffic before ordering the onboard system to dial Yara's cell phone.

She picked up after three rings. "Now's not a good time."

"Nick Rutger is on his way to Anand Gristedes's house. He got into Tanya's cloud file and listened to her video diary. Tanya apparently saw Gristedes selling pills to a patient and was planning to turn him in. Nick thinks Gristedes killed her to stop her. He's got a gun and he's saying he's going to kill Gristedes."

Yara swore. "Where are you?"

"I'm on my way to Gristedes's place, too."

"No, that is a bad idea. I want you to stay out of this."

"I think it's too late for that, Yara. I'm right in the middle of this and I'm not going to let Tanya's brother throw his life away."

"Damn it, Brandon. Listen to me. If Nick is right, Gristedes already killed one person. And I doubt he could have been selling pills out of the clinic without Dr. Manning and who knows who else knowing or being involved with what was going on. You have no idea what you're walking into."

"I get that, but it also means that Nick has no idea either. I can't let him do it alone."

"Brandon, Gristedes won't hesitate to kill you and Nick if that's what he thinks will get him out of the mess he's made. He has nothing to lose."

"I don't doubt it," he said, cutting off an SUV and drawing an angry car horn. "But I can't just sit back and hope that this young man cools off before he does something foolish. Hopefully, I'm able to get to Gristedes's place and stop Nick."

"And what if you don't get there in time?"

"That's why I'm calling you. For backup."

"I'm on my way, but Brandon, do not go inside Gristedes's house. Do not approach him. He could be dangerous. Try to get Nick to calm down and see reason if you can, but if you can't, don't follow him out of the frying pan into the fire. Do you understand me? I don't want to see you get hurt."

"It warms my heart to know you care."

"Brandon!"

"I'm two minutes away from Gristedes's place. Get a move on."

This time he disconnected the call.

He really did hope he was able to catch Nick before he got to Gristedes's, but if he didn't… He'd at least try to do for Tanya's brother what he hadn't been able to do for her.

He made it to Gristedes's house in record time. The home was in an upscale neighborhood with multi-acre properties that backed onto a protected forest area. The homes were spread far enough apart that there was no way a neighbor could hear or see much of anything happening on the adjacent properties. Which may have been terrific for privacy purposes, but it meant that no one was likely to see or hear any altercation taking place at the Gristedes home.

He was driving so fast that he passed the entrance for the driveway. He punched the brakes and threw the sports car into reverse before making the right turn.

The house was a large, white brick colonial with a traditional wide, wood-planked front porch surrounded by columns. A four-car garage jutted off one side of the house, but Brandon was more concerned by the black pickup truck that sat in front of the home.

Nick had beaten him here.

He stepped out of the car and made his way to the front door. He debated whether it made sense to ring the doorbell, alerting Gristedes to his presence, or attempt to make a more stealthy entrance. Before he could decide, raised voices came from inside.

"I know you killed my sister, admit it!" Nick's voice sounded close to losing control.

Brandon peeked through the window facing the porch. Nick and Gristedes stood in the living room.

Nick held Gristedes at gunpoint.

Gristedes's voice was too low for Brandon to make out his response, but whatever he'd said, it only made Nick angrier.

"Liar!" Nick screamed.

Brandon tried the front door and found it unlocked. He pulled his gun from his waistband, but held it down against his leg. Nick was distraught, but Brandon didn't believe he wanted to kill Gristedes. If he did, he'd have shot the man by now. He was a grieving brother and if Brandon wanted to make sure he did everything he could to talk him down off the ledge he'd climbed out on before resorting to extreme measures, he had to be careful.

He stepped into the house and approached the living room. "Nick."

Nick's gaze swung toward him, but his gun didn't waver. "What are you doing here?"

"Trying to stop you from making the biggest mistake of your life."

"He killed my sister."

"I know. And so does Detective Thomas. I called her and told her everything you told me. She believed me. She believes you. You don't need to do this."

Nick shook his head, tears streaming down his face. "I do. Even if you and that detective believe me, he has money. He'll get good lawyers. They'll get him off. He has to pay for what he did to Tanya."

"And he will. He will, Nick. No lawyer in the world will be able to get him off of drug and murder charges. Tanya would not want you to throw your life away like this. Not for her."

Nick sobbed, but still managed to hold the gun steady.

"Why don't you give me the gun." Brandon moved forward cautiously. "We can call Detective Thomas and hold Gristedes until she gets here. Let's do this the right way, Nick."

Out of the side of his eye, Brandon saw Gristedes's expression darken, but he wisely kept quiet.

Nick hiccupped, then his eyes grew wide.

Brandon felt the person behind him a moment too late. He turned, catching sight of Dr. Manning before something crashed down on his head.

He staggered, falling to his knees. His gun skittered across the floor and under the sofa. It was difficult to hold on to consciousness. He could hear a struggle taking place behind him. His gaze swam, but he was able to make out Nick and Gristedes fighting for the gun. Dr. Manning stood over Brandon still holding the lamp he'd used to smash him over the head. But now he seemed paralyzed by the unusual scene before him, unable to decide what to do next.

Gristedes landed a punch to Nick's jaw that sent him reeling backward. Unfortunately, his gun flew forward, landing several feet away from Nick and far too close to Gristedes.

The younger doctor lunged for the weapon.

"Run!" Brandon yelled to Nick.

Nick took off through the opening that led to the kitchen.

Gristedes grabbed the gun from the floor, but when he rose, Nick had already disappeared through the back of the house.

"Stay with him." Gristedes shot the order at Dr. Manning as he raced to catch up with Nick.

Dr. Manning didn't show any sign of having heard him. He stood staring out as if in some sort of fugue state.

Would he stay that way long enough for him to retrieve his gun from under the sofa?

There wasn't time to attempt doing so.

A gunshot blasted from the back of the house.

Brandon pushed to his feet and ran toward the sound.

Chapter Twenty-One

A string of swears rolled through Yara's mind but she didn't stop to vocalize them. She dashed from the office, her eyes roaming the bullpen for Martin. Her eyes landed on him coming out of the kitchen with a pretty uniformed officer at this side.

"Martin. With me." The tone of her voice must have clued him in to the gravity of the situation. He thrust the cup he was holding into the hands of the officer and dashed toward her. He caught up with her as she hit the crash bar on the exit door.

They stepped outside into a crisp wind. Daytime traffic streamed by the police station, the commuters more concerned with their destinations than the two detectives dashing from the building.

"What's up?" Martin asked as they ran for her police-issued vehicle.

Yara unlocked the car and wrenched the driver's side door open. "Tanya Rutger's brother was able to access her video diary. She was having an affair with Dr. Anand Gristedes and caught him selling medication under the table. She was going to the authorities and Nick is convinced that Gristedes killed her to stop her. He's headed for Gristedes's place now."

"Have you alerted dispatch we'll need backup?"

She swore out loud this time. It looked like Nick and Brandon weren't the only ones letting emotion get the best of them. "No, do that now. And have them confirm Gristedes's address. I know he lives in one of those big houses on the block, but I want to confirm I've got the address correct."

Martin made the call while she sped through the streets of Silver Hill, the siren blaring. Gristedes's house wasn't far from the station, but traffic was heavy, adding time to the drive that she didn't have.

She finally turned onto Gristedes's narrow curved road. Martin had confirmed the address with dispatch and when they came to the house, they found the large wrought iron gates already open. She gunned the sedan up the inclined circular drive and stopped behind Brandon's black BMW. A black pickup truck was parked in front of it.

"That's Brandon's car there."

"And the tags on the truck match Nick's registration."

Yara opened the driver's side door. "Damn it, I told him not to go inside."

"That's advice we should take, too. Backup is two minutes out."

A gunshot came from inside the house.

Ice shot through her veins. "We can't wait. We have to go inside. Now."

They entered the house with their guns drawn.

Dr. Manning stood in the middle of the living room, clutching a broken lamp.

"Put the weapon down and get your hands on the back of your head," Yara barked.

Manning didn't move.

Martin yanked the lamp from his hand and pulled his arms behind his back. Manning put up no resistance. It was like his body was there, but he was lost somewhere in his own head.

"Go," Martin said, pulling his handcuffs from his belt. "I've got him."

Yara made her way through the house, clearing the dining room before heading to the kitchen. The back door stood open, and as she approached it, she could hear the sound of male voices.

"It's over, Gristedes. The police know what you did. There's no point in killing us," Brandon said.

Anand Gristedes held Brandon and Nick at gunpoint at the far end of the large yard. Nick lay on the ground, clutching his side as blood poured out through a gunshot wound. Brandon stood with his hands in the air several feet away. He didn't appear to be hurt, thank God.

"If the cops know what I did, I'm going to jail no matter what. I may as well end the people who put me there." He pointed the gun at Brandon.

Yara stepped out of the house, her gun aimed at Gristedes. "Drop it, Gristedes, or I will shoot you!"

Gristedes sent a wild-eyed, panicked look her way but kept his gun trained on Brandon. "I don't think so, Detective Thomas. You put your gun down now or I'll shoot him."

"You know that is not going to happen," Yara said, making her way toward the men.

"Stop where you are or I will shoot!" Gristedes screamed, the hand holding the gun shaking.

She stopped. "Think this through, Dr. Gristedes. You can leave here in handcuffs or a body bag, but those are your only choices right now. Think about your wife. Your kids. They wouldn't want you to do something you can't take back."

"My wife and kids," he said with derision. "My wife left

me. She took the kids. She didn't believe me when I said I had nothing to do with Tanya's death."

Smart woman. Not smart enough to get rid of Gristedes earlier, but better late than never.

"If you pull that trigger you'll never have the chance to explain things to her. You'll never have the chance to patch things up."

"I can't fix this. You know that as well as I do. I killed Tanya. She found out about my side business. A few pills here and there. To people who wanted them! Needed them! I wasn't pushing coke to kids. These were adults. How did she think I was paying for that damn apartment of hers, huh? The Mercedes? She didn't have a problem accepting the money until she knew where it was coming from. Then she wanted to get on her high horse. She should have just minded her business."

No matter how he justified it, he'd just admitted to murder.

"Gristedes, think about what you're doing here," Brandon said in a low soothing voice.

"I have thought about it. You don't have any idea how much I've thought about it. I can't go to jail. I just can't go to jail."

Gristedes swung the gun toward her, but before she could get off a shot, Brandon launched himself at the man.

They went down with a hard thud but Gristedes didn't let go of his gun. She didn't have a clear shot and she wasn't going to take the chance she'd hit Brandon by mistake.

Brandon grabbed a hold of Gristedes's gun hand at the same time the man reared up, throwing Brandon to the side. In a testament to how determined he was, Brandon didn't let go of the man's hand. Brandon banged the gun against the ground once, twice, before Gristedes finally lost his grip. The gun fell to the side.

"Freeze!" she yelled, the command aimed at both men.

But they ignored her. With them still locked in battle, she didn't have a clear shot.

The doctor reared up again, head-butting Brandon. They rolled, Gristedes ending up on top. He threw a wild punch that landed on Brandon's neck. Brandon's aim was more accurate. His punch landed on Gristedes's temple. Gristedes fell to the side, dazed but only for a moment. He noticed the gun within arm's reach and scrambled for it.

Yara got there first. She kicked the gun away and held her own on Gristedes. "I don't think so. On your stomach, hands behind your head."

Gristedes looked up at her. For a brief moment, she thought he just might try to rush her, but then Brandon was there, pushing the man onto his stomach.

The sound of sirens came from the front of the house. Martin burst through the back door, his gun drawn.

She handcuffed Gristedes while Martin kept his gun trained on the man in case he decided to make one last stand at getting away.

Officers flooded the backyard and someone yelled for EMTs to be called.

She made her way over to where Brandon crouched, now only in his undershirt, pressing his button-down shirt to the side of Nick's torso.

"Don't worry," he said to Nick. "The paramedics are on their way. You're going to be okay."

Yara watched the blood soaking Brandon's shirt and hoped he was right.

Chapter Twenty-Two

The hospital wasn't busy, thankfully, and both Brandon and Nick were taken back to be treated right away. Brandon was receiving treatment for the bump on his head and Nick had been whisked into surgery to remove the bullet in his stomach. Martin had gone back to the station to get Gristedes and Dr. Manning processed.

That left Yara sitting in the ER waiting room alone, anxious for word on Brandon's and Nick's conditions.

A little more than an hour after she arrived, Martin called to let her know that Manning was already yelling about making a deal. He'd agreed to rat out all the players in the scheme—Gristedes and several pharmacists who had been involved in one way or another in selling medications on the side. They'd been doing it for years apparently, but Gristedes had taken things up a notch in the last year, selling far more than the others thought was advisable. With a wife, two kids and a girlfriend with expensive tastes, he'd needed the extra cash. The prescriptions had caught the attention of the state medical board, which had contacted the state and federal authorities, kicking off the investigation into the Stryder Medical Clinic. The district attorney and the state medical board were working together now to permanently shut down the clinic.

Gristedes was still refusing to talk but Yara doubted they'd need his testimony. He'd all but confessed to Tanya's murder at the house while he was holding the gun on Brandon and Nick. He was going away for a very long time.

A pregnant woman waddled in, guided by her harried-looking husband. One of the nurses at the admittance desk jumped to attention right away, grabbing a wheelchair and guiding the woman into it. The daddy-to-be looked as if he might need a wheelchair of his own. Yara was pretty sure he wouldn't make it through the birth without passing out. With practiced ease, the nurse guided the couple through the registration process, then pushed the woman toward an elevator, her husband trailing behind.

A moment later, the doors to the ER swung open and Brandon emerged. She stood, drawing his attention to her, and they met in the center of the room.

"How are you?" She let her eyes trail over him. With the exception of a white bandage over his left eye, he didn't look any worse for wear.

"The doctor says I'm fine. No concussion. Just a little cut over my eye. Must have gotten it in the scuffle with Gristedes. A couple of stitches, a few aspirin—" he waved the small square pack in his hands at her "—and I'm as good as new. Any word on Nick's condition?"

"He's in surgery. The doctors can't tell me much because I'm not next of kin. His mother is here, up on the surgery floor with a friend from her church. It might be several hours before they know anything, though."

"I should go up and sit with her." Brandon turned toward the elevators, the sudden movement causing him to wince. He pressed two fingers to the bandage on his head.

She reached out to steady him. "You're hurt. You should

go home and rest. Mrs. Rutger will understand. You can call her tomorrow."

"Maybe you're right," he conceded, only slightly begrudgingly.

"Come on. I'll take you home."

Brandon was silent during the drive.

Yara pulled into a space in front of his house. That he didn't balk at her helping him to the door, taking his key and unlocking it for him told her everything she needed to know about the pain he was in. She helped him to the master bedroom and into bed, then returned to the kitchen for a glass of water so he could take his pain medication.

Brandon's eyes remained closed as she reentered the bedroom and placed the water on the nightstand next to the bed. "I think I should stay with you tonight. Just to keep an eye on you. No funny business."

He opened his eyes and smiled, cheekily. "I don't know if I want you to stay if there's going to be no funny business."

She felt a small smile bloom. Even with a head wound, the man didn't fail to be charming. "You talk a good game, but you look like you're ready to fall down. There's no way you could even manage funny business tonight."

"With you, I think I'll always be up for a little funny business."

His eyes softened, and her chest filled with emotion. She could have lost him today. The idea hit her with a force she hadn't thought was possible.

"How about you take a hot shower and then get back into bed while I get you something to eat. If you're still awake after that, I'll put on a comedy. That's all the funny business you're going to get tonight."

All she wanted to do was curl up next to him and hold him. To keep him at her side and know he was safe.

"Hey." He caught her hand as she started to move toward the kitchen. "I'm okay, you know. I'm okay."

It was his eyes, the sincerity, the honesty there, that convinced her more than anything that he wasn't really hurt.

She reached up with her free hand and rested it against his cheek. A wave of emotion welled in her chest. "When I saw Gristedes holding that gun on you, I've never been so scared in my life."

"And when you burst through that door, ready to kill to protect me, I've never seen anything so beautiful in my life. Yara, I'm not sure how it happened, but somewhere during this investigation I fell in love with you."

Her heart galloped with the force of his words. "You did?"

"I did. And I'm just hoping you feel a fraction of what I feel. I know you weren't ready before, but I'm willing to wait as long as it takes. Maybe with time—"

"I love you, too."

His eyes went wide. "You do?"

She threw her arms around his neck and leaned in to kiss him, drawing back before their lips met when he winced. "Oh, sorry. Did I hurt you?"

He pulled her in tightly against his chest. "Don't be. It's absolutely worth a little pain to hear you say those words."

She laughed, her heart soaring with the knowledge that he loved her as much as she loved him. "I'll say them every day if you want. Just so long as you keep saying them back."

He bent his head until his lips met hers. "As you wish."

Chapter Twenty-Three

Yara reclined on a lounge chair on Brandon's back deck. They were sharing a glass of exquisite red wine, watching the sunset and just enjoying being in each other's company. Brandon had lit the firepit and they sat close enough for the heat to warm them and for the flames to throw shadows across Brandon's chiseled jaw. It had been a little more than a month since she'd brought Brandon home from the hospital, and they'd spent nearly every night together. He'd recovered from his head wound nicely, suffering only a few bouts of dizziness. The hardest part of the recovery had been getting him to sit down and rest.

She'd been surprised by just how quickly she'd fallen into being part of a couple. The quick texts or calls determining what to have for dinner and whose place they'd stay at that night. She'd even acquiesced to a barbecue at Brandon's house that had brought his brothers and their families together with Sasha, Eddie and Miss Hanny. Her older brother, Henry, had promised to make a trip home soon so he could meet Brandon.

She stole another look at Brandon, her heart fluttering.

Things were moving fast, but it felt…right.

As if he sensed her thoughts, Brandon turned his head and looked at her, smiling. "You hungry?"

She returned his smile. "Starving."

They still had a lot to learn about each other, but one thing they'd already established was that if they were to have home-cooked meals beyond spaghetti, it was he who would have to do the cooking.

He leaned over and pressed his lips against hers for a quick, sweet moment before rising. "I made a spinach-and-chicken casserole. Let me just pop it in the oven."

Her phone rang as she disappeared inside.

"Thomas."

"Gristedes wants to deal," Martin said, skipping a greeting.

"Manning is talking. We don't need to make a deal to lock up Gristedes."

Manning had started talking to Morgan from the moment of his arrest and hadn't stopped giving up the names of the people involved in the far-reaching prescription drug scam. He'd given the federal authorities details on how he'd gotten hooked up with the fake prescription drug ring years earlier. After joining the practice, Dr. Gristedes had quickly figured out what was going on and demanded to be let in on the fraud, too. But Manning swore he'd had nothing to do with Tanya's murder and had agreed to testify against his former colleague in exchange for a lenient jail sentence.

"Yes, but District Attorney Morgan wants them both tied up tight. A plea will do that and put Manning and Gristedes away for most of the rest of their lives. Gristedes has admitted to coaxing Tanya into taking a drive with him. He got her to drive to Route 30, where he killed her and tried to make it look like a suicide before walking back to the interstate and picking up his car where he'd left it off the closest exit. He told us we would find the gun at his parents' hunting cabin. I've already got a warrant in the works and a call in to the local sheriff's office."

They'd searched Gristedes's home and found Tanya's computer hidden in a closet. Gristedes admitted to destroying her phone and tossing it, so they'd likely never find that. He'd also cleared Zachary Brooks of any involvement in Tanya's murder, but accused Zach of attempting to blackmail him about the fraud. That was probably one of the reasons Morgan was so keen on a plea with Gristedes. Having a key witness at trial who'd tried to blackmail the defendant while seeking a favor from the prosecution wasn't likely to boost Zach's credibility with a jury.

"How much time is the prosecutor offering?"

"Fifteen years on the prescription fraud and thirty years on the murder before he gets a shot at parole. It's not a bad deal."

It might not be a bad deal, but it wasn't good enough. But it was likely the best they'd get and nothing would bring Tanya back.

"What about Nick?" Yara asked.

Nick Rutger was going to survive his gunshot wound, but he had been charged with criminal possession of a weapon and Brandon had made it his mission to get the charges dropped or reduced.

"The prosecutor handling the case still has to talk to your boyfriend, but she's going to offer to knock the charges down to a misdemeanor. Public sentiment is not on her side and she knows it. Nick won't do time."

She let out a breath as Brandon returned to the patio with another bottle of wine.

"Oh, one more thing," Martin said. "We finally tracked down Jasper Reinholt. He really did have a family emergency. His father had a heart attack and Jasper's been in the hospital by his side day and night with his phone shut off. That's why he didn't return our calls initially. The flight records check out. He's in the clear."

"Thanks for letting me know, Martin."

"Work?" Brandon's brow rose.

She filled him in on what Martin had told her while he poured them each another glass of wine.

"I saw I had a couple of voice mails. I guess I know what they are about now."

"Do you need to go deal with them now?"

He set the bottle down on the table next to their glasses and settled himself on the lounge chair next to her, wrapping his arms around her waist.

"It can wait. I'm right where I need to be at the moment."

Warmth fluttered through her that wasn't caused by the fire. She snuggled in closer to Brandon and he held her tighter.

"You know what, counselor? I think I am, too."

* * * * *

DANGER ON
THE RIVER

TARA TAYLOR QUINN

To my brother, Michael Scott, who always has been and always will be one of my limbs. I love you. And I love us.

Chapter One

A woman's scream pierced the air and then was gone. Mid-stream. As though it had been gobbled up by the rapids. Gaze instantly sharp on the bubbling white waves of water in front of his fifteen-passenger raft, Devon Miller, aka Tommy Grainger, was no longer a recreational boating tour guide testing the aftereffects of the recent rain. He was Detective Tommy Grainger, undercover cop, needing to find the source of that scream.

Every sense fully tuned, he listened intently as he scanned back and forth, slowly, quickly, again and again, keeping the oversize raft afloat by himself with a big paddle and an even larger sense of determination.

"Hel…"

The sound came clearly enough that his gut tightened. Sending a clear message. A life depended on him getting the next few minutes right.

With the water raging all around him, he squinted against the early morning sunlight reflecting off the river all around him. Saw nothing to direct his dive.

Based on the force of the rapids, and the weak-sounding cry for help, he was only going to get one shot.

Confident that his victim was in the eight-foot perimeter he had scoped out, he calculated water directional flows, turbulence. To give himself a chance of retrieving the vessel post rescue, he'd have to push the boat with his foot when he jumped, aiming the raft toward the one small pool of still water encased by a shoulder of mountain.

"Come on," he urged, aloud, but softly. "One more time…"

Nothing.

Still nothing.

Another few seconds and he was just going to have to jump. One chance was better than none.

Movement to the right caught his attention as he took a breath before pushing off. Switching course mid-dive, he shot the boat in the direction it had to go and arced his body with a sharp throw to the left, kicking and moving his arms as though swimming even before he hit the water. He couldn't afford a trip down under and back up again.

Not if he intended to save the woman losing her grip on the leftover storm debris about to give way.

SHE WAS NOT going to die.

When Kacey had first seen the raft, she'd had a moment of weakness. With tears springing to her eyes, she'd called out.

Rafters on the Colorado River usually meant leisure time, a vacation.

No vacationer she'd ever seen manned a fifteen-passenger raft alone.

She had a better chance of staying alive if she got on that boat. Her time was running out. Death wasn't far behind.

As soon as whoever had taken her knew she'd managed to escape, they'd be on her trail, and the only way she could have escaped was by water.

Chances were good that the raft, showing up just as it had without passengers, meant the boater was one of the unknown parties who wanted her dead.

She was tired, in pain, scared out of her wits, cold and desperate, but she could still do that math.

He'd seen her.

And the pile of storm debris she'd been riding for more than an hour was about to shoot her into the rapids.

She had to make a quick decision.

Certain death, tumbling rapidly over rocks and drowning.

Probable death if whoever managed to kidnap her from outside the police station caught up to her.

Or another chance at life by giving herself up to the lone kidnapper, with the hope that she'd get a second chance to escape and swim across the river with her feet still bound.

She was not going to die.

Which made choice number three the only viable option.

DEVON WAS ONE strong stroke away when the debris broke loose. A flash of the woman's terror-filled face filled his gaze as he kicked and pulled with all his might, grabbing at the water where her body should be and...connected.

Hauling the weight in his hand upward, he felt a thrust from what he'd feared would be a supine body, flooded with relief and immediately got back to work. Narrowly avoiding the tumble into the shooting rapids, he kicked swiftly, non-stop with his feet, while he maneuvered her body around, secured a grip with his elbow under her chin and shot himself back toward the raft.

The boat wasn't lodged as he'd planned. Floating yards away, the big yellow raft bobbed in the slowly flowing current, but Devon reached it easily enough. Heaving the body in his care over the side, issuing a silent apology as he heard the indelicate thud as the likely injured woman landed, he rolled himself back inside right behind her, checked that her vitals were strong enough, and grabbed his stick.

Immediate safety came first. He expertly manipulated

the craft to the far-left bank of the river, away from the dangerously pulling current. While the ride was still bumpy and took some know-how, less than ten minutes after he'd secured the woman, he managed to push the raft up to the shore where he'd left his truck.

Other than a brief glance to make sure she was still lying there, and not bleeding to death, he focused fully on getting them docked.

Jumping out of the raft, grabbing the tow rope to wrap it around a stump he'd been using for months, he turned to find the woman with his safety kit on her lap, one hand reaching inside.

His first wave of reaction—relief that she was well enough to sit up and avail herself of the kit, was quickly replaced with pure police instinct when he saw the small knife she pulled out of his bag.

The gun under the shirt at his waist might be wet, but it would still shoot. No way she was getting close to him with that knife to do him any damage, but the raft…

The woman was bold. Blonde, he was pretty sure, though being so wet and dirty, it was hard for him to tell. Her odd choice of clothes—wide-bottomed yoga pants and a loose, long-sleeved yellow shirt that looked like pajamas—left him little doubt as to the pretty much perfect curves in the exact right places.

Whether she knew he was watching or not—his presence didn't seem to matter to her. The knife was open and aimed at the bottoms of the long, soaked, loose-fitting yoga pants.

"Hey," he called. She needn't cut off her clothes. At least not yet. "Let me help…"

Without even a hint of hesitation, her hand proceeded forward, dipping the blade beneath a heavy, dripping pant leg, snapping, and then repeating the process with the other.

That's when he saw the rope drop.

And realized that his victim had been bound.

Which potentially changed everything.

Some cop he was.

NEVER LET THEM see you sweat. A quote from the olden days of her youth, Kacey was sure. She had no idea why it was repeating in her brain, but it was all she had while she tried to appear confident and controlled. She hid her total anguish in the soaking wet bottom of what was likely a kidnapper's boat, and calmly cut the ropes away from her bleeding skin.

She was not going to die.

The ropes had to come off.

"If you wouldn't mind putting the knife back in the bag, I'm going to board the raft and carry you off." The man's voice held enough command that Kacey did as he'd ordered. She put the knife back.

She knew where it was if she needed it again.

Or would find some other means of saving her life when it came time.

"I'm perfectly fine. I don't need to be carried," she said then, as, knife-free, she put both hands on the bottom of the grounded raft to steady herself as she got her feet firmly beneath her.

And fell back to her butt.

"Your circulation has likely been lessened in your lower extremities," came the voice again. "They'll be rubbery for a bit. I mean you no harm, but we need to take stock of injuries. I'm going to lift you and carry you to my truck."

She had to get out of there. He was the means. Kacey braced for the rough grab of criminal arms, and was surprised to feel the gentle slide, in tandem, of an arm around her back and another under her knees, followed immediately with a fluid standing motion. As though she weighed nothing at all.

And he had some decency in him. He'd mentioned injuries—because he knew she had sustained some? Or because he assumed, based on having had to haul her away from near death, that she'd be hurt? Either way, it was as though he was taking care not to hurt her worse.

A criminal with a conscience?

Or—God, dare she hope—an actual Good Samaritan?

She couldn't let herself hope.

Hope could get her killed.

He set her on the back seat of his truck, legs out in front of her, and pulled the buckle down to help her get strapped in, albeit crookedly.

He wasn't tying her up.

The door shut. She braced for his weight inside the vehicle and an abrupt fast start as he sped off with her to more unfamiliar territory.

Instead, he was walking away. Leaving her alone in his truck. Or whoever's truck.

Didn't make sense to try and run when she couldn't trust herself to stand. And if the man truly wasn't connected to her captors, she was right where she had to be.

Hidden away from them.

How soon they'd know she'd managed to cut her hands free with the help of a rusty nail and hours of darkness, she had no idea. They'd left her tied up in the bottom of a rowboat bobbing in the rain a quarter of a mile from shore. Could have planned to leave her there until she died, and then cut the anchor and let her drift away to dust.

More likely, they'd already discovered her gone. Had crews out looking.

Whatever Kyle had gotten himself into…it didn't end with him. A flash of the bloodied knife she'd left at police headquarters the day before brought another debilitating shudder. Disbelief. Panic. She could still see the scrollwork. The little chip in the handle.

No. She had to focus forward, one step at a time.

Watching as the tall, lean, clearly athletic man ran back for his raft, she tried to memorize everything she could about him. Six feet or so tall. Dark hair, long enough for a decent ponytail. Hadn't shaved in long enough to be scraggly but not far enough back to have grown a beard. Blue eyes.

Wait. She'd noticed his eye color?

Maybe she should scratch that one.

Shorts. Name brand, but not fashionably so. T-shirt.

SHE'D BEEN WATCHING the man get the raft to the back of his truck without any risk of puncture or damage. She was impressed with his ability and care for his equipment.

She sat up, her glance moving back and forth between the man securing the raft quickly in the vehicle bed and the keyless ignition.

The man had a gun. She'd felt the unmistakable metal butt against her hip as he'd carried her. If his key fob was also in his pocket, she could roll over the seat, see if his fob was close enough for the truck to start and drive off before he had a chance to stop her.

If she could trust her foot to push the pedal to get the damn thing to go.

And he didn't shoot her first for attempting to steal his truck.

The last thought kept her in her seat. For all she knew, her captors were minutes away from finding her. It wasn't like she'd had a lot of escape options with the waters raging from the storm that had hit just before midnight. She could swim across the Colorado River from Arizona to Nevada, but the award she'd won for doing so didn't take storm, debris, currents, bound feet, exhaustion, pain and darkness into consideration. She'd used every one of her faculties just to stay afloat.

At the moment, she'd be relatively easy to trace. They just had to head downstream, watching shores. Particularly for any sign of human habitation.

Like a rafter on his boat...

Ducking lower in the seat, feigning sleep as her rescuer and current captor slid onto the seat in front of her and the truck roared to life, Kacey reminded herself she had one mandate.

She was not going to die.

Chapter Two

He had a victim of some kind. She'd had a captor whom he could assume was looking for her. Devon had to make her—and all evidence of anyone having been in the area that morning—disappear.

Until he had a chance to assess the situation, to know who he had, who she was running from. He'd done a quick check of her pupils, her pulse when he'd set her in the truck. She'd said she was fine.

At his first glance at the sleeping woman in his back seat, Devon surged with compassion. The woman had grit. And height, but she was such a slight little thing. Small bones. Without enough meat on them.

Because she was a drug mule?

The thought brought him up short. It was time for him to think like the great detective he'd once been certain he'd be. No more time to waste in the skin of the "don't really have a goal in life" boat tour guide he'd grown dangerously used to pretending he was.

Almost a year undercover, and he still couldn't prove that drugs were moving up into the States via the Colorado River.

Even with another, assessing glance in his rearview mirror and thinking like a cop, he had very little. Aside from the odd clothes, the obvious feminine shape, the dirty lighter-than-brown hair and brown eyes, the tenaciousness it had to have taken for her to stay alive in that water—feet bound no less—he couldn't get a feel for what he was dealing with.

A true victim?

Or a conniving woman who knew how to play whatever part was necessary to move herself through life, one goal to the next?

He'd seen a lot of people do a lot of horrible things, when pushed, to get what they'd wanted.

On the third glance, he moved fully into the conniving camp. His victim was feigning sleep. He'd been pretty sure he'd seen the telltale flutter of her lids on the first look. No mistaking that third pass. Her eyes had been slightly open, until she'd realized he'd moved.

He'd been debating calling his captain in the Henderson police. Turning her over immediately as protocol stipulated. But if doing so could blow his cover—he couldn't.

The choice was his.

And those slightly opened eyes had just settled it.

She was the most concrete lead he'd had in months. Most definitely worthy of further investigation.

He was taking her back to his place, maintaining his cover, and finding out everything he could about her. First and foremost, a check on any injuries.

Then he'd delve into those ropes she'd cut off her legs. He still had them, secured in the bottom of the toolbox in the back of his truck. He'd be sending them to the lab as soon as he was ready to answer departmental questions about them.

The plan was fluid. Would happen on the fly. If all went well, he'd be able to sell her on his cover, offer her a safe haven, and then have her under his thumb long enough to figure out the game. Anticipation swelled as he allowed himself to consider actually closing Operation Who's Your

Dealer, as he and his teammates had begun referring to their unending assignment.

And if she wasn't a mule—had absolutely nothing to do with illegal substances being transported up the Colorado River—then he was still a cop. And he had to do whatever he could to protect her from whoever had tied her up and left her to die.

That meant maintaining his cover. Pulling out his boat guide cell phone, he placed a quick call to his place of employment to call off for the day due to gastrological distress. The lie sliding off his tongue hardly fazed him. Until he realized that his fake sleeper was privy to the occurrence.

Glancing back, bumping over dirt roads that led them further and further from civilization, he caught her open-eyed gaze.

"Would you rather I tell them that I found a woman who'd obviously been held captive, and because of that, I might be a little late?" he asked bluntly as he ended the call.

"No."

Just the one word. No inflection.

Certainly, no gratitude.

But no apparent fear, either.

That last didn't bode well for his non-mule theory.

HE WAS A convincing liar. Had told the whopper so naturally Kacey had found herself wondering, for a second there, if her current captor would be pulling over to the side of the road to relieve himself of a stomach emergency. Had already been assessing her possible getaway options while he suffered in the dirt.

She'd dozed off for a second or two after he'd left the rescue site. Had to make sure that didn't happen again. The pain in her head would pound as hard and long as it wanted, she couldn't give in to it.

Sleep was a luxury she still could not afford. A few seconds in twenty-four hours was going to have to suffice.

As would the bagel and egg she'd eaten for breakfast the day before. That, and the gulps of dirty river water she'd been forced to consume as she'd swept downstream would have to sustain her a while longer.

Other than her swimming, she had no exercise routine—yoga being her physical activity of choice—but she was in excellent health. And had enough strength to lift her mother...

No! Squeezing her eyes tightly shut against the jolt of blackness that threatened to consume her, Kacey blocked all thoughts of any circumstances outside of her immediate one. She couldn't let fear weigh her down.

She had a job to do. She'd made the choice. No matter the risk to herself, the heartbreak, she'd done what she had to do to protect those who didn't have her good health, mental acuity and physical strength.

Shivering, hurting, in the back of the truck being driven by an unknown man to God knew where, was a step up from being tied up in the bottom of an old leaky rowboat in the dark. She'd had the huge obstacle of abduction placed in her path just minutes after she'd turned in the knife, but she'd managed to overcome it.

Was alive.

With chances ahead of her.

She just had to stay awake.

To focus.

He'd called off from work for the day. Had said someone would have to cover his fifteen-passenger excursion set to leave late that morning. And then gave a thorough assessment of the river's current, post-storm condition.

In terms that had impressed her.

Had that been for her benefit? If he was one of her captors, he'd know she was an avid swimmer and rafter.

At least she had to assume he would. She had no proof
that the men her twin brother had gotten involved with
were actually familiar with their small river town—or them.
Maybe they didn't even know the two of them were related.

Could be they'd just seen her retrieve the knife. Maybe
they'd been watching her to see what she'd do. And she'd
taken them straight to the police station with her.

Or perhaps they hadn't known about her at all until she'd
shown up at the station?

If that was the case, someone from inside the police station would have had to be in on her abduction, right?

Unless Kyle was in so deep, he'd given her up?

Thoughts flew. She allowed them as long as they per-
tained to assessing the situation at hand. Emotion couldn't
enter into it.

Her captor had turned at least three times. Right. Then
left. Then right again.

He was taking her back upstream from where she'd
floated. Back to Bullhead City? Could she be so lucky as
to be taken back to the small hometown she knew so well
she could walk it with her eyes closed?

They were on a dirt road. The Mohave Desert was filled
with them. He could also have crossed the river into Nevada
or California. She just couldn't be sure. Had no real idea at
all how far downstream she'd washed. She'd tried to figure
out a way to keep track of the time she'd been in the water,
but with the darkness, and the constant bumps and swirls
as rapids caught her up, then her desperate hold on the pile
of debris that had come to save her…

She'd had to relax and let herself go with the flow as she
could. Conserve her energy.

The man driving the truck hadn't returned the raft he'd

been floating on. Meaning he didn't really have a group waiting for him? Or the company owned enough that they wouldn't miss the one he still had?

He was a private contractor for an adventure company and the raft belonged to him?

All were viable options.

There were too many of them.

After the one time he'd spoken to her, she'd been careful to keep her eyes closed at all times. She'd already seen everything there was to see inside the vehicle. And she needed him to think she was unconscious.

Just seemed safest, somehow, to not be accountable to consciousness.

At least until she was in a less vulnerable position.

He'd put her on the seat, not the floor.

The cushion, even buckled in as she was, felt…kind. Soft. Comfortable.

She couldn't let it trick her, though. Or make her weak. If she gave in to the temptation to rest, she might miss the chance to keep herself alive.

And the only constant she had, the only thing she knew for certain, was that she was not going to die.

"WHAT'S YOUR NAME?" They could go on pretending that she was asleep.

He was over it. There were too many questions. Answers that were growing increasingly more urgent to Devon as he drew nearer to his property. The hundred acres and small cabin had been a product of the job, at first. Something he'd purchased as part of his cover, but somehow over the past several months, he'd begun to feel more at home in his wilderness hideaway than he did in the lovely ranch-style home he owned in the Las Vegas suburb where he was officially employed.

She wasn't answering him. Big surprise there.

"You were tied up. Logical conclusion, someone who wanted you that way could be upset to find you gone and come looking for you. I need to know who might be hunting me."

"And I need to know you aren't one of them."

Her voice, hoarse, somewhat weak, flew at him full of attitude.

Interesting.

She didn't know who'd kidnapped her?

At the very least, she wasn't sure how many of them there were. Or who they'd befriend.

"Why were you taken?" Interrogation was a no-brainer to him. He could keep at it day and night—and would—until he got the information he needed to do his job.

"I'd rather not say."

"I'd rather not die without a chance to defend myself."

"Use your gun." She'd lost some of her moxie, but clearly did not intend to give him anything.

He threw the truck into Park so fast it nearly gave him whiplash. No matter who she'd been dealing with in the past, he would show her she'd met her match. From the time she'd slid down in the truck seat shortly after he'd set her there, she hadn't once raised her head. Because it was hurting, or because she didn't want to be seen, he could only guess. And he was done guessing.

"Look," he said, turning in his seat. "We're half a mile from my place. It's a shack in the middle of nowhere. I paid a good price for it because I like my privacy. Now, either you tell me what I need to know, or I take you back to the highway and call the police to come get you."

He wasn't sure he'd actually do that—didn't like anything about the feel of that one—and wasn't used to making false threats, either. One of the things that made him so good at getting people to talk was the fact that his word always carried weight.

"If you like to keep your place to yourself so much, why bring me there?"

Her voice was definitely weakening, though he was pretty certain her bravado was still intact.

"Because I'm a good guy and something stinks about the way I found you. I couldn't just leave you there."

"Why not take me straight to the police?"

Ah…that's where it got dicey. Or would if he hadn't been undercover for so long. "Because I don't trust them," he told her.

And had a true life story to back up the assertion, too, though in all the months he'd been undercover, he hadn't had any cause to tell it yet.

"Well, we can agree on that then," she told him. "I was kidnapped as I was leaving the police station after turning in evidence from a crime. That's all I'm going to say right now, but I would appreciate it if you'd take me to your place."

For the moment, she'd said enough. Devon started the truck. They were already on his property, but he was antsy to get her secure inside and check out the feed from the security cameras he had set up all over his acreage.

The nameless woman could be lying. Could know all about his past and be playing him.

And if she was, he needed to keep her in sight long enough to figure out why.

Chapter Three

He hadn't told her his name. She'd noticed the lapse but could hardly ask for information she wasn't willing to give in return. She didn't trust him. At all.

But she had to take life one step at a time…and staying with him for the moment seemed like the most expedient step. If he was part of whatever Kyle had gotten involved in, then she had a chance to find out more. If, by some miracle he really was just a Good Samaritan set in her path, then she'd be a fool not to accept the gift.

And if he was some not-so-good guy who just didn't happen to be involved with Kyle's particular group of bad guys—she could be putting herself in an entirely different kind of danger.

None worse than death.

He'd opened the back door and reached for her as though he was going to carry her inside. With a shake of her head, she slid down to the ground herself, telling her damned feet they had no choice but to go to work for her. Surprisingly, they'd complied without complaint.

At least her circulation system was working.

The shack was actually a log cabin. Old, but solid and in great shape. Two rooms off a main L-shaped living and kitchen area. With what was clearly a newly added on full bath off the back. He showed her there first, turning on the light, laying out a towel.

"I've got basketball shorts or sweats, and a T-shirt to offer," he told her, and waited as though expecting more from her.

If it was an invitation to join her, or even gratitude at that point, he'd be disappointed. "The sweats please," she said, as though certain that was the only choice he'd been offering. Didn't matter that it was midsummer and Bullhead City more often than not had temperatures above a hundred. He'd driven north. The air was a bit cooler. And basketball shorts were too thin and revealing.

With a nod, he headed across the main room, disappeared through a door just past the couch, and returned with clothes in his hands.

Taking them, she saw the calluses on his hand—a working man's hand—and felt a twinge of...well...feeling. Something she couldn't allow. But said, "My name is Kacey. What's yours?"

She gave, but she had to get, too.

"Devon." The word was followed by his immediate retreat from the room. He pulled the door closed behind him.

And Kacey braced herself for whatever she was going to find when she peeled the clothes off her aching body.

She'd given up trying to get a count of the bruises, but as she opened the bathroom door fifteen minutes later, Kacey was confident that she could rely on her body to do whatever she'd need it to do over the course of the coming hours. A few minutes sleep would help her figure out just what those to-do items would be. But a girl didn't always get what she wanted.

By a long shot.

She'd make do.

Stick to the plan. Get the job done.

Which included figuring out what in the hell she was going to do next.

"I've got a grilled cheese sandwich and some soup waiting for you in the oven," Devon said, appearing almost immediately in front of her when she vacated the bathroom. "As soon as we get you checked over you can eat, and then catch some sleep."

Whoa. Hold on. No checking her over and no one else coming up with her plan, either. "I'm fine." Though the food smelled good. And if she didn't have some, she wasn't going to be any good to herself or anyone else.

If she was not going to die, she had to eat. She headed toward the aforementioned oven.

"Hold it." The man beat her there. Stood facing her, with his backside pressed up to the appliance. "I don't mean to be rude, but since I brought you here and you're in my care, your well-being is partially on me."

Reaching down to a chair, he pulled out an emergency medical kit. "I've got EMT training." He shrugged. "Not good for business if a client has an issue on the river and I have no means to help." With a look straight at her, he said, "You let me check your vitals, do a brief check for alarming tenderness and broken bones, and you get all the food you want."

For a second there Kacey's normal, easygoing self appeared, ready to agree, but it shut off in a blink. She couldn't take orders. Couldn't give up autonomy.

"I have training, too. I already checked for tenderness and broken bones." She faced him, eye to eye.

"I do the vitals."

Knowing they were fine would build her confidence. She nodded. Held out her arm for his blood pressure cuff. Submitted to his fingers at her wrist, and his pinpricks of light in her eyes, too. But when he reached for her foot, she fought back. Kicked at him.

Seated in a kitchen chair facing her, he managed to keep a hold of her heel, and she kicked again. A swimmer's kick. Rhythmic and strong.

Dropping her foot, Devon put both hands on his thighs and leaned back. "I'm not going to hurt you, Kacey. We need to tend to those rope cuts or you're going to be infected by morning."

He was right, of course. She'd already figured she'd have to sneak his first aid kit at some point, but...

She wouldn't be able to see the backs of her ankles as well as he could. Couldn't tell if she'd picked out all the debris. And wouldn't be able to dress them as well.

She needed her feet workable.

She was not going to die.

With a nod, and pushing back against any sense of relief, she lifted her foot to him.

SHE WASN'T APPEARING WOOZY. Wasn't throwing up. Showed none of the signs of dangerous blood loss he'd been taught to recognize.

But as he finished dressing wounds on Kacey's ankles that could have used a few stitches in a place or two, he said, "You're exhibiting signs of shock."

The blood pressure. Discoloration of her fingernails. Among other things. He wasn't a doctor. Didn't think she was in any imminent health danger. But...

Taking the warming tray of food from the oven, he placed it in front of her. "I'm guessing your mind is firing at you on all cylinders, but your emotions, not so much."

If she felt any reaction to his words, she didn't show it. Because she was a consummate actress? A woman into things that got her kidnapped?

Because she was in shock?

It bugged him that he couldn't read her.

He could always read people.

Even when he read them wrong, at least he'd gotten the read.

Grabbing his own sandwich and bowl of soup, he sat down across the table from her. "What evidence did you turn in?"

She didn't even glance up. "Why do you live all alone in the middle of nowhere?"

He got the message. He had to give to get.

And he might give and not get.

"I'd like to help you."

She ate with manners. Bite, chew with her mouth closed, swallow. Spooned her soup from the side of the bowl. Leaned over to take the bites so she didn't spill. And never looked away from the food.

If she was curious about her surroundings, she'd managed to take them in without his notice. Other than the brief look as they'd walked through to the bathroom, she'd shown no interest.

"How do you figure someone who takes vacationers on tubing adventures for a living is going to help a woman in my situation?" Without seeing the look in her eyes, or her full facial expression, he couldn't be sure she was being purposefully rude. Sounded as though she'd just made a logical observation.

Either way. "I managed to save you from near death, and then get you out of the vicinity without being followed, have given you a hiding place, provided the means for a shower, tended to your wounds and have provided a warm meal." He just stated the facts. "I'd say that's not bad work for someone who'd been expecting to check some rapids and then navigate a boat of vacationers down the river for the rest of the day." He kept eating.

He was hungry. Had missed out on the omelet, bagel and oatmeal he'd had waiting for him at the dock's eatery, ready to consume before his rafting party arrived.

"I can offer you a room that locks from the inside."

Her mouth paused on the way to her spoon.

"You're an attractive woman, Kacey. Most particularly now that you're not dragging river sludge around in your hair. But I don't have sex with women who keep secrets from me. Nor do I have sex with traumatized women, so you're safe on both counts."

She'd just been kidnapped and was in the middle of nowhere, alone with a man she didn't know. She had to be leery. It just made good sense.

"Not to brag, but I've never had problems finding companions when I wanted them."

He'd just grown bored of wanting them. Same basic modus operandi. Generic conversation, some movies and meals, a bit of drinking, maybe a concert, body parts with varying shapes and sizes that all did basically the same things, the building up for a minute or two of release, and then...

Thoughts of catching a drug operation in full force excited him a hell of a lot more.

And if Kacey was somehow attached to it...

Just seemed odd—the woman showing up during the twenty-four hour period he'd been told to look for movement.

If she'd let him feel her stomach, he might have been able to tell if she was carrying a balloon.

For all he knew, she could have passed it while she'd been in taking a shower.

"It was a bloody knife. The kind worn in a sheath on a

belt. Had silver and gold scrollwork all the way down the side. And a chip in the wood at the bottom. Shaped like a C."

Her words stopped him mid-chew. She still wasn't looking at him. But he'd heard the words clearly. She'd turned in a bloody knife to the police the day before. And could describe it in such detail?

"Who used it?" Was he harboring a murderer? Except that, who'd bound her then, and left her for dead in a storm?

"I don't know."

Watching her, Devon was pretty shocked when she glanced up and met his gaze on that last word.

She wasn't lying to him. She didn't know who'd used the knife. That was big. He went back to eating like it wasn't.

"How'd you come to have it?"

"I found it."

"Where?"

She stood. Carried her empty bowl and plate to the sink. "I won't bother you for long, but if you wouldn't mind, I'd like to avail you of your locked door offer just long enough to get a little sleep before I head out."

With a flick of his thumb, pointing to the door behind him, he took a bite of sandwich and chewed. "And Kacey," he said, food in his cheek. "If you're planning anything or know of someone who's going to be showing up, be prepared. I shoot to kill."

The apoplectic look on her face as she stared, mouth hanging open, for the split second it took her to collect herself, might have given him a brief bout of guilt. If he hadn't been so busy enjoying the very odd moment.

He'd surprised her. Forced a natural reaction out of her. It felt good.

As did the fact that she clearly hadn't thought, for a second, that he could be onto her.

If there was anything to be onto.

She was in the room he'd assigned her. The cabin's second bedroom. The sheets had been on the bed when he'd bought the place. He'd never touched them.

"Devon?" Her pretty blond head poked around the edge of the door, sending a current through him that he couldn't place. He put it down to so many months living alone, living a lie, and to the fact that she was the first human guest he'd had since he'd moved in.

He watched her. Didn't say anything. If the sheets needed some kind of solution, she'd figure it out.

"I'm pretty sure that anyone who might approach this place, on my behalf or otherwise, would pretty much expect you to shoot to kill."

With that she closed the door.

Slammed the lock into place with obvious force.

Leaving him sitting in his kitchen looking like a goofball with a big grin on his face.

Chapter Four

Heart pounding, Kacey sat up straight. Where was she? Darkness showed her more darkness. Choking on fear, she flew off the mattress, getting tangled in sheets, and cowered at the side of the bed.

Bed?

She'd been in bed.

Her ankles burned like they were in flames. Her toes were cold. On…hard floor.

Her room was carpeted.

She wasn't home. She'd been…

Icy calm settled over her. She welcomed it as the friend she knew it to be.

She was in Devon's cabin. Had crawled in the bed herself.

Sliding her hands along her hips, she verified that she was still wearing the lightweight sweats she'd lain down in. Moved her hands up the oversized T-shirt.

She'd been going to put her bra back on, but the thing had been so caked in slime and dirt—had stunk—and once she'd seen how big the T-shirt was that Devon had brought to her, she'd opted to go naked underneath. It wasn't like her small breasts were going to be bobbing along anywhere, drawing attention to themselves.

Clothes were as they should be.

On all fours, she crawled toward the end of the bed, seeing more and more shape in the shadows as her eyes adjusted to the dark.

She focused on the floor by the door. Saw the darkening, drew closer and reached out a hand to verify that the stack of books she'd placed haphazardly against the door—at angles, so they'd have to fall, not just be pushed if the door moved—were all just as she'd left them.

Which meant the only problem was the darkness.

Summer in the west, even in the wooded wilderness, didn't see sunset until past eight. There'd been a sweet short window running along the top wall of her room. She'd been looking at it as she'd fallen asleep. Black showed there when she tried to find the glass again.

Had she really slept over eight hours?

Please, God, don't let it have been longer than that. Like a day and eight hours.

She had to get moving. To determine her moves and make them. She couldn't afford to waste hours or days or…

Standing at the door, she listened.

And froze as another thought struck. She'd eaten right before she lay down. Everything Devon had put in front of her.

Had he drugged her?

Had Kyle and his bad guys already finished whatever they'd started? Would there be more? No way men fought like that over a small, one-night thing. There'd been lives at stake. Her brother's, for one. And the man whose throat she'd seen Kyle's hands around.

The others, she didn't know how many, hadn't been able to get a definitive shadow count before they'd moved to the back of the house.

Had started to approach the back door before someone else had approached the whole group of them.

Those were the things she needed to remember.

To piece together. Find some kind of sense and then act upon it.

Those men had been going to enter the house...

Fear choked her again. She tried to draw air. Couldn't and...

One step. Icy calm returned.

The step right in front of her. Leave the bedroom and find a way back to Bullhead City. Half an hour? Half a day, from there? Find out.

Leave bedroom. Determine current location. Then find way back to Bullhead City.

She'd known a plan would begin to form if she could just get some sleep.

The door opened without a sound. Her bare feet on the floor were like angel whispers. There, supportive, yet undetectable. Liking the analogy, she adopted it and tried to see the clock on the stove.

Was Devon there?

Had he left her at the cabin alone all day?

Was he in bed asleep?

Nine. It was only nine o'clock.

The day she'd been rescued? Or the next?

Eerie, how quiet the cabin was. Not even a breeze from outside, or the flow of water in the river. Were they on the river, still?

Things she should have wondered, and ascertained, before ever allowing herself to lose consciousness.

A flicker of light on the living room ceiling caught her attention. Pressed against the wall, moving slowly, silently, she rounded the corner into the living area, saw light coming from another space.

Another room?

Had she seen Devon enter it before?

Keeping her back to the plaster, she made it down the

length of the living area, was close enough to see the doorway just ahead. Definite light flickers coming from the
space.

A television?

With no sound?

Maybe he had an earbud, was trying not to disturb her
sleep.

Shaking her head at the absurdity of that one, she reached
the door. Pasted her body tight against the wall and, tilting
only enough to allow her face to zip in and out of the opening, she took a quick look.

Plastered her face immediately to the wall again.

And felt her heart pounding in her chest.

The room appeared vacant of humanity, but the flicker-
ing was a screen all right. An entire wall of them. And even
as a non-techie, first-grade teacher, Kacey knew she'd just
discovered a very expensive surveillance system.

Question was, who or what was Devon watching?

Why?

Did it have something to do with her?

And where in the hell was the man?

SEEING HIS HOUSEGUEST plastered against the living room
wall when he came in from outside, Devon had his gun in
hand, straight in front of him, ready to clear the room, before
announcing himself. With nothing visibly out of place, he
turned to the right, to the left, and then, keeping his back to
the wall, ducked into the laundry and pantry closet because
it was closest to Kacey, then one bedroom, the second, and
the bath, before dropping his gun to his side.

The woman hadn't moved from the wall outside the oversized closet, though she was leaning more than shoving
herself against it.

"You okay?" he asked, turning on lights as he approached

her. Looking for signs of sleepwalking or panic. She'd been out more than eight hours. He'd been standing guard outside her door for all but an hour of that time.

Right up until he'd glanced at the viewing screen on his phone and had seen two men on his property, thirtyish, white. Tuning the screen to the only cameras covering his cabin, he'd shot out of there with night goggles on. It hadn't taken him long to catch up with the guys, but when they'd jumped in the river and he'd seen the rowboat heading away, he'd made the choice to let them go.

He wasn't leaving an unprotected woman alone on his land.

Of course, all the way back to the cabin—watching the cameras almost constantly—he'd had to wonder if she'd known the men were coming.

If she'd somehow alerted them—though he couldn't come up with a way she'd have been able to do that, or a reason why she'd run from them and then call them to her—it was much more likely that they'd somehow tracked her. Her clothes had been burned, but it was possible they'd injected her with some kind of homing device.

Possible, too, that someone had seen him loading her into his truck. His truck's license plate had been visible to anyone watching.

Kacey no last name had gone mute again.

He didn't have time for cat-and-mouse games. Not with someone breaching his space. Related to her?

Or not?

Had his cover been blown?

He had to know.

"Two men were on my property." He approached her with his phone, screen filled with the best image he had of the men. "You know them?"

Pulling back, her head touching the wall again, she glanced from his phone screen to his face.

"Who are you?"

"I told you who I am. Who are these men?" There was no kindness in him at the moment. She would not blow his nearly year-long cover, and let children continue to die from the drugs being brought up the river.

"Why do you have surveillance screens set up in there?" She moved her head slightly along the wall toward his laundry closet.

"Because I'm paranoid as hell." He told her the truth. "I have every inch of my property covered. Now you. Who are these men?"

She glanced again. Reached for his phone, which he grudgingly let go of, and enlarged the image with two slender fingers.

Shook her head. Looked him right in the eye and said, "I honestly have no idea. I don't think I've ever seen either one of them before in my life."

Didn't mean they weren't associated with her. She hadn't known her abductors.

"Did you get a good look at whoever took you?"

Another shake of her head disappointed him, frustrated him, but relieved him a bit, too. Assuming she wasn't lying.

"I was approached from behind, something hard and cold was put at my back and I was told to walk or someone I loved would die. I walked. Was told to climb in the side door of a van being held open for me, and I did. From there, something dark and mildew smelling was thrown over my head, my hands and feet were tied, as the van was driving off."

"So there were at least two of them."

"I'm pretty sure there were at least three," she said, surprising him by her openness. A trap? He had to consider all possibilities.

"Why is that?"

"There were two right feet walking me to the van. I didn't see much, but when we stopped, just before I was told to get in, I could see two right feet. One on the right side of my right foot and one on the left, keeping my feet apart."

Detail. Either rehearsed, or truth.

"What kind of shoes?"

"Tennis. One white with fluorescent green stripes. The other just...dirty. White, I think."

Standing there trying to decide whether or not to holster his gun, Devon was leaning more toward believing she was telling the truth.

She handed back his phone before he had to ask for it. Or force the issue.

"Maybe one of the shoes was the driver, while the other tied you up in back," he said then, but she was already shaking her head before he'd finished.

"Maybe, probably, but someone was already in the van. I saw a hand, as though to help me step up, but my wrist was grabbed instead, from behind the captain's chair in the second row and my arm was pulled practically out of my socket. The black bag thing went over my head before I could see anyone."

He'd interviewed a lot of victims over the years. She'd noticed more than most. But then, if her story was true—and he couldn't find any obvious inconsistencies or reasons to believe it wasn't—she'd acted differently than most people by risking her own safety, which presumably hadn't already been at risk, to turn in a bloody knife.

The woman had gumption.

If he believed her story.

For the moment he was inclined to do so.

Right up until she said, "I'm rested now. I'd like to leave."

And his cop instincts went back on red alert. What

woman would just walk out into the wilderness in the dark, most particularly after having been abducted and knowing that said land had just had shady trespassers breaching the property?

"You want me to take you to the police station?" The locals didn't know about his cover. Less than half a dozen people in the world knew.

He'd told her he didn't trust the cops. She'd claimed she'd been abducted outside the police station. Could be true. Might not be.

"No."

"Where then?" He hadn't yet decided if he'd comply or not. He needed to know her plan.

"Where are we?"

Was she playing him? Pretending she didn't know? She'd had up to an hour alone in the cabin while he'd been out. Didn't mean she'd been awake that long.

"You ever hear of Quartzite, Arizona?"

She nodded, with a frown forming slowly on her face.

How well did she know Quartzite? With a population less than three thousand, the small Arizona town didn't even have a full grocery store.

"It's about forty-five minutes from here. And the closest town," he told her, letting her know just how remote they were.

"Are we still on the river?"

The great Colorado. "Yes."

"California or Arizona side?"

She apparently knew the river well. Because she'd traveled it? He watched her as closely as she was watching him. Prey at a standoff.

"Arizona."

With a nod, but seeming less pleased, she clammed up

again. Wrapped her arms around herself. Looking upward toward the windows high in the wall in the living room.

Just stood there against his wall as though prepared to remain frozen in place until he vacated.

He wasn't going anywhere. The place was his—giving him the upper hand in that particular head-to-head. Devon didn't say so.

There was no need to rub in the obvious.

Instead, he turned on some lights against the darkness that had fallen while he'd been out running two male strangers off his land and set about making stir-fry for dinner.

Letting the woman stand against his wall for as long as she liked.

She could have some dinner. She could go to bed hungry. She could walk out the door into the night.

That choice was hers.

And while he hoped she opted to stay, at least for the night—mostly because he didn't want to have to leave again to follow her—he was up for what came, either way.

It was all part of the assignment.

Undercover, he was on the job twenty-four seven. He knew what he'd signed up for. And would do what it took to get the job done. He was his father's legacy, and his family name was going to shine again.

Chapter Five

Kacey left the wall when the aroma of Asian food hit her nostrils. She was hungry.

And a guy who walked away from an argument he was pretty much guaranteed to win—to cook—didn't seem as frightening to her as the one who had a wall of monitors set up in his laundry room.

She didn't relish going out into the night. Most particularly not if what he'd said about two men being on his property was true. Having seen the time stamp on the photo on his phone, she was inclined to believe that part.

Question was, were they working with him? Was he holding her for them?

She was alive. Dry. Rested. Needed her ankle bandages changed. Had no footwear that fit her. No means of transportation.

And no immediate plan for the next step she should take.

Standing several feet away from him, she watched from the side as he tossed veggies in a wok. "How do I know you aren't one of them?"

He didn't even glance up at her question. "How do I know you aren't into something illegal, got in over your head, and almost got yourself killed?"

The question threw her.

He doubted her?

But…

"My name is Kacey Ashland. I'm from Bullhead City. I teach first grade. You can look me up on the school's website."

All stuff her abductors would have known. Or could have easily found out. Facts he might already know.

Things she hadn't wanted to tell him if he was unrelated to her abduction, but still some kind of creep.

She had many valid reasons to doubt her rescuer.

She'd never even considered that he'd doubt *her*.

Was he just gaslighting her? Trying to confuse her, to take her attention away from what he didn't want her to see or figure out?

When one couldn't trust one's own brother and police force how could she possibly discern the trustworthiness of a complete stranger?

Devon, if that really was his name, had pulled out his phone, typing and scrolling with his left thumb as he continued to stir with his right hand. The man was competent at a lot of things. She'd give him that.

Putting down his phone, he grabbed a squirt bottle with some dark liquid concoction in it, doused the vegetables before adding cooked rice from a bowl.

That was it? She'd come clean and he was just going to… cook rice?

What was it with men?

The thought shook her. Until that week, she'd been quite fond of the opposite sex.

"How do you know those two men aren't already back on your property? Heading toward us?" She was in trouble. Way over her head. Cooking wasn't the answer.

"I have an alert set on my phone. It goes off anytime

there's any movement on any of the cameras, and before you ask, every inch of my land is covered by them."

Wow. That went beyond paranoid.

What kind of weird freak had she inadvertently floated into?

One who'd saved her life.

But why?

"So you'd know if I snuck off during the night," she said, making sure they were on the same page.

"Yep. But if I saw the movement was you, I wouldn't do anything to stop you. I'd just watch to make sure you got safely off my land."

He was dicing chicken he'd taken from another pan.

"That system must have cost you a load of money."

With a shrug, he didn't miss a chop as he said, "Peace of mind comes at a cost."

He'd said he didn't trust the police. At the moment, she didn't trust anyone. Peace of mind seemed like a pipe dream.

She had to eat to stay alive. Her earlier thoughts came back to her.

But she had to move forward, too. She couldn't just not die. She had to figure out who she was running from, what Kyle had gotten into, and do whatever it took to make certain that...

Starting to tremble as a vision of the two people living in the house next to hers came to mind, Kacey used every ounce of strength she had to block all feeling. To keep her mind on one step at a time.

As long as the attention was on her, as long as it was thought that she was the only one who'd seen anything, who knew anything, the others would be safe.

She had to believe that.

And if whoever took her thought she was dead...then the threat died with her, right?

Was that her plan, then?

To stay temporarily dead?

Until she could figure out what Kyle had gotten into, or the police could. If they even bothered. The fact that she'd been abducted right after turning in the bloody knife didn't bode well. Were the police in on whatever was going on?

She couldn't stay dead indefinitely. Her mom was doing well. But another flare-up would come, rendering her physically incapable of caring for a ten-year-old on her own.

And the worry of Kacey being gone would exacerbate the situation. Stress would bring on the rheumatoid arthritis that made it impossible for her to walk even with her walker.

Unless Kyle had Kacey covered on that one. Made up some story about her visiting him up at his place in the mountains and deciding to stay a few days to help him with…whatever…during her summer break from school.

Mom would believe that. And since there wasn't cell service up there, no one would be expecting to hear from her.

Surely, her twin would have done that much.

Her host was dishing up dinner. Two plates. He put one on the table. And then moved toward her to hand her the other.

She knew when she took it that, by doing so, she'd made her decision. She wasn't heading out just yet.

She had no plan.

Pulling out the chair furthest from Devon at the table, she sat on the edge of it, plate in front of her, and picked up the fork he'd laid across it before handing the meal to her.

She still didn't trust the man. Living alone in the middle of nowhere. All those screens. He'd said he didn't trust cops. There was something very odd going on with him.

But she'd watched him prepare the food and spoon his own out of the same pan from which he'd taken hers. Since he was eating it, since she hadn't died eating the sandwich he'd prepared earlier, she figured the sustenance was safe.

And so, she ate.

"WHY DON'T YOU trust cops?"

The question came at Devon just as he was relaxing into his meal. Used to eating alone, to enjoying the simple pleasure of good taste, he didn't welcome the interruption.

But he didn't want her to run off into the night, either. Whether she was part of his sting operation or not, the woman was in some kind of trouble. He needed to find out what it was. To help if he could.

A first-grade teacher. She'd checked out just as she'd said she would. Not just on the school website. He'd sent off a quick text to a friend of his at Sierra's Web, too. He'd helped out the firm of experts on a missing baby case in Vegas the year before, and had brought them officially into his current situation, as well. They also were handling a very private matter for him.

"My father was framed by them." He chose the words carefully. Purposefully.

She suspected that she'd turned in a knife that someone in the police department didn't want found. She hadn't specifically said so, but the implication had been there.

He instantly related to her predicament.

If he could form even a small bond of trust with her...

She'd stopped eating. Was looking over at him, that blond hair falling around her face like a partially open curtain.

"He was found dead, with a significant amount of contraband in his trunk, and a key to a storage unit that was also filled with it." All sickeningly, frustratingly, true.

"Oh my God, Devon. I'm so sorry..." The shock on her face couldn't have been faked. And shouldn't matter to him, either. He didn't know her.

Didn't intend to get to know her, beyond doing what he could to see that she was safe. And arrested, if she was in any way associated with the drugs traveling on the Colorado River.

Schoolteachers weren't immune from making money on the side—given the right, sometimes desperate, circumstances. Or from substance abuse disorders, either, though Kacey wasn't exhibiting any signs of needing a fix.

"The official theory was that he'd been heading up some national distribution channel of illegal goods, starting with DVDs back in the day, but also ammo, tobacco, alcohol and even makeup—all illegally imported and sold tax-free across the States. They say he knew the cops were onto him and so he loaded up his SUV, took the key to the storage with him, and attempted to drive his SUV over a cliff and into Lake Mead." All true.

Just leaving out the part that Hilton Grainger had also been chief of detectives in Las Vegas at the time. And the fact that his only child, Devon, had been a rookie cop.

He also didn't bother to mention that the year before, his father had been caught having an affair with a detective from Colorado. The old man had owned up to the wrongdoing and had been spending every free minute of his time making up to his wife and son, repairing the emotional damage he'd done.

There was no doubt in Devon's mind—nor his mother's—that his father had been sincere in his regret. And in his desire to make things right.

Just as there was no doubt that his father was not a crooked cop. Just the fact that the case had never made the news, he'd never been charged...his mother had received his father's full pension...too much had been wrong about the whole thing.

Bottom line for Devon being that he was his father's son.

Had grown up in the man's shoes, walking side by side with him, learning from the very beginning, what it took to be a man who risked his life every day to keep others safe. No way Hilton Grainger would ever, ever have dishonored the badge.

"The official theory?" Kacey's question, still seeming to brim a bit with the compassion he'd first heard moments before, brought him up out of his muck.

"There was never any proof found that linked him to any of the covert operations. And the accident, upon investigation by an independent agency, was ultimately ruled just that, an accident."

The taste in his mouth was not good. No fault of his cooking.

Maybe not his best move, bringing it all up. "It happened almost ten years ago," he quickly inserted into the conversation before things went any further.

He'd wanted to give her reason to bond with him.

Not to pour out his guts. Or gain sympathy.

What he also wanted was his father's name cleared. And had Sierra's Web, nationally renowned as the best of the best, working on taking care of that.

Devon in the meantime set about solving a seemingly impossible case and bringing at least a five-state-wide commendation to the Grainger name. Arizona, California, Nevada, Utah and Colorado each had one person, and only one person, actually working the operation he was heading up. The detectives and their corresponding captains, a total of ten people, were the only people who knew about the sting.

Because, like him, others believed that whoever had been moving contraband all those years ago never stopped.

And that the merchandise had changed to lethally charged substances being sold to high schoolers.

Granted, he was the only one who strongly believed that the distribution channel from the past was one and the same as their current, untraceable, transportation service.

But then, he was the only person on earth who'd grown up hearing Hilton Grainger's thoughts every day.

"What did your father do for a living?"

"He worked for the city."

"Quartzite? Was he the mayor or something?"

He shook his head. "Las Vegas. He worked for the mayor." Technically. The police commissioner did. Hilton Grainger had served at the pleasure of the commissioner.

And Devon had just given Kacey Ashland his last truth.

He needed her to trust him enough for him to get what he needed from her. And *for* her, too, if she was truly an innocent victim who'd just been trying to do the right thing by turning in a bloody knife.

He did not need to get tangled up with anyone. Especially not her.

Just didn't sit well with him that she'd shown up right where he'd been—his proposed route for the day had already been logged with the recreation company for whom he worked—bound and left to die. That a suspected middleman had been booked on a tour that day. And that Kacey was from Bullhead City.

The known hub of at least some of the drug activity. Stuff confiscated in Bullhead the previous fall had been tested against illegal narcotics killing kids in Virginia. Same exact product.

Directly across the river from Laughlin, Nevada—a town nearly an hour's drive from Las Vegas and yet still in his father's jurisdiction.

Had her supposed near death been staged, waiting for him to appear, to involve him?

Strange that he saves Kacey and then immediately has trespassers on his property.

Something just didn't feel right about it all.

Just as Hilton Grainger had suspected something off in the weeks before he'd died. His father hadn't said so. Had been too busy trying to make amends with son, Tommy, to talk much to cop? But Tommy had known Hilton had been having trouble with some of the guys at work. With the police commissioner. Tommy thought, at the time, it was because of the affair. His father had not only fooled around with a detective, but she'd been the daughter of a Colorado commissioner.

In the end, there'd only been one man Hilton Grainger had trusted who'd deserved that trust, an old army buddy whose life Hilton had saved.

A man who'd turned out to be wealthy in his own right, though he hadn't wanted anyone he served with to know that. Billy Collier had just wanted to offer his life for his country like everyone else. Coming from a wealthy family didn't give him the right to let others die for him, he'd said.

And when Hilton had died in shame, Billy had been the only one who'd risked his own reputation to stand up for Hilton at his funeral, and afterward.

Billy had been largely responsible for getting Tommy's mother her pension.

Kacey Ashland, even if she was innocent, was not a Billy Collier. She wasn't a friend that he could trust with his life.

And Tommy, who'd become Devon over the past year, was his father's son through and through. Raised so much in his likeness he sometimes felt like they were twins born in different generations.

One thing his father had given him was a strong sense of self. Devon knew who he was. And who he wasn't. He'd learned from Hilton's mistakes. He wasn't trusting himself to be faithful to a long-term relationship. And he wasn't trusting anyone else, period. He was just going to get the job done.

Whether the past and present situations were related in any way or not.

Chapter Six

Las Vegas. Devon was from Las Vegas? His father had been powerful enough to work for the mayor?

Had he really been framed?

Or was Devon hiding out in the middle of nowhere because his father had been guilty and he'd been shamed out of town?

Either way, figuring him to be around her own age, thirty-one, he'd lost his father just as he'd been starting his own adult life.

Something she could relate to. When he fell silent, she was suddenly feeling like the support system, not the victim.

A bizarre twist in the moment.

And yet, not so strange when she considered the fact that her entire adult life had been dedicated to watching out for and helping others. To the point of living next door to her mother and never having been in a relationship that lasted more than a couple of months. Her family came first. Young men starting out in the world didn't want to be saddled with that.

"I lost my father a little over ten years ago, too," she said to him as she slowly made her way through the delicious dinner he'd offered her. Her stomach was in knots, but she had to eat.

And didn't know what she was going to do when she got up from the table. Just stand there some more?

Ask if she could stay and then lock herself in the room she'd been assigned earlier? And worry about the cameras he probably had set up in there, too.

Or be thankful for them if they meant that she'd be safe from intruders.

Him aside, of course.

Funny, she wasn't worried about Devon intruding on her bedroom. If he'd been assigned to watch her, he might very likely turn her over to her abductors at some point. But she just didn't get any sense that he was going to take advantage of her.

Could be she just had too much else to worry about.

He hadn't responded to her father comment. Hadn't even looked up at her.

"He was a marine. Special Forces. Was killed in Afghanistan." And her entire life had spun on an axis that hadn't quit spinning ever since.

Devon stood from the table. Took his empty plate to the sink. Carried his fork to the stove and took a couple of bites out of the leftovers in the pan.

"You know how to use a nine millimeter?"

Had she had food in her mouth, she'd likely have choked. "A handgun?"

His nod didn't ease the tension in her any. What was the right answer as far as he was concerned?

All she had to give him was the truth. "My father taught me." And Kyle and their mother, too. That last trip home. They'd just found out that Allison Ashland was pregnant. Steve hadn't taken the news well—not wanting to leave his nearly forty-year-old wife alone with a late-in-life pregnancy to deal with.

It was almost as though he'd known he wouldn't be coming back...

Devon had left the room. Came back with a small pistol which he set on the table beside her plate.

"You can take that, and my old four-wheel-drive off-roader—it's also rated for general driving and is parked out back. You don't need a license to carry in Arizona. I'll report the gun stolen in the morning, so use it only if it's to save your life."

The blood drained from her upper half. She felt it go. Felt the stiffness, the chill left in its wake. "You're kicking me out?"

"No. You were the one who said you were leaving. The room is there if you choose to stay."

She couldn't figure him out. He was giving her a gun? Just on her say-so that she knew how to use it?

"You aren't worried that I'll use it to shoot you?"

"No."

Because he trusted her?

Or because he figured she'd be dead before she got a shot off?

"I turned off the cameras in your room this afternoon. Outside is still covered, but you're on your own inside the walls with the door locked. And...just for clarification... while there are movement detectors in the bathroom, there are no cameras."

"Thank you." He was doing what he could to make her comfortable. As one who spent most of her waking moments concerned about the comfort of others, that mattered. And because she was impinging on his space, she asked, "Are you working tomorrow?"

The night would end. The day would come. And she had to do something besides just hide out.

"Not if you're here."

Was he asking her if she would be?

She had no idea what she was going to do. Had to talk to Kyle.

"I need to make a phone call. How do you suggest I do that?"

"Honestly?" He stood there, leaning against the counter, fork still in hand.

She nodded.

"Who are you going to call?" Instinct told her not to say. But it was also telling her to run and hide and she couldn't do that.

"My brother." He knew who she was. All he had to do was search her name in Bullhead City and Kyle would come up, too. "He holds the state record for high school football passing yards," she said, as though once she'd started talking, she couldn't stop.

Silence was safer.

She needed Devon's help.

And still didn't trust him. It wasn't that she thought the things he'd told her had been lies. It just didn't all add up right, somehow.

Not with the man she'd witnessed that morning. Or since she'd seen him enter the cabin with gun drawn, either.

"He's also my twin." She gave him what he'd easily find. Hoping it would be enough to get her the call.

"I'll get you a burner phone. We'll need to leave the property. Choose a place to call from that he could reasonably expect you to be."

The man was a walking safety net. She'd never met anyone like him.

At the moment, though, his attentiveness to staying alive drew her to him.

"I thought burners were untraceable," she said, inanely.

Wondering where she could call from that would send Kyle after her, without her being found.

Because she had to expect that when she contacted her twin, someone would likely be coming after her. She knew the risk. Had to talk to Kyle, anyway...

"The phones themselves can't be traced. But the signal can be tracked to whatever tower it pings from."

Right. She should have known that. She watched television. Not that you could believe everything you saw there.

Standing, she took her own plate to the sink, stopping by the trash to scrape away what she hadn't been able to force past the tightness in her throat. Grabbing the handheld wash wand she'd seen him use earlier, she washed her plate, and his, leaning them in the drainboard to dry. Same for their forks. Would have gone for the wok, but he was standing directly in front of it.

"We're downriver from where I was found," she said then, standing toe-to-toe with him. The closest she'd been to him since he'd tended to her ankles. "And, obviously, I was downriver from where I was being held. So, I suggest going upriver from Bullhead City. There's a place where I swim..."

Where she trained for long-distance river swimming.

She was supposed to be competing later in the summer in Laughlin, Nevada—directly across the river from her hometown. Wasn't sure she even wanted to get back in the water again.

"And really, I can go there alone. If you meant what you said about lending me your off-roader. I have money in savings, can send it to you electronically, right now, to cover the cost in case you don't get it back..."

Grabbing his clean fork, he took another bite from the pan. "You can go alone, of course, but I'd rather go with you."

She was going to argue, but he held up his fork, forestalling her, and silence seemed like her better option at the moment. Like it or not, she needed the man's help.

It wasn't like she'd be smart to walk through his deserted acreage barefoot and show up on some dirt road alone with no money or identification—even in daylight. Maybe she'd get lucky and meet up with a good person who'd help her.

Chances were more likely that she wouldn't.

Most particularly considering the intruders Devon had just chased off his property.

"Like it or not, I'm involved now," the man said slowly, picking up the now empty pan and carrying it around her to the sink. "I have no idea who's after you, or why, but it's wholly possible that they saw me take you out of the river. Until I saw you cut those ropes, I thought I was rescuing a vacationer. Had no reason to try to conceal my identity or the rescue. Those men on my property might or might not be related to having you here, but it's the first breach I've had since security went live. They might think I know something, that you've talked, and could continue to come after me even if they get you back."

She hated every word.

Mostly because they all made complete sense. By letting him save her life, she'd inadvertently put him in harm's way.

"I'm sorry." Way too little. Too late.

She saw his shrug from behind, as he leaned over the sink to wash the pan. "I'm not. Life happens. Given the choice, I'd still have saved you. My father would turn over in his grave if I just let you die. But you're my only link to finding out who could be after me. What kind of danger I might be in. For that reason, I'd prefer that we stick together for now."

Kacey hated the relief that flooded her. Knew it was a sign of weakness.

But his reasoning was still sound.

"Okay," she said and, turning abruptly, scurried off to the bathroom, locking the door behind her.

IF KACEY ASHLAND was involved in the Bullhead City drug trade, Devon had just made a major step forward in his case.

If she was not, everything he'd just told her was still true.

He'd just delivered his message with other priorities in mind. He wasn't so much worried about his own well-being. But it would be easier to keep a watch on her with her cooperation. He'd just won that battle.

Sending a 911 to Hudson Warner, the IT partner—and his current contact—at Sierra's Web, he stepped outside to take the video call that immediately came back to him, while his rescued victim was still in the bathroom.

First asking for a full rundown on Kacey Ashland from Bullhead City, and anything they could find on a possible bloody knife turned in to the Bullhead police, he then walked the perimeter of the cabin, listening intently through his earpiece to Hudson's report.

"We got facial recognition hits on your intruders," the computer expert reported. "They both have records for misdemeanor trespassing and shoplifting. They're a team, brothers—run a two-bit private investigative firm, licensed in Nevada but the only address is a post office box out of Laughlin."

Right across the river from Bullhead City. Again.

"Winchester's team is doing what they can to find any connection between them and anyone on your radar," the expert continued. "We could do a whole lot more with an official warrant to look into them based on them being on your clearly marked land."

"I'm not risking my cover over this," Devon said barely above a whisper, but with enough force to be clear. He suspected Hudson had already surmised as much. And then

Devon added, "Do me a favor. Keep this between us for now. Bill my private account for all of today's services."

Someone had set up his father. For all he knew he could be the next target. Maybe his case and his father's weren't linked at all. But if they were...someone on the inside would want Devon shut down. Which was why so few knew about the covert operation.

Didn't mean someone hadn't found out about it.

And if they had, whoever wanted his investigation shuttered could have used a small-boned first-grade teacher as prey, to make Devon falter.

Uncaring that he sounded paranoid, he told Hudson Warner as much. Adding, "I was married, six years ago. To a blonde woman of small stature." Amy hadn't looked anything like Kacey, but if he had a type... "We divorced a year later."

"Why?"

He didn't like questions. But knew that Sierra's Web could only do their jobs if he was straight with them. And he wanted them to do their jobs more than pretty much anything.

Even if, in the end, they proved that his father had been guilty of illegal behavior—Devon needed the truth. He'd spent a lifetime idolizing the man. Using Hilton as his example as he'd shaped his own life.

And the past ten years, most particularly since his mother's death four years before, he'd been unable to find his own peace. Did he come from scum? A crooked cop? Did he love a criminal? How much was Devon truly like Hilton?

Hudson's *why* hung in the silent airwaves flowing between them. The man had the patience necessary to work with an undercover cop who barely trusted his own shadow.

"I was attracted to another woman."

"You were unfaithful."

"Hell no." But he'd most definitely noticed her. And had appreciated what he'd noticed.

More silence.

"I didn't trust myself to remain faithful for the rest of my years. I wasn't going to have kids, make a family and then see it torn apart." He coughed as he finished. Choking on his own words. Over having said them at all, let alone to a man he respected.

Guys like Devon didn't do stuff like that.

Unless it might help save lives. Hudson knew the score.

The bathroom light had gone out. Time for Devon to go in.

Ending the call, he made it inside soon enough to hear the lock click into place on the solid wood guest room door. Heading straight there, he knocked.

"Yeah?" came from inside.

He could communicate through the door. Wasn't feeling inclined to do so. "We need to talk."

The door opened immediately. He didn't want to like her any better for that. Didn't want to like her at all.

Her small frame was swimming in his sweats and T-shirt. She'd already slept in them once. He should have offered her another set of clothes.

"I'd like to leave before dawn," he told her. "To be in place for the call around sunrise. That'll keep us in shadows from the bank on the east shore."

When he found himself assessing her for more than compliance—wanting to know that she was emotionally okay—he turned to go. He'd issued his order.

She could comply or not.

"Devon?"

He stopped. Didn't turn. The woman was unsettling him. His lifestyle. His home. His case.

"Would you mind re-dressing my ankles?" she asked. "I

tried, but I think there's something in the deepest cut in the back of my left heel and I couldn't find a mirror to help me see what I'm dealing with."

She'd been going through the stuff in his bathroom looking for a mirror? The first thought did not do him proud. So she'd know what brand of deodorant he used. That he shaved with a disposable blade. And his toothpaste had both whitener and breath freshener.

"Of course, have a seat and let me get my kit," he told her, moving more quickly than the situation warranted. He needed space between them. A moment to breathe.

The kit was still in the kitchen. On the shelf above the stove. He had another in his bedroom. Went for that. Glanced at the bed. Swallowed. Shook his head. Grabbed the kit.

"I like the tweezers in this one better," he said, feeling the need to explain his odd behavior, as he took the seat next to her. "They come to a sharper point."

She didn't say a word as, one by one he took hold of her feet as he had that morning, lifting each to the table where necessary so that he could more clearly see the underside of it. Using the light from his phone, he could see that she was right. A very small piece of brown river debris was deep in the cut he'd cleaned out that morning.

"Hold on," he told her. "This numbing spray isn't the best, but it will help."

Working as quickly as he could, he sprayed, located and extricated. Kacey didn't speak, didn't flinch. She just sat there and took it.

Raising her up another notch in his estimation. He wouldn't have blamed her if she'd jerked. Cried out. Wouldn't have thought less of her.

Still, he admired her grit. "Slimy river sludge," he said, turning off the light on his phone and holding up the silver tool in his hand for her to see.

He was looking at the probable infection carrier, telling himself not to look at her face, or anywhere close that might cause inadvertent eye contact, when, suddenly, he couldn't see anything but shadows.

The lights had gone out.

Leaving the cabin in total darkness.

Chapter Seven

"Devon?"

"What the hell…"

Kacey's heart was pounding as they spoke at once.

And then Devon was moving. Grabbing the kit, and Kacey's hand, he pulled her, ankle stinging like hell, into his room, shutting and locking the door behind him. Soundlessly, he positioned her in the front corner of the side wall, shoved at what she thought was a throw rug with his foot and bent over to the floor.

"Down," he leaned in to whisper in her ear.

She was already on the ladder he'd exposed beneath a trapdoor before he got the word out. Moving quickly to get out of his way, her bare feet landed on dirt in seconds. He dropped beside her from the floor above, leaving only inches between them.

The empty space, with dirt floor and cement walls, clearly wasn't meant for long-term stays.

"What's going on?" She had to start taking full accountability. No more just thinking about one step at a time. Life was careening out of control all around her, getting ahead of her.

"The lights are programmed to go out if any of the cameras are compromised," he said softly. "If someone's approaching the cabin, they won't be able to see inside."

"But your phone didn't make a sound, did it? Aren't you alerted when someone's out there?"

"To be truly effective, every safety measure needs at least two-point security. Nothing is foolproof."

His words chilled her to the bone. What in the hell had she gotten herself into?

What had Kyle gotten them into?

"It could also just be an electrical outage," he added. "A drunk driver hitting a pole..."

Okay. Good to know that every activity in his world, her world, too, didn't necessarily mean possible death. It sure felt that way, though.

"The cameras are embedded in tree trunks and branches, mostly," Devon was saying in his same soft tone. "Could be as simple as an animal getting into one." The deep voice glided over her, as though coating her in some sense of safety.

"Has it ever happened before?"

He was looking at his phone. Glanced at her, and then said, "Never," before returning his attention back on the screen.

"Can you see anything out there?" He'd said he had screens on his phone, smaller versions of what was in his laundry room. He'd shown her the one with the still photo of the two men...

"Everything looks quiet, but a camera's down on the west edge of the property, down by the river."

She didn't need him to tell her—somehow she just knew—but she asked anyway. "The one where you saw those two men earlier today?"

"That's the one."

All hopes for safety evaporated. Kelsey started to shake.

And prayed that her mother and little sister were okay.

HE DIDN'T HAVE phone service belowground, but Devon could still use his phone and local network to tap into the surveillance screens in his laundry room. And knew that Sierra's Web would have been alerted to the emergency lighting activity and would be also watching his security feeds.

It couldn't be coincidental that he'd been in his place for almost a year without a single breach and then in the less than twenty-four hours since he'd hauled a drowning victim out of the river, he'd been invaded twice.

No matter how intensely he kept his gaze glued to the screen, he didn't see any cause for alarm. The cameras all had the most up-to-date nighttime technology. While the images were gray and a bit grainy, he could still pick out all his landmarks. He'd seen some movement, as he did a lot of nights when he sat alone, watching life happening around him.

Animals that were invisible during the day were kind of entertaining to watch at night. They ate. They mated. They played.

There was no sign of human invasion.

But he had a dead camera.

After an hour, during which he'd at least completed his first aid activity on Kacey's ankles, he deemed it time to move forward.

"You stay down here," he told her, wishing he could hand her his phone.

Not because it would keep her safer. But because he knew it would make her feel that way.

Her feelings couldn't become his problem. Not unless they were getting in the way of the investigation. Or investigations.

"I'm heading up to take stock."

"You're going out there, aren't you?"

He'd rather she hadn't asked, but he wasn't going to lie to her. "Yes. If I'm not back by morning, you're on your own."

He didn't mean to be cruel. Nor could he promise to be superhuman and make everything alright. Hell, he didn't even know what everything was.

"Have you got your gun down here?"

Pulling up his T-shirt, she showed him the butt of the gun stuffed into the waistband of his sweats, tied in bunches around her slim belly.

The skin would be soft. For a bizarre second there he envied his private weapon.

"If you need to get out, use this stick to push upward at the second rung of the ladder," he told her, showing her how to trigger the trapdoor to open, allowing the ladder to spring slowly down. "If at all possible, wait until I open it from above."

"How will I know when it's morning?"

He gave her his watch. It was a smart watch, not that it would do her any good with no service. And separated from his phone. It would still tell time.

"If you come up, and I'm in the vicinity, you'll see the watch connect to my phone. You'll be able to find the phone from there. Hopefully I'll still be attached to it." He grinned, but knew that the remark was off-color, given the circumstances.

He didn't apologize. Offering emotional sustenance wasn't in his job description.

Or so he kept telling himself.

Which was why he couldn't explain the way he reached for her neck just before he could get his foot on the first rung of the ladder. Sliding his fingers beneath her hair, he simply held her softly. Let her feel the warmth of his hand while he looked her in the eye.

"You're going to be fine," he told her. "I won't be long."

She didn't believe him. Even in the darkness he could tell that much. But when he heard her softly uttered, "Thank you," as he let go, he knew that he'd keep his promise to her.

Or die trying.

A LIFETIME PASSED. Kacey stood for a while. Then slowly slid down the wall to sit in the dirt. She shivered, but not from cold. If anything, the cell in which she was willingly staying was unusually comfortable as far as Arizona summer temperatures were concerned.

The idea that Devon's bed was directly above her took away some of the sting of sitting barefoot in the dirt in the dark. Being beneath the space he slept in every night brought a curious kind of security to her. One she couldn't indulge.

Instead, she faced reality. Her old life...it had died in the water she'd grown up loving. What was ahead was nothing but blankness. Filled with stark question marks.

There wasn't time or space to grieve. She had to let go to move forward. Period.

What would be would be.

And where she could affect it for the better, she would.

Fear sent chills through her. And she bore them. As she'd take on whatever she had to face in order to keep her mother and little sister safe.

That was it for her.

The new life.

She'd known, turning in the knife, that she'd been putting herself at risk. And hadn't hesitated, even for a second. She'd seen things.

Her mother and sister, one too sick and the other too young to defend themselves, had to be shielded from them.

Period.

Nighttime had taken on new meaning as well. Rather

than a time of rest, it had become a challenge of survival. The night before, floating down the river that would likely kill her—the same river she'd once felt master of—her goal had been not to die.

And the night that currently held her in its trap? She had a gun, knew how to shoot it. And a hole to hide in. The rest remained to be seen.

Jumping, as she heard movement above her—a door?— she glanced at the watch she still held in her hand. Two hours had passed.

Gun cocked, and in hand, she hardly breathed as she listened.

She'd never even aimed at anything but a target at a shooting range. But if it meant staying alive…gun in right hand, she held that wrist steady with her left hand.

"Kacey, it's me."

Her heart recognized Devon's voice, even muffled through the floor, as though he was her savior. And an image of Kyle in the dark outside their mother's home flashed before her eyes. Then another, when the men were gone—the knife she'd found in the bush beside her mother's house.

Devon might not be alone.

Or acting of his own accord.

He could be a criminal just like the men who'd taken her. Even if he wasn't associated with them. He'd been keeping her alive, believing that she was of some use to him.

Maybe they had what they wanted from Kyle, or her twin had given her up just as she'd done to him when she'd turned in the knife she'd seen in his hand. Devon's usefulness would be in making sure she died for real this time.

The trapdoor didn't open. She wasn't sure she wanted it to do so.

He knew she had the gun.

He didn't know how well she could shoot.

Was he betting on the fact that he could outshoot her?

She sucked in harsh air as another thought occurred to her. She'd checked to see the gun was loaded, but the bullets could be blanks. Or the gun could be jammed. She should have taken one shot, just to be sure she was truly armed.

She should have left the underground cell while she had the chance.

She had his watch. If his phone was near, she should be able to connect to it. With eyes accustomed to the dark, she punched at the screen. There was no connection.

"The cabin's secure." Devon's voice came again. "Lights are on and all screens are clear. I'm opening the door."

Gun cocked, she held it in front of her face, pointing upward. In that second, she wasn't afraid. She was determined.

She was not going to die.

THE SECOND HE saw the gun, Devon backed away out of Kacey's range. He didn't blame her, at all, for trying to protect herself. Given the circumstances, he was kind of impressed.

But he wasn't eager to deal with a bullet wound. Neither hers nor his own.

"I'm going outside," he called down. "You'll hear the door shut, and then you'll hear pounding on the side of the cabin to let you know I'm really out there. You come up, check out the cabin and let me know when you're satisfied. If you fail to do so, I'll be back ready to fight for my life. Your other option is to stay down there and perish." The cop in him just took over.

He'd never had a case anything like Kacey's—but dealing with a total lack of trust came natural to him. He understood living that kind of life.

Just as he knew that there were times a person had to act on trust even when they didn't feel comfortable doing so.

His current case in point. It was clear that the drugs pouring into the five-state area were protected by someone with the power to see that protocols didn't stop them. Which meant the only way to get to the source was to go undercover. He couldn't do that alone.

And was trusting his life to the five law enforcement officers who were working the case with him.

Out the front door, he rounded the cabin to the wall directly outside his bedroom. Kicked at the wood several times with his tennis shoe. Waited a few minutes, and then, gun drawn and ready to shoot, went back in.

Kacey stood, hands open and up at her shoulders, facing him. He could see the gun he'd given her openly sticking out of the waistband of his sweats. Ready to grab.

And his admiration for her grew. The woman made moves, choices, that he'd make himself.

He still didn't trust that she wasn't a part of his drug sting operation. And needed to know more about that bloody knife.

"Did you find the source of the electrical issue?" she asked, as though she'd been sitting on the couch watching television for the past couple of hours.

"The camera was compromised as suspected. A branch was protruding into the lens area." He gave her the facts. Nothing more. Sierra's Web had already been in touch with him. There was no evidence of human occupation on his land. But from the direction of the damage, the branch could have been shoved at the camera from a boat in the water. Perhaps the same boat the two men had escaped in earlier that day. He'd taken down the damaged device. Replaced it with one of the extras in his shed. Would be shipping the damaged one to Sierra's Web in the morning, hoping the experts there could get some footage of the branch's trajectory.

"You think the wind did it? Or an animal?"

Wind, no. There hadn't been any. "It's a likely possibility."

"So, it's safe for us to get some sleep?"

As safe as it ever was. And he couldn't solve the case, or cases, if he didn't rest. "Yes. There are enough inland cameras to alert us if anyone gets close to the cabin." He'd sleep because he had to, but his mind wasn't going to make it easy on him.

Was his cover blown and someone from the drug operation was out to shut him up? Had Kacey Ashland brought thugs to his property?

Or was the Sierra's Web probe into his father's case bringing out law enforcement worms who knew who Devon was, where he was, and wanted him dead, too?

"Go rest," he said to the woman who was still standing her ground, watching him. "I'll knock on your door in a few hours so we can head out."

And as soon as he heard the click of the lock inside her door, he took his phone to bed with him, placing it on the pillow beside him, and closed his eyes.

Oddly, the last thought he remembered having wasn't about any of the possible sources of danger surrounding him. It was of the petite framed blonde woman sleeping in his clothes on the other side of the wall.

He'd like to be in that room with her.

Just to guard and protect.

And make certain that she stayed safe.

Or so he told himself.

Maybe what he really wanted was to hold her for a little while.

Chapter Eight

Not only was there a knock on Kacey's door, waking her up before dawn, but when she opened the door to head in to the bathroom, she noticed a bag hanging from the outside knob. Inside was a pair of men's underwear, another pair of sweats, a T-shirt, an unopened toothbrush that looked as though it had come from some cheap motel, a small black comb, and a pair of too-large flip-flops, barely used.

She'd used her finger and some of Devon's toothpaste to clean her mouth the day before. And had borrowed his brush, too, figuring he wouldn't notice a few long blond hairs in with his as-long dark ones.

Apparently, she'd been wrong on that one.

The man's awareness of her needs, his willingness to tend to them, warmed her, even as she told herself that he was only doing what he'd done because they were going to be out in public, or at least out and possibly being seen, and a scraggly-looking, barefoot woman would be sure to draw attention.

He didn't have to take her out at all.

Except that he wanted answers for his own safety as much or more than he wanted to help her stay alive.

She hated dousing any good feeling that tried to surface in her. But she had to stay aware. Couldn't let herself get soft. Others were depending on her, even if they didn't know it.

All of that aside, how could she possibly trust a stranger when she couldn't even trust her own twin brother? The one person on earth she'd thought she'd known as well as she'd known herself.

The man was nowhere to be seen when she walked through the kitchen to the bathroom. But he was waiting, dressed in shorts, a T-shirt and tennis shoes, by the front door when she re-emerged, showered, shaved—she'd borrowed the razor he still hadn't used—and with her blond hair clean and soft again as it hung around her shoulders. The black flip-flops were a few inches too long, but they stayed on her feet just fine.

"We can stop at a box store along the way and get you some clothes that fit," he said as he grabbed keys and held open the door for her, motioning for her to precede him out into the darkness.

"I don't have any money on me." She stated the obvious. But…she had an online mobile payment account. Named it. "If you have an account, I can send you funds from there."

He was shaking his head before she'd even completed her sentence. "Too easily traced," he said. "Confirming that you're with me to anyone who might not know. I get paid in cash and will front you the money. We'll keep a tab and as soon as you're safe, I'll expect cash in return." He tossed a new phone at her as she climbed into the front passenger seat of the white truck he'd hauled her home in the day before.

His order-like words might have prompted her to argue with him, if he hadn't made such good sense. And if she didn't very much want the opportunity to shop that he'd just offered her. If she could dress in her own clothes—new as they would be—in clothes that fit, have shoes on her feet she could run in, and brush her hair, she'd feel better.

And, she hoped, get out of her disoriented state and begin to think more like herself.

"I suggest you get on there and pick out what you want from the store. Put the items in a cart and then I'll take the phone in with me and use your cart as a shopping list."

"But…"

He shook his head, his stony expression visible to her in the darkness via the lights from his dash. "I'm all about staying alive here, Kacey. In case whoever wanted you dead doesn't know you aren't, it's greatly to both of our benefits that it stay that way."

Again, he made sense. How in the hell did the son of a city worker—no matter how high up in the mayor's office Devon's father might have been—a rafting guide who was something of a hermit, know so much about living in danger?

The thought kept her on edge as they passed through miles of one-way roads and totally black uninhabited desert on their way north to Bullhead City from which they'd be continuing upriver another thirty miles. She wanted to demand that, when they reached her hometown, he let her out. Instead, she went online to shop, wondering what he'd make of her choices. A couple of outfits, including underthings. Both pairs of shorts had pockets and the shirts were long enough, loose enough, to cover a gun in the waistband. Tennis shoes, though she never wore them at home, preferring flip-flops and sandals year-round. Basic toiletries. Scrunchies for her hair. And a large box of the granola bars she ate every single morning.

The last was strictly for her comfort, but she kept them in the cart.

As lights from Lake Havasu City came into view in the distance, he slowed. "I'll shop here in Lake Havasu. The store's open twenty-four hours," he told her. "I'd prefer if you get down before we hit town and stay down until we're back out of it," he continued, slowing. Dawn wouldn't be arriving for another hour, at least. "I'll be quick," he told her as he parked close to the store, jumped down and locked the truck with one click.

He had no way of ensuring that she'd comply with his orders, but she did so. If his mandates kept him alive, chances were good that they'd keep her from getting killed, too. As long as he wanted it that way. She had to add the last sentence.

A very necessary reminder to herself.

She might feel as though she had a partner in the horrifying twist her life had taken, but she was completely and totally on her own.

In a danger of her own making.

Kyle had begged her to leave the knife where she'd found it. To stay out of it. Whatever *it* was.

And maybe, because he was her twin, she would have if he hadn't brought his altercation to their mother's home, where their little sister lay asleep in her bed upstairs.

As she sat on the front passenger floor of Devon's truck, Kacey thought about the choice she'd made to turn the knife in. And knew, in her heart, she'd have done so even if the weapon hadn't been left in her mother's bushes. What she'd seen...if people didn't stand up and speak about the criminal activity they witnessed, none of their communities would be safe.

It's what she taught her kids in school—to always come to her, or another adult, if they ever felt afraid or saw something that they knew was wrong.

She had to talk to her brother. Figured it was no mistake that Devon had taken her new burner phone with him into the store. Yeah, so he could see the exact items in her cart.

But she didn't kid herself that he trusted her any more than she trusted him.

It was a curious thing, the state they were in together.

Something she'd think about in the future, if she got to an emotional place where she could think about the danger that was ruling her life.

Gun in hand, though kept down on the floor by her thigh, she heard people passing outside the truck. Could hear voices—one male, one female—froze when they suddenly stopped. Certain that she'd been seen. Had sparked curiosity if nothing else.

She had to warn Devon!

Car doors slammed close by. Followed by the sound of an engine starting. The voices she'd heard? And then lost? Simply because the speakers had climbed into their vehicle?

Was she becoming as paranoid as Devon?

For good cause?

Minutes later she saw flashing red lights reflecting off the ceiling and windows of the truck. An emergency vehicle?

Close by?

Her fingers held tight to her gun, poised to reach for the trigger.

Listening for anything that might tell her what was going on outside, Kacey was careful to remain completely still. Movement from the truck would draw attention to it.

A couple of minutes after the lights had first appeared, she was no closer to knowing what was going on. She just kept breathing. And then heard the unmistakable timbre of Devon's voice.

Couldn't make out his words.

Again, she was trapped, waiting, holding a gun—and hearing his voice. Feeling relieved. Safer. The whole thing was becoming too much of a habit, a way of life in her new world.

It had to stop.

But she waited, just the same. If they took Devon off...

No one knew she was there.

Could she hope to slide out to the ground before anyone confiscated his truck? He had the fob...would he hand it over to authorities if asked?

Why would he be arrested?

Should she show herself?

Ask for help?

Questions flew, growing in stature, until the driver's side door opened, a large bag flew in her direction, landing half on the seat and half on her head, and Devon was climbing inside.

Ignoring her completely.

He pressed the start button but didn't to seem to be in any hurry about it. Put the vehicle in Reverse, and, checking his rearview mirror, pulled slowly out of the parking space.

A tense five minutes passed with him saying nothing. He knew more than she did about whatever was going on—he'd told her he didn't trust the cops and why, though his experiences had been in Las Vegas. Because she wasn't feeling all that enamored of the Bullhead City Police Department, which was closer, Kacey took her cue from him. She sat half-hidden by the things falling out of the bag Devon had thrown.

Saying nothing.

And hoping that she'd just chosen to trust the right side of whatever hellish battle she'd gotten herself into.

DEVON DROVE IN silence for longer than was probably necessary. He'd needed to be absolutely certain he wasn't being followed.

When they were once again out in the middle of nowhere within the blackness of the Arizona desert, he said, "You can get up now." In lieu of the praise he wanted to give the woman who'd kept her cool, asking no questions—trusting him?—while her life lay in the balance.

She didn't immediately comply. But she moved the bag he'd thrown over her as a cover in the event that anyone tried to get a look into his truck as he drove past.

"I didn't ask for jeans," she said.

A quick glance down showed her leaning against the door of the truck, facing him, staring at him with what looked like a frown on her face.

"You didn't ask for fishing gear or a flannel shirt, either," he told her, his gaze back on the darkness of the road in front of him. "But in case I was on camera coming out of the store, or, as it turned out, was stopped, I didn't want someone seeing me carrying nothing but women's things." In his job, most particularly after his father's demise, he had to think of everything.

Always.

"You were stopped?" Her frown had grown deeper.

"Two officers from the Lake Havasu police. Said they were looking for a white truck, same make and model as mine. But the license plate didn't match."

"Did they say why they were looking for the truck?"

"No."

"Seems kind of odd, doesn't it? That a truck exactly like yours has a bolo out on it?"

He held back a smile at the lingo. Because she was right. "Too odd for my liking."

"But they let you go. Said the license plate was wrong…"

"Could be someone saw me loading you into the back of my truck, called it in, got the plate wrong." Could be a lot of things.

Most of which he didn't like.

His cover could have been blown, first and foremost.

Coming in a close second was the fact that whoever was after her really must have police contact on the inside. Which was how she'd been abducted so quickly after turning in the bloody knife.

But they'd let him go.

Thanks to Sierra's Web's official work for the Henderson Police Department—creating his Devon Miller persona so completely that he'd check out even if he tried to join the Secret Service. "The truck's plate number checked out clean, as did my identity," he told her. "I have no police record, and they didn't have a warrant."

Didn't mean they hadn't placed his truck with Devon Miller. Only that they hadn't acted on the information.

Yet.

If they knew he was Detective Tommy Grainger from the Henderson Nevada police force, they hadn't let on.

"Did they ask you anything about me?"

"Not a word."

And he didn't know what to make of that, either.

Except to hope that he really had managed to get her out of the river, and to his place, without anyone knowing.

She'd been gone more than twenty-four hours.

Had anyone reported her missing? And if not, why not?

He'd have more answers about her soon enough. Hudson would be calling with an update later that morning.

There was one he wanted right then.

"You saw the flashing lights," he said. She couldn't have missed them unless she'd been sitting there with her eyes closed the entire time she'd heard him back there talking.

"Yes."

"Yet you didn't get out of the truck, ask the police for help."

Her silence gave him some gratification. Not enough. And he needed more than just a good feeling.

If she was running from the law, he had to know about it. He was a cop. If he was harboring a fugitive, he could be held culpable.

He was his father's son.

"I'm wondering why."

Still no answer.

"Kacey. I need an answer on this one."

"Because I trust you more than I trust the police right now. Bullhead City is the next major town over. Police cover large jurisdictions. They know each other. And if your truck has been flagged as one to watch, there's a chance that whoever took me knows I'm alive and is still looking for me. And is connected to the Bullhead City Police Department."

He'd entertained some of the same suspicions based on the story she'd told him. Wanted to believe her.

"I need to talk to my brother."

"You think he knows something?"

"He's my brother. I just need to talk to him."

She'd said they were twins. He'd heard of multiple birth siblings sharing close affinities. Figured if he was in her position, he'd be more likely to trust someone who'd shared a womb with him. There was no logic to it, though.

He didn't like that.

"I'd like to listen in on the conversation." Not something he could force. He could take away the phone he'd given her. That was about all the power he had on that one.

"Then you might as well turn around. I'm not calling him if I can't speak with him alone."

He liked it better when they were in his home and he could pretty much call the shots. But said, "Fair enough," and let the matter drop.

She trusted him more than she trusted the cops. Ironic, since he was one, but that wasn't for her to know, or find out. He had to help her. Even if she had nothing to do with his current assignment. The woman was in trouble—whether of her own making or not—and the man he'd been raised to be could not walk away from that without doing all he could to get her safely out of harm's way.

Had nothing to do with the badge.

And everything to do with the sense of honor that defined him.

Chapter Nine

"What's your last name?" Riding in the dark, in the middle of nowhere, with a man she'd just chosen to stay with rather than approach the police for help, Kacey was fighting back a major case of looming anxiety.

He glanced her way. Said nothing.

"I told you my last name." She pushed.

"It's Miller."

"Devon Miller." She tried the moniker out loud. Sounded harmless enough. But then famous criminal names probably had too, before they'd been associated with hellacious wrongdoing.

"You can look me up," he told her. "I'm from…"

"Las Vegas," she said. He'd already told her that part. And wondered how many Devon Millers she'd find listed there.

But if his father had worked for the mayor's office…ten years before…she did a search on the new phone he'd given her. Found out who'd been mayor of Las Vegas ten years before. Did a search of his name with the name Miller.

Came up blank.

Then looked for Devon Miller.

He came up right away.

"You won the lottery?" she exclaimed, staring from his picture to him.

He didn't even seem to blink. Just kept driving.

"That's why you're so paranoid…and why you can afford such high-tech security…"

She stared at him some more. Just couldn't help herself. He didn't glance over.

The article didn't say how much he'd won. Or what lottery. But it had a photo of him, standing in a kayak on what looked to be the Colorado River, with his long hair hanging around his shoulders, bristle on his chin, and a big grin on his face.

When she found herself starting to smile back at that face, Kacey clicked off the phone screen and stared out the window. Just because Devon had gotten lucky—and apparently shared an affinity with her for the mighty Colorado River—didn't mean that she could suddenly trust him wholeheartedly. Or with her heart, at all.

It was mind over emotion for her current situation. That was the only way she was going to make it through. She had to stay mentally sharp. Figure out a way to find out who was after her, why, and how to make it stop.

And if the police were involved?

One lucky river-boating enthusiast wasn't going to have the ability to take that on. His family had already lost that battle once, albeit in a different state within a much larger police force.

She understood his need to be a part of her investigation, since his saving her could likely have involved him, making him a possible target, too, but beyond that…she was on her own.

Something that she had to remind herself of when—at her request—Devon vacated his truck to allow her privacy for her phone call with her twin. Not only could she not rely on her current companion, she'd also severed a major connection with the twin who'd been in her camp since the day they were born. She'd turned her back on him, gone against his wishes, and handed his bloody knife in to the police.

She had no idea if he'd pick up the phone. Or ever talk to her again.

But she dialed—looking out over the small parking area where she'd left her little car countless times to swim across the rapids below. Dawn was just gracing the area with her presence and Kacey pictured the water she knew would be flowing at the end of the short path leading to the bank. Waited for the mixture of peace and excitement she felt every other time she'd sat there.

For the first time in her life, the water wasn't calling to her.

And her brother wasn't picking up.

Maybe because he didn't recognize the number? Kyle was clearly in trouble. Made sense that he wouldn't answer an unknown caller, didn't it?

I was supposed to be named Annabelle. She typed the words as they came to her. Sent the text.

And then dialed again.

"Kacey? Is that you?" Kyle's frantic voice came before the first ring finished sounding.

And her eyes flooded with tears—thankfully not within sight of Devon Miller. "Yes. Kyle, you have to tell me what's going on." She didn't know how much time she had.

Or even if he was alone, free to talk.

"Thank God." She heard a break in his voice. "When you didn't come home…"

"Have you seen Mom and Lizzie? Are they okay?"

"Yep. At Mom's place. Cynthia's with them."

She caught the secret message, understood the wording, right away. While she flooded with relief, Kacey's heart also sank. Her brother had sent their mother and sister out of the country. That didn't bode well.

Mom's place—their moniker for a vacation spot they'd all visited once when Kyle had received a lovely year-end bonus at work. Allison had been suffering from a particularly bad RA flare-up and her doctor had told them about the hot springs in Italy that were free of charge. He'd known their father. And owned a condominium not far from the springs, which he'd offered to them. It was the best vacation they'd ever had.

"Does Cynthia know there's trouble?" Their mom's divorced and childless best friend had been a lifesaver many times in the years after Steve's death.

"Cynthia loves Mom's place."

She took that as a no.

"Are you alone?"

"I can't talk, just needed to confirm…"

That it was really her. Her text about Annabelle, something no one else would ever have cause to know…

"I have to know what's going on, Kyle." Her stern tone of voice…not something she ever used with him.

It hadn't ever been necessary.

They'd been born of the same cloth. Understood things without words. They knew each other that well.

They'd known each other that well.

Or had she just thought they had?

"I have to go. And you…stay gone."

His harsh tone froze her blood.

But she got the message. She most definitely wasn't safe.

And something else came through, too.

No matter what Kyle had gotten mixed up in, no matter that she'd turned him in, her twin brother still loved her.

Devon stood far enough away to give Kacey privacy on the phone, but he had his hand on his gun, and kept watch as though their lives depended on it.

Because they might.

With his back to the concrete wall that marked the public access to the river, he watched Kacey's expressions as she talked. And kept track of the area around them as well. That early in the morning, there was no traffic on the road. And he didn't see any activity down in the river, either.

The second she was off the phone, he was at her door, pulling it open. "Give me the phone," he said, reaching to take it whether she offered it up or not.

She let it go without a fight and he ran to the path leading down to the bank. Hurled the phone into the river, and then jogged back to his truck, jumping inside and taking off.

In case anyone was watching her brother and attempted to trace the call.

"I've got another burner you can have back at the cabin," he told her then, feeling like a clod for snatching away her only means of communication with the outside world. "But it's only to be used for calling out in case of emergency, and then needs to be immediately destroyed."

She hadn't said a word.

She hadn't told him to stop the truck and let her out, either.

"What did your brother say?" He had to ask. Didn't expect much of a response.

"My mom and little sister are safe."

She hadn't said her brother was. Did he assume, since she'd talked to him, he was fine?

"Why did you need to speak with him?"

"To let him know I was okay. And to make sure my family is safe."

Made sense. Except that he'd seen tension on her face, tears in her eyes at one point, and at the point of hang up, maybe even some anger.

"What aren't you telling me?"

The silence stretched out between them as he drove, heading away from the river. He'd backtrack at some point, get to the cabin, but not before he knew more.

He wasn't being followed.

Police could keep a fairly good trail of him just with his license plate, if he drove through areas with traffic cams. Which was why he was avoiding all civilization.

"Kacey, we can't just stay at my cabin and fight off intruders for the rest of our lives. I'm in this up to my neck. I'm helping you. I need to know more."

And he would. As soon as he spoke to Hudson.

But he needed her to tell him. He wasn't fond of that fact. Yet there it was.

"I heard an argument outside my window, late the night before I was abducted. It woke me up. I looked out, saw my brother arguing with three guys. They had their backs to me. Were hunched. My brother kept shaking his head. Then I see the three of them leave, and my brother throws something in the bushes before he takes off, too…"

His gut sank. Really low.

Nothing about what she was telling him was good.

"The bloody knife," he said then.

She nodded. "I ran out, but Kyle got in his truck and chased after the SUV the other guys had been driving. I called him and he didn't pick up. Not then. The next morning, after I found the knife, he told me to put it back. To stay out of it. And he hung up on me."

"He didn't know you were turning him in?"

"He wouldn't pick up when I called him back."

"But he did today."

"Yes."

"And?"

"I already told you. My mom and little sister are safe."

"Don't lie to me." His tone wasn't threatening, but it wasn't kind, either.

"That's really all I got. Our mom has rheumatoid arthritis. She was pregnant, at forty, when our dad was killed, and was diagnosed before the baby was born. Lizzie is almost ten now. Kyle and I have been watching out for both of them ever since. He turned down Big Ten college scholarships to stay local. I commuted to college in Kingman." The Arizona town closest to Bullhead City on the way to Phoenix.

"And when I graduated, and got a job, I bought the house next door to them."

Another chilling piece of the puzzle just hit him. "He threw the knife in your mother's bushes?"

Her nod was slow. Filled with a weight he recognized. It had landed on him when he first heard about his father's affair. And had grown heavier when the contraband had been found in his father's vehicle after his death.

"The three guys, did any of them look injured when they left? Was anyone holding what could be a bleeding wound? Limping? Walking oddly?"

"No," she said after a second. "No, they walked like they had purpose, you know. All three jumped into their respective doors at the same time. When the car left, it just pulled away, not like they were in a hurry or anything."

But her brother had been? If he'd chased after them…

"What do you *think* is going on?" he asked then. Facts mattered. But so did perception, if the truth was going to be found. Facts could be made to appear as something they were not.

"Kyle's in trouble. Someone thinks I know something. My brother isn't talking to me, really talking to me, as in confiding in me, for the first time in our lives. I don't know if it's to protect me, or because he doesn't want me run-

ning to the police with any information he might give me.
Could be both."

He believed her. He wouldn't go so far as to think she
was being completely straight with him. But he didn't think
she'd just lied to him, either.

"What kind of trouble might your brother be in? Was he
into anything…excessive partying…drugs…"

"Absolutely not. He's production manager at a sawmill
up north in the mountains. Makes a lot more money than
I do. He has a small two-bedroom place up there, on the
property, and comes home for dinner once or twice a week
and on weekends whenever he can. He's the most responsible, hardworking man I know."

Sierra's Web would be checking out that information as
soon as Devon could get with them.

"Did he have any run-ins with anyone? A discontented
employee, maybe? Someone he might have fired? Or maybe
an angry boyfriend of someone he might have had a drink
with?"

If she knew her brother as well as she seemed to think
she did, she probably had more information than she thought
she had. He just had to get it out of her.

"Kyle's had a slew of girlfriends. Nothing serious, though.
Personally, I think he doesn't want the responsibility of a
family of his own. He's got enough of that with Mom and
Lizzie to suit him. He likes his freedom. He doesn't want to
be like our dad, living with an inner call to go serve, while
being held back by commitments at home. He's kind of got
the best of both worlds right now."

Devon didn't completely buy the assessment, though he
had no reason not to do so. "He tell you that?" he asked.

"No. He says he just hasn't met the right girl yet."

Or, could it be that Kyle Ashland was so tired of being
a family man that he'd plotted to get himself free? Didn't

explain the bloody knife in the trees. At all. Still, Tommy Grainger had to look at all options.

"Have you ever been up to Kyle's place?"

"We all have. Many times. Last summer, when school was out, I went up and painted the interior walls for him. Mom and Lizzie go up often during the summer because it's so much cooler up there. And we spend weekends up there sometimes during the winter so Lizzie can play in the snow."

She was talking a hell of a lot more. Had lost a good bit of her bravado.

Her phone call with her brother had obviously scared her.

And while that wasn't all bad, if it helped him get her out of the mess she'd walked into, and kept her safer while he did so, he hated to see her lose some of her spunk.

Didn't like seeing her suffer, either, but that one came with his job on a regular basis.

Detectives didn't often have cause to interview happy, untraumatized people.

He couldn't help but sympathize.

And told himself that was all he was feeling for his unplanned houseguest as he turned his truck back toward the river and the place that was feeling more and more like home to him.

Chapter Ten

You...stay gone.

Kacey couldn't get her twin's words out of her head.

There'd been no mistaking the almost desperate warning in Kyle's tone.

She'd escaped death once. Her brother didn't think she'd be able to do so a second time.

"I don't know what to do." She let the words fall into the cab of the truck, as Devon drove. "I'm putting you in danger. Anywhere I go, I'd put whoever is around me in danger. I don't trust the police—at least not in Bullhead City—and I have no means, equipment or training to conduct my own investigation."

When she heard how pathetic she sounded, she added, "But I'll figure it out. First things first, you need to drop me off someplace where there's no chance of anyone seeing you."

She'd figure it out from there.

She was not going to die. Her mother and Lizzie would need her in the months and years to come, just as they had during the ten that had just passed.

All she had to do was find a place to stay alive and trust Kyle to either get himself out of trouble, or turn himself in.

"Dropping you off doesn't ensure that I'm out of danger."

Devon's response was slow and steady. "We've already been over this. There's a good chance that I've been implicated."

"Yes, but there's a chance you haven't been…"

Didn't seem likely, considering the intrusion on his property—twice in the twenty-four hours or so she'd been there—and then that morning's police stop. But the possibility was there.

"I've got the setup to keep you safer than you'd likely be anywhere else."

She couldn't argue that. Every "stay alive" instinct in her body was telling her to stick with Devon. But instincts were feelings. Not facts.

"It makes no sense," she said aloud. "Kyle lives a quiet life. I cannot figure out what, or how, he'd be involved in that is something big enough to warrant any of this."

How did she let entities that wanted her dead know that they had nothing to fear from her? That her brother hadn't told her anything?

That while she'd heard angry voices the other night, she hadn't been able to make out any words?

Why couldn't she stop looking in the rearview mirror—and watching both sides of the vehicle as Devon drove? There hadn't been a car on the road with them in the past half hour. And none that could have in any way been suspected of following them.

She was getting paranoid.

More feelings when what she needed were thoughts.

What had she missed? What was she forgetting? Something that could help identify either the men outside her house that night, or those who'd taken her.

And it hit her.

"There were three men, both times," she said aloud then. "Arguing with Kyle in the yard the other night, and then the next day, with the van…" Maybe it was nothing. But… "It could be the same three men."

"Any thoughts on size? Height? Weight?"

"Nothing that stands out," she said then. "They weren't huge, not overly tall or heavy, and they weren't short. But then, I was looking at them from above—through an upstairs window."

"Hair then…did the moonlight shine on any heads? Was one lighter than another…"

Closing her eyes, she tried to remember. Shook her head. "I was paying attention to my brother. And grabbing my phone. It all happened so fast. By the time I woke up, got to the window…there were only seconds before the men left and Kyle took off after them." After tossing something into his mother's bushes.

Why had he done that? It just made no sense. Why leave evidence of a crime on your own mother's property? Most particularly when you were getting in your vehicle and could have unloaded the thing anywhere?

Kyle's behavior scared her, mostly because for the first time in their lives, she didn't get him at all.

"Maybe I should call the police," she said, shivering at just the thought of doing so. But, "If they weren't involved, they could use surveillance cameras in her neighborhood, and compare them to cameras at boat docks in the area. I was definitely on a dock."

"Could be a private one. They're a dime a dozen on the river. And without a crime, the police can't force neighbors to give up video cameras."

He was right on both counts, but she had to *do* something.

Devon's phone vibrated. If she hadn't been sitting there next to him, and it hadn't been touching the seat belt buckle, she'd have never known. As it was, she watched as he looked at his watch—obviously hooked back up to the phone. And was surprised when he turned a very serious, assessing look on her.

Had something just happened that changed his mind about keeping her around?

"I hired a private, nationally renowned firm of experts to oversee the planning and installation of the surveillance system on my property."

His words made about as much sense to her in that moment as Kyle's lack of them had done earlier.

"Okay." The man had won the lottery. Made sense that he'd have the money to hire the best.

"Yesterday I hired them to find out what they could about any crime involving a bloody knife in or near Bullhead City a couple of nights ago."

Oh.

"I need to make a call," he said then, pulling over into an alcove of desert brush and exiting the vehicle.

She thought about following him.

But didn't. If he'd wanted her to hear the conversation, he'd have had it sitting behind the wheel. And she was in no position to barter with him.

A couple of minutes later, he was climbing back in beside her.

Mouth dry, she stared straight ahead. Waited. Needing to know.

And dreading the knowledge.

"There were no crimes that fit the description reported in Bullhead City, Laughlin, Lake Havasu or Kingman."

The relief was palpable. So maybe...

"However, through a contact in a lab in Vegas that does private forensic testing for smaller police forces as well as individuals, I'm told there was a bloody knife that came in yesterday. The contact didn't know from where at this point. It had gold and silver scrolls, a C-shaped chip out of the bottom—and the blood on the blade was most definitely human. It was run through a DNA database..."

The hiss of her indrawn breath was as loud as his words had been. Shocked at herself, needing to cover her ears against what was coming, Kacey covered her mouth with both hands, instead.

"There was no match," Devon finished quickly, seeming to be watching her like a doctor watched a patient, or something.

And then, with a glance in the rearview mirror—one she copied through her own side mirror and saw nothing but empty roadway behind them—he pulled back out onto the road.

"This private firm is sending an expert investigator to canvas your neighborhood, as well as public and private boat docks along the river, asking for surveillance video, under the auspices of looking for evidence of a reported domestic situation. No one will be compelled to give any, but we could get lucky."

How had fate had it that this lottery-winning rafting enthusiast and guide had been on the water right when she'd needed him? Surely that meant that she was destined to stay alive.

To do everything she could to protect her family. And anyone else, besides Kyle, the bullies after her brother were hurting. The men who'd taken her had most definitely not been amateurs. The confidence with which they'd felt they could take a law-abiding citizen at their will...

She had to stay alive to be able to testify against them. Send a message that people like that couldn't just terrorize good people.

The thoughts were powerful, invigorating...but still left her sitting as a passenger in a truck that was not her own. Going to a cabin where she was welcome at the pleasure of the owner only for as long as he chose to let her stay there. And without a plan.

But Devon seemed to have one. Even if it was only to keep himself safe, he was her best shot at finding out what was going on so she'd know how to take care of it.

"I'm assuming that you also had them check me out," she said then, referring to his firm of experts.

"Yes."

"And?"

"You're an accomplished river swimmer. The list of awards is impressive."

She shrugged. "What good did it do me? I'd have died in that water if not for you."

His glance felt personal. Warm. "You'd have died in that water if not for your skills," he told her. "Even with your feet bound, in a storm, with raging rapids, you managed to keep your head above water."

"My father used to help me train," she told him, the thought giving her strength. "He taught me that if I ever get in trouble in the river, I have to find debris to hold onto, and just ride until another option comes along."

Devon had been that option.

With help from her father, who she liked to believe was watching over his family still?

She didn't want to get too emotional, or fanciful, but because the thought of her father having worked through Devon gave her a renewed sense of strength, she allowed it to hang around.

KYLE ASHLAND HAD a spotless record. With a chance at the National Football League ahead of him, he'd walked away from the sport after his father's death to provide for the family his dad had left behind. He'd started out with Greenland

Logging and Sawmill at eighteen and had worked his way up to production manager.

He had no arrest or criminal record. Not even a traffic violation.

And even though Kacey's twin was on-site at the saw-mill most of the time, he still managed to be active in the Bullhead City community, using his two-week vacation every summer to run a high school football camp, among other things. The full report would be coming to Devon via email later that day.

And Kacey had been voted teacher of the year three times.

Too good to be true?

Tommy Grainger had a hard time not thinking so.

The bloody knife bothered him more, though. If Kyle had stabbed someone, the narrative changed drastically.

Out of supreme caution, he'd kept his phone in airplane mode during much of the trip up north, only turning it back on when they were within thirty miles of his property. In the event someone was tracing Kyle Ashland's calls, Devon didn't want his phone to be found anywhere in the area of Kacey's burner phone.

If the police were involved, they'd have the means to put pieces together.

Which was why the cops checking out his truck earlier that day was bothering him more than a little. Thankfully Kacey hadn't been in sight at all in town. Any surveillance footage would show him alone in the cab.

He still didn't like being on anyone's radar.

Which was why, as soon as he was back at the cabin, he excused himself from Kacey under the auspices of check-ing the area where the camera had been hit the night be-fore. He was heading to the river to do just that. But had his Tommy Grainger phone in hand as soon as he was out of earshot of the cabin.

If Kacey wanted to spy on him, was watching him from the screens in the laundry room, she'd only know that he was making a call.

Rachel Wallace, aka Bonita Donaldson, a decorated detective out of Phoenix, his second in command in the undercover operation, picked up on the first ring.

"Hey, baby, it's Devon, how are you?" he asked, using a low sexy voice. She was a cop. But he'd only known her as Rachel. Just as she'd only known him as Devon. Going in as strangers had been a requisite he'd set for the job.

"Had a date yesterday, tough guy." Her response sent his heart rate up a notch.

Either of them having dates meant they'd made contact with one of their major suspects. "You trying to make me jealous, woman?"

"Nope. Just letting you know if you don't take care of me, you'll look for me and I'll be gone."

"This guy...was he as good as I am?"

"I'll let you know..."

She hung up.

And Devon's blood flew through his veins. Rachel had made contact with the suspect who'd been on the rafting trip the day before. The one they were now certain was selling the exact drug cocktail they were looking for. She'd managed to talk him into selling her some opiates. If the guy delivered, they were one huge link closer in bringing down the chain.

He had to get back to work.

Chapter Eleven

He'd said that if she was at his cabin, he wouldn't be going into work that day. And yet, there she was, an hour after they'd returned from her predawn phone call, watching his truck drive away from the property.

Leaving her there all alone.

With a gun and screens to watch.

And a new burner phone with his cell number programmed in—along with instructions not to use it unless it was a life-and-death emergency.

She had no right to be unhappy with him.

The man was bending over backward to help her.

But now that they were back at his place—that felt like a fortress—and she had feet on solid ground, the sense that something was off about Devon started to attack her again.

Pushing the paranoia away, she moved to the laundry closet. Watched the screens carefully, noting landmarks on each one to use for comparison purposes.

And wondered why a man who'd won the lottery was working as a recreational river guide. Why, with his life in possible peril, had he chosen to go into work?

As if that was the worst of her problems.

Devon Miller had absolutely nothing to do with Kyle, the

bloody knife she'd turned in, or her abduction. Anything going on in his life had nothing to do with her.

Unless...

Staring at the screens with cameras giving her views of the river, she thought about Devon's rescue the day before.

Had it been planned?

Had Kacey's captors intended all along to keep her alive? They'd left her to possibly die in the anchored rowboat, but if the storm hadn't come in, she'd have been fine. Uncomfortable, certainly. But in no real physical danger. She was the one who'd put her life at risk by leaving the boat in the middle of the storm.

When they'd found her gone, had they sent Devon after her?

Horror struck as she considered that he might have been one of three men outside her mother's home. One of the three who'd kidnapped her?

Oh God, had she played right into his hands? He'd gotten her to tell him what she knew. And what she didn't.

Other than Kyle's last mandate—*you...stay gone.*

From what she'd said that morning, Devon now knew that she hadn't heard a word of the argument between the three men and her brother the other night. And he knew that Kyle hadn't given her any more information that morning. He also knew that she had little to no description on the three men.

Him included?

He'd asked specifically about hair. To see if she knew one of her captors had hair as long as hers?

She'd seen a couple of pairs of tennis shoes. Easily thrown in the river to sink to the bottom and get lost in the sludge. Or shredded or burned.

Shivering, she looked around the cabin, as though she needed a way to escape. When she could just walk right out the front door.

And Devon would see her do so. He had his phone, his camera screens.

She'd known she wasn't dealing with amateurs. Devon's setup at the cabin was definitely of the professional variety.

Working herself up into a paranoid frenzy, Kacey took herself back to the laundry closet, studying the screens again. Devon had them there for a reason.

They'd been there before she'd shown up in the river the day before.

What was he looking for?

Or doing out there?

Was it really just a case of winning the lottery? But if so, why was he working as a river rafting guide?

Because he loved the water and needed something to do with his time?

Did the people he worked for, or with, know of his lottery win?

Studying the screens, she allowed the questions full rein. Needed to keep an open mind until some kind of proof told her the truth.

His reasons for letting her stay…because saving her could have put him in danger, too, and she might have answers she didn't know she had…made it seem true that they were better together. She was safe at his place. He was just a decent guy trying to do the right thing.

While staying out of the headlines.

Could be true.

He'd also expressed doubt about her innocence in whatever had gotten her kidnapped.

Did he still harbor those doubts?

He'd left her alone at his place with a gun.

To send his men after her? Was she a sitting duck, standing there looking at screens, thinking she had view of the entire property?

That she'd be safe as long as she kept watch?

Was someone walking his land right now, ready to ambush her?

No one other than Devon, or whoever he told, knew where she was. Not even Kyle. But her brother had clearly known that if she was found, she'd be killed.

Who'd look for a remote cabin in the wilderness?

How would they ever get by the people watching Devon's cameras to rescue her?

And what in the hell was it all about?

What could possibly matter so much?

Money, obviously. A ton of it.

But where was it coming from? What was making so much that multiple men were willing to kill for it?

And why was Kyle still alive?

They knew where he was, right? Or had he gone into hiding, too?

He must still have something they wanted that they could only get with him alive.

Maybe killing her had been their way of threatening him to give whatever it was to them. But even that hadn't caused her brother to give in.

To tell them what they needed to know.

Or they wouldn't still be after her.

And now that he knew she wasn't dead, his resolve to stand strong against their intimidation had grown. Which was why he'd implored her to stay gone.

Or...he was involved with them and still loved her and wanted to protect her.

Nothing else made sense.

Nor did that boat bobbing in the water. Stepping forward, Kacey stared at the screen in the far-left corner of the wall. A river view, but quite a bit upstream from the screen where the camera had been altered.

It wasn't a raft, or a kayak. More like a rowboat.

The one she'd been held captive in? Had her captors lifted the anchor and set it free when she'd disappeared? Thinking that she'd gone overboard and her body would never be found?

Had whoever had taken her been so sure that no one would look for her?

Probably not as far downstream as she'd been taken. She was known to swim in Bullhead City and places upstream from there.

The boat was small. Maybe a three-seater. No one was manning it. Just bare seats bobbing in the sunshine, caught in a slow-moving, almost stationary, bit of water close to the shore. As though something under the water was slowing the velocity.

It happened, especially after storms when branches and sediment built up.

Chest tight, Kacey stood there for a few seconds, and then, taking note of the landmarks she'd been studying for more than an hour, she was out of the cabin.

If the boat practically mooring just off from Devon's land was the same one in which she'd been tied up, she'd be able to tell. She'd just have to see the bottom of it.

And if it was, she had solid evidence that could link whoever was in that boat to her abductors.

There was no movement on Devon's land. She had her gun.

And, finally, something to do.

If Devon was out on the river, it could be hours before he even had a chance to look at his screens. And longer before he could make it back to her.

She couldn't let the piece of evidence just float away with hopes that they'd find it later.

And if it wasn't her boat?

She'd have spent the afternoon doing rather than just sitting. Trying.

Which was better than letting her fears run away with her mind.

Not that she was discounting her concerns. She put on her new tennis shoes and traipsed across desert land dotted with bunches of Palo Verde trees and various forms of cacti—some sprawling, some not—amidst hills and valleys from the surrounding mountains. Kacey fully acknowledged to herself that her boat appearing on camera during the time that Devon was away was a bit too much of a coincidence to be one.

It was a very convenient way to draw her down to the river.

She could be walking straight into danger.

But the water was calm. She knew she could master it.

She had the gun.

And if someone was there, with a plot to kill her, they'd get her up at the cabin, too. At least this way she was on the offensive.

And could dodge bullets by moving like a fish through the water, underwater, only bobbing up for quick air if necessary.

The river would be muddy brown after the storm, making her harder to track underneath the water. And the dark sweats she had on, while somewhat cumbersome to swim in, would also help hide her from exposure.

She'd planned, upon returning to the cabin, to shower and put on some of her new clothes.

After Devon left, she'd thrown the clothes in the washer first, instead, preferring to stay close to the screens while in the cabin alone.

While she was a bit nervous, not having the screens on her burner phone, or the ability to watch them as she walked, as Devon did, Kacey moved swiftly over the acres. She had purpose.

Was fighting for her life. Her freedom to return to it.

Fighting for her brother and the right to be present to watch over her mom and Lizzie.

She stepped carefully, as quietly as possible, keeping herself hidden in the tall brush and trees when she could, feeling the sun's heat on her head, her bare forearms, knowing she'd be burned, but still welcoming the warmth.

Arizona's sun was a living entity to her. At the moment, a companion on what could be a life-threatening journey.

She thought about sending a text to the number Devon had programmed in her burner. He'd said life or death.

It wasn't that yet.

If Devon was one of the scum who were after her, they'd all be watching her. The idea sent wells of panic through her, but she didn't let it show.

They were obviously good enough at what they were doing to have Kyle running scared. Or to have sucked in a good decent man to their dark activities.

But she was smart, too.

And she wasn't going down without a fight.

A few more acres out, she took a few sips from the bottle of water she'd brought with her. Had to keep hydrated.

Put her free hand on the gun tucked into her waistband under her T-shirt.

Criminals intent on killing her weren't the only things she had to worry about out there alone. Rabid coyotes were sometimes out during the day and would attack humans. Mountain lions or bobcats would come down out of the mountains looking for water. Javelina—smelly, hoofed, piglike animals—had been known to be aggressive to humans and inhabited lands not far from Quartzite.

Ears constantly straining to hear any sounds around her,

she continued to move at a quick, sure, steady pace, as though she knew exactly where she was going, and what she was going to do when she got there.

When she saw the branch protruding out of the big, five-foot boulder—one of the landmarks she'd been staring at back at the cabin—her heart started to pound. Another acre or so and she could hear the river.

Landscape changed around the water. Bigger leaves, more greenery to use to hide. Kacey was thankful for its thicker cover, making it easier for her to approach without being seen by anyone in the water.

The boat's seats had been empty. There'd been no movement in the water from the moment the small vessel had appeared on-screen. Didn't mean there wasn't someone close by, aware of the cameras, watching her approach.

Panic flared, and she let anger push it back. Her mother, Lizzie, herself…they didn't deserve any of this.

Maybe Kyle didn't, either. She couldn't think about her brother's involvement right then. Couldn't let emotion weaken her.

A few yards from river's edge, she stood in some six-foot-high greenery, assessing the shoreline. Looking for a place to enter the water with the least chance of being seen. The boat was nowhere in sight. Perhaps it was gone. She'd made the trek for nothing.

There'd been that possibility from the start.

She wasn't leaving until she knew for sure.

The last couple of feet happened almost naturally. She'd been entering the Colorado River from her various shores since she was a toddler.

Braced for an initial shock of cold, she hissed against the sting to her ankles as she slid in down to her shoulders without making a sound. Turned a complete circle, saw nothing, and moved further out slowly. Head underwater, she swam a few yards, then popped up again, just long enough to take in air and then was down again, heading straight downstream, allowing the water to do most of the work for her.

Her third time coming up for air, she saw the boat. Just feet from her. Heading toward some rapids, which would suck it away from her. She couldn't let that happen.

Head under, she kicked and pulled with all her might, shooting herself across those feet three times as fast as the river was flowing. Touched the side of the boat. Shot herself up in the water as far as she could, reaching for an edge, anything she could grasp hold of, use to pull herself up. The boat kept moving along, growing closer and closer to the rapids. She didn't have much time.

Propelled by a need for answers, to save her family, to get her life back and end the nightmare consuming her, she shot up one more time, grabbed hold of the empty rigger, managed to tilt the boat enough to get an elbow over the side. The small boat rocked, as it hit a wave burst, almost capsizing on top of her, and then, the force of the water yanked it out of her grasp.

As the boat swept away, Kacey turned and swam with all her might. Channeling her father, hearing nothing but his firm words of instruction as she reached, pulled, kicked. The familiar rhythm, soothed even as she used every muscle in her body to fight the current trying to push her into the rapids. To get herself to shore.

She was almost there when a flash of color caught her eye.

Something bobbing in a splay of reeds down shore from where she'd entered the water, but still upstream from where she'd ended up. Filled with adrenaline, she barely felt the exhaustion in her limbs as she changed course, heading against the current to make it to the shiny substance before it broke loose and was swept away.

Taking a long breath, she did a deep dive, swimming closer to the river's bottom where the current would be less. And when she came up for air, she was only feet from her prey.

A small, square-looking object. Close enough to shore that she could touch bottom and walk her way in.

Off Devon's land, she wasn't sure she could be seen, but she stayed under cover of brush and leaves as much as she could. Keeping in shadows when she couldn't.

Another minute and, heart pounding, she reached for the article.

It was hard, slim, covered in river slime, but…familiar-feeling.

Rinsing it in the water, she got her first glimpse. Took another look, and almost dropped the thing.

It was a DVD. Still packaged in a CD case.

And judging from what she could make of the picture on the front, and the title, it was nothing she wanted to see, nothing her students or sister could legally see.

She almost dropped it back in the water. Had been trained young not to pollute the majestic Colorado River. She could enjoy it. Swim in it.

And was to always respect and care for it.

She was just downstream from Devon's property. He'd been down to the river even since she'd been there.

Could the pornographic movie be his?

There was nothing illegal about that. Figuring she'd take it back to him, just in case, Kacey tucked the plastic case into the back of her sweats, swam back to where she'd entered the water, climbed out and back into her tennis shoes, and, soaking wet, started the trek back through Devon's desert land to his cabin.

She'd been on a fool's chase. But at least she'd been back

in the water. Like falling off a horse, you had to get right back up on it. Or, in her case, in it.

And she'd tried to help herself out of the mess she was in.

What Devon would have to say about it all, once he saw the day's films and knew she'd been to the river, she didn't know.

What she was certain of was that if she had to do it over again, she'd take the very same action. She had to do all she could do.

Always.

Her father had expected no less of her and Kyle, and whether her twin had buckled or not, she wasn't going to accept any less than all she had out of herself.

Devon could understand that, or not.

With every step she took, she grew stronger in determination, in her sense of having done the right thing.

While a small part of her hoped that Devon Miller would agree. And maybe even admire her a little bit.

Chapter Twelve

Devon was ready to pop a gasket. Tense, frustrated, he drove to his place feeling as though he'd held his breath for hours and it was pushing at the seams of his skin, ready to explode out of him.

How could the woman have exposed herself to danger from all sides? Alone. With no one anywhere nearby to call for help.

More to the point, *why* would she?

He had been out on the water with a family of five. He'd gone to work so he could head to the bar across the street from the dock when he finished the two-hour trip and see what Rachel was up to. His watch had vibrated the second Kacey left the cabin. He'd seen the abandoned boat, too. He'd checked the surveillance app on his phone, had seen Kacey walking out into the desert on her own, figured she was getting some exercise.

He'd checked on her periodically over the next hour, saw her heading toward the river, afraid the boat was her target, hated that she was exposing herself out on his land when they still didn't know who the two men were who'd been on the property the day before.

Or why they'd been there.

But she was a free woman. Free to stay because he'd offered her the room. And free to go. He couldn't risk his cover because the woman had chosen to put herself in potential danger.

As much as every instinct within him was urging him to get off the raft and into a motorboat that could take him to whatever trouble she might be walking into, he knew he couldn't do so. He wasn't her babysitter.

And he most definitely was not going to blow his cover, blow a many-months-long case, because the woman he'd rescued was getting to him.

Most particularly not when they'd had their first real break in the case. Rachel tended bar at the dive across the street from the docks. Had a room upstairs.

She was their eyes and ears at the dock they'd pinpointed as a major source of the drugs. The others were in similar positions along the river, in Utah and Colorado, at other suspected ports.

Places chosen for the number of young people turning up in area hospitals with drug overdoses—all with similar symptoms, caused by the same hallucinogen as the cases they were seeing across the country.

Virginia was handling the influx of drugs on the East Coast in their own way.

His job was to stop the flow into the country. There'd be others. He didn't kid himself. But if people didn't fight against them, there'd be a pandemic that could take control of them.

Rachel had made the score she'd set up with Belen Alexopoulos. Devon had seen it go down. She'd be sending the drugs to her captain in Phoenix to have them tested.

She'd also agreed to meet up with the guy for drinks later that night. It had taken months for them to identify the source of the drugs causing the overdoses. They'd known they were coming from the river, knew, by process of elimination, that they had to be traveling via recreational boating.

What they didn't know was how much this Belen Alexopoulos was transporting and selling. The good-looking young Greek man seemed to travel among the lowly and most of the drugs were being distributed to the wealthy. They knew of one high-school-aged dropout who'd bought drugs from him. And then distributed them at a party, where another high schooler bought some. From there drugs went through two more buyers before they'd reached the girl who'd overdosed.

Thankfully, she survived.

Rachel's job, once the current drugs were tested and confirmed to be their same recipe, was to find out as much as she could about Alexopoulos.

And, at Devon's insistence, she was to text him as soon as she was locked in at home for the night.

He'd told her nothing about his housemate.

They didn't talk about personal stuff.

Keeping himself focused as he drove home, Devon took a lot of deep breaths. Kacey had made it back to the cabin safely. Had spent time in the bathroom and come out looking fresh and clean in a pair of the shorts and one of the loose sleeveless blouses he'd picked up for her.

When he caught himself thinking about the panties and bras that had also been on her list—he forced a quick swerve to his thoughts again.

He had to stay pissed at her. Not admire the guts it took for her to head out on her own. He'd keep those thoughts to himself.

Kacey wasn't going to get the chance to hold out on him. If she expected to stay with him, she had to spill her secrets. He wasn't going to have her bringing danger upon herself under his watch.

And he didn't much fancy the idea of her bringing it to his home, either.

His place in the woods...he liked it a hell of a lot more than he'd expected to. Having grown up in Vegas and spending his entire life in the city and her suburbs, he'd expected the hardest part of his current operation to be the cabin in the woods.

And perhaps it would be, with his rescue of a strangely invigorating petite blonde woman that he didn't wholly trust and his subsequent invitation for her to stay with him.

Something about Kacey's story just seemed off.

He was certain the Colorado River was being used to transport drugs...but people dumping bodies there? Leaving them to die?

But then, when he considered Lake Mead—a huge reservoir on the Colorado just outside Las Vegas—and the number of bodies that had been found there recently as the water lowered...

Devon was shaking his head as he pulled onto his property. Tamping down any sense of anticipation he felt as he parked the truck and headed toward the front door.

He hadn't decided if he was going to reprimand his guest, give her an ultimatum, or just ignore her until he had time to think clearly about her actions that afternoon, as he stepped inside.

She came out of the laundry room, looking...attractive... in the shorts and colorful top...until his gaze landed on the fresh bandages around her ankles and he wondered if she had river sludge in her cuts again.

Turning away from her before he said something he'd regret—something inappropriate like insisting that he look at those ankles—he noticed the plastic case on his table.

"What's this?" he asked, picking it up.

And then, seeing the image under the sealed plastic, threw it back down to the table.

"I found it, down at the river."

He hadn't noticed her picking up anything. And he'd viewed the reels from the day while he'd been sitting at the bar nursing a lemon-lime soda with a lime wedge, made to look like an alcoholic beverage, waiting for Rachel's hookup.

"It was downstream from your place, stuck in some reeds. I didn't know if it was yours..."

"Hell no, it's not mine."

He didn't need to watch sex. If he wanted to enjoy bodily pleasures, he knew where to find women who'd expressed mutual interest in sharing it with him.

"Just to be clear, while prostitution is legal in parts of Nevada, and in Vegas, where I grew up, I've never paid for sex. Just not my cup of tea."

What in the hell had he thrown that out there for?

He'd never said anything so asinine in his life.

She didn't flinch. Or even blink. Just shrugged and said, "Seems like an odd thing for the men who'd been on your property to have left behind, but do you suppose it could be theirs?"

He supposed it could have floated downriver from a lot of places. He didn't give a damn about the movie. Other than...

He glanced at it again. A DVD in a CD case. Seemingly professionally packaged, albeit on a low budget.

Probably someone in a houseboat on the river who lost possessions during the storm. It happened. As light as the case was, it could have floated. Been caught on debris. Washed up onshore.

Or it could have been part of some kind of illegal distribution. His thoughts flew as he stood there, aware that his houseguest hadn't moved from the doorway of the laundry room.

The boat he'd seen on-screen—while newer looking than the one she'd described being held in, and metal, not wood, was about the same size.

She'd seen it on-screen and had risked her life to swim out to it.

Because she knew there could be something of value in it? Not just one movie, but other things? Drugs, maybe?

His suspicions grew, even as parts of him didn't want to buy what he was thinking. He'd grown soft on the woman. He couldn't listen to those parts.

"Why did you go down to the river?"

"I saw a boat with no one in it. It was just too odd. A seemingly empty boat floating downriver only miles from where I'd been tied up and anchored, in a similarly small boat only two days before? I had to go. What if someone had been in the bottom of it, as I had been? Or what if I recognized something about it?"

His tension started to dissipate. Until he thought of the way she'd moved in the water. As well trained as he was on surveillance, and as much time as he'd spent staring at his own screens, he'd lost her as soon as she'd gone down the bank. Out in the water, a lot of the time she'd been outside his camera view. But during those last seconds...

It was like she'd been trained, too. To stay hidden.

"And the movie?" he asked.

"After the boat went over the rapids, I saw something glinting by the shore. Turned out to be the plastic case."

"After the boat went over?" he asked, honing in on what he could deal with at the moment.

"Yeah."

"Is it possible the case came out of the boat?"

"Not while I was holding on to it," she said, taking a step closer to him. "The boat, I mean..."

"You held onto the boat."

"I had to see what was inside."

"And the boat went over the rapids."

She looked him in the eye. Nodded.

"You could have gone over with it." The air in his lungs constricted.

"It's a chance I had to take, Devon. I'm well trained to handle the water. If not for the ties at my ankles the other night, I probably would have survived the storm."

His admiration for her grew.

He wasn't happy about that. Figured maybe he needed to keep her on the same level as Rachel. Nothing personal at all between them. Not even talk.

Except that it was possible he was being personally associated with her by those who wanted her dead. He had to know everything she could.

"What was inside the boat?"

"Nothing. Not even the oars."

"Likely something that broke away from a dock or pier during the storm. It could have been traveling the river since yesterday morning." He put the possibility out there. Wasn't buying it.

But had to acknowledge that he had no other viable explanation at the moment.

If she was to be believed.

What if she'd known the boat would be coming downriver and had gone to intercept it knowing it would be carrying contraband? Because she was a part of whatever Kyle had gotten involved with, or to get some kind of leverage to help out herself and her family, he didn't know.

Either could be possible.

The drugs he was after were not the only contraband flowing up and down that mighty river. With borders along Arizona, California and Nevada, and flowing to Mexico, the river was a potential hotbed for interstate trafficking of all kinds of illegal goods.

And he was purposely positioned at a known hub. A recreational boating mecca. The legal revenue alone from water activities up and down the river was astronomical. As were the numbers of vacationers who passed through the area between Quartzite and Bullhead City. And that was just on the Arizona side. Directly across the river, in California, the business was equal or even greater.

"Did you take your gun with you?"

"Yes."

"Into the river?"

"Yes."

He was both relieved and bothered by that. Glad that she'd had the wherewithal to protect herself as much as possible.

And wondering if she'd gone into that water knowing she was taking on the men who'd kidnapped her—even just by trying to confiscate one of their boats or known contraband.

For that matter, he had no way of knowing if the one movie on his kitchen table was all she'd brought back to the cabin.

"Do you mind if I search you?"

The question was all wrong.

And all mistrustful cop.

She held out both arms. Submitted to his pat down.

First time he'd ever done one where grazing a breast with the back of his wrist distracted him from his job.

He stepped away. Searched the bathroom. Came back out to find her standing right where he'd left her. "And now your room?"

He knew she hadn't stashed anything anywhere else on his property or in his cabin. He'd viewed the tapes.

Wordlessly, she motioned toward the door.

He made quick work of going through the space he'd allotted her. Returned to the main living area with a mixture of regret and relief. Focused on the relief.

"Thank you," he told her.

"You still don't trust me."

"Don't take it personally," he told her. "I don't trust anyone."

She nodded. "You want me to leave?"

"No." Solid truth. On many levels. At least one of which he wasn't going to explore. Ever. He couldn't like having her there for personal reasons. Period.

"You want me to make meat loaf for dinner? I saw you have hamburger thawing in the refrigerator."

"I was planning on just grilling up plain burgers, but if you want to, knock yourself out." No. Wrong words. Insensitive to say to a woman who'd nearly been knocked out permanently.

And why did he keep saying such ludicrous things about the woman? He'd never had a problem conversing with a female in his life.

"My mother used to make a great meat loaf," he said then, to soften his inadvertent blow.

Kacey didn't show any reaction—either to his gaffe, or his attempt to make it better. She moved with her usual softness to the kitchen. Giving him a view of the back of her ankles.

Both bleeding through the gauze she'd wrapped around them.

"Let me take care of those ankles, first," he said then. Reaching for the first aid kit he'd left on a table by his bedroom door.

And considered himself forgiven when she immediately took a seat and let him tend to her cuts.

The skin was raw, painful looking, and she'd left a small piece of sludge in one of the cuts. He was as tender as he could be, caring that he had to be hurting her, feeling her pain as though it was his own.

And reminded himself—she could just be allowing his attention because she knew she could be facing infection if she didn't let him do so.

Because she needed her skin to heal quickly and allow her to get on with whatever questionable, likely illegal, business she was getting on with.

Problem was, he wasn't believing a word of it.

Chapter Thirteen

As soon as he'd finished bandaging her ankles, Devon asked for Kacey's gun. She supposed it was inevitable—her activities that day had blown what trust he'd had in her.

She handed over the weapon without a word. Started on the meat loaf. And ridiculously started thinking about his bigger, warm hands skimming her body moments before. He couldn't have been more impersonal—and yet the blood in her veins had grown instantly warm. Like he was some kind of infrared wave.

Turning to the refrigerator to get an egg to add to the meat mixture in the bowl on the counter, she saw him. And warmed all over again.

He'd taken her gun apart. Was drying it by hand with a small towel.

Didn't mean he was going to give it back to her. But he hadn't taken it just to punish her, either. He'd asked her if she'd had it in the water. She'd thought he'd wanted to know if she'd protected herself. Had been glad to say that she had.

She should have thought about gun parts that could rust.

Back at the counter, her hands in a mixture of ground beef, oatmeal, catsup, onion, egg and a couple of spices, she was startled again when the gun appeared beside her bowl. Devon didn't say a word. About her hands in the glob in the bowl, the day—or the weapon. Just set it there and walked out.

When she saw him on his phone outside a few minutes later, she understood his abrupt departure. He'd obviously had a text from that firm of experts again. Requiring another phone call.

Though she knew she shouldn't, she placed the finished loaf, already in its pan, in the oven and then stood there and watched the man who'd been her only companion for the two worst days of her life.

His shoulders, while broad, weren't huge. Yet they seemed stronger to her than even her brother's. Who'd trained his whole life and took on bruisers on the football field.

The long hair had seemed odd to her at first, not anything she'd ever be attracted to, but as he stood outside in the desert wilderness, staring off into the distance, a frown on his face, she thought the hair he'd set free when he'd come home suited him completely.

He was wild and unpredictable.

And yet…she felt safe with him.

More than that, she was hot for him. Growing hotter by the hour. Maybe some kind of Stockholm syndrome, but she didn't think so. Devon wasn't holding her hostage. To the contrary, he'd made it clear that he'd help her leave anytime she wanted to go.

She didn't want to go.

She liked Devon's cabin. She liked being there with him. She liked him.

Still standing there with the thoughts, not yet having had time to process them, she watched the man—in shorts and a T-shirt and flip-flops—hang up the phone and head for the cabin door.

One look at his face and she knew that whatever had

made him frown on the phone had to do with her. Not his father's cold case.

"What?"

He looked her in the eye—his expression serious, and something more. She couldn't tell if he was doubting her, or worried about her. "What?" she asked a second time.

She'd deal with it, whatever it was.

"Your brother reported you missing today."

A swallow got caught in her throat. She choked. Thinking about the words. Coughed until tears ran down her face.

When Devon came closer, she put him off with an upheld hand. She just needed a minute.

Swallowed. Took a deep breath. Her mind scrambling.

And coming up empty.

"Why?" she asked, blinking through wet lashes as she looked over at her host. "Why would he do that?"

The obvious reason, that he wanted the police to get a hold of her, struck terror within her. Was her twin giving her up to save himself?

Because she'd turned traitor by turning in the knife?

Then why tell her to stay gone?

"My guess is that now that he knows you're alive, he wants to make it look like he doesn't know you were abducted. Doesn't know where you are. It puts suspicion off from him. You live in a relatively small town. You know people. You said your mom and sister are on vacation, but there are others who will begin to wonder when no one sees you around anyplace. Neighbors who don't see sign of life at your house…"

Good. Right. It all made sense.

And was far more palatable than the hell into which her mind had immediately fallen.

"It also lets whoever took you know that you haven't been found," Devon said more softly, dropping down to a chair he pulled out from the kitchen table. "Which might calm them into thinking that you drowned in the storm. Or strengthen a belief that you did, if they were already thinking as much."

"And Kyle would likely know if they *were* thinking that."

"There's more…"

She nodded. She'd take as much as she had to take to get her family back together safe and sound. "He said that he last saw you at the spot on the river we went this morning, late afternoon, the day that you were abducted."

"After I was kidnapped?" She shook her head. It was like her twin had been taken over by some kind of alien. "He knows exactly where and when it happened because I just told him this morning. The only reason I can think of that he'd lie about it is so that no one investigating my disappearance looks at footage around the police station to try and find out what happened…"

"He's protecting your kidnappers."

Maybe. It sounded that way. Her heart couldn't buy it. Not yet.

Devon's eye-to-eye look, his continued frown, had her taking a seat as well. "This also means that unless you want your whereabouts to be known to the police, you need to stay hidden. Every cop in the state is going to be on the lookout for you."

She'd already figured out that much. "Why would Kyle want that? Why would he do that to me?"

A shake of Devon's head was her only answer.

And it wasn't good enough.

SHE'D CALLED HER brother and then the man had sicced the police on her. Or put bad cops under notice that cops all over the state would be watching them.

Devon didn't know what to think. He needed to know not just what Kacey was saying, but what she was thinking.

He had to know how to keep her safe. Even if she was involved in something bad. He'd turn her in if he found out she was guilty of any crimes. Once he knew that she'd be treated fairly by the law.

In the meantime, Devon ate meat loaf. Thought about Rachel on her date. Waited for the detective's text.

And tried not to enjoy every move Kacey Ashland made in his home. Tried not to like having her there.

Or think about how quiet and empty the place would seem when she left.

Life would return to normal—as normal as Tommy Grainger's life ever got—he knew that. He'd been under-cover before. A week or two and he'd acclimate back to his real life.

Until the next assignment.

At least until Sierra's Web found out who'd framed his father. If they found out.

Hilton Grainger had been unfaithful to his wife. It was possible he'd been unfaithful to the job as well.

Tommy wasn't ready to accept that.

So he allowed himself to be consumed by Devon's life. His current world. It's how he did the job so well.

And stayed alive.

Tommy out. Devon in.

And Kacey Ashland… Devon's world, not Tommy's. Not real life. No permanency.

But if he could help her get her real life back…he'd like to be able to do that.

Even if it meant she went to prison?

The thought stopped him. Until his phone vibrating against his leg from inside his shorts pocket took him out-side again.

"Rach? What's up?"

He listened. Gave her a one-word affirmative, and then rushed back inside.

Kacey glanced up from the new burner phone he'd given her. She had internet access. He'd determined that he had to give her all the freedom she needed to lead him to her truths.

Reality was, she was free. Had had the wherewithal and guts to free herself from her captors. And he wasn't going to do anything to take that sense of liberty away from her again.

Except, maybe get her killed? He'd barreled into the cabin, mouth open, breath taken, ready to speak. Saw her sitting there, so beautiful. So fine. And said nothing.

"What's wrong?" She'd looked up from her phone.

For a split second, he considered lying to her.

To protect her.

"Devon, what's going on? Is it Kyle? Did someone hurt him?"

Her fear, and the strength with which she stood, as though she was ready to beat the truth out of him, brought him back to his current reality.

The truths were hers. As were the choices.

"I know this bartender… Rachel. She works at the place across the street from the marina and docks that I work out of…"

Her glance fell, and then when she looked at him again, was completely deadpan. "You want to go on a date?"

Then, before he was even fully on board with where she'd taken his lead in, her brow raised, and she said, "Oh, you want to bring her here. And I'm…you need me to go." Turning, Kacey moved toward her room.

"Kacey."

Just the one word. Filled with so much…dread, worry, anticipation, energy, and far too much caring.

He didn't know how much got through to her, but she

turned back, her gaze filled with emotions he couldn't decipher, as she just stood there.

"She's a…friend…but not like you're thinking. There's nothing—and never has been—anything romantic between us. She's had a few troubles at the bar. I step up when I can. That sort of thing." All true. Just nothing to do with her work as a bartender. "Anyway, today after work, I stopped in. I asked her if she'd seen or heard of three guys in a rowboat the night of the storm. I told her I knew a woman who was looking for them because they knew her brother. She hadn't heard anything, but said she'd keep her eyes and ears open…"

Kacey sank into her chair, mouth open, eyes wide as she kept her gaze on him.

"Rachel thinks they're at the bar right now," he told her. "Playing pool. She lives in the apartment upstairs. She offered to let you in—there's a vent in her floor above the poolroom. You'd be able to hear them talking…"

She hadn't seen any of them well enough to give any kind of usable description, but she'd heard them talking. It was a long shot.

One that had earned him a raised brow, but no questions, from Rachel when he'd briefly mentioned the situation that afternoon.

"And she doesn't think that's odd?"

"She works in a bar that serves all kinds of people," he told her, a truth, but not the full one where she was a hotshot detective who could generally get anyone to tell her anything. "She's heard it all. And stays alive with her live and let live motto. People tell her things. She keeps them to herself." All Rachel. Not Detective Bonita Donaldson who used her training to keep herself safe.

Kacey stood. "Then why are we sitting here? Let's get over there before these guys take off…"

Walking straight into a building that possibly held her captors and not even a second's hesitation? Or hint of fear in her eyes?

What was he walking into?

"Maybe you should put on a T-shirt, to hide the gun in your waistband," he said to her, nodding to the 9mm that was still on the counter where he'd left it earlier. Without waiting for a response, he went to get one of his shirts, tossed it to her, as, gun in hand, she was heading for the door.

Giving him serious pause. "Kacey."

Stopping at the door, she glanced at him over her shoulder. "You're walking straight into potential danger here. If these guys really are the ones who took you, and possibly the ones arguing with your brother, they want you dead. You get that, right?"

She shivered, and he figured he could have been a little less blunt with his words.

Wrapping her arms around herself she gave him what seemed like a really long look. A real look. It was as though she'd given him access to her deepest places—letting him see the fear, the desperation, that was driving her determination. "I get it," she told him. "I also get that, though I'm alive, these men, and whoever else might be involved in whatever Kyle got mixed up in, have already taken my life. I can't go anywhere, do anything, without fear of death. I've been here two days and am no closer to knowing anything, other than that the knife I turned in had human blood on it. I can't stay here forever, Devon. I walked into this danger of my own accord—to protect my family—and if any of us are going to have a chance to get our lives back, I have to finish what I unknowingly started by walking into that police station."

With that she turned, and walked out to his truck, opening the passenger door and climbing inside.

KACEY KNEW DEVON would follow her out. That he'd take her to his friend's apartment above the bar.

She hoped he didn't know how very much she was praying that he'd go with her upstairs, stay with her and then get her safely back to his place. If he didn't, if he just dropped her off at the apartment and went on his way, she wouldn't blame him.

He hadn't signed up for life-and-death drama. He was just a Good Samaritan who'd saved a drowning woman. One who carried a gun. And had a spare for her.

And a stash of burner phones, too, apparently.

One who was as paranoid—so as watchful and careful—as she'd become.

They made a good team.

"As soon as we're off my property, you're going to need to get down. With that missing person's report out, I'll be stopped if you're recognized."

Right. In the adrenaline-induced hurry of the moment, she hadn't thought of that. His paranoia was much more honed than hers. He'd been at it longer. Had had more time to acclimate.

"The staircase up to Rachel's apartment is enclosed, with a locking door at the bottom. I'll text her when we get close and she'll see that the door gets unlocked. I can pull up right to the door, will open my door, get out, open hers and you'll climb over my seat, stay below the truck door window and get inside. I'll follow you up."

And anyone looking would only see a male friend of Rachel's heading up to her place.

The plan was good. As failproof as one could possibly be.

And most of all, it meant that Devon would be with her.

It was that information, not thoughts of her family, that gave Kacey the most strength of all.

Chapter Fourteen

There were so many things that could go wrong. Kacey being seen and stopped by the police for one. News getting out that she was alive before they knew who wanted her dead.

And he was taking chances on the possibility that the three men playing pool in the bar were actually Kacey's kidnappers.

The only thing he felt good about as he drove toward the bar at the marina was that he'd get a good look at Rachel's date, Belen Alexopolous. She should be sitting with her drug-dealing companion, enjoying an after-dinner cocktail. Hopefully Devon would be present when the date ended to see his partner safely make it to her apartment.

The Phoenix detective didn't need Devon's protection—any more than he needed hers. He felt better being able to offer it just the same.

And wished he felt half as confident that Kacey was going to get out of her current circumstance unharmed.

If the three men in the bar were indeed her captors, he was driving her into a hub of danger that could get her killed.

And giving her the chance to find the beginning of the answers that were her only way back to her life.

Glancing at the woman sitting with her knees up to her chest, her back to the passenger door of the truck, he had to tamp down the need to turn around and get her back to his place.

"After the bar closes, Rachel can get us surveillance tape of the three men," he said, figuring Kacey had to be fighting her own set of nerves, and feeling compelled to help. Forcing himself to stay on track. He wasn't involved in some kind of heroic rescue mission. "And remember, it's only legal for you to shoot at someone if they're an imminent threat to your life."

"Self-defense," she said. "I know. I own a small pistol. I don't like it in my home, but my mom insisted on it when I moved into my own place. She might be a widow with RA, but she's my dad's partner through and through."

The words, the glimpse she gave him into her personal life, touched him far more than the situation warranted.

Not completely trusting Devon in that moment, Tommy Grainger took note. Was he in too deep? Losing objectivity?

He didn't trust Kacey, either. He wasn't being blinded by the woman. He was just human—a guy who felt a bit drawn to a woman he'd met.

Didn't mean he couldn't—or wouldn't—do his job.

The thought brought him full circle back to his father. Hilton Grainger had been drawn to a woman he'd met on the job, too. He'd given in to the temptation to be unfaithful to his wife. That did not mean that he'd grown lax on the job, too.

Devon knew a few great law enforcement officers who'd had affairs. Didn't make them stellar husbands, but it didn't make them crooked cops, either. And since Tommy had already long since determined that he didn't trust himself to be a faithful husband—and thereby would never again be married—he had no reason to give the matter any more thought.

If anything, his growing attraction for a woman he met on the job served to strengthen the decision he'd already made for his life.

Confident that he was on track and ready, Devon texted Rachel that they were almost there, and a couple of minutes later, pulled up close to the door leading to Rachel's apartment. Reminding himself that if things went awry, he had a top-rated detective in the room with the three men—one who was armed and trained to take down the worst kind of criminals—he shut the truck door as soon as Kacey was in the stairwell, following her up to the apartment.

She paused at the top of the stairs, standing back to let him enter the living area in front of her, an action he was hugely fond of. Gun in hand, he led her through to the kitchen vent. "The air-conditioning in here travels through a vent in the poolroom," he said softly. "Rachel discovered soon after moving in that if she didn't keep some kind of soft music, or the TV on, she could hear conversations down there."

Kacey gave him a long, assessing glance. He guessed that the source of her curiosity was his relationship with Rachel, but quickly dismissed the thought. He had no relationship with Rachel—not in the man-woman sense, and he'd already told Kacey that. He didn't like deceiving Kacey about how he knew the other woman.

And threw that thought out, too. He had absolutely no reason to feel guilty about the lies he told regarding his association with the bartending detective. He was doing his job.

On his way to saving the lives of countless young people—and others—who were going to die of overdoses if he didn't get the lethal cocktail off the streets.

A minute or two after they'd entered the kitchen, he heard

Rachel's voice, asking the men seated in the corner of the poolroom if they'd seen anyone coming out of the restroom with a red purse.

He watched Kacey as at least two nos sounded, pretty much simultaneously. She didn't react, but then, he wasn't sure he'd have been able to pick out any distinguishing sounds from the double answer.

"I'm sure I left it in there," Rachel's voice continued, sounding a bit confused—and somewhat needy. "I've had a bit to drink, but I know I took it in with me about an hour ago. I'm on a first date…" Devon was impressed with the sexy little worried tone in her voice. Knowing how completely out of character it was for the detective in her real persona.

Kacey, with her serious gaze focused intently on the vent, seemed to be buying it. He felt a twinge, not telling her that the woman she was listening to was the same one whose apartment she was currently inhabiting, but shoved it aside. Focused. "And I went in specifically to finish my makeup. I didn't need it again until just now, when I noticed it was missing…"

"We weren't here an hour ago," one man said, his tone all male, wanting to come to the aid of a helpless woman. Rachel had played the scene exactly right.

Impressively on target. And Devon felt not even an ounce of attraction for the slender, dark-haired detective.

"But I did see a couple of women head back to the restroom since we arrived," another offered. Both sounding like regular guys. Reasonably educated. Somewhat amused, but not overly disrespectful.

Nothing notably thug-like, threatening or murderous about them.

"One was a redhead, slender, about your height," a third voice confirmed.

Kacey's gasp hit him as hard as the fingers suddenly clutching his arm. She didn't say a word, just stared at the vent, completely white, as though planning to listen to whatever came next.

But he'd heard enough.

Texting his partner, knowing that the double vibration she'd programmed into her phone would alert her, he grabbed Kacey's hand, peeled it off his arm, and pulled her toward the door. Getting her out of there had become his prime objective.

She met his gaze at the door. He saw the fear there. And the anger, too. Motioned toward the stairs. She nodded.

She was with him.

They had no time to step softly. He couldn't risk the sound of two sets of feet heading down the stairs, or voices either. Grabbing her up against his chest, Devon jogged down to the truck.

READY WHEN DEVON dropped her on her feet at the bottom of the stairs, Kacey waited long enough for him to get his truck door open, and then dove inside, sliding across the floor hump and onto the passenger side while he was climbing into the driver's seat. As panicked as she felt, as badly as she needed to know who those three men in the bar were, she was not going to put Devon Miller any further at risk.

Or his bartender friend, either.

She didn't relish facing death at their hands again, either.

"It's hard," she said as soon as Devon had started the truck and pulled away from the building. "Just letting them go. I feel like we should call the police. But…"

She didn't like the idea. At all.

"But what?"

"I know we aren't in Bullhead City, but if one of those

guys has connections with the Bullhead police, all it would take was a phone call down here to local police and..."

Paranoia had her in its grip. She knew it. Couldn't think straight.

Finding that knife, having her twin refuse to confide in her, turning him in, being kidnapped and left for dead... she couldn't expect herself to process anything normally.

Nothing about life was normal anymore.

"And with Kyle having listed me as a missing person... we call the police, I'm found." With all that entailed.

"You said your friend could get you surveillance tapes from the bar? Pictures of the guys? Maybe we take a look at them, first," she said, focusing on the immediate moment. "Assuming I'm still welcome to stay with you."

"You want to see if you recognize any of the three." His words were more statement than question. So she didn't answer him.

He still didn't trust her.

The knowledge shouldn't hurt. At least not nearly as badly as it did. What Devon Miller thought of her didn't matter.

She didn't need him to like her.

She just needed him to not get hurt because of her.

"The voice you recognized, was it from the night of the argument, or the kidnapping?"

He was watching his rearview mirror as he spoke, so even though she was facing him, focusing on him to give her strength, she couldn't see his expression.

He'd been watching the mirrors religiously since they'd left the bar.

"The kidnapping," she said, looking straight at him. "He was the one directly behind me, telling me to walk normally. And then to get in the van. I also heard him after I was in the boat. He told someone to double-check the anchor."

"He was the one giving orders, then?"

"I don't remember hearing any orders. Mostly, everything happened in total silence. Like they all just knew what they were doing."

"And the other two?" He glanced briefly in her direction, though, in the darkness, she had no way of knowing if he could see her. The lights in the dash kept him visible to her.

"I didn't recognize the voices, but, as I said, there was very little talking."

He seemed as though he was going to say more, but closed his mouth, tight-lipped, and sped up. A few seconds later, he slowed down.

And then made a quick turn.

"What's going on?" She felt powerless again, huddled on the floor, unable to see outside. Reminding her of the night before in the crawl space beneath his room.

He didn't respond. Just continued to drive. And watch his mirrors.

It was as though she wasn't there.

Were they being followed? Had someone been on their tail since they left the bar?

If that was the case, why hadn't he said so?

A few more turns happened in quick succession, throwing her against the seat, and then in the next second, as she flung back, she hit her head on the glove box.

Fear engulfed her, taking her air. Making rational thought seemingly impossible. Had she been right in the beginning, to mistrust her rescuer?

Was Devon on her side?

Or not?

Was he associated with the men who'd taken her? For all she knew he could be one of them. Maybe they'd seen her slide overboard in the storm and he'd been sent downstream to see that she didn't make it to freedom.

And the evening's activities…the friend Rachel…the apartment…had all been a setup to see if she could identify her kidnappers?

Or at least one of them?

For all she knew the other two male voices in the bar could have been anyone off the street—taking part in superfluous conversation.

For all she knew, there was no Rachel, bartender friend. The apartment she'd just vacated could belong to the man whose voice she'd just clearly recognized.

And Devon could be taking her to her death.

Shaking, her hand on her gun, she thought about her chances of survival if she shot the driver of the vehicle in which she was traveling.

And knew they didn't matter at all. Because there was no way she could shoot Devon. The man had been good to her. He'd taken her to call Kyle.

Had tended to her ankles when he clearly didn't have to do so. If he wanted her dead, he could have simply let infection fester in her cuts.

He'd given her a gun.

He'd snatched her away from that bar more quickly than she'd have believed possible. Before anyone could have known that she'd recognized one of the voices.

He'd told her about his father, though that could have been a lie.

"You up for a hike?" he asked then, his voice dropping like a bomb into the silence, making her jump.

"Why?"

"We were being followed. I've lost them for now, but we're not taking any chances. Up ahead is a steep ravine. Below it is one of the deepest holes in the river that I know. The truck's going over the cliff. If the fates are with us, it'll sink into the river, never to be seen again. We're about ten miles from my property. You think you can make it?"

To stay alive? "Absolutely."

"Get up and get a good grip on the door handle. When I say now, open the door and jump out."

She climbed into the seat. Got ready to let herself out.

He could be leading her to her own death. Making it look like a suicide.

The thought occurred. Struck terror within her.

He was driving along a road that bordered the river. Looking out his window, all she saw was eerie darkness, with occasional glints of light far in the distance. The opposite shore.

California side.

Visions of her dad flashed before her eyes. Her mom. Lizzie. Kyle…

Brother, what have you done?

The truck swerved sharply and so did she, bumping her head on the window. They'd slowed down drastically. Only darkness lay ahead.

"Now!" Devon yelled out.

She pulled, jumped out the opened door, hit the ground and rolled, realizing, too late, that Devon hadn't pulled when she had.

He'd still been sitting there, watching her.

Lying in a huddle, she cringed at the sound of metal hitting rock, branches breaking, an avalanche so loud she couldn't hear anything else, thought she might go deaf from the sound.

Until she did. Her head filled with nothing but eerie silence.

And all she could think of was Devon Miller, going down with his truck, as she laid there on the hard desert ground and sobbed.

Chapter Fifteen

Devon heard the crash. Didn't give a whit about it, or his truck as he raced to find Kacey and get them the hell out of there.

He'd seen her land just before he'd taken his own dive for the ground. Was certain he'd seen the hump of her body on the ground a distance across from him while the truck made its stupendously loud descent into the Colorado.

But when he started running toward her even before fully standing upright, he couldn't get his bearings. Circling, even as he continued jogging, he didn't see her lying anywhere. She'd been there. He was certain of it.

She couldn't have just vanished.

Running full speed, he covered the ground where she'd jumped from the vehicle. She'd landed. Rolled. He'd made certain...

With a frantic glance toward the cliff, as though to be certain that she hadn't been in the truck when it went over, he ran in that direction. If she'd gone over...

Panting, he stopped just short of going over himself. Glanced down.

And saw movement.

Downward movement.

Just yards away from him.

Kacey was descending the ravine?

Purposefully?

Shaking his head, he stood there for a second, as though not sure he could believe what he was seeing.

She was trying to get away from him?

Made no sense.

She'd definitely been tied up. Had clearly recognized the voice of one of the men at the bar. And if she hadn't, why lie to him about it?

For that matter, why cooperate with him to get in his truck if she…

He was over the side of the cliff and following her before the thought finished.

She had to have heard him, but she didn't turn around. Rather, she sped up. So he did as well. Knew, no matter how athletic she was, he could catch her. Put his mind to getting it done as quickly as possible, sliding on the side of his bare leg in the dirt to that end, gun in hand in case she turned to shoot him. Was almost upon her when he said, "Kacey."

The sound had a peculiar effect on her. She froze. Just stood there. Both hands—gunless—at her sides.

"Kacey?" he said again, quickly holstering his own gun before taking a small step toward her.

Had she been knocked out? Lost her memory?

Frowning, engulfed with concern, he stood still, knowing he had to proceed with caution.

She turned then, close enough to him that he could see the tears on her face.

"Kacey?" he asked, taking a few quick steps to reach her, hold her by the shoulders and gaze into those wet eyes. "Are you hurt?"

Shaking her head, she stared at him. "I…thought you'd gone over with the truck…"

And she'd…

She was going after him?

"If you were trapped... I had time to get to you... I'm the strongest swimmer I know...and..."

The way she was looking at him, so wide-eyed and sincere, the emotion, tears, words, the moment... Devon didn't seem to be able to think.

He could only do.

And so he did.

Pulling her up against his chest, he held on tight, lowered his lips and mingled his life breath with hers as he kissed her with every ounce of his being.

KACEY HELD ON. Floated. Flew to heaven and stayed firmly on earth, as she lost herself in the taste, the male scent, the strength and warmth of Devon Miller.

She barely knew the man. He had secrets. He didn't even trust her.

And yet she was consumed by a need to be as close to him as humanly possible, for as long as the night would leave them alone.

She thought he'd...

A huge rumble of metal and rock shocked her into pulling her head up for air. Devon's arms held her; she'd wrapped hers around him and didn't pull them away as she glanced downward.

Watched as the large body of white metal slid into blackness.

"We have to go," Devon said then, dropping his arms as he stepped away from her body, but grabbing hold of her hand. "We've got to get you back to my property before dawn."

He said nothing of the kiss. And as soon as they were on level ground, he dropped her hand, too.

Kacey pretended to herself that she was relieved. That

she wanted it that way. For a second or two, anyway. One of the lessons both of her parents had taught her growing up, and that life had taught her even better, was to always be honest with herself.

And in all honesty, she wanted Devon's arms around her again. She wanted his body naked, holding hers. In hers.

Thoughts of having sex with her recluse rescuer kept her adrenaline pumping, and the fear at bay, as they started out. "I can do a fifteen-minute mile," she told him. Wanting him to know that while she'd pretty much fallen apart after the truck went over the cliff, she had the strength to take on whatever lay ahead.

Sex with him, or another tangle with death.

"Stay close," Devon's response came quietly. "At night like this, we've got wildlife to contend with as much as anything else."

She'd known that. Wasn't going to panic over it. "Most shy away from humans," she said aloud, something he'd know. Energized by the connection with him. "And we have guns."

Something else he clearly knew.

Making her contribution little more than jabber, she figured.

"You're one of a kind, you know that?" He turned his head, giving her a glance, and their lips were almost close enough to kiss again. If they both leaned in far enough.

Neither did. She caught a glimpse of the moonlight's glint in his eyes and shot her attention straight forward again. "Why do you say that?"

She'd rather talk than not.

And would much rather the conversation be about something other than danger and death. They had to talk about who'd followed them. At the moment, she needed her emotional strength for all of the steps immediately in front of her.

He climbed up a hill of rocks. "No matter the trial, the constant threat, you seem to focus on whatever little positive might be there."

Right beside him in the rocks, she tried to shrug off the warmth that flooded her at his words. Suspected she'd only managed to shrug. "Growing up with a father in Special Forces who was always leaving to fly off into danger, I learned that the best way to be happy and get good grades until he came back was to think about how strong he was, how well trained. And remember that he was surrounded by people who were equally qualified. I couldn't make him stay home. But I could control my own head. Replace thoughts of fear with knowledge of the strengths I had around me to combat the bad stuff." She was definitely rambling, but didn't much care. Whether he was taking in her words, or not, she needed their reminder.

"I can relate to that," Devon said, surprising her. "My father's work with the high-powered rich and famous in Las Vegas had his associating with some scary guys. But at least he came home every night."

Until he didn't, based on what he'd told her earlier.

As hers hadn't.

She'd tried to find anything on the internet that talked about a Mr. Miller, associated with the former mayor of Las Vegas and who'd died in a car accident, or had been suspected of anything ten years before, but she'd found nothing. "Did you have siblings?" she asked him.

"No."

"I'm lucky that I had Kyle. All through school, it was like I was never really alone."

Mention of her brother made her stomach clench, so she quickly turned her thoughts back to Devon. "Did you play sports in school?"

"Nope." She should be put off by his one-word responses. Should stop asking questions.

The dark of the night, their solitary trek through miles of desert that held unseen dangers, drove her on anyway.

"Have you always liked to raft and kayak?"

"Yes."

"Where did you learn to cook?" She threw out the next question almost as a challenge to get him to give at least two words in response.

"My parents," he said. And then added, "And the internet."

Okay, so innocuous was the way it would go. "What's your favorite food?" she asked next.

Discovered that they both shared an affinity for Asian and Italian dishes, liked to try new things and disliked the same greens. Spinach and Brussels sprouts.

He hadn't been to a movie theater in years. He didn't watch much television but occasionally streamed old sitcoms. Or Westerns—the gunslinging kind.

It was kind of like a first date.

A surreal one. Encased in constant danger. Where the guy didn't know he was on it.

And he got a text right in the middle of it. Kacey stopped talking as soon as he pulled out his phone—figuring that since it was after eleven, and they'd left her apartment so abruptly, that the communication was from Rachel whatever-her-last-name-was.

Knowing full well she had absolutely no ownership of feelings for Devon Miller, rights to his time, or even a place in her real life for the lottery-winning rafter, she pushed against the twinge of jealousy she felt when he read from his phone, and then dialed.

Jealousy? Seriously? She'd never been jealous over a man she'd dated.

And she wasn't even dating Devon.

Had to be the trauma. Her near death. Having to stay out of sight. Kyle's betrayal.

Just like the paranoia she'd been experiencing. Some kind of stress syndrome taking effect. If she didn't get over it when she returned home, she'd get some therapy...

Devon's conversation consisted of one-word responses. Kacey was hit by another ridiculous thought as they walked, arms bumping into each other on occasion. The Rachel woman, if it was her, didn't elicit any more of a response than Kacey had. No reason to take it personally, then.

"The bar doesn't close until two," he said as he hung up the phone, confirming her suspicion that he'd been talking to the other woman. "Rachel'll be sending footage over shortly after that."

If their journey didn't take any unexpected detours, or experience delays, they'd be back at the cabin before then.

And there'd been far more to the conversation than that. He'd given several "okays" in response to whatever the bartender had told him.

If it had been about the three men in the bar, she deserved to know what had been said. Had to know.

She just wasn't sure enough that she wanted to hear the news out in the dark with at least a couple of miles to go before they were safely on Devon's land, to ask for it.

And didn't feel like engaging in any more first-date banter, either.

At least one of the men who'd kidnapped her was close by. Drinking in a bar as though planning to hang around.

For all she knew he was from the area.

Maybe—most likely—somehow connected to whoever had followed them?

And there she was walking through the desert as though she'd planned the outing as some form of entertainment.

"The three men in the bar said they're vacationing in the area. Hoping to catch some largemouth bass in particular." Devon spoke as though relaying the plot of a boring television show. "They said they lost a crate of supplies off their boat during the storm. Asked Rachel if she'd heard of anyone finding it."

Kacey's blood ran cold. "A case of supplies?" she asked, affronted. "You think they meant me? That I'm their case of supplies?"

"I have no idea." Devon didn't miss a step, didn't even glance at her as she stumbled, caught herself, and kept up with him.

"Vacationing?" she said then, knowing she had to quit fantasizing and take her troubles head-on. "They aren't from the area, then."

"If you believe them."

A generic you? Or was he being personal again? Doubting her, as well as the men in the bar from whom he'd just saved her? To the point of sinking his own, relatively new, clearly expensive truck.

He'd done that for her.

Or rather, for himself, because of her.

"Do you believe them?" she asked then, having no patience or time for useless worries about what her host thought of her.

"I don't know."

Yeah, she didn't know, either. Far too much.

"You think they're hanging around until my body turns up, so they know for sure I'm dead?"

"Or maybe long enough to ensure that it's not going to turn up." He looked at her, then. "If you drowned, a century could pass without any body being found."

"With the missing person's report, they could be waiting to see what sightings the public might turn in on you," Devon continued with a glance in her direction.

She met his gaze.

And wished he'd stuck with his one-word replies. They'd been much easier to hike with.

"Thanks to you, I haven't been..." Her words cut off as Devon's arm flew out in front of her, stopping her forward progress. He gave one short, succinct nod in front of them slightly to their right.

And she saw what he'd seen.

A family of javelina—at least eight of them, were staring right at them. The forty-pound pig-looking mammals weren't necessarily dangerous to humans—but could be lethal if they attacked. If they felt threatened. By the stance of the squadron facing them, she and Devon were in trouble. During the hot season the animals were mostly nocturnal, looking for food, and out in the desert like they were, far from civilization, she and Devon would clearly be considered intruders.

She started to back away, saw Devon take a step back as well. She heard the "woof" sound only a second before the entire squadron started to charge right at them.

"Run!" Devon called, grabbing her hand and taking off the way they'd come, only to face another eight or so of the beastly mammals. "Toward the water," he said then and she was right with him, step for step, as they headed for the river. The landscape had changed as they hiked. The shore was just yards away down a slight incline and Kacey ran like she'd never run in her life, diving into the cold river just one beat ahead of Devon.

Kicking off her tennis shoes, she treaded water, making certain that he came up close by—watching for any sign that the potentially dangerous animals weren't following them into the water. She saw the squadron stop several seconds before she could pick out Devon's head above water and made it to him in record time. "Lose your shoes," she shouted to be heard above the current.

"Already done."

"How far can you swim?" she asked him, taking charge, as though she owned the water.

"As far as I need to," he told her, treading water beside her in the way-over-her-head water. "I'm a certified life-guard. Part of the qualification to be a guide."

Without a word, she took off for the roughly two-mile swim, tired, feeling the sting of the water against her soaked bandages, and comforted to be in familiar surroundings, too. Thankfully they'd been upriver from Devon's place and a large part of the trip consisted of staying afloat to ride the river, while guarding against any sudden thrusts that might send them up against rocks or crashing into the mountainside.

In the dark, the feat was exhausting. Animals came down to the river to drink. Could be a bobcat, or worse, on the shore. She'd swum at night, many times, but only in the area whose shoreline she knew as well as her own backyard.

With rocks and limbs looming, looking alive, she shook as she reached and pulled, kicking with the natural rhythm that generally helped to keep her calm in the water.

Devon stayed right beside her. Matching her steady stroke for steady stroke. And when he glanced her way, his expression serious, she knew that she'd keep pulling for as long as it took if it meant that they lived to get out of that water together.

Chapter Sixteen

His phone was waterproof. Her burner wasn't. He didn't give a rat's ass about that. He had several more of those in the box in the shed outside his cabin.

Scanning the shore as he swam, Devon pulled stronger, kicked harder as he recognized the riverbank he owned.

He climbed out, ignoring the scrapes to his bare lower legs as he turned to give her a hand up only to see her standing a foot or so downriver from him.

Pulling some bark, leaves and desert vine from the immediate vicinity, he fashioned footwear for her first, using the vine to tie the leaf-covered bark to her feet, and then repeated the process for himself. Dripping wet, their feet were bound to slide some, the hike wouldn't be comfortable. "This isn't going to be pretty, easy or all that effective, but it should help prevent either of us getting punctured by cactus needles," he told her.

"Thank you." Her response was short. To the point. She hadn't looked him in the eye since they'd reached land.

Or complained about the trek ahead.

She didn't seem out of breath. Just quiet. He liked it better when she was talking.

At least then he had a shot at knowing what she was thinking.

He couldn't look at her without thinking about the kiss

he'd planted on her. After he'd told her she had nothing to fear from him on that score.

He'd never done anything so asinine in his life.

And...had she liked it? Anywhere near as much as he had?

The hot Arizona night air dried his clothes, took away the chill, and fed his physical hunger to do more than just kiss Kacey Ashland.

He couldn't touch her sexually again.

Had he offended her? Scared her off?

Didn't seem so.

But then, if she was using him, she'd take a kiss in stride until she no longer needed him.

Hadn't felt like she'd just been going through the motions.

More like spontaneous combustion on both their parts.

Maybe just the circumstances. Life and death could do that to you.

Who wouldn't want to go out kissing a beautiful woman? Or celebrate not having died in the same way?

Rachel had let him know during their brief phone conversation that Belen had left the bar shortly after Devon and Kacey had. He'd told Rachel he had a drive ahead of him but asked the bartender for a date later in the week.

She planned to ask for a bigger score during that rendezvous.

She'd also heard from the city lab in Phoenix. The drugs she'd scored and sent to them were the same lethal recipe as the ones on their radar.

Finally, they had the proof that they were on a solid path.

He had to hold on. Couldn't let his compulsion to keep Kacey close until she was safe screw up the bust of a lifetime.

Period.

Too many lives were at stake.

And that kiss…had he imagined how different it had been from anything else he'd ever experienced?

A product of the circumstances, he reminded himself. Several times, as they stepped carefully, having to half drag their makeshift shoes, and stop to pull up new vines and retie them, too.

The trek back to the cabin took twice the time it would have during the day with real shoes on their feet. With his surveillance screens up on his phone, Devon could diminish the constant worry of danger just around the corner, could see where wildlife was feeding and avoid the areas. And with a backtrack, he was assured that his property hadn't been breached in their absence.

He shared the news with Kacey.

She nodded.

Kept pace beside him.

And he could no longer hold concerning thoughts at bay in the name of staying alive. "It seems pretty clear, since you're certain that the voice you heard tonight was one of your kidnappers, and then my vehicle is followed, that they know I'm associated with you."

"Unless someone saw me during the split second I climbed from the floor into the doorway."

There was a chance. A minute one. But only if someone had been close by. Watching.

The outside of the bar, maybe? Keeping a lookout while the three kidnappers were inside? Or at least one of them was?

Another option, one Rachel had already mentioned during her call to him in the desert, was that Rachel was being watched by Belen's people. Had she been made?

Belen could have had someone outside the bar, a witness to Devon's visit to Rachel's apartment. A brief stop without even heading into the bar to see her. Something that had looked suspiciously like a drop-off or pickup? That had maybe put him on their radar, too?

"I'm in the area all the time." He told Kacey what was pertinent to her. "Today, for hours. And I haven't been followed. But the night you identify the voice of a man inside the bar as one of your kidnappers, I'm suddenly tracked?"

The theory held weight. A lot of it.

"You think one of the three men who took me saw you rescue me?"

It had been a theory all along. "Seems to make sense, don't you think?"

Kacey didn't answer. She didn't speak again until they were only about five minutes out. "What time is it?" She'd looked at her ruined phone once, shortly after they'd exited the river, and then shoved it in her pants pocket.

"Few minutes before two."

She'd ridden on the floor of the truck, heard her abductor, jumped out of a moving vehicle, hiked, swam and hiked some more. Her feet had to be uncomfortable at the very least. Her ankles with their dirty sagging bandages sore as hell. All after a full day of fighting for her life in one way or another.

And he hadn't heard a single word of complaint out of her.

He couldn't help noticing. Admiring her fortitude. And remembering what she'd said about dealing with her father's danger-filled absences growing up.

Those words, it had been like she'd been inside him, seeing his own thoughts growing up. Thoughts that had led him to keep his feet firmly in every one of his father's footsteps.

Until the man had strayed from their family.

One weekend.

That had changed everything.

Like his couple of days with Kacey seemed to be doing.

Shaking his head as he unlocked the cabin, he held the

door for her to enter before him. He noticed her backside, and instantly raised his gaze to the straightness of her back.

The solidness of her shoulders.

And then down to those bandages.

He was in the throes of trying to help find out who wanted her dead and why. Once that was done, like any other case, he'd walk away.

And anything he might be experiencing where she was concerned would fade with the memories that would one day just be vague images of a side case in his past.

Conclusion firmly reached, while Kacey shut herself in the bathroom, he tapped his phone to log into the specially encrypted site that would allow him to view Rachel's video, or stills, at the highest quality possible.

"It's here," he said as his houseguest reappeared a short minute later, still in the same river, desert and sweat-covered T-shirt and new clothes she'd had on since he'd returned from work.

She stood close to him, her breast pressing up against the back of his arm, as she leaned down to look at the screen he held.

The image was a little grainy. Black and white only. Not bad for surveillance tape. He maximized the size, scrolled in to pinpoint faces.

Looking at men who seemed to be just what they'd sounded like they were—regular guys, family men, longtime decent job holders, out for a fishing vacation. In shorts and short-sleeved shirts and tennis shoes, they appeared about as harmless as a group of men could get.

"Do you recognize any of them as someone you might have seen before? Someone Kyle knew, maybe?" he asked, not moving lest his body start to show physical reaction to Kacey's closeness. He just needed a few minutes, a few cold showers maybe, to let the memory of her mouth hungry on his fade some.

"No."

And then, "Can I have the phone a second?"

He pulled it back, quickly pushed to download the still images to his phone. Opened the gallery that usually only held still images of animals on his property, and then the files he'd just downloaded, and handed the device to her.

She clicked, scrolled and gasped. Was visibly shaking as she enlarged some more. "Look at those shoes, Devon," she said, handing him a screen with nothing but a pair of oddly striped tennis shoes visible.

"Those are the shoes I saw. Maybe not the same exact pair, since I can't verify the color, but ones just like them. The stripe was lime green."

Every sense in his body sharpened. Went straight to work. "What about the other pairs? You said you saw two pairs."

"The others were dirty white. Nothing I can remember distinguishable about them. Either of the two other pairs I see here could be them. Or not..."

With a nod, he sent off a quick text to Rachel.

Offered Kacey the shower first, while he awaited a response.

And was waiting for her, on edge, feeling more emotionally torn than he should be, when she returned to the kitchen fifteen minutes later, dressed in his sweats again and the original T-shirt he'd given her. "I washed them this after..." she started in, but when she glanced at his face, stopped midsentence. "What?"

"The stripes were lime green."

LIME-GREEN STRIPES DIDN'T mean the shoes were the same. Made by a popular brand, and closely copied by others, there were likely plenty of them floating around. But she knew the voice. Even if the shoes didn't belong to one of her kidnappers, that voice had.

Meeting his gaze head-on she said, "Can you ask Rachel which man made the comment about the redhead? Was the voice I recognized the man wearing the striped shoes? If not, we can pretty well assume that at least two of the three who kidnapped me were together in that bar tonight."

She wasn't going to hide from the truth. To the contrary, she had to find it. There was no other way to get her life back.

"Already done," he told her. "The voice you recognized came from the corner stool." He held out his phone, showing her the clearest image of the three another time. Gave her time to look at the face of the man whose voice she'd recognized. And to notice that he was not the man wearing the striped tennis shoes.

At least two of her kidnappers had been in the marina bar that night. "They couldn't have been the ones following us, though, right? Rachel would have known if they left the bar when we did."

"They left about ten minutes after we did."

"How soon did you know we were being followed?"

"Less than a minute after I pulled away."

She'd seen him watching his mirrors. But he hadn't mentioned anything...

Because he still didn't trust her? Had been trying to spare her? "In the future, if you're aware of imminent danger, can I please be privy to the information from the onset?" She cringed as she heard her words. As though she was taking for granted that they would be continuing to fight the current battle together.

"I sent the bar footage to Sierra's Web to see if they can get identities on any of the three men. And I gave them as much of a description as I could of the dark truck that was following us when we left the bar. Since Arizona doesn't require front license plates, and his headlights and the darkness pretty much blinded me to any identifiers, there's very little to go on there." He hadn't given her any agreement that he'd abide by her request, but he'd basically just done as she'd asked.

She knew that, as a lottery winner, he had the money to spend with the expert firm and was spending it on his own behalf because he believed Kacey's kidnappers were after him, too. But Kacey's heart still gravitated in his direction again.

When he insisted on tending to her ankles even before he showered, she secretly gave up fighting her attraction to the man.

She might live. She might die. Reality was, she was in one hell of a mess with a strong possibility of being killed.

And all she could think about was getting the most out of life while she still had it.

At the moment, Devon Miller comprised every single part of that "most."

DEVON DIDN'T LIKE the idea of Rachel being watched. If his partner had been made, he would be too. Neither of them was ready to give up on the operation. As she'd said in their phone call, it was possible that, yes, she was being watched, but the eyes on her could be because she was a new active link in the chain the two of them were trying to pull apart.

And he knew Kacey's kidnappers could be the reason someone was watching for his truck outside a bar in which the abductors were sitting. If the men were powerful, as he was beginning to think, they'd have a lookout wherever they went.

Rachel didn't ask how he knew the woman who'd supposedly wanted to know about the men at the bar because they knew her brother. He'd told her, initially, it had nothing to do with their case, and she'd respected his privacy on the matter. If it got to the point where he had to read her in, he'd do so.

They weren't at that point yet. There were still too many unknowns, suppositions and unsubstantiated possibilities. They were in the gathering stage and one small tip of the wrong hand could blow either case in an instant.

Back at the cabin, immediate threat to their lives abated for the moment, touching Kacey's calves and feet as he tended to her ankles, he had to guard against a vastly different but equally powerful danger.

His desire to lose himself in Kacey Ashland was unlike anything he'd ever experienced. In the danger-induced passion grown from the fact that they'd both gone over the cliff after his truck, seeking each other, he'd kissed her. That had been his one and only warning. He couldn't let sexual need get such a hold on him that he made a horrific mistake. He'd promised her that she was safe from any advances from him.

He would rather die than be the man who broke that promise.

As he stripped down, got in the shower, he forced himself to focus fully on the case.

Turned the shower on cold. Stood there with the droplets stinging the front of his body, having little effect on the enlarged organ between his hips.

And heard a knock on the bathroom door.

Immediately shoving in the knob to stop the water, Devon grabbed a towel and his gun, and went to the door. "Kacey?"

Had someone found them? Penetrated his property in the ten minutes he'd been in the shower?

"Yes." She didn't sound frightened. Or coerced.

She sounded…inviting.

He opened the door a crack, ready to shoot if someone had a gun at her throat.

His jaw dropped, instead.

Chapter Seventeen

On fire like she'd never been in her life, Kacey stood naked except for the towel she'd wrapped around herself and smiled at her dripping-wet host.

"You said that you'd never proposition me, but you didn't say you were opposed to being invited." She said the words she'd been rehearsing for the past five minutes. And then, when he opened the door wide and stood there, openmouthed, staring at her, she just kept talking. "These last two days have taught me like never before that there is absolutely no guarantee in life. I've nearly lost mine a few times in the past two days and there I was spending precious moments standing in the kitchen alone when where I wanted to be was naked in here with you."

He hadn't moved. Hadn't said a word.

She saw the telling bulge in the front of the towel at his waist. Licked her lips without thinking about what she was doing and felt naughty in a totally invigorating way for having done so.

"The way you kissed me earlier made me think that you had some interest in seeing me naked." She glanced pointedly at the juncture between his thighs.

He hadn't moved. Wasn't speaking.

But the truth was a living being pulsating back and forth between them.

"It's your turn," she told him.

"You said you wanted to be naked in here with me." His voice sounded a bit thick. But completely coherent.

"That's right."

"Yet you're neither in here nor naked."

Desire swirled heavy and hard in her lower region as she lowered the towel. And continued to grow as she stood there, watching him devour her with his gaze.

She took a step forward, placing herself just inside the bathroom, inches from his wet towel, and leaned forward to lick drops of water off his shoulder.

Devon's gaze was on fire and yet he stepped back. "Kacey, our lives outside this cabin diverge. It's too complicated..."

"I might never have a life outside this cabin. I'm making choices based on the one moment I have, as I have it." She kissed his neck, smelling the soap she'd recently used, and shivered at the sexual chills that shot through her. "Life is too precious to waste and when you have a moment like this one..."

He did not back away again, and, completely serious, she looked up at him. "I don't know how many more times I can escape death," she told him. "But I do know that if and when I meet you in the afterlife, I want to be meeting up with a lover."

DEVON COULDN'T GET enough of her. Couldn't touch everywhere at once, or thoroughly enough. He couldn't see enough. And didn't want to waste another second standing in a puddle of water on the bathroom floor.

Letting his towel drop, he picked Kacey up and, avoiding the cameras he'd placed himself, walked with her to his bedroom, depositing her in the middle of the crumple of sheets covering his unmade king-size mattress, and slid down next to her. Half on top of her.

His room, like the bathroom, was motion detector only.

Neither of them spoke. He had no words to convey any of what he was feeling. The need. The tenderness he felt toward her. The sexual drive. All mingling together, feeding off her hungers, reaching for more than he'd ever had before.

"Now," she yelled out at one point, spreading her legs, and he touched her, had her crying out with pleasure in seconds, and then began to titillate her again, her nipples, her neck, behind her knees. His creativity came out of nowhere, driving him to touching in ways he'd never done, never even thought about doing. And every brush of his skin against her brought new heat borne of a liquid fire that consumed him.

When he finally entered her, barely holding himself together as she sat on top of him and slid the condom down his painfully swollen length, he heard his own cries from far off.

As though they belonged to someone else.

Until that moment—the moment Kacey had chosen to take her life in her own hands and share it with him—he'd been a completely silent lover.

If they ever did meet in the next life, she'd have that to put her on a pedestal above the rest.

She was the one who'd received everything he had to give.

KACEY AWOKE TO the sight of dawn's purplish haze showing through the row of small windows lining the top of the wall in Devon's bedroom. Lying still, she savored those first seconds, feeling cozy and happy in bed with the man who'd given her more life in a couple of hours than she'd ever imagined possible.

And then, hearing the coffeepot in the kitchen, turned

over to find herself staring at an empty mattress with an indentation in the sheets where his body had been.

That's when the next negative thought hit. She'd left her towel on the floor outside the bathroom door. Had nothing to cover her nakedness except the sheet wadded on Devon's bed—or clothes from his drawers.

While she didn't relish taking another's possessions without permission, she most definitely was not going to walk out into the kitchen completely nude.

She'd had her moment. Had lived it to the fullest. And was back to the job of staying alive.

Sitting up on her way to the dresser across from the bed, she saw the clothes just beyond her feet at the bottom of the bed. The sweats and T-shirt she'd put on after her shower the night before.

Donning them hastily, lest her host hear her moving around and came in before she was fully covered, Kacey felt a little let down as she entered the empty kitchen. And saw Devon outside the cabin, talking on his phone.

For all she knew, the man had an early morning river trip that he had to get to. She had no business having any other expectations of him—or of being disappointed that their night together included no intimacy on the morning after.

In shorts, a T-shirt with the logo of the recreational boating company he worked with and tennis shoes, he put a hand to his head, looked off in the direction of the river, and paced around a small portion of his desert land as he spoke.

She stood there, watching, waiting, because his conversation could very well have something to do with her life.

Was Rachel on the phone? Giving him more information about the three men in the bar the night before? Or maybe asking him about the woman he'd had up in her apartment?

Was it Sierra's Web, his firm of experts, giving him the identities of the three men who'd kidnapped her?

Shivering, she didn't make her necessary trip to the bathroom. Didn't even go for coffee. She just watched the man she'd shared her body with the night before, feeling as though he was a somewhat intimidating stranger in a world from which she had to escape.

The sensation dissipated some when he re-entered the cabin, seeing her there, meeting her gaze with a look that seemed to hold recognition of what had passed between them during the night.

"That was Rachel."

The bartender sure was up early for someone who'd been at the bar at two in the morning. And her catty thought had no place in Kacey's life. Just because Rachel had been up before her, had spoken to Devon before they'd had a chance for at least a tender smile to start their morning after, didn't give Kacey any cause to resent the woman.

Her thoughts came. They went. She waited silently for whatever her host had to tell her.

"The police woke her up half an hour ago. A man was found dead in a Colorado River lagoon not far from here."

Instantly fully focused, and feeling childish for her slow-moving brain that morning, Kacey asked, "Does she know him? Was it one of the kidnappers?"

"No," he told her. Holding up his phone. "She sent a photo."

Kacey looked and felt her chest tighten around the air sucked into her lungs. "Is that one of the men you ran off your property the day I got here?"

With a tilt of the head, a half shrug, Devon took his phone back. "Looks like it, doesn't it?"

"Do you know who he is?"

"Nope. Neither did Rachel."

"Why did the police go to her, then?"

"The man had the address of the bar written on a marina business card in his wallet."

"Something's going on at that bar, Devon." And it was beginning to look like his woman friend was involved in whatever it might be.

Involved with whoever wanted Kacey dead?

Throat closing in on her, Kacey felt herself go cold. Had Devon told the woman about Kacey? Including that she was staying with him?

Before she could get the question out, Devon was speaking again. "There's more. The man was found crammed into an empty packing crate."

According to Devon's bartender friend, Kacey's kidnappers had been looking for a crate. Filling with horror, she stared at the unrelenting man standing before her with no hint of tenderness on his face at all.

"The bottom of the crate had a piece of plastic wrap stuck to it," Devon said. "A partial label for a pornographic movie…"

Devon had said he'd sent the movie she'd found by overnight express to Sierra's Web in Phoenix.

"Have you heard back from your expert firm about the movie I found?" she asked then, growing more frightened, feeling more powerless, by the second.

He shook his head, then, watching her closely, asked, "Is there anything you want to tell me before I do?"

If she hadn't already been sinking back into hell, his question would have slapped her down there quickly. "You still think I have something to do with all of this?" She met his gaze fully, held on tight. "That because the kidnappers mention a missing crate of supplies right before a crate turns up with a dead man in it that had a partial movie label matching a movie I found means I'm somehow involved in it all?"

"I don't think it. Viewing all the current circumstances, I see it as a logical possibility."

He still didn't trust her.

And really, why should she think he would? Sex didn't magically create trust. Nor, apparently, had running for their lives together.

With a nod, she moved toward the bedroom he'd loaned her. Planning to get her stuff and…what? Head out?

Where could she go and stay hidden?

How would she get there?

And then what?

How was she going to find the truth that would allow her to put her life back together?

Show herself at the marina bar that night and take on her kidnappers alone—assuming they were there?

Call Kyle again and demand that he talk to her?

Her previous run-in with her abductors had nearly cost her her life. And Kyle had already refused to tell her anything. On two separate occasions.

"I need to get dressed," she said, realizing that putting on underwear and clothes that fit her, brushing her teeth and hair, using the restroom, were the activities that would serve her best in the moment, as she prepared to protect her life for another day.

WHERE WAS THE dead man's companion? The two had clearly been together the day Devon had chased them off his land.

Had one killed the other?

And the crate…he'd heard about a missing crate the night before, feasibly from Kacey's kidnappers who were missing one they said was filled with supplies for their fishing trip. And then a trespasser on his property suddenly showed up in one?

Pieces were oozing out like worms. Yet he had no clear indication of how they went together. Which pieces answered what questions.

Sitting at the table while Kacey showered, Devon used his stylus to draw a chart on his phone just to organize the information in his head. Three cases, in three different corners. Hilton Grainger's old case that Sierra's Web was investigating. Tommy Grainger's current undercover assignment with the Henderson police. And Devon's involvement with the kidnapping, near-murder and rescue of Kacey Ashland.

And then he listed anything he could think of that could be a part of any of the three. The men at his property were listed twice. Under Kacey's kidnapping since they appeared the day that he'd found her. And then she'd risked her life the next day to go chasing after a boat and came home with a pornographic movie. A case of which had been found in the crate housing one of the two trespassers.

As she'd pointed out, Kacey's kidnappers had mentioned a missing crate. Could be the same one. Or just something else for the unrelated corner.

But that movie, if there was a crate of them as the bottom of the dead man's crate would imply, then they also had to be added to his father's case, as the movies were likely illegal contraband on the river.

The trespassers ended up in that corner, too. The dead man had had the address of the bar in his pocket written on a marina business card. Which could implicate both Devon and Rachel.

He put those two men in the fourth corner as well—the one that had nothing whatsoever to do with anything he was investigating.

He had no idea why Kacey had been kidnapped, other than a knife bearing human blood. Wrote "knife" only in her corner.

Possible police misconduct went in Kacey's corner, too. Along with his father's.

His own corner contained Belen Alexopoulos. And the critical confirmation that the drugs the good-looking Greek man had sold Rachel were from the same source as those traveling across the country. Ironic how his own potentially dangerous undercover case seemed to be the only easy corner he had.

The random rowboat floating down the river? Shaking his head on that one, he entered it in Kacey's corner, as well as the one reserved for unrelated material. For all he knew, the thing could have been his trespassers' boat. Or, as he'd said earlier, a random boat knocked loose by the storm that floated downriver.

Brother in trouble and four-man-argument-at-night went only to Kacey.

Kidnapping, another rowboat, ropes, all just in Kacey's corner.

He'd yet to hear back on the ropes he'd shipped to Phoenix, to Sierra's Web. Wasn't expecting much out of them but put them on the list that had started as Kacey's corner but was taking up much of the screen.

Being followed—that went in Tommy Grainger's case column as well as Kacey's.

Hearing the shower turn off, he quickly saved the chart as a hidden file on his phone and was preparing to make some breakfast when he got a text from Sierra's Web.

While the blow-dryer ran in the bathroom, he called Hudson Warner, his Sierra's Web contact.

"There's nothing on the ropes," Hudson said straight off. "Kind commonly purchased at any big box or hardware store. No fingerprint hits. The way her abductors got her so quickly, managed to get her away and on that boat without her even seeing them…these guys don't seem like amateurs to our team. The supposition is that they wore gloves."

Devon listened intently.

"No obvious hits with standard facial recognition on the images you sent, but we're just getting started on our identification processes."

A disappointment, but not a surprise.

"Bigger news is the movie you sent and that's why I texted the 911. There's a layer of powder, in a thin compartment under the movie. We need to know if you want us to process it or turn it over to Detective Donaldson's contact here in Phoenix." Detective Donaldson, Rachel's real-life persona. Her contact in Phoenix, her current boss, was someone Tommy Grainger—with Sierra's Web help—had vetted and then handpicked for his operation.

Still, he'd had Sierra's Web process the small buy Rachel had made. As paranoid as he was, Devon wanted to keep as much as he could within the private firm he was trusting with his father's case. Instructing Hudson to analyze the powder and get back to him, he hung up, just as he heard the blow-dryer stop.

And knew that there was no way he was filling Kacey Ashland in on his newest information. She's the one who'd brought him the movie case. Granted, it had been sealed, but he had only her word that she'd found it tangled in reeds on the shore of his property.

Was it possible he'd let his rescue of the beautiful woman get to him? Blind him to connections he should be seeing? She'd clearly been left for dead—which meant she'd pissed off some bad people. Didn't mean she hadn't been associated with them beyond the argument she said she'd witnessed and the subsequent knife she'd turned in to the police.

And it didn't mean that she wasn't currently trying to work her way back in with them. Perhaps on instruction from her brother during their phone call the day before? Giving her a way to get back in their good graces?

Had sleeping with Devon been a way to throw him off track? The way she'd come on to him…showing up naked to his shower…a pretty bold and sure way for a first-grade teacher to distract a riverboat guide from figuring out that something illegal was going on right under his nose.

His gut didn't react to the theory. There was no instinct clamoring to confront her. But it made some sense and so he kept it close, harboring it as the possible weapon it might turn out to be.

And maybe hoping that his unexpected houseguest had cause to use it one more time before Tommy Grainger solved his case, or Devon Miller solved hers, and their little saga came to an end.

Chapter Eighteen

"I have to go to work." Devon's announcement came as Kacey exited the bathroom and her first thought was that he obviously didn't need the money so must want to get away from her. Put distance between them.

She didn't altogether disagree with the idea. The man was growing on her and allowing that to happen would just create an entirely new set of problems for her.

"I've got three back-to-back shorter trips scheduled," he said as he dished up a toasted bagel with egg and cheese and put it on the table. Obviously for her. He took a bite out of one that was three-quarters gone as he worked.

Their morning after might consist of sharing a meal, but they were clearly not eating it together.

She didn't like the choice, but she approved of it.

And couldn't stand the tension he was exuding like sweat on a cross-country run. She'd clearly made a huge judgment error when she'd intruded on his shower the night before. It was up to her to fix the situation. Lord knew, she'd already dumped a life load of stress on his remote little hideaway…

Finishing his bagel, he turned toward her. "I can't just sit here," he said, feeding her compulsion to set him free from the night before, but he didn't give her a chance. He just kept talking. "If your kidnapper is hanging out around the marina on a supposed fishing adventure, I've got the perfect cover for being there, to watch out for him. Or them."

Oh. *Oh!* "But you were followed last night. What if they recognize you? I can't have you getting hurt because of me, Devon. This has just gone too far. I need to go." She passed on the bagel she'd been about to sit down and eat and headed toward her room.

"My white truck was followed," Devon said, following her to the door of her room. "It's gone. I'll be driving the off-roader, which means that you're going to be left without transportation."

Heart constricting, she forced herself to concentrate on the immediate moment. "You don't know that you weren't seen."

"The men in the bar didn't see me. We know that for sure. And maybe whoever followed us has the hots for Rachel and wanted to know who'd pulled up to her apartment."

She opened her mouth to argue, and he threw up a hand. "Regardless, I have to take the chance," he told her. "With the body in the crate, these guys aren't fooling around. I need to find out what I can while Sierra's Web does their thing, and then we're going to have to figure out how to proceed. Maybe we go to the police. In Phoenix, where Sierra's Web is located, if nothing else. They won't have jurisdiction here, but because we're afraid of police misconduct in the area, they might be a place to start..."

His gaze was steady on her, filled with serious intent, and she nodded. "That sounds like a good plan." She wasn't sure it did. Where would that leave Kyle?

When she'd thought she was merely turning in her brother's troubles to the police, where he'd have rights and protection, she'd been certain she was doing the right thing. But with men who were willing to murder...and after hear-

ing the terror in her brother's voice when he'd commanded
her to stay gone…she couldn't just sign his death warrant.

No matter what he'd done, he was her twin. She loved
him. And wanted him to have all chances afforded to him
by law.

Not be executed before law enforcement had a chance
to investigate and find out who, of the local jurisdiction,
might be on the take.

But neither could she continue to allow Devon's life to
be in danger. Thoughts of the trespasser in the crate, when
her kidnappers were looking for a crate, sent waves of terror through her. She was in way over her head, even without adding in the adult movie correlation, and needed the
help of trustworthy authorities.

"Maybe we should both just stay out of sight until we hear
back from your firm of experts," she said then, her heart
leaking out a little bit despite the strong hold she had on it.

When Devon shook his head, she knew she'd lost him—
or whatever part of him had held her so tenderly, touched
her body with such passion. "If these guys are around town
looking for anything unusual, I become an instant suspect
if I suddenly call off work again. The marina area is fairly
tight-knit. The locals all know one another. We notice when
someone is missing. All it would take is for someone to tell
anyone asking that no, they haven't seen me around as much
the past few days, or to mention that I canceled another day
of trips, when I've never done that before…"

As much as she wanted to, she couldn't argue with his
logic.

"It's also safest for me, as well as you, if you stay here,
hidden, as dead as we're assuming the kidnappers hope you
are, at least until we know more."

She understood that, too. Her tension eased drastically at
the thought that she didn't have to leave. That not only was

it in Devon's best interests that she stay but that he wanted her to do so.

For his sake, yes.

But she was still, for safety reasons, welcome.

Being weak with relief over the idea was not okay. She'd deal with that. Would apparently have most of the day alone to work on herself.

Before that, though...

"Devon?" she said, as he turned to leave.

He stopped, didn't turn back to her. Which made what she had to say a little easier.

"I apologize profusely for my completely inappropriate behavior last night. Interrupting your shower...the rest... I take full accountability. It was wrong. It won't happen again."

Her heart leapt when he swung around. "I'm a grown man," he said, looking her straight in the eye. "If I had, in any way, been offended by your actions, I would have rejected the invitation."

Feeling a smile sliding around inside her, she had no idea how to respond. So she just stood there. And nodded.

"But it won't happen again if you would rather it didn't," he said, still watching her when she really needed him to exit her space long enough for her to have a stern talk with herself about overreacting where he was concerned.

It wouldn't...if she'd rather it didn't. Did that mean...it sounded like he was open to...

Warmth rushed through her, pooled in her lower belly. Swarming around with an urgency that shocked her.

"Would you rather it didn't?" he asked then.

Sex with Devon Miller was the only thing that filled her up with good feeling in the hellish nightmare her life had become.

"No." The word escaped before she could stop it. "I would rather it did."

While she was there...trapped in his space by circumstances neither of them could control.

With a nod, he knocked his fist on the doorframe once, and was gone.

DEVON HAD THREE short trips scheduled that day—but not on a raft, or kayak, which would preclude him from keeping an eye on the surveillance screens on his phone. It was his day to run one of the riverboats and his turn for the hour-long round trip scenic tour. With the slow speed he'd be traveling, and a crew onboard to serve the customers beverages and snacks of choice, not only could he keep an eye on his phone, but he'd also have full, close-up, slow speed view of the banks on either side of the river.

And for added protection, he called Sierra's Web on his way to work and allocated personal funds to have someone physically watching his cabin surveillance cameras at all times during the hours he'd be on the river. Whether Kacey was somehow involved in whatever was happening, or was as innocent as she claimed, he needed her safe. Period.

He went in early. Hung around the breakfast bar across the parking lot from the marina. Ordered a burrito and took as long as he could to munch on it. Watching the vacationers milling around. Saw families heading to boats they either owned or had rented for a day on the river. Noticed others walking around the small array of shops.

He did not see a threesome of men, lime-green-striped tennis shoes, or any individual that stood out as someone on the grainy tape he continued to view on his phone.

Nor did he get any sense, or see any evidence, of anyone paying him any particular attention. Keeping his back to the wall, he was prepared to act if there was any sign that he was raising suspicion.

Could be that anyone who wanted him—either because his cover was blown, or because of his association with Kacey—just wasn't present in the area.

It was also possible that whoever had suspicions about him only had his white truck to go on. Not enough of a visual to identify him.

The trespassers on his property were a bit of a thorn in the theory, except that they could have been watching for his truck. Had maybe seen it nearing his property.

And there was always the chance that they hadn't known they'd strayed onto private property.

Kacey risking her life to run to the river and coming up with the movie that matched a label found in the dead man's crate worried him. The white powder in the movie's case bothered him more.

Narcotics was his specialty.

In his experience, the people who dealt them, from the top down, were unrelenting, unforgiving and ready to do whatever it took to protect their livelihood.

His morning tour was so uneventful, families on vacation, laughing kids, and scenic views that he got off the boat for lunch feeling uneasy.

Calm before the storm.

Tempted to call Kacey, just to hear her voice and make sure she was okay, he studied his surveillance screens while he waited for the soup and salad he'd pre-ordered at Rachel's bar to be brought to his table along with the usual soda.

Kacey was hanging out almost exclusively in the laundry closet.

Keeping vigil for safety purposes?

Or watching for some sign that she was to make a move?

If he and Rachel had been made, it was possible that

Kacey knew that Devon was make-believe and she'd been staying with Detective Tommy Grainger. Her brother could have told her during their call.

Could be that Kyle had let her know that the way back into the good graces of those who'd left her for dead was to deliver Devon to them in some fashion.

Or to help them play him until they found a way to change the course of their operations and disappear.

He couldn't let that happen.

Rachel delivered his lunch to him, sliding into the booth on the opposite side of his table.

"The dead man—Antonio Hardy. Twenty-five. Has a brother, Jerome, twenty-seven. They're two-bit thugs, registered as PIs in Nevada, but have multiple arrests between Bullhead City and Lake Havasu for shoplifting, mostly. Convenience stores. Jerome has a bar assault from eight years ago. No one knows where he is."

Devon quit eating. Focusing his expression as he listened to his partner. Antonio and Jerome Hardy. The two-bit PIs Sierra's Web had identified from his security camera photos. The two who'd been on his land the first day Kacey had been with him...

Were now officially a part of Tommy Grainger's case. He had to tell her. At least the part that involved them.

"The plastic movie label found in the crate... I had a still sealed movie show up on my shore a couple of days ago." He was careful not to say how he knew that. "I saw these two on my property, chased after them. They jumped in a boat and took off. I sent the movie to Sierra's Web and just heard back on it this morning. There's a sealed compartment on the case that contains white powder. They're checking it now."

He managed to reveal the information without implicating Kacey. Or exposing her existence. For the moment.

But he had to divulge to Rachel anything that sat in his corner of the file he'd made that morning.

He told her about being followed, too.

And ditching his truck.

She listened intently. "And the three men last night?" she asked him.

He shook his head. "My asking about them had to do with a personal matter, something I heard while out on the water the other day. Had to do with a woman, not drugs." He looked her straight in the eye. "I'm not liking that they were missing a crate."

"Why would they announce the news if they knew one was going to turn up with a dead body in it?"

He'd been asking himself the same question. But when he heard his partner pose it, he had an answer. "Because they knew it was going to turn up and were ridding themselves of it in the event that anything on it led police to them. They were here last night specifically to establish an alibi for having lost the crate."

Rachel's nod didn't surprise him. It did unsettle him. For Kacey's sake. What in the hell had she gotten herself into? Either inadvertently, or otherwise?

"And for their whereabouts," Rachel added, "I'm guessing when time of death gets back to us we're going to hear that Antonio died during the time the men were in this bar last night."

Yeah, he was guessing that, too.

His gut was sinking more by the second as he wondered if he'd ever had any chance in hell of getting Kacey out of trouble and safely back into her classroom when school started in August.

But he also knew that as long as he had even the slightest chance to protect her and help to get her the miracle she said she wanted, he wasn't going to stop trying to do just that.

Chapter Nineteen

Kacey had expected the day to be excruciating. As it turned out, sitting in the laundry closet of Devon's home, watching the screens he'd had installed to keep his property safe and secure, was comforting. Knowing that he was watching them, too, knowing that he could see her, gave her a thrill she hadn't expected.

It was as though they were spending the day together.

Mostly she sat there because she wanted him to be able to see her at a quick glance so that he didn't waste energy worrying about her.

She was the safe one. He could be putting his life on the line just leaving the property.

Those thoughts brought panic. Which she fought by stopping by the door of Devon's room. Looking at the rumpled sheets. She didn't stay long enough to draw attention. Didn't do anything rash like going in and taking a nap there. She just took a deep breath, promised herself that he'd be okay, and went back to the laundry room.

She was sitting there, having a granola bar for a late lunch, when she noticed movement on-screen from the camera that showed Devon's furthest shore from the cabin. Moving in closer, watching intently, she was pretty sure she saw the toe of a shoe. Black.

Was that a hairy ankle? She enlarged the video until only the area in question was visible on the big screen.

Showing utter stillness in the foliage she'd been studying, half convincing her she'd been imagining things. Or had seen a small animal that had briefly come ashore from the water. Probably a beaver. Due to the Colorado's flow, the mammals had to build their dams on the shore—a lesson she'd taught to her kids for science the year before.

Sitting back, she was ready to accept her explanation, and a leaf seemed to fill up right before her eyes. As though there was something inside it. And underneath it, the tips of two fingers, touching the ground. Pulling back.

Not claws. She'd seen fingernails.

She had to get more of a look than the camera was showing her. Burner phone in her pocket and her gun at her waist, she burst out the front door, running until she had to slow to catch some breath, and then speeding up again. Continuing that way until she was almost close enough to the shore to be heard. Bending at the waist, her hands on her knees, she caught her breath for a second and then, slowly, silently, approached the area she'd been watching on-screen.

Heart pounding, she kept low, hidden, using desert brush for cover. With the hot sun beating down overhead, she was sweating in rivulets, but didn't risk movement to wipe them away. Her plan was to see. Period.

No way she was going to take on a potential murderer out in the desert alone. Or risk giving Devon more reason to be suspicious of her. But if she could see what the camera could not...could see how the man traveled, what kind of boat, which direction he went when he left the camera view...if she could get a good enough look at him to give Devon a decent description, some kind of identifying characteristic... he could let his experts know and maybe they'd be closer to finding the truth that was going to set them both free.

And show Devon that he could have trusted her all along.

She understood the man's struggle to have faith in anyone. His belief that his father had been framed and killed. And then, with the lottery win—there were stories all over the internet about lottery winners whose lives had been ruined by the huge influx of cash. About people coming out of the woodwork with their stories. Once-trusted friends. Using, hounding...

She got it.

She just didn't want his doubts shining on her.

If for no other reason than because her heart cried out for him to have one person in his life he'd learned he could trust. If she could leave him with that...

Brush moved down shore from her. Off Devon's land. She watched from the shelter of a wall of Mexican Birds of Paradise plants, peeking through the curtain of orange flowers on the tightly growing thin branches. A man moved rapidly, bent over, from place to place. Occasionally glancing over his shoulder.

And searching under every piece of brush, debris and plant along the shore.

The other trespasser? Companion to the man who'd turned up dead in a crate the night before?

Chest tight, Kacey pulled out her phone. Snapped pictures. Afraid, from her distance, they wouldn't enlarge clearly enough. She had to get this right.

To contribute, not just be needy.

In long shorts that hung to his calves, and what looked like water shoes, the man's T-shirt was tight around a slightly protruding stomach. Looked more sloppy than athletic. And his skin...browned from the sun? Or ethnicity? She couldn't tell. Dark hair, maybe black. With the sun shining so brightly, and his hair looking wet...

She looked for tattoos on the exposed skin of his arms, his neck.

Maybe there were some. There had to be something.

He was too far away to tell for sure.

What else might help Devon recognize him?

Calming herself with thoughts of the man she was helping, more than thoughts of helping herself, she made herself tune out everything around her and focus only on the body, trying not to panic as the man moved further away.

He stood straight—she had him for around five ten—was facing further downstream away from her, though. *Show me your face,* she implored silently. Snapped another photo anyway.

Saw the man run and feared that her camera lens in the sunlight had somehow alerted him to her. Started to shake as she lost sight of him. Then caught sight of him again. Further away from her, not closer. Nearer to the water where the bank was steeper. Moving as quickly as she could from one safe spot to another, she lost sight of him, gained it back again, lost him, and…found him just in time to see him attempting to carry and shove what looked like a heavy container of some sort—a crate?—inside a large cluster of the same type of brightly flowering Mexican Bird of Paradise she'd been hiding within.

Shooting as many pictures as she could, she saw the man down on his knees, giving one last shove with his shoulder. She snapped one more shot, glanced at the photo on the screen, saw the plants, with nothing else visible.

She had to know what he'd hidden. What if Devon didn't make it back before the man returned to claim whatever it was he'd found?

She could wait until he left. If he left.

At least get a picture of the crate.

Keeping her male prey in sight, she was already studying the landscape for a safe path she could take to his stash while staying out of view, when she saw him freeze. His back was to her, but his head was turned to the side facing the desert.

Had she made some sound that had traveled?

Following the direction of his glance, she almost stopped breathing. A pack of coyotes stood between Kacey and the man, looking in both directions. On first glance, she figured seven adults, at least. Maybe as many pups. Her guess was that they'd been sleeping under or near where the man had shoved his find.

The only way she knew of to scare off coyotes was to make a lot of noise.

She couldn't do that. And didn't figure the man wanted to draw attention to himself, either, based on all the looking over his shoulder he'd been doing.

While some of the wild animals seemed to be trained in her direction, more were facing the man. Holding her breath, Kacey stayed completely still, watching, and saw the man run toward the shore.

One of the animals took pursuit, followed by one more. As far as she knew only packs that had become humanized by exposure chased after people, but she watched as the dogs flew at the man's ankles, one at least nipping him, as he jumped over the bank.

Whether he hit the water deeply enough to survive, she had no idea.

And didn't wait to find out.

Picking up as many rocks as she could find while staying hidden, she took off her shirt, placed the rocks in it along with her phone, and started shaking the shirt as hard as she could to make noise, while slowly backing away to a cluster of cholla. The tall dense cactus stalks had needles that were known to jump out at anything that got too close, so she didn't, but with any luck, the coyotes would move on.

She didn't want to scream, to alert any other human beings who could be lurking, to her presence. Slowly, keeping her eye on the animals, she backed toward Devon's land, with the sun beating down on the untanned skin of her back and midsection, covered only by the bra Devon had purchased for her. If the coyotes came at her, she'd throw the shirt. Took the phone out of it, pocketing it, so she'd have the pictures, and then picked up another, larger rock, one that barely fit in her hand, to throw as well, if she needed to do so.

Shaking, near tears, she wanted to run so badly she ached with the need, but continued her slow, steady backward pace, taking herself closer to the water, but careful to stay out of sight of the river in the event the man was down there, swimming to wherever he'd come from. Probably a raft tied somewhere onshore.

She didn't so much see the coyotes turn away. More like, they didn't follow her far. Once they were out of sight, she turned and started walking as swiftly as she could, dropping the rocks from her shirt and sliding back into it. Keeping watch behind her as she did so.

Her gun was loaded. Within reach. She could shoot an animal coming at her. Her abilities didn't extend to taking down a pack of them. Nor did she have enough bullets to do so.

By the time she got back to land she knew was Devon's she took her first full breath. And felt it catch in her throat, too. The man…the crate he'd hidden. She had no idea what was in it.

But knew it mattered.

And couldn't avoid the obvious conclusion, either.

Her kidnappers were somehow involved. The trespassers had been on Devon's land her first day there. He'd never been breached before.

At least one of the men who'd abducted her was looking for a missing crate of supplies.

Someone had been found dead in a crate the night before.

Lying on a partial wrapping from an adult movie.

Akin to the one she'd found on the shore.

It was all adding up to something.

She just couldn't figure out what.

But had a feeling her time to save herself, or Kyle, was running out.

Devon, though…she'd die saving him.

GUN IN HAND, Devon was canvassing his property like the top-rated detective he was, searching for anyone—his houseguest or any possible compatriots—when he saw Kacey walking several yards to his right, heading at a quick pace toward the cabin.

To make it back home before he did?

He'd seen her move in close to one screen in the laundry room. Had had a 911 from Sierra's Web when she'd left the house. They'd both been back over the tape she'd been studying. Saw what looked like a beaver briefly showing itself on his land.

As soon as he'd docked the riverboat, he'd jumped in his vehicle and sped home.

She wouldn't be expecting him for another half hour at the earliest. Longer if he stopped in the bar to see Rachel. Which he would have done.

Should have done.

Because it was routine.

Instead, there he was, practically stumbling over himself at the sight of her well and able and heading home.

Relieved that she was safe.

And thankful that she'd returned of her own accord.

None of which pleased Tommy Grainger at all. He'd enjoyed the company of a lot of women. Not one of them had called him back as Kacey Ashland did.

Keeping his distance, watching her, he dealt with the battle going on inside himself, and came out the cop he knew himself to be. A man who had to wonder why the woman had left the only place she was relatively safe, risking her life—and possibly his—by heading down to the river.

He hadn't taken the time to study all the video yet, but Hudson Warner had filled him on what the team there had seen, which had been very little. She'd run the entire way from the cabin to just short of the river. And then had quickly disappeared after that. Most of whatever Kacey had been up to had happened off-screen.

In the space of about twenty minutes.

And then she'd been back. Pulling her shirt down over the waistband containing her gun.

He hoped to God she hadn't used the weapon.

Felt a bit sick at the thought that she had.

And had to consider the most obvious explanation for her hurried departure. A lot of people knew he'd been expected at work that day. The three men in the bar could easily have found out. A simple question at the marina regarding the day's trips would have told them.

Did Kacey get a signal telling her to get down to the water? Something prearranged with her twin during their phone call? The one she'd insisted on keeping private?

The idea that there'd been some kind of rendezvous was the only thing that made sense.

So why wasn't he shoving her out the door? Calling the local police and reporting what he knew? As Devon Miller, recreational river guide?

He followed her to the cabin. Knew the exact moment when she saw his vehicle and knew he'd made it home before she did.

She'd stopped. Looked around.

And then picked up her pace to the cabin? Like she was eager to see him?

Or to explain away her absence.

She'd have answers ready. He had no doubt about that at all. She knew he'd see the screens.

But if she thought he was going to be blinded by her combination of innocence and allure, toughness and sweetness, strength and vulnerability, then she was in for a surprise.

Devon Miller was done being played.

KACEY BURST INTO the cabin, words fighting to tumble themselves over her lips. The container. With him home early, they had a better chance of getting back to the container before the current trespasser did. When she didn't see Devon in the kitchen or living area, she made a beeline for the laundry closet.

Was about to turn away from the emptiness there when she saw movement on a screen close to the cabin. Heart pounding, fearing she'd somehow brought trouble closer to home than ever, she moved in.

And recognized the purposeful gait of the man getting closer with every quick step he took.

He'd been behind her?

Following her?

Without calling out?

He'd been spying on her.

Maybe he hadn't gone to work at all. Just driven far enough away to be out of his property's camera range and had been sitting there watching the surveillance screens on his phone, watching her, the entire day.

Filled with urgency and anger, she was standing by the couch, leaning a shoulder against the wall, arms crossed, hoping she appeared calm, when he walked in.

His tense expression collided with hers immediately. He didn't trust her. That was his problem. She had nothing to apologize for.

To the contrary, she had important news to report.

He'd get that information when he quit looking at her like she was some stranger.

She'd taken on coyotes, she could handle Devon Miller. And had no time.

Chin up, she kept her gaze shooting solidly into his for a full thirty seconds. Time they weren't going to get back.

"What in the hell were you thinking?" he finally blurted out. His gaze held steady. He didn't approach. "You have some death wish you need to tell me about?"

His words pierced her heart. Flooding warmth through her veins when only adrenaline should be there. He'd been scared for her. Maybe he knew that. Maybe he didn't.

Didn't much matter to her what Devon was ready to acknowledge. The fact that he'd cared melted the armor she'd pulled up around herself before he'd walked in.

She had no intention of letting him know that, however. They were equals, or they were nothing at all. And had business at hand.

"I was thinking that I had a chance to help figure out what's keeping me a prisoner in my own life. Thinking that I'd rather risk that life than just sit around and wait for others to risk theirs to help me. I knew that turning in that bloody knife could have negative repercussions for me. A heated argument in the dark? A bloody knife? Getting involved in that, even just by having to testify to what I'd seen, wasn't going to be a walk in the park. I chose to do so, anyway. Now it's up to me to deal with whatever I unknowingly stepped into. To find a way out of it. If I can prevent it, I am not going to die."

He didn't relent. Much. A softening of his shoulders, maybe. "You figure a desert rat or some other small animal scrounging on the shore has something to do with the mess you're in?"

Not the kindest way to describe having been kidnapped. The man almost didn't deserve to hear what she had to tell him. Except that he'd rescued her from death.

Had been attentive, kind, welcoming, in spite of his doubts.

Was still asking questions, rather than storming in and demanding she leave. Her mind calculated. Her heart was on hold.

"I figure an animal doesn't have fingernails," she told him, and while she would have liked to walk to the laundry room, showing him her images, knowledge of the crate that was likely going to be taken away, if it hadn't been already, was pushing at her more.

She'd had her minute of standing up to Devon. Life mattered more. Walking toward him she pulled out her phone, shoved it at him, gallery open.

"Who is this?"

"How should I know?" she said sharply, and then added, "I was thinking maybe the second trespasser? I never got a look at his face."

Devon's thumb moved rapidly, scrolling through all the photos she'd taken. And then he was out the door, jumping into his off-roader. She had no doubt he'd have roared off without her if she hadn't run after him, jumping in the passenger side. He gave her a glance, but didn't argue, just pushed the pedal to the floor and sent her head back against the seat as he tore off across his land.

Chapter Twenty

The container was gone when they got there. Devon could see exactly where it had been. He'd had Kacey send the photos she'd taken to his phone and knew, comparing branch to branch, they were in the right spot. And saw evidence on the ground, in real time, too. There were no discernible footprints, but a fresh ditch in the hard desert ground beneath the tall sprawling plant gave him at least the length of the container that had been there.

A small boat had come ashore just below it. Some kind of long flat surface had been run from the vessel to the plant as best he could tell by the surface of the shore.

A ramp of some kind. Maybe even just some two-by-fours.

His guess was that whoever had returned for the container had dragged it down the ramp.

"He sure got back here quickly." Kacey's voice came from behind the thick wall of six-foot-high thin flowering branches. He'd suggested that she stay back, out of view of the shore. No sense in taking chances that boaters would go by and see her.

"Probably had a shore runner moored close by."

"That's what I thought, too, but I think he was hurt."

After taking a few quick photos of the scene as he'd found

it, Devon scrambled up to Kacey, feeling sick again. "He was hurt? You didn't think to mention that before now?" He had a flash of the gun she'd pulled her shirt over.

"There were coyotes," she told him as they walked back to his off-roader and climbed inside. She'd been completely silent on the trip to the shore, but filled him in on the details of her afternoon of amateur detecting on the return journey. Impressed by her quick thinking, her capability in the face of danger, he wasn't at all pleased about most of what he heard.

Except that she'd made it back safely.

"Do you think this guy's the other trespasser?" she asked as he pulled up out in front. "And if so, could that container hold more of those movies?"

"Seems likely," he told her, scrambling to put the pieces together. Antonio was dead, and Jerome had been out looking for something? Found a container, hid it, returned for it? He had to talk to Rachel. To Sierra's Web.

Had no way of proving whether the man in Kacey's photos was Jerome.

He had to know what the white powder was in those movie cases.

He wasn't going to call in local police until he had to do so. Wasn't going to let some two-bit thugs undo almost a year of undercover work. Not now that Alexopoulos was in the picture, selling Rachel the drugs they'd been looking for. Authorities had known they were there.

Local police had been able to trace small buys.

He and Rachel getting to know the local kids hanging out at the marina had been key to finding Belen. If she was able to pull off the larger buy later in the week, things could start to tumble in their favor very quickly.

After months of establishing his identity, becoming known as a water lover with no real ambition, Devon would move into the picture, want in on the action, come up with money to make a huge buy, but only be willing to deal if he got in on a bigger piece of the organization. The higher up he went, the more heads would topple.

Assuming they hadn't been made, it could all be done within the week.

"It's a bit frightening to me that these guys show up on your property the day I do, that I subsequently find a movie, then what seems likely to be one of them shows up dead in a crate with part of the same type of movie label in the bottom of it. And then some guy with one of my abductors says they're looking for a crate of supplies they lost."

Driving, with an eye on his phone screen showing him areas of his property, Devon nodded. It concerned him, too. Hugely. He knew that one of the trespassers was dead.

And he couldn't be sure she wasn't more involved than she let on.

He wasn't really Devon Miller. If someone knew that...

Rachel wasn't really Rachel Wallace, either.

He knew that Kacey Ashland really was a first-grade teacher from Bullhead City, but that didn't mean that she couldn't also have a secret life.

Maybe a summertime job making a load of extra money on the side? He'd heard teachers were grossly underpaid.

Or even a worried twin attempting to help her brother out of something he fell into. Hometown football hero, getting offers from top universities based on old Boulder City news reports, who's forced by family tragedy to skip his entire future to work at a sawmill for the rest of his life? Devon could see the man being tempted by the big money he'd been headed to make.

What if her whole near-drowning had been a setup to specifically reel him in and he played right into it?

Would a woman who'd been left for dead, who'd been

through as many life-threatening situations as Kacey had in the past few days, really go barreling out into the desert alone, alerting no one, unless she knew she had little to fear?

Except perhaps an unexpected pack of coyotes woken from their naps?

Would a decorated detective, intent on spending his life being the best cop he could be, really be so easily taken in?

Was Tommy Grainger as much like his father as he'd thought, growing up? Falling for a beautiful woman on the job to the exclusion of everything else he held dear?

Not that Devon was falling for Kacey.

And he wasn't being taken in by her either, hence the doubts. If anything, in the event it turned out she was playing him, he'd be the guy turning the tables and taking advantage of the situation.

Because he was keeping all doors open, all possibilities on the table, he'd be prepared for whatever came at him.

And because he had Sierra's Web, Rachel and the rest of his handpicked team on board, ready to notice any inconsistencies they saw, even if he was the one exhibiting them.

Which was why he needed to get Devon's butt back to town and into the bar. With a call to Sierra's Web on the way.

Feeling better, he followed Kacey into the air-conditioned comfort of the cabin, changed the bandages on her ankles, checked that everything was secure, and then told her he had to head back to the marina for a bit.

She nodded. Didn't complain. Asked if he had anything particular in mind for dinner.

Almost like they were a couple.

Which had him heading faster toward the door as he told her he liked all the food in the place so anything there would be fine, silently thinking maybe he'd eat at the bar. He was almost out the door, pulling it closed behind him, when he turned back.

"You did a great job out there today," he told her. Meaning every word. No matter what life she was living, the woman was pretty incredible.

STAY GONE. KYLE had told her.

For how long?

Were more dead people going to turn up? Possible thieves?

How would she know when it was safe to return? It wasn't like Kyle had any way of getting in touch with her.

More than twenty-four hours had passed since she'd spoken with him. For all she knew, Kyle could be hurt.

Or worse.

And yet she felt compelled to heed her twin's advice. To give him time.

Based on the likelihood that it was the trespasser in the trunk, there was a good chance what she'd seen that afternoon, taken photos of, had been something illegal. She didn't trust Bullhead City Police, but down by Quartzite, she should maybe go to the police.

Doing so would most definitely bring her back to life.

Which could endanger Devon, since her abductors might very well be onto him.

To his truck, obviously. He'd been followed to his property, with a probable dead trespasser and likely the other back again.

But maybe it was just his truck that had been exposed, not his person, yet, or he wouldn't be doing his job and coming home without mishap, right? Unless she went to the police. She'd have to expose Devon, too, as the pictures she took were on and near his property.

So was she to think that whatever Kyle was into had to do with adult movies?

She couldn't imagine it.

But if there was one topic she and her twin didn't share, ever, it would be their sex lives.

Maybe Devon was going to the police without implicating her, which should keep him safer from her kidnappers. Saying he took the photos. The timeline would be a little off, depending on how long he'd been home, following her that afternoon.

Had he seen her with her shirt off?

Like it mattered under the circumstances.

Still, it kind of did. Privately. To her. She just wasn't sure if she wanted him to have had the view, or not.

Checking the laundry closet screens every fifteen minutes, scrolling back to see all that had gone on during that time, she put together a baked, bacon-wrapped chicken dish for dinner. Figured she'd serve it with steamed broccoli and cauliflower.

Surely Devon would inform her if he was taking her evidence to the police. At least give her a heads-up.

When she saw his vehicle enter the property, she put the foil-wrapped pan of chicken and mushroom-soup-based sauce in the oven. Telling herself it was good news that he was back so soon.

But knew it wasn't.

Trembling, she was kind of watching for police to arrive with him, ridiculously fearing that he was having them take her away, when he came in and asked her to have a seat.

He looked her in the eye as he made the request, his expression serious, but not hard as it had been earlier that afternoon.

She chose the couch. Needing what comfort she could provide for herself.

When he sat, too, Kacey drew a slightly easier breath.

She knew that, ultimately, she was completely on her own. Would have to accept, would be completely accountable to, whatever consequences ended upon her for the actions she'd taken. But Devon's nearness calmed her.

Gave her some kind of odd strength. Because he'd saved her life? Offered her refuge?

Because she'd taken him into her body the night before, as though he was a part of her soul?

Because he hadn't ditched her when her advent into his life had created major difficulties for him?

A full minute passed and he hadn't said anything. She glanced over to find him watching her. Oh, Lord, was he getting ready to tell her she had to go?

Not that she blamed him, but... "Just tell me," she blurted.

"The dead man in the crate was a man named Antonio Hardy. You know the name?"

Frowning, her stomach in knots, she shook her head.

"The man you saw today is his brother, Jerome. They were the trespassers the first day you were here. Jerome's body was just discovered floating in the river ten miles from here. He had a bullet in his stomach. Please tell me you did not put it there."

"Of course I didn't!" How could he...

"I need to see the gun I gave you, Kacey. I need to know whether my bullet could turn up in a ballistic report."

Shaking inside, but with steady hand movements, she removed the gun from her waist and handed it over to him.

Watched as he systematically checked the gun. Counted bullets.

Had he gone to the police already then?

Implicated her?

Before she'd had a chance to talk to them herself?

If her twin brother was in trouble, it stood to reason that she was involved? Guilty by association?

"It hasn't been fired," he said, as though imparting some big news.

"I told you that."

He nodded. Gave the gun back to her.

Shocking her.

She took it as though she'd expected it to happen. Slid it back into her waistband.

His doubt—him thinking there was even a chance she'd have shot and killed a man and tried to cover it up or lie about it—angered her. For starters. The rest she wasn't going to think about.

The fact that he'd handed the gun back emboldened her.

"How did you hear about this so quickly?" she demanded more than asked. He could tell her to go to hell.

At the moment, she didn't much care.

"I stopped in at the bar. The police were there, questioning Rachel again."

"Did this Jerome have the bar's address in his pocket, too?"

"No. But because he was Antonio's brother, they came back to talk to the employees a second time. Rachel was on duty."

Right.

Was Rachel the reason he'd gone back?

It shouldn't matter to her one way or the other.

Once she had her life back, had some control of her destiny, it wouldn't matter.

"Had she seen either of them before?"

"No, and from what I understand, bar surveillance tape doesn't show them there."

"Did you tell the police that I'd seen Jerome? Show them the pictures? Did you tell them I have a gun in my possession?" He wouldn't have been wrong to do so. She had to know what she was facing.

"No. I think, after this latest development, for your safety and mine, it's best that you stay missing…"

She glanced at him. Met his gaze. Felt the silent communication that passed between them, a return to some kind of "them."

"If my gun had been shot, and because you hadn't mentioned shooting it, we'd be heading into them right now," he told her softly.

"I wouldn't expect any less," she shot right back at him. With complete sincerity.

He sat another minute. Studying her. As though assessing.

"Is there more? Did they find the container?" Had it been full of the same adult movies as the one she'd found? Had Kyle gotten mixed up with someone dealing illegal contraband? Maybe by purchasing a movie?

"They didn't," Devon said, more thoughtful than tense, an arm along the back of the couch. Not touching her. But close. "Which kind of makes you think that whoever shot Jerome has it."

"It kind of does." It made her nervous, how much she was thinking it. "The guys in the bar last night...missing a crate...you think it's Jerome's container?" Say no. Say no. Say no.

"I think it's possible."

She needed there to be some other explanation.

"While I was at the bar, I saw another photo of Antonio in the crate," Devon dropped almost casually into the room. "The police were showing it around to a few people."

That had to have been hard to look at. She almost said so. Something held her quiet.

"The crate could have been any of the photos you took of that container today," he said then.

"The brothers were dealing with stolen goods," she said slowly, and from that drew the painfully obvious conclusion. "The three men last night...they wanted those movies."

Devon's fingertips touched her shoulder. Not in a sexy way.

More like he was just making her aware he was there. With her.

She wondered if he had any idea how badly she'd needed to know that.

Chapter Twenty-One

He'd shown Rachel the photos of Jerome Hardy hiding the crate just yards from Devon's land. Hadn't said who'd taken them. She'd naturally assumed he had.

If he was making the wrong call, maintaining silence about his houseguest, he would be the only one going down for the information.

He was the lead detective on his undercover assignment. It was up to him to determine what truths to tell and which ones to conceal to protect not only the integrity of the operation, but also the detectives working it.

A call from Sierra's Web had let him know that while the powder found in the movie case was a form of heroin, it consisted mostly of sugar and starch with a minimal amount of morphine, and therefore was far less potent, less effective, and much less addictive than the lethal form of the opiate his team was following. He'd discussed with Rachel the possibility that the three men in the bar the previous night were dealers, just on a smaller scale, a much less professional, local operation, peddling more of a small-high party drug than dangerous opiates. Not worth risking their operation, blowing their cover, even with the local police.

For all they knew, local law enforcement cooperation could be the way their drugs were passing through the ma-

rina and across the United States. Made sense that the same
crooked cop or cops were taking kickback for the passage
of other illegal substances as well.

She'd agreed.

They decided together to keep a watch for the movies,
the once again missing crate, and to keep an eye out for the
three men who'd been in the bar the night before. To find
out what they could, with a possible tie to a mutual link in
the supply chain from their marina for illegal contraband.

There was no indication that Belen and the three men in
the bar were connected. But that didn't mean they didn't
share some distribution channel.

The discovery of which could be the piece they needed
to solve their case and get astronomical amounts of lethal
drugs off the streets and away from the kids who were dying
while partying with them.

All they really had at the moment was one movie, and
knowledge of a crate being hidden before the hider was
killed. And they had crates that looked alike, one with a
partial movie label on the bottom, but no proof at all that the
crate Kacey had photographed that afternoon had contained
more drug-concealing adult movies. He felt sure that it did.

But before he went any further up his professional ladder with the news, he needed more.

He'd asked Sierra's Web to log the movie, and its cover
and contents, as evidence, and hang onto it. The firm had
been retained by the Henderson Police Department to help
on his undercover operation. He'd discovered the movie
while working that assignment.

He'd been given a specific job. But he was still a cop, with
temporary jurisdiction in the state of Arizona. Detectives
regularly worked more than one case at a time.

Not at all happy with the turn of events of the past few
days, Devon gained a measure of peace in terms of his pro-

fessional decisions with the mental self-check. Which left him to wallow in a quandary of a more personal nature.

He'd never before been in the position of having to have "The Talk" after having had sex with a woman. In Devon's world, and Tommy's, that conversation was like putting on a condom. It had to happen before he got intimate with a woman, or he didn't get intimate. Period.

Looking over at Kacey, seeing her determination and ability to stand back up every time she got knocked down, he had trouble getting any words out at all. She was clearly at a low point in her life. All alone. Unable to reach out to anyone at all because she had to appear to be dead. Devon didn't want to join the list of circumstances pushing her to the ground.

She'd done right by him more than once. He'd known she was out by the river that day. She hadn't had to take photos. Or to show them to him.

If she'd known Jerome was heading to his death, she could have taken the time stamped pictures as a form of protection for herself. An alibi of sorts. Proving he'd been alive at the time she'd been present.

The theory fit.

He didn't feel strongly about it.

And then he saw it. A speck of orange hiding underneath the top layer of blond hair at the back of her head, by her neck.

A flower from the Mexican Bird of Paradise plant.

The only way it could have gotten there was if she'd been underneath one.

She'd said that she hadn't gone near the crate. That she'd taken her pictures from afar, that Jerome's shoving of the crate had disturbed a pack of coyotes, that the man had run for the river, maybe being nipped by a coyote and then had detailed how she'd dealt with the pack to make her own escape.

Other than getting a little dry-mouthed, thinking about her walking out in the desert in only the bra he could picture well because he'd purchased it for her, he'd taken it all in as fact.

"What?" Her word brought his gaze from the back of her hair to her face.

Frowning, she still seemed to ooze her strange brand of compassion and, as usual, he was like a magnet to its force. He couldn't keep getting sucked in.

"You have a Bird of Paradise flower in your hair." He heard the accusation in his tone, though he hadn't purposefully put it there.

Reaching back, she slid her fingers through her hair. "I hid under a wall of them to watch Jerome." The small delicate orange bloom was still twisted in blond strands. Pulling the burner phone he'd given her from her pocket, she scrolled, tapped and held the screen up to him. An earlier photo of Jerome in the distance, bent on the shore—insignificant except for the obvious orange foliage in the forefront.

The look in her eye, when he glanced from the screen to her face, dripped with resignation.

He didn't trust her. She knew it.

Pulling the flower out of her hair, he handed it to her. "I was married once." Not the way he'd ever entered the conversation he'd meant to have. And not Devon Miller information, either.

He'd have to have Sierra's Web get Devon married and divorced.

The rest wouldn't be in any record. "My father was unfaithful to my mother. It ripped our family apart. I've always been a lot like him. Everyone said so as I was growing up, even into my early adulthood. And they were right. I saw it myself."

Too much.

"After I was married, I found myself attracted to another woman."

He was looking at her. She didn't speak.

"I got out of the marriage, thankfully there were no kids involved, and will never, ever marry again."

There. Went around the block, but he got there.

"Because you were unfaithful."

"No." He glanced at her, saw no judgment in her gaze. Or…hurt or…anything he'd half convinced himself he'd find. "I got out of the marriage before that happened."

"And the woman you were attracted to? That didn't last?"

"I never told her. Never acted on it." The whole thing had been a turnoff.

Her brow showed confusion. If he had to spell it out, he would. "It's not just you I don't trust," he told her. "I don't wholly trust anyone. Including myself."

And that should be that.

Not quite his usual *this can be for now, for mutual pleasure, but I'm not looking for a relationship* speech. But the point had been made.

"I'm not sure how much I trust anyone right now, either." The softness of her words, the warm look in her eye, hit him before the actual words made it through processing in his brain.

"You're trusting me to keep your secrets. To provide you safe lodging." He spoke without stopping to choose his words. *What are you doing?* What the hell. He was pushing her to trust him when he'd just told her he didn't trust himself?

Sexually. To be faithful. He didn't trust himself to be

faithful to one woman for his entire life. Otherwise...he was a good guy. His entire life was about getting it right.

"Yeah, I'm trusting you to keep my secrets," she said, the funny half smile on her lips turning him on. In an obvious way. "And you trust me enough to keep my secrets. To give me a phone and a gun and to let me stay here."

That wasn't trust. His mind instantly refuted her words. He knew better. He'd made well-thought-out calculated decisions.

He opened his mouth to say so and, "What about you? Are you in a serious relationship?" came out. The other part of the conversation that always happened before sex.

The shake of her head kept him hard. Not a good sign.

But he'd had his say. She knew he was never going to be a long-haul guy.

"There've been a couple of guys I thought could eventually get there, but I come with a mother that needs care and an almost ten-year-old sister. That's nonnegotiable."

"The guys you dated didn't want to sign on for instant, every day, family obligations." He translated.

"Right."

"Then you weren't dating the right guys."

"That's what Kyle said."

Oh, yes. Her twin. Devon had been so caught up in the immediate drama around him, Kacey's afternoon activity, another dead body, a cheap rendition of heroin showing up in a movie case...thoughts of her brother had temporarily slipped off his radar.

Kacey would have already put together that the trouble her brother was in likely had to do with adult films. She didn't know about the heroin connection.

And he was not going to tell her.

Sidestepping that conversation, he said, "I'm not that instant family guy, either."

"No kidding…" Her tone dripped with sarcasm. But her eyes were resting gently on his. "And if this conversation is because you've somehow gotten the idea that because we got caught up in the adrenaline and passion of the moment last night that I'm going to be expecting a proposal, or even a date, you can relax," she said, holding his gaze the entire time. "I'm not opposed to finding pleasure in the moment, while we're caught up here, to help my sanity, but that's it, Devon. When I get home… I have no idea what I'm going to be facing. But I know for certain, I'm going to be one-hundred-percent focused on Mom and Lizzie…"

Ironically, words that were meant to comfort him, to assuage his tension, had the opposite effect.

Devon didn't ask why. He didn't want to know.

Tommy Grainger disappeared completely. Kacey didn't know him. Would never know him.

"About that pleasure in the moment," Devon said, grappling to rid himself of perceptions and feelings that didn't fit his life—which, by nature, was only temporary.

He was going to make love to her. Only in the moment, as she'd said.

Because the moment was all a make-believe guy like Devon had to worry about.

THEY HAD SEX—in Devon's bedroom in front of motion detectors, not cameras. They ate chicken and vegetables, sitting as homeowner and rescued guest, not close, not touching.

And then had sex again.

In her room.

She didn't care if he had a kiss on tape to remember her by. Kind of liked the idea, really.

But respected his insistence that no part of their physical relationship would be recorded on tape.

It kind of endeared him to her more…the way he was holding their time in bed together sacrosanct.

They did dishes midevening. Took a shower together, and without either suggesting a word, both gravitated back to his room.

Touching Devon, being touched by him, took her so completely out of herself, she had no fear, no worry—just pure euphoria, for an hour at a time. Wanted to doze and wake with him next to her and do it all over again, for the rest of the night.

Morning would come. Trouble would be there waiting.

If she could just get…

Half-asleep, she thought she heard his phone vibrate on the nightstand next to his bed. He'd left it there with his gun. Picked them both up every time he pulled on his shorts and left the room. Either bedroom. And laid them right next to him again when he disposed of the shorts.

It was like clockwork with him. Ingrained habit. His phone that only vibrated—she was thinking different rhythms. Like ringtones. And that gun. It made her sad. The idea that the man so mistrusted everyone in the world around him that he couldn't separate from the device that held his surveillance screens and gun that he believed kept him safe.

The only things within his power, his control, to protect himself…

And like clockwork, he was sitting up, phone in hand, staring at the screen.

"Are there deer?" she asked drowsily. She'd spent enough time in the laundry closet to know how much wildlife he caught on his screens—most particularly at night. "You should sell some of that footage," she said then, groggy with sexual satiation and the sleep that had been about to overtake her. "You could make a video and put it up online."

It took her a second to realize he wasn't listening. Setting down his phone, he pulled on his shorts and T-shirt.

"What's going on?"

"I have to make a call," he told her, leaving the room. She was already in her own shorts, pulled her shirt over her braless chest when she heard the front door open and shut.

He must have had a text, not a surveillance notification.

Ten o'clock at night...she'd bet it was from Rachel. The immediate wave of resentment quickly passed as, fully awake, Kacey removed her arms from her shirt, put her bra on, and then, after her shirt was back in place, her tennis shoes.

Were her kidnappers back? Had something happened?

Was someone in the bar, or on the streets close by, selling movies?

Why did he always have to talk to Rachel in private?

Before she could get outside with Devon, or have it dawn on her that if she was welcome in the conversation he'd have made the call in the cabin, he was pocketing his phone and heading back to the door.

The intensely focused look on his face as he came in struck terror within her. He looked at her but didn't connect. Not even a little bit.

"When your brother filed the missing person's report, he gave the police your hairbrush. A common request during such investigations, for identification in the event a body is found." She nodded, couldn't breathe.

Had a body turned up?

But its DNA wouldn't match her hairbrush. It couldn't. She was standing right there.

Devon knew that.

"Sierra's Web got access to that DNA. It was a match for the blood on the knife you turned in." His chin trembled a bit with tension as he watched her.

"You think I cut myself and then turned in the bloody weapon?" He'd been over every single inch of her body. Thoroughly. Other than the cuts on her ankles, which he knew firsthand came from the ropes with which she'd been tied up, he knew there were no injuries that could possibly have been made by a fixed blade knife...

And it hit her. She was a twin. Had a twin. Who'd have similar DNA. He hadn't said an identical match. Just a match.

"Kyle..." She felt the blood drain from her face, the energy seep from her body, as she stared at him. "They stabbed Kyle..."

While she'd been standing at her window upstairs in the dark, watching shadows in between her house and their mom's. Horrific thoughts tumbled one after the other. Had Kyle pulled the knife from the wound, thrown it in the bushes, to run after the men who'd attacked him?

He'd been able to run. And had sounded fine when she'd talked to him on the phone...

The worst of the devastation came to her when, ready to break with worry, with the weight of her imploding life, she looked back up at Devon. And saw the cold question gazing at her from those expressive blue eyes.

There were no witnesses to her having been in the dark in her upstairs bedroom window, watching the argument between Kyle and those men that night. "You think I stabbed my own twin? And then made up the story of the argument and turned in the knife saying I'd just found it? To turn suspicion off from me?"

For a second, she couldn't even comprehend the idea. Felt like she might sink to the floor in a puddle.

But the backbone her father had given her—and Kyle— held her upright.

She had to think. Not feel. Provide solution. Not need.

Devon was just…being Devon. He didn't trust anyone. Not even himself. He hadn't been kidding when he'd said those words earlier that night. He'd been deadly serious.

He knew himself. His failings.

And Kacey finally understood why the man had sequestered himself alone in the desert. Because of the lottery win, yeah, she got the trust ramifications that came from such a windfall. And his father's having been framed. She got what had made him the man he was.

But she'd already known both of those things.

What she hadn't realized was that he was broken in a way that couldn't be fixed. He knew it. And would never, ever be a man who could give a woman what Kacey had just then realized she so very much wanted from him.

A future.

Chapter Twenty-Two

There was no organ tissue on the knife. Just skin and some blood. The blade hadn't gone deep. A warning from those with whom Kyle had been working? Or the result of an amateur who, when it came right down to it, couldn't bring herself to stick it to her brother and so had only ended up with a surface wound? He was a cop. Had to keep his mind open to all possibilities, palatable or not, and let the evidence tell him the truth.

As soon as Kacey turned her back and went into her room, Devon went to bed. Slept a few hours and then showered and left for work. He didn't make coffee. Or make any attempt to see or speak to his houseguest.

He needed distance. Had to make certain he maintained clarity. He and Rachel had spent months infiltrating marina society, becoming locals. They'd learned things. Made small buys, testing to find them inferior to the recipe they were seeking. Finally had a contact who they suspected moved large amounts of the heroin they were after. Had just had a small buy of it confirmed. Were ready to move in for bigger buys, showing the money to do so, but needing to know more about the operation before they made the spend. They were on the cusp of infiltrating the right organization and bringing a successful close to their mission. They could take down Belen. And someone else would just move into his place. But if they could just get in far enough to know how the drugs were traveling away from the river and ending up in Virginia, they could shut down a lethal, nationwide chain claiming the lives of teenagers.

He couldn't let a woman get in the way of his successful completion of the job.

Had that been what had happened to his father?

Had Hilton lost sight of what was going on around him? Lost clarity? No way his dad would ever have knowingly turned dirty, but had things slipped by him because he'd been distracted by sexual desire? Making it easy for someone to put contraband in his vehicle and frame him for something he hadn't even known was happening?

Sierra's Web had talked to a lot of people about Hilton Grainger over the past months. The partner in charge of everything science related, Glen Thomas, had his lab of experts going over what physical evidence they—and Tommy—had been able to access from ten years before, which hadn't been much. Because the framing had to have been an inside job, they had to tread carefully where the Las Vegas police were concerned.

Sierra's Web had a contact there—a detective they'd helped on a case—and while Sierra's Web had been able to irrefutably verify that there hadn't been enough hard evidence to definitively prove that Hilton Grainger had been a crooked cop, they hadn't yet been able to pinpoint that he hadn't been.

Devon used his time on the water that morning, taking a young family of five on a beginning rafting trip, to clear his mind. To ground himself.

And to keep an eye on river traffic and shoreline—as he'd been doing every day he'd worked since he'd signed on for his job as river guide. And for weeks before that, too, out on the water in his kayak.

When thoughts of Kacey crept in, he shoved them away. Focused on a shadow in the water. Or started conversation with his clients.

He never told her that her twin hadn't been badly hurt. He should have done.

"Hey, Charlie, you enjoying your first time on a raft?" he asked the seven-year-old son of the family in his craft.

Saw the boy's nod. Heard the conversation between family members that ensued. Responded with nods of his own, and smiles. Not really taking any of it in.

He didn't watch his surveillance screens, either. His phone would vibrate if there was activity on any of the outside cameras, including around all windows and doors. Intruders couldn't get in—and houseguests couldn't go out—without him knowing about it. Just as they couldn't penetrate his property without a vibration happening against his leg. And a notification from Sierra's Web, as well. As long as his phone remained still, the place was secure.

Kacey was free to leave. If he got notification that she vacated the premises, he was not going to stop her. She wasn't under arrest.

End of his circles of control and concern.

He'd just checked himself on the thoughts, found himself in good standing, as he pulled into the dock. Wished his passengers a good rest of their vacation when he saw a man—average height, athletic, blond, come out of a public restroom by the marina and disappear around the back of it.

The clandestine movement got his attention, but the brief glimpse he'd had of the man's face sent his radar humming at top speed. He'd seen a few images of Kyle Ashland. And had been harboring a woman who looked a lot like him for the past few days.

Making a beeline to the boat storage area behind the restroom, he got there in time to see the man out on the guest dock, jumping into a small motorboat. He snapped a picture with his phone. Didn't get enough to make a positive identification on his own, but he sent it to Sierra's Web. With their software, they'd be able to match the image to others they had of Kyle Ashland and find out if facial, head or body parameters matched.

Devon didn't need to hear back from experts to know that Kyle Ashland had been at the marina. And had left in a hurry.

Had he been looking for his sister?

Meeting up with Kacey's kidnappers?

It couldn't be coincidence that the man had shown up.

Or that two men were dead—one buried in a crate that had had wrapping from a movie case in it similar to one that had been filled with drugs. And the other killed just after hiding a crate identical to the grave of the first.

And Kacey had been in possession of one of those movies.

Kacey had also been left to die in a boat anchored not far from the marina.

And her kidnappers had been in Rachel's bar two nights before.

She'd called her brother. Could have easily told him where she was.

And Kyle could also be following his own leads and was out looking for her. He'd headed upstream. Too fast for Devon to commission a boat and catch up to him.

Didn't think it a good idea, in any case. Why would a boating guide go chasing after a man using the public marina restroom?

One going the opposite direction of Devon's property which was miles in the other direction.

He pulled up his surveillance screens, though. Just in case Kyle turned around and headed toward Kacey. No way was he going to have his property used for illegal activity. There would be no suspicion, ever, of him being dirty.

No way he was going to let Kyle hurt Kacey on his watch, either. If that's what the man had set out to do. Even if Kacey had tried to hurt her twin with that knife.

Could have been self-defense.

Just as it might not have been.

Or been her at all.

Her kidnappers had been asking for a crate the night they were at the bar. Antonio had had the bar address on him the night he'd been killed.

The same night.

Keeping all mental channels open, he crossed the street to check in with Rachel—as he always did before leaving the marina area. Grabbed a burrito on his way, ate it sitting at the bar, washing it down with the soda she slid over to him.

The look she gave him as she did so…she had something to tell him. There were others at the bar, asking questions about the area. Wanting her opinion on the best things to do, which boating tours to take, what stops they involved. And he chewed slowly. Seemingly lost in scrolling on his phone.

More like, he was glued to his surveillance screens.

Kacey was in the laundry room, watching them, too. As she had the day before. Right before she'd rushed out in time to see a crate show up onshore. Had she been watching for Kyle?

The twins wouldn't be so careless as to have Kyle show up on Devon's cameras, but there could be some signal to her to get down to the shore. Off camera. Like where the crate had been shoved under the Bird of Paradise plants.

That flower in her hair…

His fingers in it so soon after…

Or… Kacey could be watching the screens so diligently because it was the only thing she could do to try to get her life back. Looking for any evidence that might lead to her freedom…

Boats on the water, going by his place was common.

Them coming close enough to shore for him to see them on camera…

Not so much…

Rachel's head appeared in his vision, tipping to see what he was looking at on his phone. Looking like a nosy bartender friend. "A guy came in. Early twenties. Wanted to know if I knew Jerome and Antonio. Said he heard Antonio had the bar's address on him. He'd known his friend was meeting up with someone and was about to get rich. This guy was nervous but figured someone here could help him make some money off of some movies. Said he didn't want to hold onto them, since they got his friends killed, but he needed the money bad. Seemed more like he needed a fix worse…" She looked him in the face as they talked, smiled a time or two. They could have been lovers having a little lunchtime tête-à-tête. Or good friends, sharing a good story over his glass of soda.

Devon smiled in response. Tapped his phone. Glanced at the screen.

"He said the brothers happened upon a broken case of porno movies during the storm. Stray movies from it were going downstream. They collected as many as they could. Found another case in the process, and then another. Thought they hit on a gold mine…"

Explained how movies—and Jerome—ended up at Devon's place.

"What'd you tell him?" Devon asked Rachel.

"The truth. I have no idea why Antonio had the address to this place."

Picking up a towel, Rachel wiped the counter around him, told him that Belen had been in touch to say his contact was open to conversation, and with another one of her sexy smiles, headed off to take the order of a couple who'd just taken seats at the bar.

Leaving Devon more frustrated than ever.

SHE HAD TO get ahold of Kyle. Kacey spent the morning watching the surveillance screens. Because...that was the only thing she could do during her current existence to feel as though she was taking action toward solutions.

But as the hours passed, one truth got louder and louder in her head.

She had to contact her brother. Period.

He'd been knifed. He hadn't told her—even when she'd turned in the weapon to the police. There was nothing about that that made any sense to her.

Nothing that made his situation look good.

But he was her twin. Her family.

She had to talk to him.

Even if it meant leaving the cabin permanently.

There was nothing keeping her there any longer except her own safety. And Devon's belief that he was safer if she stayed hidden.

He was probably right about that.

Stay gone. Kyle's words had been in her head all morning as well. Over and over and over again.

It was a match for the blood on the knife you turned in, hit her up as often. Followed by the vision of the cold question gazing at her from her lover's blue eyes.

She couldn't stay gone forever.

Nor continue living indefinitely with a man who might have feelings for her but was never going to trust her.

She couldn't let life trap her on a stool in a laundry closet.

She had nowhere to go. No way to get there. No identification. No money.

She had a phone.

Could call a friend from Bullhead City. Ask someone to come get her. Take her home where she had everything she needed.

Except protection.

She couldn't bring anyone she knew into her world. It was too dangerous. Her brother had already been hurt.

It seemed likely, with mention of the missing crate, that her kidnappers had had something to do with those two brothers turning up dead.

All over adult movies?

Thoughts rolled around, and as many times as they passed by again, they still made no sense to her.

She had to contact Kyle.

DEVON WAS STILL sitting at the bar, when his phone vibrated against the wood in front of him. And then again, and again. As he tapped on the screen, trying to find out what was going on, a 911 text from Sierra's Web popped up. Followed by another vibration.

The noise was distracting enough, Rachel glanced over. Smiling an apology in her direction for anyone who might be watching, he tapped to get back to his screens. They'd blacked out.

All of them.

At once.

Only one way that could have happened.

He pushed speed dial for Kacey's burner phone. It went straight to a voice mailbox that hadn't been set up.

His heart sinking, causing his thoughts to stagger, he dropped money on the bar, left and ran to his vehicle. He had it moving before he'd even fully closed his door and broke every speed limit as he devoured the miles between the marina and what had once been his private haven.

Kacey had shut down his surveillance system. It could only be done, all at once, from inside the cabin. No one else could have entered without him, or Sierra's Web, being aware of it. One vibration to him, not dozens of them.

Just as she couldn't have exited without being seen.

He'd trusted her, dammit. Left her alone at his place, believing that she wanted to be there, that she'd respect his property, at the very least.

He'd hoped she'd keep herself safe.

His security system being disabled...was Kyle there? Were they setting Devon up to take a fall for illegal drug distribution via porno flicks?

Was she okay?

She must have made the choice to disable the system.

No way anyone could have gotten to her without him knowing.

Unless, the day before, she'd given the number of her burner phone to someone.

He'd trusted her with that phone.

What in the hell was she doing?

Nothing safe. That was guaranteed.

She had a target on her head.

And he had no idea who was behind the trigger.

Why hadn't she trusted him to help her?

Every muscle in his body was tense, the blood racing through his veins, as he chewed up the miles.

And he thought of the last words he'd said to her. *It was a match for the blood on the knife you turned in.* There'd been accusation in his tone.

Borne of fear.

If she'd stabbed her brother, he couldn't help her.

And borne of doubt.

He was a man who'd always have difficulty trusting.

He tried her phone again. Same result. Either she'd shut it off, was hitting end call the second she saw it was him, or...

What?

Rachel called as he was nearing his turn in. Not wanting to take attention away from Kacey, he told his partner that it was a private matter and hung up.

And then called her back. He was a good cop.

"I've got something going on at my property. Connected, I think, to those movies. I'll keep you posted."

It had nothing to do with their operation. She couldn't blow her cover to help.

And he wasn't blowing his to ask for help.

Not unless he had to.

There was no sign of tire tracks other than his own larger off-road wheels in the dirt leading onto his land. The drive was hard desert ground. Plants, cacti, rock all looked as they had the hundreds of times he'd driven to and from the cabin in past months.

The cabin, when he careened within view, appeared... unremarkable. Just as he'd left it. No broken windows, or bullet holes in the wood. Front door intact. Closed. No sign of a vehicle, other than his own.

Had Kacey decided to take her own life? And turned off the tape so no one had to see?

He'd given her the gun.

Heart in his throat, tears close, he tore into the building, practically breaking the door when the lock got in his way. He could still have time to save her.

God, please don't let her die.

His last words to her had been full of accusation...

He'd never said anything about the way he admired the hell out of her ability to stand up when life knocked her down, or how she was the one woman he'd have wanted to marry if he trusted himself to do such a thing. Not even a word about how much he liked her cooking.

In the door, his gaze flew faster than his feet.

Nothing out of place in the kitchen.

Her room. The bathroom.

The living room.

The laundry closet. He turned the security system back on. Scanned the screens like a madman.

Looked at the rooms he'd just been through.

No blood.

No sign of struggle.

Back out in the cabin, he took a quick look in his room. Avoiding more than a cursory glance at the unmade sheets, he eyed the rug over the trapdoor. She couldn't get down there and then replace the rug, but someone could have…

The rug flew across the room as his hand let go of it, landing on the bed, and he pulled up the opening to his small bunker.

Not one damned thing down there.

Where in the hell was she?

And then it hit him.

She was an award-winning swimmer.

The river.

Chapter Twenty-Three

Kacey hiked for miles. Her phone was turned off and in a sealed kitchen storage bag in her pocket. Bottles of water and granola bars were in another sealed kitchen bag tied up in a shirt to the belt loop at her waist. And her gun was shoved in the other side of her waistband. She was careful to stay as hidden as she could in the never-ending tall desert brush. Walking along mountain edges for coolness as often as she could. When Arizona's blistering hot sun got too much for her, she climbed down to the shore and swam downstream for a while, her goods on her person and secured, then got out and hiked some more. The river was the quicker and less tiring way to travel, but she'd also be more likely to be seen there.

By drones, if nothing else.

Not that she was getting fanciful, or dramatic.

She was being practical.

Trying to stay alive.

She had to get far enough away from Devon's place to make a call without leading anyone anywhere near him. And then she was throwing the cell in the river.

Just as Devon had taught her.

She'd left him a note—on his pillow because she had to believe that some of what they'd shared there had been special to him, too—apologizing for shutting down his system. And thanking him for all that he'd done for her.

She'd researched cell towers in the area. Had to get fifteen miles to be assured that her phone would connect to a different service than the one the cabin used. Two miles was possible, because there was a tower at the marina that could reach out another ten. Ten was safe, due to the rural area. Fifteen guaranteed her that she wouldn't be able to connect to the smaller tower that provided signal to Devon's place.

Stopping to eat granola bars in shaded coves, to sip water on a regular basis, she didn't let herself think beyond the next horizon. What she'd find out when she got her brother on the phone...that was to worry about in that moment.

Where her next meal would come from, if she'd have a pillow somewhere to lay her head on that night, if she'd be alive by morning...all things currently out of her control to know.

She had to talk to Kyle.

She'd planned on twenty-minute miles. Three miles an hour, five hours to destination, give or take five-minute breaks for resting and eating. Longer if she happened upon wildlife. When she grew discouraged, she reminded herself that swimming helped cut down the time.

And she thought about the previous night in her bed, and Devon's. Before she'd gone to bed alone. The way he'd touched her, the tenderness...it brought tears to her eyes just thinking about it.

When she figured she'd gone eight miles, she leaned against the side of a mountain, about a hundred yards from the river, and pulled out her cell phone. Opened an app that let her see what tower she was connected to, and nearly wept when she saw that she'd gotten lucky.

That fate, or her father's angel, was watching out for her.

She could make her call.

With shaking fingers, she dialed her brother's number. She'd hear his voice. Connect to her real life. Threaten to turn herself in if he didn't tell her what was going on. She couldn't *stay gone* any longer.

The phone rang. She took a deep breath.

And heard that the number she was calling was no longer in service.

THE SECOND THE trapdoor had slammed back into his bedroom floor, Devon had called Sierra's Web, telling them to track one of many burner phones they'd given him—his only way to do an immediate search for the woman who needed to remain dead even after she was found. If she was found. And giving them a no-holds-barred directive to find Kyle Ashland.

He'd been halfway to his own boat dock by then, had jogged and jumped downhill the rest of the way, and had been on the river ever since. Up and downstream. Slowly. Searching banks. Shorelines. Looking for any sign of Kacey. A piece of clothing. A tennis shoe.

A granola bar wrapper. Whether she had them with her or not—he hadn't taken the time to find out—he figured her for being prepared when she'd left.

Of course, if Kyle had picked her up just beyond Devon's dock, she'd have needed no other preparation.

As a couple of hours passed with no sign of her, his tension grew. As did his return to thinking like the full-time star detective he'd been. Kacey didn't fit the profile of a suicide victim. Not on any level.

Didn't mean she couldn't have gone to the river to die. Profiles were only suggestions, supposition. Guesswork based on data.

After he'd done enough searching to be convinced that Kacey wasn't swimming the river, he headed back to search his property—and beyond—on dry ground. Until he heard from Kacey, or heard that she'd been located, he would be in his vehicle, driving every inch of desert setting out from his cabin.

He was not going to rest until she'd been found.

SITTING ON TOP of a five-foot boulder Kacey tried Kyle's phone one more time. To hear the same recording. Looking at her screen, to make sure she'd dialed correctly, she could hardly make out the numbers through her suddenly tear-blurred sight. She allowed the wracking sobs to rip up from deep inside her, let them have their say.

For a minute. Just until she could make them stop.

She couldn't afford to cry. Heatstroke, caused in part by dehydration, was the most common cause of death in the Arizona wilderness. She had to conserve her bodily fluids. Her father's words from years gone by sounded in her brain.

Sitting up straighter, she took note.

Sipped from her second water bottle. She had two more. Hadn't figured she'd be hiking further than fifteen miles, expecting Kyle to either come get her or send someone he trusted, and hadn't wanted to weigh herself down.

The more weight, the more danger of tiring sooner and falling prey to heat exhaustion.

She had her phone. Other than the brief seconds to make her calls, she'd had it off. But if she was going to risk exposing herself, she could send money electronically.

Where? Where would she send it?

How would she get there to pick it up?

Without putting someone at risk for having been associated with her?

And then it hit her. She needed to call the sawmill. She could disguise her voice, just ask for the production manager. Perhaps pose as a lawyer, with the threat of a lawsuit.

Or a doctor. Some kind of call that Kyle would definitely want to take.

Or make someone at the mill more apt to give Kacey a number where she could reach him if he wasn't there to come to the phone.

She doubted Kyle was at work. But her brother was always available to the mill by phone.

Always.

Feeling energized, purposeful, she stood on the boulder, on top of the world, albeit hidden by the leafy six-foot ground cover in front of it, and dialed.

There was hope in her voice as she tipped it up an octave, gave it her rendition of a Southern accent and asked for Kyle Ashland.

Only to be told that her brother was no longer working there.

Phone off again, Kacey sat.

Alone in the desert wilderness, with late afternoon turning into early evening, she had no time to get back to Devon's before darkness fell and the desert's live creatures came out for the night's hunt.

Not that she was going back to the cabin.

Or to Devon.

She had to take care of herself. Rely only on herself.

There was a solution to every problem. It was up to her to solve, not need.

So why was her heart crying out in such a desperate way for a man who couldn't trust her?

One who'd taken her in, tended to her ankle wounds, provided her with clothes, given her a gun and a phone, driven her to call her brother, helped her identify—through bar surveillance footage—at least one of her abductors...

She couldn't go back there. That look in his eye when he'd told her about Kyle's blood on the knife...if Devon was convinced that she'd stabbed a man, he'd turn her in to the police. And do all he could to see that she was treated fairly.

The man had a code of honor like none other.

Not only would she then be in the custody of the people who very likely betrayed her when she'd turned in the bloody weapon to begin with, but if she were to be charged with a felony, she'd lose her job.

Her career.

She could lose her home next door to her mother. Her insurance benefits…

Panic swirled, making her light-headed…

Or was it the heat?

She had to drink. Took a sip. Then another.

She had to find a place to spend the night. Maybe if she climbed a tree. And drifted off to sleep and fell out?

Under some brush?

Prey to any animal that happened upon her?

If she could find a small mountain cave…the early settlers in the area had lived in them. Centuries ago.

Standing again, using her boulder to peruse the mountainous landscape rather than the river side, she sought out the most likely source for an overnight dwelling.

Saw a couple of ground level indentations in the distance. There was no way to know if they'd suffice until she reached them. But she had a plan. A step to take.

And so she started taking them. One at a time. One foot in front of the other.

With one thought in mind.

She was not going to die.

KYLE ASHLAND WAS nowhere to be found. He hadn't been to the mill where he worked since the day Kacey had witnessed the argument outside her bedroom window. Was no longer employed there.

His residence on-site still appeared to have his possessions in it, but no one had seen him there in days.

His wireless number had been disconnected, by him, the day Kacey had called him.

Devon didn't ask how Sierra's Web had come by the information revealed to him during a phone call as he drove, but he knew that whatever the means, no laws had been broken. The integrity of Sierra's Web was one thing he knew he could trust.

He also suspected Kacey's twin was going off-grid. Maybe forever.

Which left Kacey—and eventually her mother and little sister, too—hanging out to dry.

Most particularly if Kacey was going with him.

Or was murdered because of him.

As the sun moved dangerously closer to the horizon, giving him only a few hours left to find any sign of his missing houseguest before darkness fell, Devon debated going to the local police for help. If she was hurt, or...

What?

She was a free woman. She'd obviously chosen to leave his place of her own accord. No one else had been on the property to shut off the security system.

Stopping back by his place on his back-and-forth grid search across the desert, he grabbed more water for himself—leaving the extra he'd already thrown in the cooler in the event that he found her hurt out in the desert—and grabbed some fruit, too. Turning back to the cupboard when he remembered her granola bars. The woman couldn't get through a day without one of them.

The box wasn't there.

It was empty, in the trash.

There'd been at least six bars left that morning. He'd

grabbed one for himself, but, thinking of how they'd left things the night before, had put it back.

On his way out, passing his bedroom door, he hesitated. Glanced in, remembering the hours they'd spent on that bed before Sierra's Web had called with the news about Kyle's blood on the knife.

The rug he'd thrown on the bed...ruined the memory. With the water balanced with one hand and arm against his chest, he grabbed the edge of the rug. Threw it to the floor. Just like he needed to do with the myriad feelings he couldn't seem to escape where Kacey was concerned.

Something fluttered on the bed.

A piece of paper.

He grabbed it.

Read the two lines.

I apologize for shutting down your security system. Thank you for all that you've done for me.

It was signed simply, *K.*

A goodbye letter.

Clearly.

He had to let her go.

Chapter Twenty-Four

The second cave worked. It took Kacey a couple of hours to get there and get settled. She'd turned on her phone only for a few seconds to use the flashlight to scope out the small crater space, making certain that the enclosure ended at the six feet or so in, as it had appeared, and that she wasn't sharing it with any critters. Next had been finding and hauling in the soft brush and leaves she'd used for a cushion to sit on. Then setting up piles of rocks under a randomly running perimeter of brush set haphazardly around the opening. Nothing would get close without her hearing stones move. And finally, pulling part of a fallen tree, and breaking other taller branches from ground plants to create a door in front of her.

Satisfied that she'd done all she could, she stood at the entrance where she'd be more likely to have service and turned her phone back on only long enough to try Kyle one more time.

For all she knew he'd taken his SIM card out of his phone and was putting it back in only when needed. She had no idea how those things worked, in terms of a wireless phone with a no-longer-in-service message. Hadn't ever had cause to care.

Receiving the same message a third time, she turned off

her phone midway through the verbiage. Battery was at seventy percent. She needed to conserve. Had no idea what the next days would bring.

The lack of phone left her with nothing but shadow inside the cave to keep her company. And an imagination that kept her picking her feet up and putting them down, brushing the area around her little makeshift mat with a big leaf on a twig. Sweeping up her area, she told herself. All in an attempt to make certain that no spiders or scorpions were getting close to her.

When she started thinking about rattlesnakes, she stood up. Nearly hit her head. Went out and grabbed more twigs, searching until she found a few logs big enough to fit across the front of the cave, dragged them over. Put some pebbles in her two empty water bottles and balanced them on top of the makeshift half door. If nothing else, a slithering ground animal would inadvertently topple the bottles, alerting her, were she to have a trespasser during the night.

About an hour into the darkness, early enough that she could see still the light of deep dusk outside, she heard the snort.

Knew it from the night she and Devon had met up with the pack of javelinas. Remaining completely still, she hardly dared breathe. The forty-pound smelly animals didn't hunt humans. She wasn't in their path. She should be fine as long as she didn't somehow make them feel threatened.

When she felt pretty certain that the danger had passed, she cried a little. Only a few tears. She wouldn't waste the liquid.

But, damn. How had life gotten so completely out of whack? She'd gone to bed a regular daughter, sister, first-grade teacher. Had woken to ugly voices out her window.

And everything had changed.

In that blink.

And Devon?

She'd never in her life slept with a man without going on several dates, first. And she'd never fallen in love.

Not that she was saying she had with Devon, either.

But she'd come close.

She missed him.

Wondered what he'd done when he'd seen her note.

If he'd seen it yet.

He could still be with Rachel at the bar, for all she knew. She hadn't seen him all day. Another few hours and it would have been a full twenty-four since she'd laid eyes on him.

So, what, she was going to count the hours with him, now? Or the hours after him?

Shaking her head, she nixed that idea.

Had it really been three mealtimes ago since he'd slid hungrily on top of her? Inside her?

Was she going to sit there all night and torture herself?

Something touched her ankle. Jerking back, she slapped her hand against the skin. Felt nothing but…herself. No bug. No bite.

Kyle, where are you?

Thoughts she'd been fighting so hard to keep at bay were caving in on her.

Was her brother dead?

He couldn't be. She'd know. Right?

Twin thing.

She didn't know.

Whether he was alive.

Or if he wasn't.

And her mom and Lizzie? They'd be gone at least a week. But after that? Since it was summer, and Lizzie wasn't in school, had Kyle booked them longer?

She missed them both.

Tears sprang to her eyes again as she thought of her little

sister's sweet blue-eyed face, with the soft long blond hair falling around her. She still had a bit of a baby face, with cheeks not quite matured into their final shape.

Lizzie was bright. And funny.

She hated that everyone in the family had known Steve Ashland but her.

And loved having her big sister at school with her. Every chance she got, she visited Kacey's class on her way to recess or during lunch. Rode to school with her. And came down to Kacey's room and waited for Kacey to take her home, too.

Outside had grown as black as the interior of her refuge. Shadows lurked everywhere. The moon's glow hadn't yet come over the mountain to bathe anything in light.

She needed the light. Turned her phone on long enough to see the time. And then, walking just short of the opening of the small cave, turned and surveyed her abode. To check more carefully for any little live creatures. The light helped. She'd burn a little battery.

Checked her ankle. Scratched at it again.

Grabbed a granola bar, sat back down, unwrapped the top, took a bite, but practically choked trying to swallow it.

She sipped water to wash it down. Quickly recapped the bottle. She had no idea how long she was going to need to make it last.

Turned off her phone.

She'd head to the river in the morning. Swim downstream until she came to some form of civilization. Or could flag a boat on the water.

She had a plan.

She was not going to die.

DEVON WAS JUST finishing up frying some fish for dinner when his phone buzzed a 911 from Sierra's Web. They'd identified the man Kacey claimed was one of her kidnappers. He was a well-respected man from a small Utah town. And the CEO of the mill in Arizona where Kyle Ashland had been employed. He was also CEO of two other sawmills. One in Utah. One in Colorado.

The man had money. Not enough to be famous, but enough to live well. Owned a home in a well-to-do neighborhood in his hometown. Had a summer ranch house. A houseboat.

And took his family vacationing in the Caribbean every winter, based on their social media accounts. He was a family man.

Not a kidnapper.

There was also no physical evidence of him being in Bullhead City. In Arizona.

Or in a bar in a marina anywhere on the Colorado River.

No credit card usage. No gas receipts. No flight records.

The one thing that rang true from any information he'd had on the kidnapper, was that the man was on a fishing expedition with a couple of his friends.

Except that Eli Sanders was in northern Colorado. Staying at a friend's cabin. Off the grid.

A yearly sabbatical they'd been taking since high school.

The next piece of information he and Hudson discussed in more depth was equally unsettling.

They'd known Kyle Ashland no longer worked at the mill, his place of business since giving up his football career to help his family.

But had the man been fired, become a disgruntled ex-employee?

Had Kacey been trying to get her brother to see sense and things had gotten out of control?

Or, more likely, had her brother been trying to make up

the money he was missing from his lost job by peddling cheap drugs via porno flicks?

His mind was racing so fast he almost missed Hudson saying, "that burner phone you wanted us to trace. It has to be on long enough for us to pinpoint a tower."

So if she'd talked to her brother, she'd known not to make the call too long.

"It was just on long enough," the man told him. And Devon turned off the oil cooking his fish. Ready to rip into the man for not giving him that information, first.

Not that Hudson would have any reason to know which piece of information was more important to Devon. On the face of things, the Kyle information was… "And?" he asked as he slowed himself down.

"It's connected to Wi-Fi so as soon as it stayed on long enough, we were able to triangulate the number to a small tower out in the desert. Only has a range of about two miles. Apparently, it was put there for a fairly sizable RV park by the mountain. The park's only open during the wintertime so activity on that tower is pretty much nil."

A closed RV park? Any that he'd been in had public restrooms. Showers. Even with the water off, it would offer shelter.

A hiding place.

"How close can you get me to the phone?"

"It's off again, so I can't do that. But I can tell you the co-ordinates, within six feet, of where it was when it was on."

Grabbing his keys, Devon was still on the phone when he headed out into the night.

SHE WASN'T GOING to lie down. Kacey had made that determination from the beginning. She was sitting up with her back to the end wall of the cave. Facing the entrance, with her gun beside her.

After she'd settled in, telling herself she had to get some rest, she'd sat there practicing with the gun's location. Closing her eyes and reaching for it. Moving it an inch and trying again.

Before she was allowed to sleep, she had to be able to pick up the gun, having it pointed at the entrance, with her finger on the trigger, all in one move. In one second.

No fumbling.

She'd ended up with the side of the butt of the pistol up against her leg.

The weight of it there gave her comfort. Almost like it was a live companion. A gift from Devon.

And she could use her leg to hold the gun steady as she grabbed it.

Satisfied, she'd just closed her eyes, panicked that sleep wasn't going to come, when she heard the unmistakable sound of rocks tumbling outside.

Her makeshift security system.

Just the one crunch and tumble.

And then total silence.

That couldn't be good.

Had Devon turned her in? Given the police her phone number to track? Reported his gun stolen?

Were they coming to arrest her?

Or worse, had her kidnappers somehow found her? Because she'd called Kyle's phone so many times?

Could they track that kind of thing?

There were apps…she knew a little bit. Not nearly enough.

The gun in her hand, pointing at the entrance of the cave, happened in one move without her even being aware of trying. She'd never shot a living organism in her life.

But if some fiend thought she was going to be found floating facedown in the river…she'd shoot.

She was not going to die.

HE'D FOUND HER. A mile closer to his place than the deserted RV park. Devon stopped when his tennis shoe, set carefully down on a leaf, crunched pebbles on a bigger rock which rolled. He'd been watching every step. Not well enough.

He'd located the makeshift wall. Had been heading toward it. And missed the perimeter of random brush.

Over pebbles.

He'd gotten ahead of himself.

And Kacey Ashland was one smart woman.

Was she in there alone?

Or still in there at all?

He was more than half an hour behind the phone's ping. Surely she wouldn't have set up a structure and then gone out alone into the pitch-black night.

He listened for talking.

Whispering.

Anything to indicate if more than one person lurked behind those limbs. Or close by.

Watching him?

No technology, no experts, no evidence was going to help him with this one. It was all assessing what he could see, listening for what he couldn't, and relying on instinct.

She had a gun.

So did he, but until he had an eye on her, she had the advantage.

Tommy Grainger was in full work mode. Gun out. Pointing.

He took one step back, off to the side, so he wasn't standing in her line of fire. In case her aim was that good.

The cave. The fallen trees and brush at the entrance. That perimeter. All impressive.

He'd bet they were things her father had taught her.

The Special Forces marine.

A man Devon would have liked to have known.

One who'd raised a daughter to risk her life for others. To get up when she fell, brush herself off and move on. To push herself, physically and mentally. To serve her family with an open heart filled with love.

Devon was sure the man had not advised his daughter to fall in love with a complete stranger. And yet...she had. Not love. She hadn't loved Devon. But she'd made love to him with an open heart filled with acceptance. With honor and liking and care.

"Kacey?" He lowered his gun but didn't move otherwise. She'd have to shoot through the mountain to hit him. Or Kyle would.

Someone else their father would have trained.

His call was met with total silence.

"I'm alone," he said then. "Sierra's Web tracked your phone for me. I've been out here looking for you since the security system went down. Except for a brief time when I let myself be convinced that you didn't need my help. Please, just let me know you're okay."

"Did you report the gun stolen?" He almost dropped to his knees when he heard the strength in her words. Like she was going to use the weapon on him then and there if he had.

"No." Just the one word. Partially because his throat was thick with emotion. He blinked. Looked up to the sky.

Thank God.

She was still there.

And wasn't going to shoot him. His heart had known that all along. Kacey gave everyone the benefit of the doubt. Even after they'd hurt her.

Unlike Tommy Grainger—and through him, Devon Miller—who never would.

"I'm afraid Kyle's dead. His phone's saying it's not in service." She hadn't shown herself. Didn't sound any closer.

He remained off to the side of the cave's opening. Wasn't going to trap her. "I saw him this morning."

Devon barely heard movement before he saw her, standing there covered from the hips down by her natural gate. Her hair looked tangled. Her face, what he could make out of it, seemed to hang with weariness.

"You saw Kyle?"

"Yes."

"Where?" She still hadn't come out. Didn't trust him. Or want to be with him. Either way, he didn't like it.

If she was involved in something bad, he had to help her.

By the law, but he'd pull every string he had to pull. And find others if she needed them. He'd pay Sierra's Web to contact whoever they had to contact to make things as easy on her as possible. "At the marina. He came out of the public bathroom and jumped in a boat tied up at the visitor's dock."

Her wall fell forward so quickly, he jumped back. And then, unable to help himself, moved toward her, turning on his phone's light and shining her as she stood there. His beam covered every inch of her.

He had to know she was okay.

"What kind of boat?" she asked, not even squinting in the brightness.

She'd been crying. Streaks of dirt followed what would have been tears down her cheeks.

"An older one. Motorboat. Small, but powerful judging by the way he took off out of there." He knew so much more about her and her brother than he had the last time he'd seen her. First and foremost, that the man she claimed had kidnapped her was a well-to-do businessman from Utah. Not something he was going to offer. He was still a cop.

"With a red stripe down the side and a gold bulldog on the back?" Her voice shook.

Bulldog. Marine mascot. He should have put that together.

"Yes."

He'd turned off his flashlight but could still see the glisten in her suddenly widened eyes. "Can I use your boat?"

"*We* can use my boat." That was nonnegotiable.

She nodded. "We have to go, Devon. Now," she told him. Moving quickly, as though she was going to lead the way.

Heading off in the wrong direction. That strength. The determination. The getting right back up and moving forward. He almost hated to call out to her.

"Kacey?"

"Yeah?"

"The off-roader is this way."

He waited for her to catch up to him. Would have started toward the vehicle, but she stopped right in front of him. Almost standing on his toes.

"Thank you for coming to get me," she said, then.

And he pulled her into his arms.

He couldn't help it.

The woman had gotten to him.

Chapter Twenty-Five

For a second, Kacey let herself lean on Devon. She fell into him, hung on.

And then let go.

Heading off in the direction he'd indicated. He'd keep up with her. She knew that much about him.

"Last I knew, the boat was out of commission," she told him, her tone giving away none of the relief that had consumed her when she'd felt his body against hers. "Something about the engine. Kyle must have had it fixed." He hadn't mentioned it, which seemed odd, but not nearly as out of character as fights with strangers, bloody knives and refusing to confide in her.

And that was all for a future moment.

In the current one... "My dad insisted on a tracking device for the boat," she started telling the only man who was currently in a position to help her. "We lived a block from the river and rather than restricting us from going there alone, he taught us how to enjoy the water safely." The vehicle wasn't in sight yet. They had a walk ahead of them. She wasn't going to let time in the dark with Devon push her off track. "He practiced what he preached. Even his fishing boat had a tracker because he said you never know and you have to be prepared..."

"I'd like to have met him."

Her heart tugged. Her dad probably would have liked Devon.

Other than the thinking his daughter was a criminal thing.

No.

She wasn't getting personal.

She had to find Kyle and one way or another, get her life back. Period.

"It's an old device," she said after a long second's pause. "A little radio transmitter. There are four receivers. Mom has one. Kyle and I each have one. And the fourth one is buried under a rock in the shore right by our dock. Mom's friend Cynthia knows to check there if we don't make it back."

What had always seemed normal to her, good sense, sounded paranoid as she walked in the dark with a man she'd only known a few days.

A man who'd never met her family.

And who was convinced that her brother was a bad guy.

Even if Kyle had fallen into something off-key, there'd be some kind of explanation. Maybe not one that would keep him out of jail, but her twin was a good man.

Bone-deep good.

If he had to do jail time, he'd be a model prisoner. Kyle was just that way.

"You're suggesting that we take my boat to Bullhead City, to look under a rock for a receiver that's been buried there for years?"

"I dug it up last year, the last time we had the boat out actually, to change the batteries," she said. "And yes." It was the day the engine had gone out. She'd had Lizzie on-board with her.

"The man wouldn't talk to you, tell you what was going on, even after you were kidnapped and left to die," Devon's tone was stern. "How on earth can you still think he'd leave you a way to find him?"

"That's not why he's in that boat. Kyle has his own boat. He has access to a marina of them. The only reason he'd take Dad's is because he's in over his head. Anytime he's struggling, he uses Dad's tools, or wears an old shirt of his, or goes fishing in Dad's favorite spot. I know my twin. He's feeling desperate."

And if he wasn't…if he'd thrown out the radio transmitter in the boat…she at least had to try. Even if she had to hitchhike back to Bullhead City and take her chances to remain undiscovered.

"He's no longer at his job."

She stumbled. He kept walking. And she kept up. She'd known, but…

"How do you know that?"

"I paid Sierra's Web to see what they could find out."

For her. He'd spent his own money to help her. Granted, he'd won the lottery. Money wouldn't mean to him what it meant to her. Still, that he'd done that…

"Did they say anything else about him?" Like who those men were who'd been with her twin that night by their mother's house.

"No."

She nodded. Wanted to thank him for checking for her.

Was afraid she'd crack and take him back into her personal space if she did.

Instead, she just kept on walking.

BECAUSE THEY COULDN'T operate a personal watercraft on the river between sunset and sunrise, Devon suggested that Kacey get some sleep on the back seat of his vehicle while he drove the nearly two hours up to Bullhead City. With everything escalating, and him not feeling as much in control of the situation as he'd like, he wanted to keep her out of sight more than ever.

She didn't argue.

She wasn't saying much of anything.

She'd accepted the water he'd offered her. Had taken down an entire bottle at once. But had shaken her head when he'd offered food.

Though he kept a close watch, and was ready for trouble, the trip across one-lane mostly uninhabited roads lacking any kind of lighting was completely uneventful. Either whoever had been after him only knew his truck, as he'd suspected, or they no longer had an interest in him.

Because they thought Kacey was dead?

As the miles passed easily, he relaxed a bit with the thought that Tommy's cover hadn't been blown.

And didn't think Kacey slept at all. She'd been restless. He'd heard none of the long steady breaths he'd listened to when she'd been asleep in his arms.

Seemed so long ago.

He followed her directions to a public parking lot near her family's dock. Expected a fight when he told her to stay down in the off-roader while he went to dig up the receiver. Instead, she'd told him exactly where to find the device. And he'd done so in a matter of minutes, careful to fill in the dirt and reapply the rock exactly as he'd found it. Verifying that he'd done so with the picture he'd snapped on his phone before beginning. And taking an after photo for her sake.

As he headed back out of the small river town, he tried to picture Kacey growing up there. Completely silent in the back—not even a thank-you when he'd handed her the receiver—she didn't mention which street she lived on in the small town. Didn't point out an area, much less a house.

From what he could see in the dark, lit only by a few city streetlights, there weren't a lot of two-story homes.

What she'd also never mentioned during their acquaintance, but which he'd full well known, was the brightly lit strip of casinos directly across the river from her hometown.

Laughlin, Nevada. Once his father's responsibilities. Though the casino strip was an hour and a half from Las Vegas, it was still under the LVPD jurisdiction. Tommy had been there many times. With Kacey, unknowingly, just a quick walk across the bridge.

Devon Miller's portion of the great Colorado River bordered California. Kacey's bordered Tommy Grainger's home state.

Not one to put any credibility in omens, he still figured that for a bad one.

Tired, and yet filled with the adrenaline that kept Tommy Grainger on the job for thirty-six hours or more when needed, Devon made it back to his cabin with a few hours to spare before sunrise.

Charged up that he wasn't going to spend the night in his home alone, as he'd been thinking when he'd been frying fish he hadn't wanted, he wasn't even put out when Kacey excused herself to the restroom the second he unlocked the front door. And then, with a quick word about seeing him just before dawn, went into her room.

The lock he heard click in place after her pretty much told him where she stood.

His body drooped a little with the message, but, as he cleaned up the dinner mess he'd left, the rest of him was completely on board with her choice.

Their time to fool around was done.

He was an undercover cop. Kacey was a victim, and possibly a suspect.

There was no more between them than that.

KACEY SLEPT WELL. And was already awake before she heard Devon moving around in the cabin. Unlike the morning before, when she'd purposely stayed in her room until after he'd left, she was up and had the coffee going before he exited the bathroom.

Her turn was quick. Just basic necessities.

She had to get out on the river.

And away from the reminders of who she'd been in that cabin. With him. Because she knew herself. With just a small bit of encouragement from him she'd be right back in his arms. In his bed. In his life for however long he wanted her there.

His inability to trust was a flaw. Most definitely.

But she understood it. He was aware of it. Acknowledged it.

And everyone had faults.

On the other side…the man had been faultless in his support of her. Respecting her choices. Being honest with her. Risking his life for her.

Even after she'd left him, he'd come to find her.

Was helping her find Kyle.

He was tender. Aware. Paid attention.

And…her heart burst open when he came out of his room in shorts, a T-shirt and tennis shoes, his long dark hair pulled back in a ponytail. She loved the man.

The day before, she wouldn't let herself think about never seeing him again. Or to acknowledge how bad leaving him hurt. She wouldn't let herself cry for him.

Didn't seem possible that she could love him. She'd known him less than a week. But they'd faced possible death together. And lived a lifetime in those few days.

"You ready?" he asked, all business when she was melting all over the place.

Saving her again. From herself.

"Yes," she told him, holding up a shopping bag filled with bottled water, granola bars and fruit.

His nod as he reached into the oven and pulled out two bagel-and-egg sandwiches, handing her one, didn't express approval. Or the opposite.

What was, was.

She took the bagel and ate, following him out the door.

FOR AN OLD device with outdated technology, the tracking system worked like a charm. He should have figured. A marine would have had access to the best of the best.

Tense as he steered his small motor craft, Devon was channeling Tommy, all cop, watching everywhere. Ready for anything. Kyle being at Devon's marina the day before had not been an accident. Or a coincidence borne out of bathroom necessity.

The man clearly had some kind of business there.

With Kacey's kidnappers? Someone had abducted her. Tied her up. Left her to die. Someone who'd argued with Kyle in Bullhead City.

Or else Kyle Ashland was the unluckiest human being Devon had met in a while, stopping to pee and being spotted by an undercover detective, who happened to have rescued his sister. The man's days of escaping accountability for whatever he'd gotten involved in were done.

Worried about Kacey, about how it would all go down, how he'd protect her, Devon followed the coordinates he was receiving, watching for anyone else on the river.

He wanted Kyle Ashland to pay for whatever he'd done. He did not want to lead killers to the man's boat.

As they got closer, he slowed. And before approach, turned off his motor. Grabbing the oars to propel them.

"Sit at the wheel," he told Kacey. "Be prepared to throttle up and get us out of here."

She was there in a second. Watching around them intently, one hand on the wheel, one hand on the key.

"Stop." He heard her whisper. She pointed. Run aground in a cove almost completely covered naturally by the low-hanging branches of trees above, was the boat.

He nodded, letting her know he'd seen it.

And a shot rang out.

"FULL THROTTLE!" DEVON'S command came in the very next second.

Kacey held tight to the key, ready to pull it from the ignition if Devon approached.

Kyle had shot in the air. Kacey heard the bullet burst through the leaves and branches above them.

And she saw Devon aiming for her father's boat.

He wouldn't miss.

"Kyle," she called softly. Just once. He'd have scoped out the area. Wouldn't have shot if he thought whoever he was running from was nearby.

He'd been warning any curious onlookers to leave him alone.

Even if he hadn't secured his surroundings and didn't know he wasn't alerting her kidnappers to his location, he'd know her voice.

Devon wasn't going to give him a second chance. He was aiming.

Sweat poured down Kacey's back.

Then, hands in the air, Kyle appeared.

Devon lowered his gun.

And Kacey wept.

DEVON WATCHED, CHIN tight, poised and ready to jump into action as Kyle Ashland boarded his boat.

Devon stood there, gun in hand, chin still tensed, as

he watched brother and sister gravitate to each other. And hold on.

The whiteness of the other man's fingers as they wrapped Kacey's back told Devon how much strength was in that hold. Kyle's eyes were closed for the first seconds.

And then wide open, peering at Devon, before he shoved Kacey behind him. "I don't know who you are, or how you know Sanders, but you're going to let my sister go. You've got me. I'll say I did it all. I'll take the fall, knowing that if I don't, if I ever breathe a word to anyone, even a cell mate, Sanders will be after my family. I've got the message, loud and clear. Now you're going to let Kacey board my boat. She's going to drive away, and I'll turn over my gun. If you don't want to play it my way, if you hurt me again, or in any way harm my family, an envelope is going to show up at the Sanders home, another with the FBI, and a third with the Utah state police—all being held by a secure source, in a secure location, to be sent if Kacey, my mother, Lizzie and I can't all be contacted for proof of safety. If you need proof, or Sanders does, of what's in those envelopes, I have copies, right here, on my phone."

The man was good.

Taking Tommy Grainger by surprise. He'd had Kacey's twin pegged for a weakling who'd let his sister take a fall for him.

"If you've got such strong proof of something on Sanders, why not just go ahead and send it and be done with it?"

"You don't know, do you?"

Shaking his head, Devon told the truth. Listening for the lies.

"He's a...friend... Kyle," Kacey said, coming out from behind her brother. "His name's Devon Miller. He's a river guide. He saved my life and has been letting me stay at his cabin. Since you told me to stay gone, I haven't been seen in public at all..."

Hold everything. Kyle had told her to stay gone? And she hadn't told him. Devon's hand tightened on his gun. With a thought to the badge he didn't have on him.

But the mention of Sanders, the man in the bar Kacey had named as her kidnapper...kept Devon quiet. For the moment.

Staring at his sister, Kyle then turned a dark glance back at Devon. "You were watching me at the marina yesterday..."

"He's been trying to help me find you." Kacey spoke again, preventing any lies Devon might have told. "He's seen pictures..."

Did she leave out mention of Sierra's Web on purpose? Or just didn't see a point in clouding the issue?

The idea that she was protecting him, his privacy, came and went.

"If this is true, can we get to wherever you've been keeping Kacey?" Kyle put Devon on the spot.

But one glance at Kacey, the expectancy there, and Devon nodded.

With a sick feeling in his gut.

Chapter Twenty-Six

Though it hurt to do so, Kacey fully agreed when Devon and Kyle both insisted that they leave Steve Ashland's boat in the cove where Kyle had spent the night.

It was early enough that they made it back up to Devon's place before seven. He was due to go into work at ten. No more was said on the boat during the trip back.

She'd checked her brother's side, saw that the wound was superficial and already partly healed. As were her ankles. Funny how skin healed even when hearts were broken.

She needed to hear about that knife wound. About all of it.

Including whoever this Sanders was.

But with the sun up, and Kyle with her, she was taking no chances on them being seen. She'd insisted Kyle lie down, keeping his back to a side of the boat.

She sat on the floor between the two seats.

Glancing at Devon more often than she'd have liked. Needing to read him. To hear what he was thinking.

Frustrated that they couldn't talk openly.

Not until they knew what was going on.

If Kyle was into illegal activity, she wasn't going to have Devon implicated. No way he was going to be charged with harboring a criminal.

At the same time, her heart was pounding in leaps and bounds. Could it really be ending? She'd get the truth. The three of them would figure out who to trust, how to proceed.

Whatever Kyle had been about to confess to, he obviously had evidence on someone else. Enough to get him a deal?

Witness protection would be better than jail. Or death.

It could mean she'd never see her twin again. His disappearance would devastate their mother. Could trigger a worsening of her disease...

Kyle started talking the second they were inside Devon's cabin. Her brother didn't look around, didn't check to see that she had her own bedroom. He just dropped into a kitchen chair, looking more exhausted, more hopeless, more defeated than she'd ever seen him. And words came pouring out.

"Eli Sanders is the CEO at my mill and a couple of others." His mill. Kyle had lost his job. Wouldn't have any way of knowing she and Devon both knew that. "I've only met him a few times, but he was the one who interviewed me for my latest promotion. The one who chose me to be production manager. So when I discovered that someone was using logs with the middles sawed out to ship contraband, I went straight to him."

Kacey's chest thundered. Her nerves shattered.

Devon pulled out a chair, dropping down perpendicular to her brother. Leaned forward, an arm on the table.

"What kind of contraband?"

"I only saw adult films. But I did my own investigating before I went to Sanders. I needed to know the scale of the problem, who could be involved at my mill, our contacts at the destination points. I figured these were all things I could find out while no one knew anyone was onto them..."

"Which could implicate you..." The words came with

Devon's voice. But sounded nothing like him. Completely intent, his attention appeared riveted on her brother.

"Right," Kyle said, his gaze also astute as he talked to Devon, with an occasional glance in her direction.

"I found three distribution points. One in Iowa. One in Alabama. And one in Virginia."

Devon sat up straight. His back leaning on nothing. "I need you to stop talking for the moment," he said. He'd turned completely away from Kacey. "My name is not Devon Miller. I'm Tommy Grainger, an undercover detective with the Henderson, Nevada, police, and you've just crossed into information that could be what I've been seeking. As you aren't under arrest, you're free to go. If you're willing to continue this conversation, I need to get my partner here. And to record everything you have to say."

Kacey lost track of Kyle. Of her brother's reaction or response. All she could hear was ringing in her ears. As her body was consumed with shock.

And the greatest heartache she'd ever known.

Devon Miller didn't exist? She'd fallen in love with a fake? Had trusted him with her life? Her brother's life?

Had given him her heart and he hadn't even given her his name.

He'd been her strength. She'd been his undercover informant?

Excusing herself, Kacey made it to the bathroom. Slid down to the floor by the toilet. And lost her breakfast along with her heart.

HE THOUGHT HE heard her retching. Couldn't be sure. Tommy couldn't stop to find out. Every instinct he had told him Kyle Ashland was ready to hand them not just a link in the chain, but the whole damned thing. Getting Rachel on the phone, he told her he needed Bonnie at his place as soon as possible.

He offered Kyle something to drink. To eat.

The man went to see to his sister. What was said, he didn't know. Knew it wasn't his place to care. His mind was on the case. It had to be.

So many young lives...

He shook with the anticipation of preventing more death. Of completing the job he'd started. Setting up the video equipment that would record the upcoming interview, he was aware of Kyle's return. Again, he offered the man something to eat or drink.

Kyle, looking wearier than ever, shook his head. Wasn't looking at Tommy at all.

"I begged her to give me back the knife," he said, his head in his hands. "I'd stopped by my mom's to fix a leaky faucet and they were there when I came out. Letting me know what I was risking if..."

Throat tight, Tommy Grainer held up a hand. "Hold it just a few more minutes," he said, adjusting the small tripod he'd brought out for his phone. Heard water running in the bathroom.

"She's stronger than any woman I've ever known, but she's not cut out for this," Kyle said, as though explaining his sister to a man who didn't know her. "She said you gave her a bedroom that locked from the inside, showed me the gun...we owe you our lives..."

Tommy's jaw clenched. He swallowed. And found his air when he heard Bonnie's car pull up.

"Detective Bonnie Donaldson, from the Phoenix police, meet Kyle Ashland," he said as soon as his partner walked in.

He heard the bathroom door open.

Saw the way Bonnie's eyes widened, as Kacey entered the room, taking the seat at the table closest to her brother.

His houseguest would be out of camera range, was the only thought Tommy allowed himself. He wouldn't need to see her image when he went over and over the tapes. Or, if all went well, watched them in court.

His seasoned partner said nothing, just took the seat next to Tommy, who hit record.

And got the job done.

KACEY UNLOCKED THE door to her home, stumbled to the couch, and started to cry. Kyle, who'd stopped to thank Detective Donaldson one more time for driving them home, came straight over to her, the second he followed her in.

Hugging her. Rubbing the top of her head as their father might have done. Awkwardly. Telling her it was over.

She knew better. For her it would never be over.

But the moment wasn't about her.

Memories faded with time.

She'd get over it.

And Kyle...he truly was the hometown hero. And had been through far more than she'd ever have been able to take.

Through his diligent, quiet investigating, he'd found evidence of nearly a decade's worth of contraband being shipped in the middle of sawed-out logs, from his sawmill to the destinations in Iowa, Alabama and Virginia. He'd thought the manager of the mill had been responsible. He'd seen, and filmed, the man overseeing the placement of cargo into a shipment of logs.

Come to find out, the man was only a middleman. Getting paid a hefty sum for watching packages get loaded and shipped out and keeping his mouth shut.

Sanders had been the one running the operation. When

Kyle had first gone to him, a couple of weeks before, the CEO had offered Kyle a ridiculous amount of money to look the other way. And when Kyle had refused, saying he didn't want to get rich that way, the man had started with threats. First Kyle's job. Then seeing that Kyle couldn't get decent work anywhere close to his family. Sanders had let Kyle know that Sanders had friends in the Boulder police, and the next night, Kyle had been stopped for an offensive taillight that hadn't been broken until the officer broke it. And finally, the night that Kacey had witnessed, Sanders had shown up in town, at their mother's home, with two of his henchmen and threatened Kyle.

One of the men with the CEO had stabbed Kyle. Telling him it was only the beginning.

That's why Kyle had begged Kacey not to turn in the knife. He didn't want Sanders to retaliate. He'd panicked, had to go after the three. He would say he'd take the money, and figured along the way he'd find a way to expose Sanders. He'd ditched the knife in case he got stopped with it in his car, didn't want any ties to it. Unaware that Kacey had seen the encounter, he'd planned to go back before dawn and secure the knife until he could figure out what to do.

He hadn't caught up to the three men that night.

But had managed, by talking to a close friend at the mill, to find out more about Sanders. About some of his contacts. Apparently, Kyle wasn't the only who'd been threatened into complying with the shipments. And he'd found out that the marina where Devon and Rachel had been working had been one of the three hubs on the river that supplied the three sawmills with contraband. From lethal heroin to handbags and jewelry.

Kyle had found proof that the other two sawmills Sanders owned were running similar operations before he'd been fired.

One of Detective Grainger's and Donaldson's next challenges would be to conduct interviews and investigate police departments until they could find the officers Sanders owned.

Or, Kacey figured, until someone offered Sanders a deal to expose those under him. The ones who'd done the actual dirty work.

She'd come through the ordeal with her life.

She'd lost her ability to believe the best of people during the scuffle.

It might return.

Or maybe she'd learned a valuable life lesson. You couldn't believe in the best of people unless you wanted to get run over.

Either way, it was time to stand up, brush herself off and move forward.

Because she was alive.

TOMMY'S WORLD WAS consumed with conducting interviews, following up on leads, and traveling. Arizona to Nevada, to Utah, to Iowa, Alabama, Virginia and back to Nevada. He, along with his partners, slowly found the evidence federal prosecutors were going to need to prosecute Eli Sanders, and many of those who worked for him.

He'd personally spoken to the two men who'd followed him. One, the fiend who'd tied Kacey's feet, and been told to watch the boat, but who'd gotten drunk instead, only to find her missing. He'd seen Kyle's truck leave the area and had followed it.

The other, a friend of Belen's who'd been watching Rachel, wanting to know everyone she associated with before going to his bosses with her offer.

Eli Sanders had found a way to beat a lot of the charges Tommy wanted to stick to him. Sanders thought he was clear of the kidnapping of Kacey Ashland, and the subsequent near death she'd suffered. According to him, he'd merely walked up behind her as she'd left the police station where he'd just had lunch with a friend, telling her to watch her step. He'd gone his own way and had no idea that two other men had stepped in and forced her into a van. The other two had confirmed Sanders' testimony.

It would be Kacey's word against Sanders.

Tommy had almost punched the guy when Sanders said as much. The CEO had an alibi for the rest of that evening. He'd caught a charter plane back to Utah.

And he'd gone on a fishing trip in Colorado, too. Only flying out one night when his friends were in the boat for an overnight catch. He'd been back in their cabin when the guys had come out of their rooms at noon. Not that Tommy had found evidence yet to prove that.

But he knew it. He'd been told under the condition of anonymity so that Tommy would find the evidence.

Sanders was smart. Thought he had it all worked out.

Tommy wasn't resting until he had enough to put Sanders away for life.

So far, he hadn't found the evidence he needed to hold over the guy. To get him to cry like a baby and ask for leniency. For a deal.

That was when Tommy planned to line the table in front of Sanders with pictures of teenagers who'd died from his drugs.

They'd arrested Belen Alexopoulos, and the Arizona middlemen who'd not only killed Antonio and Jerome Hardy, but who'd accepted shipments from an older couple, posing as grandparents, from Devon's marina, and taken them up to the sawmills. It would all fall in place.

Someone would take the deal and roll on the rest.

Tommy needed it to be Sanders. The guy had been personally responsible for Kacey's abduction. For making her suffer through a nightmare that would haunt her forever. The guy was going to pay.

By the law.

Always by the law.

Overall, Tommy figured life was good. The commendations and congratulations rolling in didn't puff him up as he'd thought they would. Even an offer to lead the narcotics detective squad for the LVPD didn't faze him much. His parents were the ones who'd suffered the most from injustices in their past. His dad, being murdered, and made to look like a dirty cop. His mother, having to live with the aftermath.

And on that front, Sierra's Web hadn't yet found hard evidence to exonerate Hilton Grainger. Tommy had begun to accept that they never would.

Life didn't always play fair.

But Tommy and his team, thanks to Kyle Ashland, had saved lives.

Had helped Kacey Ashland get hers back.

And that had to be enough.

KYLE RECEIVED MORE than a year's worth of pay in a severance agreement. With all the money he'd saved, living alone and frugally, over the past ten years, he'd be independently wealthy for a while. He was talking about going to college to get his teaching degree, but also to pursue a dual major in athletics. He wanted to coach football someday. Had already applied to both degree programs at the University of Las Vegas, an hour and a half away.

In the meantime, he was moving in with their mom and Lizzie, planning to fix the place up so they weren't moving from one leaky faucet to the next. He'd start work as soon as he could convince their mother that he was allowed to spend his own money on her home.

Kacey figured he was coming to her for help in that venture when her twin called a couple of weeks after they'd returned home to say he needed to talk to her.

He wanted her to meet him down at their dock.

While she hadn't been out on the water since her return, she saw how her brother was killing two birds with one stone. Getting her cooperation in working on their mother, and getting Kacey back to the river she loved, too.

She wasn't opposed to a ride on his boat.

Hadn't figured he'd have their father's craft geared up to go. The boat had appeared at the dock the day after they'd returned to Bullhead City. Kyle had never told her how it came to be there. He'd just let her know it had arrived.

She could have asked for details.

She hadn't wanted them.

Still, climbing aboard the old vessel gave her heart a nasty twist. Visions of the last time she'd seen it floated before her mind's eye. She kicked them out. Most of her waking hours were spent not thinking about any of the days she'd spent with a fake persona. She battled constantly with her heart and mind to redirect herself every time he appeared. And there she was, on the boat that had ultimately ended it all.

Kyle's nightmare.

Her own run for her life.

And her belief in love at first sight. Or true love at all.

She'd fallen for a man who didn't exist. How in the hell could she ever trust her heart after that?

A couple of miles downriver, when Kyle had done no more than exchange small talk with her, asking her about running times, her newly implemented workouts at the gym, and other normal summer activities, Kacey was ready to head back.

"How far you planning to go?" she asked, standing by

her brother at the wheel. Out on the water, all she could see was Devon. All she could hear was his voice.

"I need to talk to you about that," Kyle said, maintaining position in the middle of the river, and a speed that precluded anything but holding on.

She had a life jacket onboard. Hadn't actually worn it in years.

"I've had some interviews with Tommy Grainger," he said. And she shut down. Sat down. Far enough away that she couldn't hear him.

Kyle was worried about her. She knew. A twin thing.

But no way was she going to talk about a man she didn't know as though he was any part of her struggle to readjust to normal life.

Being kidnapped, on the run, almost killed...it would get to anyone. She'd talked to a therapist about those three things.

When the motor slowed, and she heard the anchor splash overboard, Kacey scoured for things she could tell Kyle that would satisfy him enough to leave her alone.

The secret in her heart would never be spoken.

"He told me about his father," Kyle said, coming over to sit in the seat next to her. "He's had me talk to a couple of people from Sierra's Web, putting together pieces of the case, and he mentioned that he originally hired them to help him clear his father's name."

So that part had been true.

"Did he also tell you that he's paying for that with lottery winnings?" she asked sarcastically. And didn't realize until her brother said, "He mentioned a life insurance policy from his mother," that she'd been half hoping that Devon's story had all been true.

Just under an assumed name.

His mother's life insurance. Not a lottery win. Bitterness filled her up and she let it. At least for the time being. Sure beat crying.

"His father was a Las Vegas cop."

She'd already found that out.

And… Devon being a cop…she remembered the night he'd told her he could never be in a long-term relationship. He was like his dad…

"The thing is, Kace, I think I can help him prove that his father was set up. Just like I was."

Her heart missed a beat. She glanced over at Kyle. Saw the earnest need in her brother's gaze. And couldn't be bitter about that. "Then do it. Please." If he thought she'd be hurt because he was helping the man who'd played her…

Kyle didn't know that part.

"I want to. But I'm not going to unless you go with me."

"What?" Frowning she did another check. Was her twin losing it?

"There's more between you two than you're telling me. Something happened at his cabin. It changed you…"

"I was kidnapped, Kyle! Left to die…"

She broke off as Kyle shook his head. "I know you, Kace. This is more than some kind of PTSD. You trusted the man with your life. And I also saw female underwear twisted in the end of his sheet as I walked by his room…"

"You did not. I packed up both pairs of my underwear when I left…" Too late, she stopped. Felt foolish. In so very many ways. A simple, "well, they weren't mine," would have been so much better.

"He hurt you." Kyle's words were filled with knowing. Not question. "I just need to know if he forced anything…"

"No!" The word came out strongly. She followed it up with, "Absolutely not."

Kyle's nod, his serious look, was telling. As though he'd already been certain of the answer.

"You're playing me," she accused then. Men. They were all alike.

"In my own sloppy way, I'm hoping I'm getting you to see the truth. But whether I am or not, I have to tell you, Tommy Grainger is a man possessed."

"Of course he is. All he cares about is solving his case. Makes sense, with his father having died with his name smeared in the mud. A Las Vegas cop. Who'd been set up." That part, the dying with the name smeared part, of Devon's story had been true. In a very weak, middle-of-the-night moment, she'd looked up Tommy Grainger. Read about a few of his cases that had made news. And had devoured everything there was to find about Hilton Grainger, too.

"He's solved the case. He and his partner had already found the dealer who'd lead them to the group selling the lethal heroin to Sanders. My information led them to the supply chain. It's not that. He's hell-bent on making Sanders go down for your kidnapping. Sanders has an alibi for that night. From what I hear, Tommy's obsessed with finding some piece of evidence to prove that the man told you to just keep walking like you said he did."

She frowned. "What does Sanders say he said?"

"That he told you to watch your step. And that he walked off and never saw the two men who took you. He swears they were acting of their own accord."

Looking her brother in the eye, she said, "He told me to just keep walking, Kyle. I'm one hundred percent certain of that."

Kyle's nod was almost nonchalant. "Grainger is, too."

"Sanders was at the marina, too, Kyle. In the bar…"

"He's denying that it was him, at this point, but the truth's coming out. And that information just proves that he had dealings with two of his underlings and that's already a done deal. They've already tied him to them. And we've gotten way off point. I'm not helping Grainger with this thing with his dad unless you go with me to talk to him."

"Why not? That makes no sense."

With a shrug, Kyle said, "I'm just not."

Her brother wasn't kidding. He also wasn't telling her something. "How certain are you that you have something that might help him prove his father was innocent?"

"One hundred percent." He gave her words back to her. "That I might be able to help."

"How could you not do it then? Kyle…"

He shook his head. Cutting off her words. He wasn't budging. Just like when he wouldn't tell her what was going on with the knife.

He'd done that for her.

And her response came clearly. "We owe Detective Grainger our lives, Kyle. So yes, I'll go with you to deliver your information." She'd be fine. It was the right thing to do. And whatever Kyle's reasoning, she trusted her brother. "When do you plan to do this?"

"Right now." Kyle moved back to the wheel as he spoke, pushed up the throttle and sped downriver.

"Kyle, we don't even know where he is." She raised her voice to be heard.

"I do," Kyle hollered back. "Detective Donaldson says he's still based at his cabin. And is working from there today…" Her twin's words flew off on the wind.

The memories they invoked within Kacey wouldn't let go of her.

TOMMY'S PHONE LET him know something had breached his property. Gun in hand, he moved to the laundry closet for the best view of the screens. He'd rattled a lot of cages over the past weeks. Had left some unhappy families in his wake.

A teenager set on retribution for taking his dad away…

someone on Sanders' payroll he hadn't yet reeled in. It all came with the job. Calm, unfazed, his gaze went from screen to screen.

Got to the dock, and his heart started to pound. He would never forget that boat.

Nor, he feared, would he get the woman out of his system. Not in a dozen lifetimes.

What were they doing there?

If someone had threatened them...cops giving them trouble...he'd...

He met them halfway up to the cabin. Would just as soon take care of business out there. Getting Kacey's scent... her presence...out of the cabin was already proving to be a challenge.

He didn't need to make it any worse.

Kyle said hello first.

Tommy shook hands with the other man. Respecting him. But could only give a second before his attention had moved to taking in every inch of Kacey's face.

The woman met his gaze. With the eyes of a stranger.

He got it. Needed it to be that way.

Breathed a little easier, while reality settled over the energy raging within him.

"Can we talk inside?" Kyle's question interrupted Tommy's attempted return to peace. Kyle had been almost solely responsible for solving Tommy's case. He could hardly deny the man's request.

But he noticed that Kacey lagged behind her brother.

Almost as though she didn't want to be inside the cabin any more than he wanted her there. Good to know. Would help during those times when Kacey's optimism and endurance, her strength and vulnerability seemed to take over his home.

No matter how many times he sprayed cans of disinfectant.

Inside, he showed them to the kitchen table. It was more businesslike.

Odd how Kacey's gaze stayed right there. On the table. And the wall across from the seat she'd pulled out. One she hadn't sat in during her days with him. The rest of the cabin could just as well not have been there for all the attention she failed to give it.

"How are you doing?" He hadn't meant to ask aloud.

"Fine." Her nod told him nothing.

Kyle opened his phone, as though the two of them weren't there. Leaving Tommy in an awkward as hell position he did not appreciate. Nor did he know what to with it.

So he glanced at Kacey. Looking to her for guidance.

She was staring at the wall.

"Tommy, you had a thing with my sister." Kyle's words weren't sinister. But they weren't filled with joy, either. The man still held his phone but was most definitely giving Tommy the eye.

A glance at Kacey told him that she was giving it right back to Kyle. Her twin just didn't seem to be noticing.

Returning his gaze back to Kyle he said, "I did." Loud and clear.

"While you were pretending to be someone else." Yep. That was him.

He heard Kacey's sharp intake of breath. Oddly, recognized it from a couple of other times that came to him clearly. When she'd heard Sanders' voice in the bar.

And when he'd told her Kyle had reported her missing.

"I was."

"You were using her."

Instantly angry, Tommy didn't even let Kacey appear in his peripheral vision. Keeping his gaze solely on her twin.

"Absolutely not."

"How would you describe who you were when you were

personally involved with her?" Tommy had never under-estimated a man as much as he had Kacey Ashland's twin. Kyle Ashland had been in the wrong profession all his life. He needed to be an interrogator.

"What the hell is this?" Tommy asked, not proud of how he was letting the other man's words get to him.

And even less happy that Kacey was hearing it all.

"Just trying to sort out the truth," Kyle said. "I…"

"Need to shut up," Kacey said, standing. "Devon… Tommy…whoever the hell you are, I apologize for my brother. He seems to have lost his mind. He told me that he has information that might help you exonerate your father, but he wasn't going to give it to you unless I came along. Kyle, either put up or I'm leaving."

Tommy's heart burst. Right there. All over his table. The cabin floor. The pain, and something much bigger, was so intense he half expected to see it oozing in some kind of color out of his body.

"You want to help me clear my father's name." He was speaking only to her. Holding her gaze. Because she was letting him.

Holding his.

"You gave us back our lives." Her words came out sounding weak. The emotion in her eyes…he recognized it. Had a feeling he was never going to be himself again without it.

Maybe not even with it.

He was changing, right there before his own eyes. He couldn't stop it.

Wasn't sure he wanted to.

"I…um…just sent you your proof," Kyle said, standing, putting his phone in his back pocket, and heading toward the door. "Kace…if you need a ride home, call me. Tommy, I better not get that call."

The door shut behind Kyle and Tommy still sat there. Staring at it.

Kacey hadn't moved, either.

Just stood there.

And it hit Tommy. "You didn't go after him. Leave with him." She could have. He looked up at her, standing a couple of feet away.

She didn't speak. Just stood there, her eyes looking half-stony. Her chin trembling.

"I'm never going to be good in the trust department," he told her.

"I know." She still stood there. As though undecided whether to walk out the door or sit down. "I'm not so good in that department myself anymore."

A direct hit. He deserved it.

"You came back." It was all he had to fight with. And he suddenly felt as though he was in the battle of a lifetime. He was aware of his phone on the table. The supposed gift of a lifetime Kyle Ashland had just said he'd sent to him. Which didn't even compute. At the moment, he had no interest in that mystery.

He was waiting for Kacey. Was she staying? Leaving?

What did she want from him?

Could he ever hope to have enough to give to keep knowing her?

She deserved so much more.

"You're trustworthy, Devon." She stopped. "Tommy." She sounded as though she might be gritting her teeth.

"I like Devon," he told her. "When it's just us. Like a nickname."

"I'm not going to pretend."

"Devon knew how to give you something Tommy would never have dared let loose," he said, and suddenly, he knew. Standing, the constriction around his chest loosening, he went to her. "The name was a cover, Kace," he said, running the back of his fingers lightly over her cheek. Trembling when she didn't turn her face away. "What we shared…was all completely real for me."

He'd been honest with her. Tommy honest. He'd told her he didn't have forever to offer any woman.

"You didn't trust me."

"Not completely. Not in my head, anyway. And I was honest with you about that."

She nodded. "I know." Then, lifting her hand, ran a finger over his lower lip. Watching what she was doing. "I think that's when I fell in love."

That lip she was rubbing, instead of delivering instant rejection, broke into a grin. "I think I'm kinda glad to hear that."

"Kinda?"

"I'm not any kind of expert on these types of situations, mind you, but based on how you own every breath of air in this cabin, and I can't seem to move back to Tommy's house in Henderson even though I really need to be in the office every day… I might have fallen pretty hard, too."

"I need more than might."

That was it then. He'd known.

"I'm not going to profess a feeling I might tarnish."

"I'm the one taking the risk. Believing it," she said, standing up to him.

"I'm not going to take a chance that I'll break your heart."

"You a coward, Tommy Grainger? Because I never took Devon Miller for one. And to your point," she continued before he could respond to the challenge. "You've already broken my heart once. I survived. I'm still standing."

He'd met his match.

There was just no point in denying the obvious.

The evidence was all right there.

"I love you, Kacey Ashland."

"I love you, too, Tommy Devon Grainger." Her expression grew dark. Or, at least, serious. "I'm not expecting anything but you, as you are. And a chance. Because without you…life doesn't feel right anymore."

"I'm not sure I'll be successful at any of this."

She nodded. Studied him. And then smiled.

A naughty look. "I think I'd like to see how good Tommy Grainger is in bed. You up for that?" she asked, pressing her hips against his rock-hard penis.

He kissed her then. Hungrily. Taking every bit of her air. Giving her his. So they didn't have to talk anymore.

He wasn't great at personal conversation.

But loving her… Tommy knew he could do it. After two weeks of life without her—a hell he was never going to forget—he had no doubt that he'd do whatever it took to be the partner Kacey needed. Just as he knew she'd be there for him. They'd already lived through the hardest stuff life had to give. Faced death more than once.

And had come through for each other.

Every time.

Life wasn't easy. Human love wasn't perfect.

But it was the source of every ounce of strength he was ever going to need. Right there. In Kacey. With Kacey.

In every new family member—hers and theirs—that came to him.

And in knowing that the world was filled with people like Kyle Ashland, a man who was trustworthy to the core.

It wasn't about being perfect. It was about getting up when you were knocked down, brushing off, and trying some more.

It was about not giving up.
Taking the next step.
That he could do.

Epilogue

Kacey sat on the couch in the cabin with Tommy, hanging all over him—fully clothed because of the cameras—as he finally opened her brother's email later that night.

Saw him save the folder Kyle had sent to his device, and then open page after page of information. She read with him.

She didn't get what it all meant.

"Who's Billy Collier?" she asked, feeling the muscles in her lover's body tense. And not with passion.

"An army buddy of my father's. Dad saved his life."

She frowned. "I don't…"

Tommy read more. She followed as best she could.

When the pages in the folder came to an end, he sent the file to the man she now knew to be his captain in the Henderson police.

And shut off his phone.

He turned, his eyes closed, his mouth hungrily seeking hers.

"Uh-uh," she said pushing him back. "Tell me, Tommy."

"There's nothing…"

"Devon."

Just the one word. Torn from her heart…

He opened his eyes. Stared toward the wall across from them. "Your brother overheard a conversation between

Sanders and the manager of his plant, when they were deciding what to do about him. Sanders was being urged to pull out all his stops, use his connections, to make it all go away. And Sanders admitted that he wasn't the man at the top. So, your brother did some deep digging. Looking at shipping manifests that went back a lot further. Following them to the same destination points. Turns out that Billy Collier is the silent owner, through many shell corporations, of not only all three mills, but all three distribution points, as well as about fifty other companies. He'd been shipping contraband in his logs for thirty years. My father found out about it…"

She pulled in air so fast she almost choked. "He thought your dad would cover for him."

"By that time, Collier had friends in higher places who had friends in lower places…"

She was putting together pieces of the evidence she'd just seen. Was relieved, truly happy for him, to know that his father was the man he'd thought him to be. His trust in his father had been validated.

And yet, she worried that what Tommy had just read would put them right back on rocky ground, too. "Did you know this Billy?" she asked.

And sat with him, making him talk to her, to tell her about the man he'd known intermittently growing up, as Billy's main residence was on the East Coast. She heard how Billy had been the man to clear his father's name. To make certain that his mother got his dad's full pension.

Then she heard how Billy had tried to start something up with his mother.

"Mom was gracious, of course, but she'd already had the love of her life and wasn't settling for second best. We haven't heard from Billy since…" Tommy's words drifted off.

"I'm guessing Billy Collier doesn't understand the value of true love," she said.

Tommy turned to her then, with tears glistening in his eyes. "I get it, Kace. I swear to you. Any mistakes I make, you can count on me to…"

She put a finger over his lips. "Now's the time to kiss me," she said, climbing on top of him and kissing him with her mouth wide open.

Ready to take him in. All of him.

Always.

Because that was what love did.

* * * * *

COMING SOON!

We really hope you enjoyed reading this book.
If you're looking for more romance
be sure to head to the shops when
new books are available on

Thursday 4th January

To see which titles are coming soon, please visit
millsandboon.co.uk/nextmonth

MILLS & BOON

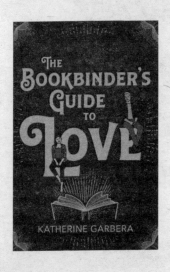

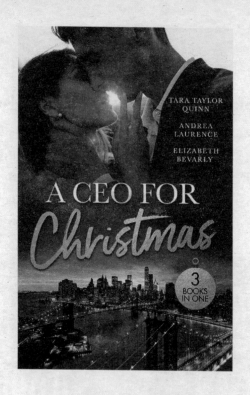

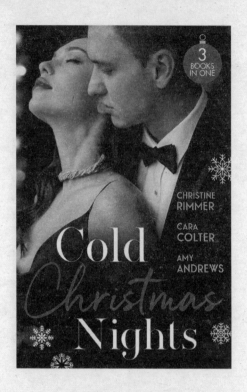